WHISPERS IN THE NIGHT

Silence thickened between them, and Cynara wondered what was going through Merlin's mind as he stepped closer and cupped her face with his hands.

"What do you know about me?" he whispered. "Nothing, my dear. Nothing! All you do is hold your chin high and look down on me in contempt. Do you think I'm powerless? Do you think you can deny your duty to me and our marriage, and that I will accept your scorn forever?" His face moved ever closer to hers.

"Let me go," she said, yet she longed to feel his lips against hers.

A sudden smile transformed his face. "What would you be prepared to give me in return if I helped to free Brandon?" His voice was velvety soft, cajoling, and Cynara pushed him hard in the chest. He only laughed. "Well?"

"I married you, as you wanted me to," she said. "What more do you demand from me?" As she looked into his eyes, she knew very well what he wanted. "Will you *force* me to do something I don't want to do?"

"I wouldn't exactly use such strong words if I were you." He pulled her tightly against his body, and she could feel the hard ridges of his muscles and the lean flesh pressing against her. And as he traced her cheek with his lips, kissing her earlobe and murmuring endearments in her hair, she felt her resistance falter. . . .

* * *

Praise for Maria Greene's *Mine Forevermore*:
"A terrific read. Don't miss this one!" *Rendezvous*

TODAY'S HOTTEST READS
ARE TOMORROW'S SUPERSTARS

VICTORY'S WOMAN (4484, $4.50)
by Gretchen Genet
Andrew—the carefree soldier who sought glory on the battlefield, and returned a shattered man . . . Niall—the legandary frontiersman and a former Shawnee captive, tormented by his past . . . Roger—the troubled youth, who would rise up to claim a shocking legacy . . . and Clarice—the passionate beauty bound by one man, and hopelessly in love with another. Set against the backdrop of the American revolution, three men fight for their heritage—and one woman is destined to change all their lives forever!

FORBIDDEN (4488, $4.99)
by Jo Beverley
While fleeing from her brothers, who are attempting to sell her into a loveless marriage, Serena Riverton accepts a carriage ride from a stranger—who is the handsomest man she has ever seen. Lord Middlethorpe, himself, is actually contemplating marriage to a dull daughter of the aristocracy, when he encounters the breathtaking Serena. She arouses him as no woman ever has. And after a night of thrilling intimacy—a forbidden liaison—Serena must choose between a lady's place and a woman's passion!

WINDS OF DESTINY (4489, $4.99)
by Victoria Thompson
Becky Tate is a half-breed outcast—branded by her Comanche heritage. Then she meets a rugged stranger who awakens her heart to the magic and mystery of passion. Hiding a desperate past, Texas Ranger Clint Masterson has ridden into cattle country to bring peace to a divided land. But a greater battle rages inside him when he dares to desire the beautiful Becky!

WILDEST HEART (4456, $4.99)
by Virginia Brown
Maggie Malone had come to cattle country to forge her future as a healer. Now she was faced by Devon Conrad, an outlaw wounded body and soul by his shadowy past . . . whose eyes blazed with fury even as his burning caress sent her spiraling with desire. They came together in a Texas town about to explode in sin and scandal. Danger was their destiny—and there was nothing they wouldn't dare for love!

Available wherever paperbacks are sold, or order direct from the Publisher. Send cover price plus 50¢ per copy for mailing and handling to Penguin USA, P.O. Box 999, c/o Dept. 17109, Bergenfield, NJ 07621. Residents of New York and Tennessee must include sales tax. DO NOT SEND CASH.

MARIA GREENE

THE RAVEN AND THE DOVE

ZEBRA BOOKS
KENSINGTON PUBLISHING CORP.

ZEBRA Books are published by

Kensington Publishing Corp.
475 Park Avenue South
New York, NY 10016

First Printing: May, 1994

Printed in the United States of America

Prologue

Belgium
June 18, 1815

The earth shook as a cannonball drilled into the soil beside Merlin Seymour, and the air shivered with the deafening noise. An excruciating pain shot through his thigh as something shattered, a rock perhaps, piercing him with jagged shards. Legs broken, the horse screamed and went down under him. Merlin swore and pulled himself away from the thrashing stallion that had trapped one of his feet.

Closing his eyes momentarily to ward off the pain in his wound, and the sorrow at losing his mount, he then lifted his pistol from the saddlebag and ended the beast's suffering. The snorts and screams, the wildly rolling eyes, stilled. Merlin scanned the area quickly for any enemy soldier advancing toward him, but no one had noticed him.

He crawled across the cold, muddy cornfield toward the English lines up on the ridge. The rest of his unit, the King's Dragoons, fled from the French Lancers after the initially successful attack on Napoleon's army. The English had made heavy inroads on French soldiers, but Merlin knew it had been a mistake not to listen to the trumpets calling frantically for retreat. The Dragoons had been blinded by success and had ridden wildly on. He had turned around at the last minute as the French reserve arrived with fresh horses. He would be lucky if he reached the safety of the ridge, but he would fight until his last breath if need be. He crept doggedly on, refusing to let pain and exhaustion defeat him.

The stench of gunpowder and fresh blood tormented his nose. Dust clogged the air. A fog blackened by fire had hung over the battlefield since the violent rainstorm on the previous night. Had this place once been a lovely Belgian farm? Now the earth was drenched with the blood of Englishmen, Prussians, and French alike.

Grimacing in agony, Merlin struggled to get up, but the torture was too much. His leg was drenched with blood and the material of his breeches hung in strips. Cursing with grim determination, he inched himself toward safety from which a fusillade of musket fire exploded at the advancing French. Dots of orange pierced the black smoke.

Dead men lay all around him, but he had no desire to join their ranks. With his last bit of strength he jabbed his elbows into the bloodied mud and pulled himself up, ever up the incline, struggling as misery sapped his power.

He had almost reached the British lines when what was left of the Life Guards, the troop which—as a last desperate attempt to stop the French—had set out earlier, returned. Horses, wild with fear, thundered past him, and men screamed as musket balls found their targets.

Merlin swore as an officer tumbled to the ground beside him, his body thudding heavily in the mud. The pale face staring up at Merlin was streaked with blood and soot. Aghast, Merlin stared into the pain-darkened eyes of his cousin, Maximilian Seymour.

"Max? Why aren't you behind the lines with Wellington?" Merlin was on his stomach, and he reached out to shake Max's shoulder. "Are you badly hurt?"

Max's eyes cleared momentarily, but his face was bleached of all color. "Merlin?" His hands were red with blood as he gripped Merlin's arm convulsively. Merlin stared in horror at the bloody crater in Max's stomach.

"Did you see? We rode in . . . literally ripped the guns from the Frogs," Max whispered, a ghost of a smile on his face. "Boney will lose this war . . . I'm glad I fought. Today we will stand . . . victorious. Blücher is coming with enforcement. We'll whip that madman Boney. . . ."

Merlin struggled to sit up. Tears made warm rivulets down his face as he watched life slowly seep from his cousin, his best friend. He'd known Max all his life, and they had always been as close as brothers, together through school and, after that, in the wars. "I will fetch a doctor for you," he shouted over the infernal din. Icy fog curled over the ground, sweeping a veil over Max's face.

"No . . . bloody too late, old chap." Max pressed his hands against the sticky stain on the front of his uniform. "I'm going to dance with the . . . angels." He smiled, then grimaced as pain evidently set his body on

fire. With sudden urgency he gripped Merlin's coat
and dragged him down beside him. His lips were cold
as he pressed them against Merlin's ear. "You must
promise one thing. . . . Can't deny a dying man . . . his
last wish."

Merlin blinked away his tears and eased his arm
under Max's shoulders. He nodded convulsively. "I'll
do anything you want. Only mention it."

Max's bluish lips worked, and sweat pearled on his
face. He fought to overcome the weakness in his voice.
"I promised to marry Cynara . . . when I returned
from the . . . war. Promised to take care . . . of her.
You must marry . . . her . . . in my place."

Merlin's eyes widened in shock. "That's a great
favor to ask, especially since she detests me."

Max pulled feebly at his arm. "You must! She's
vulnerable with . . . no one to look after her. Brandon
is . . . irresponsible and . . . and . . . her mother so
scatterbrained." Max struggled, his voice hoarse. "I
need to know that she will . . . be cared for. You're
. . . the only man I . . . *trust.*" Max's eyes fluttered shut.
"Promise," he whispered. "I love her so."

Merlin fought his own distress. Max was asking him
to change the course of his life, but how could he say
no?

"Promise!" Max shouted, tears filling his eyes.

Merlin gripped the stiff, bloody hand in his and held
it tightly. He wished his own life could replace the
force leaving Max's body. As sorrow scalded his eyes,
he battled to hold Max back—in vain. Max's hand
grew cold, clammy, weak.

"I promise."

"I shall reserve an angel for you . . . old fellow, the

loveliest of them all," Max said with a ghost of a smile. "And we shall dance . . ." His head tilted sideways, and his hand hung limply in Merlin's grip.

Grief clutched Merlin's chest, suffocating him. He could not conceive of a life without his cousin. How could anyone so full of life die? The future stretched vast and empty before him.

As pain constricted his throat, Merlin looked up, noticing that the French were advancing yet again, after battling back another English attack. The charging enemy soldiers had not yet noticed that he was alive. A huge fallen war horse shielded him from fire.

Too many good soldiers were already dead, and now Max. There would never be another like him. Merlin folded his cousin's hands over his chest and pulled off his own tattered coat. With a last look at the white, still face, Merlin spread the garment over Max.

Merlin's thigh ached so much, he feared that he might join Max sooner than he knew. Blood oozed from the large wound and dribbled into his boots. Faintness came over him, but he inched himself back to the lines. He had a promise to keep, and if death didn't claim him in this battle, he would honor that promise.

Chapter 1

Devonshire
June 1816

Faced with such a momentous step as marriage, Cynara Hawthorne wished she had a trusted confidante, someone—other than her maid, Tildy—who knew how to advice her. Mother wanted only to pursue the easiest way to solve her brother Brandon's dilemma, an immediate union between Felix Seymour and Cynara.

Problems did not usually daunt Cynara like this. She didn't hesitate to confront them as they arose, but this decision involved the rest of her life.

"Botheration! I wish there were another way out of this." Dressed only in her shift, she paced the floor of her bedchamber at the Bluewater estate. Her bedchamber measured twelve steps, and she had recited *one, two, three, four . . .* over and over for two hours at least—if not longer. If she didn't stop soon, she'd wear a groove into the wooden floor. She tossed a stray ringlet impatiently over her shoulder and halted in the middle of the room.

"I just have to wed that toad," she said for the twentieth time. "There's no other solution. If I don't marry Felix, Brandon will die." She directed this grim truth to her sturdy maid. "Brand'll get that dreaded prison fever and perish."

Tildy shook her head. "Come now, Miss Cynara. Ye don't know that for sure. Yer making a mistake. I've told ye it's no use trying to help yer hapless brother again. He always expects ye to solve his problems, but this time he's gone too far, mark my words."

"If only I could turn back time, to before the war. Then Max would still be alive. He would have known what to do."

"He would have been dead set against this marriage."

"Of course! He would have married me himself. He didn't get along with Felix, and I know why. No person in his right mind would trust Felix Seymour, and now I'm about to become his wife." Cynara threw her hands in the air. "Damn my reckless brother!"

A year had passed since Max's death at the Battle of Waterloo, the battle that had finally put an end to Napoleon's terror, at the cost of thousands of British lives. She was on the brink of getting married to one of Max's cousins, Felix Seymour. Felix was the heir to the earldom of Black Raven now that Max was dead. Max had been the son of Sydney, the previous earl, and Felix was the son of George, the middle Seymour brother. The youngest brother, Ross, had fathered Merlin, but she hadn't seen Merlin since Max's funeral.

She remembered Brandon's letter. *You must help me, Cynara. You know I didn't steal that diamond necklace. Resourceful that you are, you're the only one who*

*can find a way to get me out of this horror. I know you
don't like Felix Seymour, but as the Earl of Black
Raven, he has powerful contacts in London . . . ask him
to aid you!*

She had asked Felix, and he'd promised to help
her—on one condition. She had to marry him. According to Felix, he'd always had a soft spot for her,
but she didn't consider his coercing her into wedlock
a "soft spot." It had another name: blackmail.

She would never have accepted an alliance with
Felix if it hadn't been for Brandon's dilemma. . . . Such
shame! Had Brand felt the Hawthorne poverty so dire
that he had to resort to stealing? She knew he hadn't,
but who had made it look like he was a thief? No clues
to that puzzle.

With apprehension Cynara viewed her wedding
gown spread out on the bed. Since her father died, she
felt as if she were the head of the Hawthorne family
even if Brand was two years her senior. He was a
wholly lovable person, but without an ounce of common sense.

She longed for her father as she touched the smooth
silk of the gown. He had been a rock to hold on to, and
after his death her mother clung to anyone who offered an arm. Cynara refused to cling; she had to find
a way to manage Felix. Anyway, most alliances of her
class were marriages of convenience.

Setting her jaw and squaring her shoulders, she tried
to forget Felix's dark side. She sensed his secretive,
sinister character behind the smooth exterior.

Cynara said more to herself than to her maid, "I
want to help Brand. I care what happens to my family."

"Ye care too much, if you ask me." Tildy clucked her tongue. "Yer eyes are puffy and red, Miss Cynara. I take it you didn't sleep at all last night."

"No . . . I didn't." She glanced at her maid. "Wouldn't you worry if *your* brother ended up in Newgate Prison?"

"I don't have a brother. Now, miss, your face needs a good wash in cold water. Master Felix will notice yer worry, an' displeased he'll be."

"Besides Mother, Brand is all the family I have." Her stomach twisted into knots at the thought of the ordeal ahead. "I wish we knew some powerful man other than Felix, but we've always lived in the country. Mother doesn't have many contacts in London, nor do I."

Tildy shook her head and rolled her eyes. "Aye, an influential friend would be a blessin'." She stomped over to the bed and fingered the exquisite Mechlin lace foaming around the neckline of the gown. "Ye'd better get ready." She slanted a shrewd glance at Cynara. "Pardon me for sayin' it, but Mr. Brandon would not marry someone he dislikes just to save yer skin."

Cynara glared at her free-spoken maid. "He would! Don't be cruel, Tildy. I love Brand, and he's helped me with problems in the past."

"Compared to him, you don't have problems. You're more trustworthy than he'll ever be."

"Well . . . our gifts weren't divided equally. Brand is the impetuous one."

Tildy enfolded her slender charge in a maternal embrace. Cynara's thin shoulders shook with silent sobs.

"That sly bird, Felix Seymour, has had his eye on ye for a long time, and now he sees his opportunity to get ye. But, mark me words, in the end he won't lift a finger to help Mr. Brandon."

Cynara's golden hair, drawn back into a cluster of curls at the back of her neck, bounced as she shook her head. "You're wrong, Tildy."

Tildy released her arms and tenderly patted the bent head of her charge. "Since Max is dead, I wish that terrifying cousin of his, Merlin Seymour, had the title and the power." Tildy nodded her head. "Now, Master Merlin is a man I respect. Straight as an arrow, he is. If he weren't so frightfully aloof, I could easily fall in love wi' him. He's no sly namby-pamby like Felix."

Cynara looked up, her eyes burning and her eyelashes wet with tears. "We should not speak of Merlin Seymour. I'm sure *he* wouldn't lift a finger to help me. I have seen him only once since Max died, and he didn't even offer his condolences."

"Ye told me yerself that he's been terribly ill since the end of the war."

"Yes, he had to travel abroad to seek help for his leg wound."

"I bet he was heartbroken after Master Max's death. Those two were closer than twins. *Merlin* wouldn't let ye marry Felix." Tildy righted an unruly blond curl in Cynara's hair arrangement, and settled an orange blossom that had come loose.

"Perhaps not." Cynara let the maid slip the stays around her. She held on to the bedpost as Tildy began to tighten the strings in the back. She closed her eyes and tried to remember Max's dear face, but the memory that sprang to mind was her meeting with Merlin Seymour at Max's funeral.

Merlin had been pale and haggard, so thin he was

nothing but a shadow. The slimness had made those broad shoulders of his look out of proportion with the rest of his tall body. She knew that he'd received the wound in his thigh at the battle of Waterloo, a wound that had almost taken his life. At the funeral he had been dressed in full military regalia, but later she'd learned that he'd sold out. What was he doing now? Had he returned from the Continent?

She had known him all her life. While Max had been a boy full of pranks, of laughs and wild adventures, Merlin had always been reserved, mysterious, thoughtful. Merlin was as dark as Max had been fair—dark hair, dark eyes, and sun-darkened skin. Merlin had always been a disturbing figure with that piercing black gaze—as if he could read her every thought. She had always been a bit afraid of him, but Max had assured her that no one was as loyal, as kind, and as thoughtful of others as Merlin. Well, Merlin had always intimidated her, and that one time, when he'd tried to kiss her on her fourteenth birthday, she'd told him she hated him and his dark, haunting eyes. She had hurt him then, and he had kept his distance since.

Now she feared him even more since there were rumors that he was involved in the scandal that had cost Merlin's father, Ross, his life. She had heard that one night Ross and Merlin had quarreled terribly at White's Club in London, the row ending with Ross stalking outside and Merlin following him in a rage. She'd never found out what the row was about.

However much she resented Merlin, she had to admit that his imposing presence always set her mind fluttering and her heart racing. Ever since her fourteenth birthday, she had been aware of his virile magnetism. At nineteen, he had already been a man. Now, at twenty-six, he was even more attractive. She wished she knew why he had tried to kiss her. . . .

It was fortunate that he wouldn't be at her wedding.

She gripped the bedpost until her knuckles whitened and her head drooped. Max was dust now, and Brandon in Newgate Prison. Of the three boys who had played together, only Merlin was free, but his head might end up on the block if the rumors about Ross's death were true. He was no longer welcome in polite society since the day his father died. Everyone shunned Stormywood, Merlin's estate, since that fatal night. No wonder Merlin had fled to the Continent under the pretext of seeking a cure for his wound.

No more gloomy thoughts! Cynara pressed back the distracting memories of Merlin and Max before they could undo her completely. But her mind would give her no peace.

"There! Almost done now," Tildy said, pulling the strings even tighter. "Master Felix will find ye very lovely, dearie."

Cynara closed her eyes, fighting for breath. Felix was the strangest of the four boys she had always known. He had spent his school years at Eton and Oxford, and his holidays at Black Raven while his parents were in Virginia across the Atlantic. George Seymour, Felix's father, had emigrated to America, where he had married the heiress to a tobacco plantation.

Felix had been a strange, brooding boy. He used to pull wings off flies and legs off spiders. His eyes were as murky as a muddy pond, eyes hiding secrets in the depths, secrets as dismal as the creatures living in the mud. His voice had a soft, hypnotic quality.

Felix would always get what he wanted, even if it meant hurting others in the process. He was clever; she did not underestimate his power. If anyone did, he had the resources to help Brandon.

Jagged images of the four men—the three Seymour cousins, Max, Felix, and Merlin, and her brother Brandon—pierced her mind until she wanted to moan out loud. She hadn't been sleeping well since that day Brand was brought before the magistrates at Bow Street in London. He was at Newgate awaiting the decision as to whether he would be tried and sentenced in Surrey, where the theft had taken place, or in London.

Cynara tipped her head back and stared at the heavy gold brocade hangings around the four-poster in her bedchamber. Tonight she would sleep in Felix's bed at Black Raven. She would have to learn to endure.

Her eyes ached with unshed tears, and she was relieved when Tildy said, "Finished! Ye're naught but skin an' bones, and I wouldn't be surprised if ye faint this evening with all them petticoats and tight stays. Fair cruel 'tis! Even if ye're to become the Countess of Raven, ye'll always be me dear, dear Mistress Cy." Tildy dabbed at the corner of her eye with her apron, reminding Cynara of happier times, when life had been less complicated. Originally hailing from London, Tildy was the daughter of the housekeeper at Bluewater, Cynara's childhood home.

"I'm not going to a funeral, you know."

Tildy shook her head. " 'Tis a grim day at Bluewater."

When Cynara was ready, the gown adjusted, the lace foaming around her shoulders, and blossoms in her hair, a knock sounded on the door. It was Winslow, the butler, announcing that the carriage was waiting at the door to take her to the Black Raven chapel five miles away.

Cynara was glad that the chapel was shrouded in semidarkness. The guests ought to be spared the embarrassment of seeing a miserable bride. White lilies filled the small stone building with heavy perfume. Wax candles shivered in the breeze from the open doors. There was a leaden pressure in the air, the hush before the storm. Nature was waiting, every flower tightly closed against the rage of promised rain, every bird cowed, breathless.

Cynara kept her gaze stiffly trained on the altar. At the perimeter of her vision, she saw Felix. Deliberately, she kept her gaze unfocused, refusing to accept that a real man—not an evil phantom—was waiting for her.

Every impossible step led her closer to her doom. Clutching her bouquet and a lacy handkerchief, she walked slowly, regally, her head erect. Then one carpeted step up and she stood in front of the Black Raven chaplain. Felix's hand closed around hers. She trembled, feeling cold, so cold. His hand was fleshy, demanding. He squeezed hers, forcing her to give him a fleeting glance.

His round face shone with perspiration, the neckcloth already losing its starched freshness. His short brown hair was trimmed and pomaded. Glittering with triumph, his pale brown gaze rested on her. A gem flashed among the folds of his cravat. His eyes held that secretive air she had known since they were children. He licked his full lips, and Cynara closed her eyes as disgust filled her.

To her it sounded as if the chaplain's voice were pouring forth incantations of evil. She listened as Felix said his vows. Her hands trembled so much, she thought she was going to drop the bouquet.

Everything began to tilt, to twist around and around crazily. She could not find air, and her knees buckled. Just before she toppled over, Felix's arm shot around her waist, holding her relentlessly upright. His thumb poked painfully into her side and she wanted to moan, but her lips could not move. It was her turn to speak her vows, and Felix pushed his nails hard into her when she failed. *She couldn't go through with it.*

The first jagged lightning slashed the sky, quickly followed by a clash of thunder that left the earth trembling. A gust of wind bearing the sounds of horses tore into the chapel. Hoofbeats clattered on the paved path outside; voices whispered in the pews. Steps rang on the stone floor, and Cynara threw a glance over her shoulder. Felix's arm had fallen from her back.

In a daze, she viewed the tall man striding across the chapel. He was dressed entirely in black, and a slight limp marred his powerful stride. His hair was black, his skin dark from the summer sun. His obsidian gaze pierced her through the gloom.

There was no mistaking Merlin Seymour. Never. He was no longer the haggard, broken man she'd seen at Max's funeral; he was a man of purpose, of power.

"This wedding is canceled," he said in his deep voice. Cynara heard the words, but she was aware only of the hard width of his shoulders and the dark curls on his collar. She cringed when he reached out toward her, and stepped back into the front pew, where her mother was sitting. Voices rose in indignation all around her.

Two long strides brought him to her side, and even though she fought him, he lifted her in his arms effortlessly. Without another word he turned and carried her toward the door. Voices blabbered now, Felix jabbing at Merlin with his fists and trying to pull Cynara from his arms. Shocked, she pounded the hard chest of her abductor, but his grip only tightened. "Be still," he ordered her, and fear skittered along her spine.

"Let me down this instant." Her demand went to deaf ears.

"You can't do this, Seymour!" Felix shouted after him as he jumped down the chapel steps.

"It's already done," Merlin said. "Cynara doesn't belong to you, and she never will." He tossed her up in the saddle of his stallion, swung himself up behind her, and clutched her hard around the waist before she had a chance to slide off.

She knew she ought to protest louder, but the whole scene seemed unreal. In a daze, she watched as the wind played havoc with her handkerchief. Ghostlike, it writhed through the air to land on a tall iron cross. Cynara's eyes widened. Was it an omen of death?

A parade of faces blurred before her as the guests crowded in the doorway. They stared at her in bewilderment, crying her name and reaching out as Merlin turned his huge black steed and galloped down the path. He was closely followed by another rider, an old man who had been aiming two dueling pistols at the guests.

"You shall pay for this, Merlin," Felix cried after them as rain deluged the earth. "Mark my word, your blood shall be running ere long."

Chapter 2

"Where are you taking me?" Cynara demanded to know as they left the village and its ancient keep of Black Raven. The sea below the castle was a sullen gray. The waves crashed against the steep black cliffs, the surf snarling around the rocks as the horse trotted past Gairlock Woods and up onto the ridge bordering Lyme Bay. "I thought you would take me back to the house."

He laughed. "And leave you to Felix's machinations? I have more sense than that."

She looked up into the hard face where cheekbones slashed across hollowed cheeks, where charcoal eyelashes shaded the already shadowy deep-set eyes, where the nose was a hooked blade that reminded her of the beak of an eagle.

"Why are you doing this?" She squirmed in his arms, but his grip did not lessen. The black riding cloak flapped around him, and strands of raven hair flicked across his forehead. "I won't have anything to do with you, you know that. In fact, I loathe you, Merlin."

His gaze swept over her, and her skin prickled. "I don't care what you feel, Cynara. You can hate me all you like, but you're not marrying Felix."

"We'll see about that!" The wind tore at the soaked layers of her wedding gown, bringing the scent of seaweed and salt from the sea. Rain lashed her face, and her hands and lips stiffened with cold. "Are you going to tell me where you're taking me?"

"To Stormywood, but not just yet. Lackeys will fetch your mother, and she'll attend to you there. First I must know the answer to a burning question: Are you willing to marry *me* instead of Felix?" That dark gaze swept over her again, penetrating her deepest thoughts. There was no emotion in that hard face.

"Why in the world . . . I certainly will not!" she cried over the moaning wind. "I have no desire to marry you, not now, not ever." Aghast, she stared at him. "What made you ask such a startling question?"

"You were willing to marry Felix, so you might be willing to marry anyone."

"I am not!"

He smiled mirthlessly. "Are you now going to profess your deepest love for that snake? Please spare me."

Cynara glared, pinching her lips shut.

"You don't love him, nor do you love me, so what difference does it make whom you marry? Answer me."

"Felix has power; you don't. That's the simple reason."

Merlin reined in the horse in the shelter of a clump of trees. The man who had accompanied him to the chapel was close behind.

Cynara had never seen him before, a gnarled, bow-legged fellow with stringy gray hair sprouting below the rim of his damp hat.

"Let me down," Cynara demanded, the cold making her teeth clatter.

Merlin let go of her then, and she slid to the ground. Knowing there was no use, in her heavy dress, trying to run away from the two men, she waited until Merlin had jumped down. She wasn't exactly *frightened* of him, but there was something about him that made the hair rise at the nape of her neck—a bleak stillness, a deep sadness, as if he'd spent these last few years staring into the darkness of hell. She had seen him only at brief intervals during the war. The battles had changed him. He had never been this aloof as a boy, although he had kept to himself most of the time.

Max was the only one who had truly known and loved Merlin. Curiosity overcame her momentarily, but it was swept away as rain started pelting in earnest. All she could think of was shelter.

Merlin swept his cloak around her, but the fine wool was already damp. He led her through the trees to a broken-down cottage she'd seen on her rides but never investigated. Even though most of the roof had caved in, one corner was dry and gave them shelter. The rain beat the furze and reedy grass outside, but soon slowed to a whisper. Fog had begun to rise from the ground.

Merlin's companion said nothing, only stared at Cynara from under a hedge of white eyebrows. She was startled to discover that one of his eyes was blue, the other greenish-brown. Suddenly he winked and smiled, and her worry lessened a fraction.

His boot propped on the sill, Merlin stared out the glassless window. "I didn't mean for this farce to happen. I just arrived last night from France. Had I but known, I would have come earlier to prevent the wedding—"

She stiffened. "Farce?"

"Your wedding to Felix. I always thought you had better sense than that. As I recall, you used to be remarkably levelheaded and strong-willed." Reproach clouded his gaze as he glanced at her. "I suppose you have changed—like all of us."

Cynara wrapped the cloak closer around her, using it as a shield against his sharp eyes. "There are difficult circumstances to consider."

He adjusted one of his gloves. "If you're hinting at Brand's latest scrape, I know all about it. Even the servants know." He sighed profoundly. "But that you believed Felix would help in that matter surprises me. When did he ever help anyone but himself? He didn't ride after us, now, did he? Like a fat spider he'll try to entwine us in some web, then wait patiently for the perfect moment to pounce."

She lowered her eyes. He was right of course, but she disliked the way he had put her in her place. Who was he anyway to carry her away in front of friends and relatives? Such shame! Hereafter, she would be unable to face her peers. "You compromised me, Merlin. Don't you care that you have ruined my reputation?"

His lips quirked at the corners. "Would you have accompanied me voluntarily?" He paused, gauging her expression. She glared at him as he shrugged. "I didn't think so. I wasn't about to start an argument with you in front of the altar. Surprise is always the best strategy; first thing I learned in the army."

Like two powerful adversaries, they appraised each other for a moment. Cynara was the first to turn away. Her cheeks burned with anger and bewilderment. This man had always had the power to stir her emotions—one way or the other. Not even the worldly Prince Regent at Carlton House in London would be able to remain indifferent under such a haunting black stare as Merlin's.

"What now?" she asked as if the dire truth of her situation had just sunk in. "What are your plans with me?"

"I already told you. We shall marry just as soon as may be." He pointed toward the old man who was leaving the cottage to see to the horses. "My batman, Gideon Swift, will witness that we spent the night together here." He laughed mirthlessly. "Not the most romantic spot for a tryst, I admit, but we must remain here until the rain lets up."

"Of all underhanded—"

He smiled mirthlessly. "Cynara, your eyes sparkle with fire when you're angry, but spare me—"

She stepped up to him, so close his virile presence enfolded her, and said softly, "If you think that I will marry you, you're sadly deluded. I'm sure friends and relatives will understand when I explain that you held me prisoner."

The wind moaned in the cracks of the broken roof, and rain whipped through a hole to puddle on the dirt floor.

"There will be tattle nevertheless," he said as non-chalantly as if they were discussing the weather. "Your mother will not like to hear your name dragged into sordid gossip. She's a conventional soul if my memory is not mistaken."

"After today I'm already the center of gossip! Mother will be furious," she said. "She will be on my side."

"Don't fool yourself," he said bluntly. "Your mother will do what's expected of her. To stop the gossip, she'll be prepared to offer you up to the devil himself."

"Seems that I already stand eye to eye with him," she said, striding to the door. The fog moved dismally over the sea, crowding closer to the cottage with every breath. "Your reputation is evil, Merlin, and Mother won't have anything to do with you."

He sighed. "I take it you're alluding to my father's death?" He followed her to the door, gripping her shoulders. "So you believe I'm guilty of murdering him? I thought you might understand—"

"I know nothing about his death except for what I heard. Mother will never condone my union to a mur—someone with so wicked a reputation."

"Felix is by no means the purest of men," he said dryly. "But she would have allowed you to wed him."

Cynara longed to get away as his words wove a web of pitfalls around her. She had known it was wrong to accept Felix, but had there been a choice? "He would have found a way to acquit Brand." She took a turn around the cottage, picking her way among debris on the floor. Not a stick of furniture to sit on. Dispirited, she stared out the window, wondering what her mother was doing at that moment. Probably having one of her fainting spells with Felix hovering around her, smiling ingratiatingly. How easily Mother had been taken in by him, but then, he'd promised to alleviate the Hawthornes' poverty. He could be charming when he chose to.

Gideon Swift returned, carrying a load of blankets. "Sorry to say they're damp, Captain Seymour, but there's nothing else."

"Make up a pad for Miss Hawthorne to lie on. We must sleep on the floor," Merlin said, turning his attention to the silent woman by the window.

His heart constricted at the sight of her. She had grown lovelier over the years, and the adoration he'd always felt for her had returned with renewed force as he looked into her angry blue-green eyes. Her body was daintily built, like that of the porcelain shepherdess adorning his mantelpiece at home. Just like the fine porcelain, her skin glowed as if lit from within. Her neck was long and graceful, her features just as fine and delicate as the rest of her body; nose small and straight, lips rosy bows of sweetness. But there was nothing frail about her flashing eyes. They glared as fiercely and as powerfully as the sea in bright sunlight.

The unattainable woman he'd always yearned for was here, so close he could touch her. No one knew how lovable he'd always found her, Max least of all. In his cheerful, open ways, Max had explained two years before that Cynara had promised to marry him. Those words had hurt, Merlin thought. Cynara had slipped forever out of reach, and he'd struggled to forget her.

A quirk of fate had changed everything. Now he would step into Max's shoes, but would Cynara ever feel a fragment of the attraction for him that she'd felt for Max? It was clear that she still detested and distrusted him. Cold, paralyzing misery entered his heart at the thought that she would never love him. Perhaps no woman would, not while the suspicious death of his father was hanging over his head.

Cynara had always looked at him with disdain, and this latest escapade would surely push her farther away. He swore silently, wishing he had scotched her wedding plans sooner. He'd planned to tell her about Max's wish that she marry him, but some perverse notion had stopped him. He wanted her to marry him for himself, not because Max had requested it. Love made one too vulnerable, he thought, cursing his weakness. He wished he could get Cynara out of his mind, but perhaps he would have to be dead for that to happen.

"Sleep on these here, missy," said old Gideon to Cynara after spreading the blankets on the floor. "You must forgive Captain Seymour for these makeshift arrangements. We didn't have time to plan this better, seein' as we just returned from abroad."

Cynara threw an angry glance at Merlin. "Don't apologize for your employer, Mr. Swift. What he did this evening is beyond redemption." Without another word she sank down on the blankets. She knew she would not sleep, but she would rather sit than stand all night, staring at the darkness, as Merlin was doing. How Merlin could go on living while carrying the suspicion of murder on his shoulders was more than she could understand. Without a word or a glance he eased himself down by the door, propping his back against the wall. Though his posture was relaxed,

Cynara knew he would not let her slip past and run away.

Gideon Swift sat by the window and tilted his hat over his eyes. No more could she escape through the window than through the door. Even if she did, and managed to get back to Black Raven, she knew she had no desire to see Felix, not until she'd had time to think through her situation yet again.

If she managed to flee, there was no other estate except Black Raven for miles around. On the morrow she had to convince her mother that the weather had prevented them from riding to Merlin's country house, Stormywood. Perhaps Mother could think of a way to reverse the damage to her reputation, but in her heart Cynara knew it would be hopeless.

Mrs. Estelle Mournay Hawthorne had never quite adopted the British ways. However many years she lived on this mist-enshrouded island, she would forever be French at heart. She wound the cream cashmere shawl closer around her frail shoulders, once more cursing the fog that crept through every crevice of the ancient house of Stormywood to penetrate flesh and bone. She had lived in this land for twenty-seven years and had yet to get used to the damp, dismal climate. Even during the summer months the sun was reluctant, although she had to admit that perfect, sunny days came like bright jewels when one least expected them. This day was doubly dreary as she stared out the window of the salon next to the hallway. She wanted to be right by the door when that scoundrel, that young jackanapes, Merlin Seymour, brought her daughter to his home.

Two lackeys had fetched her from Black Raven after the horrible humiliation at the chapel. Here at Stormywood she was protected from the gossip—for the moment. She had been glad to escape the curious and pitying stares of the guests. What a disaster! Cynara was ruined, and there was nothing she could do to protect her daughter now. She couldn't bear thinking about it.

A wistful feeling floated through her. There were so many memories in this lovely old stone mansion, memories of Ross Seymour, Merlin's father. Such a wonderful man . . . such kindness . . . such manly charm and, oh . . . such patience. But their love had been doomed from the start. Besides, Edgar Hawthorne had loved her more than any man was capable of. How much had she given him in return? Had he sensed her long-ago weakness for Merlin's father?

"Mon Dieu! Merlin shall pay for this," she said, fluttering a fan in front of her face. *Imbécile.* Wicked boy. *I will never forgive you for this.* She paced the floor, her tiny slippers tapping impatiently. She was too old to deal with this sort of scandal. If only Edgar had been alive . . . In earlier days this would never have happened. He would have dealt with this crisis efficiently, as he always did. Now she was too old to handle Brandon's plight or Cynara's headstrong nature. Cynara, who looked so much like Edgar, and who had been her father's daughter to the end, daunted Estelle. She experienced a flicker of guilt at labeling her daughter intimidating. Cynara had inherited her strength from her father, there was no doubt

about that. She was British to the bone, Estelle thought. She could have acted as hostess at any gathering hosted by the Prince Regent without a flutter of nerves.

She had none of the darker, more volatile French heritage of the Mournays. Estelle threw a glance at herself in the mirror in the hallway. Many admirers in her youth had told her she had a classical beauty—oval face, regular features, dark eyes, pale marble skin. Left of that beauty was a certain brittle shadow of times past. Cynara was all gold and cream, not at all like herself, unless she had inherited her French passion. Only her future husband—whoever he now would be—would find that out.

"Merlin, Merlin . . . why did you have to ruin Cynara's life besides your own?" she muttered. "Are you so bent on destruction after the war? At the rate you're going, you'll destroy everything that Ross ever worked for. And where does Cynara fit into your schemes?"

The sound of horses' hooves echoed in the ghostly fog. Estelle tensed, worry shooting through her. She adjusted her dark curls, which were streaked with silver, and took a deep, steadying breath. Why did her children cause her so much pain? First Brand in prison, now Cynara ruined. Her daughter could not show her face in society again. With a shudder Estelle summoned the footman stationed by the curving oak staircase in the hallway.

"It's your master returning, no doubt. Open the door." Her fingers trembled around her ivory-handled fan as she peeped over the footman's shoulder. Bramble, the butler, arrived, every fat roll quivering, every inch of his moon face flustered. He wrung his white-gloved hands and waddled out on the steps.

"Sir," he began as Merlin slid from the saddle. "Such terrible weather to be abroad."

Merlin lifted Cynara from the saddle. She looked disheveled and pale, Estelle thought, and fluttered outside. "My darling—"

"Mother," Cynara cried, and threw herself into Estelle's arms.

"Have you aired the lady's bedchamber?" Merlin inquired of the butler, who bowed and smiled by the door. Merlin nodded to Mrs. Hawthorne, then strode up the stairs, his limp barely visible.

"You, young man," Estelle called after him. "I must have a word with you this instant!" She pulled Cynara with her inside. "You must explain—"

Merlin was halfway up to the second floor. "Later, Mrs. Hawthorne. You may hear all the sordid details from your daughter." A grim smile flashed across his face to disappear as rapidly as it had appeared.

Estelle started to climb after Merlin, but Cynara held her back. "Let him go. There's no use talking to him."

"His father would turn in his grave if he knew about this. Merlin has changed into a devil since Ross's death." Estelle trembled with emotional exhaustion. She viewed her daughter, noting the dark smudges of fatigue under the usually brilliant eyes. Today those eyes were shadowy and tinged with worry. Cynara was barely holding back her tears, as much was clear. The spirit of her proud and beautiful daughter was crushed.

"Did he molest you, my child?" Estelle whispered, and led Cynara up the stairs.

"No . . . we barely spoke above ten words with each other."

Estelle pressed her handkerchief into Cynara's hand. "You do understand that your reputation is ruined now. *Where* did you spend the night?"

"In a broken-down cottage by the sea, not far from Black Raven."

They reached the room allotted to Cynara, the chamber adjoining that of her mother. Estelle pushed her daughter inside, and untied the cords of the black cloak that Merlin had wrapped around her. "Do you regret that you're not Felix's wife?" she asked, tossing the garment onto a chair. She chafed Cynara's cold hands and led her to the four-poster that was surrounded by yellow and green chintz bed hangings.

Cynara shook her head as she sat down. "No . . . I see now it would have been a terrible mistake to marry Felix." She pressed her fingertips to her lips as if to force back despair.

"What did Merlin say to you?"

Cynara's eyes darkened with anguish as she stared into the distance. "Merlin hasn't explained anything. I believe he's quite mad. Merlin is set on marrying me, that's why he kept me out all night, to compromise me. I have no idea why he wants to marry me."

Estelle gasped and felt the floor tilt under her. *"Mon Dieu.* Marry? How could he—a man suspected of murder—suggest such a *dastardly* thing? His mind must have gone a-begging." She whipped her fan back and forth, noticing the dirt streaks on Cynara's lovely wedding gown. What an upset! How would she cope with this? She stroked Cynara's cold hand gently. "And you, daughter? What do you want?"

Cynara's eyes had a faraway look. "He didn't sleep at all, only sat there, staring into the darkness without moving all night. Like a ghost."

"Who? When?" The child was deeply disturbed. She'd wring Merlin's neck just as soon as she had a chance.

Cynara moved across the room like a sleepwalker. "I would like a bath, Mother. I'm so cold."

"Of course. I don't want you to get ill." Estelle bustled about the room, pulled the bell rope, and ordered a hip bath and hot water to be brought up to the chamber. "Tildy will arrive with your things tomorrow. Merlin's orders. That young man has too much gall."

Cynara was huddled in front of the marble fireplace, where a small fire hissed and crackled. The room was cheerful with its gold and green decor and flower-patterned carpet, but the towering rain clouds outside the windows brought in an air of gloom, of foreboding.

Cynara looked up, her face pale with anguish. "He's determined to marry me. How shall I escape him?"

Estelle steeled herself. This was one of the few times Cynara really needed her, and she had to find a way to help her somehow. "I must speak with Merlin this very minute."

"Mother," Cynara began, but grew silent as Estelle left the room, closing the door gently behind her. *You are on my side, aren't you?*

* * *

Estelle found Merlin in his study, legs propped on the gleaming surface of the desk. He had changed into dry clothes, a black coat, and buckskins. He wore dry topboots, but his hair was still damp and disheveled. But that was the only outward sign that he'd endured any discomfort on the previous night.

"I will speak with you later, Mrs. Hawthorne," he said, shoving aside a stack of papers and rising with a polite bow. But when she didn't leave, he reluctantly offered her a chair.

She sat on the edge of the leather wingback chair before the desk. She knew how the steward must feel every morning waiting for his orders in that selfsame spot and meeting those penetrating dark eyes. He would cringe just as she did now.

"Merlin, you have ill used my daughter, and if you expect me to stand by and watch without comment, you're sadly mistaken."

"Your daughter has a willful mind of her own, and if it hadn't been for her rash decision to marry my cousin, I wouldn't have been forced to take such drastic measures. Believe me, I had no desire to abduct Cynara from her own wedding. But a union with Felix is quite unthinkable."

"You have *ruined* her! She will never be able to raise her head in polite society again. Her chances at an advantageous marriage are nil, so how will we survive, I ask you? The Hawthornes are merely scraping by, and well you know it. Why didn't you just bring her back to Bluewater after you interrupted the ceremony?"

He ignored her questions, and that made her even

more flustered. "I will, of course, do the honorable thing and offer for her myself."

Startled, Estelle met the piercing gaze. *He was serious.* "It does you credit, Merlin, but I regret that you would do such a thing. Why, your father has been dead only a sixmonth, and with your own reputation in shreds, how could you ever think of marrying a gentle lady?"

Silence stretched unbearably. Merlin smiled coolly. "That's why. No lady would marry me, so I took matters into my own hands."

"How can you be so cold-hearted—calculating?" Faintness was creeping over her, and Estelle wished she had brought her vinaigrette bottle to provide a refreshing whiff. This man was the devil incarnate. He would drag Cynara down with him. People would whisper that she'd married a murderer—unless the mystery of Ross Seymour's death was cleared up. Fast.

"You shall not lack for comforts, Mrs. Hawthorne. This will be your home for as long as you wish, unless you want to return to Bluewater to await Brand's release."

A headache was starting to pound at her temples, and she wondered why she couldn't be as calm as this man who sounded as if he actually believed that Brand would return. She fumbled for her handkerchief inside her cuff, but then recalled that she'd given it to Cynara. "Oh, why, oh, why did all this have to happen?" She rocked back and forth, wishing Edgar were alive to deal with this mess.

"Will you give the union your blessing? I intend to

marry Cynara just as soon as I can procure a special license."

"But your father's death . . . *mon Dieu,* you're in mourning, surely for another six months."

"This cannot wait. It will be a quiet affair, just you and the servants as witnesses. Anyway, who would want to come? Everyone shuns me since Father's demise." He rose and towered over her. Fear fluttered in her chest.

"Come now, Mrs. Hawthorne, you always had a shrewd head on your shoulders. As you know, I am a wealthy man, and I promise to provide for your future. Will you give your blessing?"

Chapter 3

"I have Cynara's best interest at heart. Only she can accept you," Estelle said.

"She won't come willingly. You know that."

"Why her? Why don't you choose another bride, someone who would gladly accept your offer."

"I just explained to you that no one would accept me."

Estelle pressed her fingertips against her temples. "So you *stole* my daughter. When did you lose your good manners, Merlin? Ross would have been appalled at this conversation."

Merlin rubbed his chin as if weighing his words carefully. "You see . . . Max asked—"

"Don't blame this on Max! I won't hear of it. Of the three Seymour cousins, he was the only truly decent man."

Merlin laughed. "You must admit that Cynara would be better off with me than with Felix. He would break her spirit completely. I'm not a violent man, Estelle. I'll not harm Cynara."

"What am I to believe?" Estelle moaned.

"If you don't want to starve and see Bluewater go to ruin, Cynara must make an advantageous marriage. I'm a rather wealthy man; I'll provide for you—and Brand."

Estelle's thought whirled in wild confusion. She was torn in many directions. She then said something she wouldn't have dreamt of saying two minutes earlier. "Convince Cynara that you'll be a better choice than Felix, and if you press home more strongly that you're innocent—that Ross—" She couldn't finish the sentence.

He laughed then, cold mirth that sent shivers along Estelle's spine. Yet, as she had uttered those words, it was as if she'd placed the entire burden on his broad shoulders. Let him straighten out the problem. Another unbidden thought entered her mind . . . the realization that Cynara would be the *pawn* of this alliance. Her daughter's life would be wasted, since a loveless marriage would be tragical. Estelle rapidly closed her mind on that frightful thought. Like the practical Frenchwoman she was, she figured that love seldom was involved where marriages of the nobility were concerned. Everyone part of this particular transaction would have enough money to put the finest food on the table, including the parent of the bride. It was a sound bargain, the only one available. Surely Cynara would understand that when she spoke her vows to this dark man.

Estelle flinched as Merlin said, "I take it I have your blessing then, madam?"

Choking on her own cowardice, she nodded.

* * *

That night Merlin stood for a long time outside Cynara's door. No sounds came from within. Was she sound asleep, or was she staring into the darkness, sleepless?

This was wrong somehow. He'd much rather marry Cynara out of love. He sighed. Though he adored her, the possibility of her ever loving him was slim. Yet the only way to take care of her, to protect her against Felix, was to have her by his side at all times. With another sigh he went to the master suite at the end of the corridor.

His steps echoed hollowly along the wooden floor. Since his father's death he could barely bring himself to walk the length of this room, remembering that it had been Ross's bedchamber before. How many nights, how many *years* had his father walked this same path every night?

"I will find out who killed you, Father, and why," Merlin whispered as he closed the bedroom door silently behind him. He remembered the suspicion in Cynara's eyes, and that hurt more than the snubs of his peers at the clubs. Over and over he relived that nightmare when his father had lost his life: the stormy night, the frantic horses bolting straight into the ravine, the coach getting crushed among the rocks. If only he knew who had delivered the shot that had wounded one of the horses!

Sitting on the edge of his bed, he rubbed his hands as if to chase away the chill of the memories. Ever since Waterloo, he'd struggled to rest his eyes on beauty, to find relief from the pictures of blood and destruction that scalded his mind at night. On the outside he looked as before the battles, except for the limp that

would always remind him of Max's death, but inside
. . . inside was a battle of war and peace. War . . . war.
Even now the memories were trying to suck him down
into a hopeless void.

With a jerky movement he stood and took some
deep breaths, forcing his thoughts to the positive
things about his life. He was back at Stormywood, and
the work at the estate lent normalcy to his life. It was
a deceptive pleasure, since his father should have been
sitting behind that desk in the study—not he. Yet, he
liked the tranquility of the place, the friendliness of the
horses and other animals that didn't know to judge
him. The staff, however, treated him as if he were the
devil, all except Bramble. And Gideon Swift was the
last true friend he had, the friend who had brought
him back to reason when all had looked utterly
doomed after Father's death. Now he lived day by
day, getting more and more impatient to discover who
had wanted Ross dead.

His alert hearing picked out the faint crack of a
branch breaking. He crossed the room swiftly and
parted the heavy velvet drapes a fraction.

At the edge of the park, three horses were silhouet-
ted against the brilliance of the full moon. The riders
were silent, dark cloaks flapping, faces turned up toward him. Were they even now staring at his windows,
or at Cynara's? Swearing silently, Merlin fingered the
well-worn sword at his side, the weapon he'd carried to
stave off any trouble after fetching Cynara from Black
Raven. The dagger was in its usual spot inside the top
of his boot. Had Felix finally come to wreak ven-
geance? This was his style. He would come at the small

hours in the morning and stab you in your sleep if you
weren't careful—or hire others to do it.

The three men rode through an opening in the hedge
surrounding the grounds and advanced cautiously.
The thick grass turf muffled the sounds of the hooves.
Merlin's jaw tightened, and he waited only ten more
seconds to make sure they were truly heading for the
house. Then he slipped out of his room, and, sure-
footed, ran down to the hallway below. If they were
out for blood, they would find their own flowing.

Silvery light trickled through the tall windows by
the door, and Merlin moved through the shadows to
get a better look outside. There they were by the steps,
the three dark riders, as silent as wraiths.

Slowly, Merlin pulled out his sword. It grated
against the scabbard, the sound jarring in the stillness.
His fingers tightened around the carved hilt.

For a moment no one moved. One of the riders, his
face pale in the darkness, pointed up at one of the
windows. *Her* window. Rage possessed Merlin, but he
remained unmoving, waiting for their next move.

To his surprise, they didn't dismount. The horses
skirted the shallow steps and the long stone terrace
with its low balustrade. Merlin followed inside, walking from salon to salon toward the back.

The riders took a tour of the perimeter of the chapel
located in a copse not far from the main house. Then
they returned, but instead of stopping, they crossed
the front lawn and headed back the long drive toward
the gates.

Merlin frowned. He could have sworn he recognized
Felix's profile under the tall hat, but it could have been
anyone. Yet he sensed it was Felix. Who else would

skulk around the house at night? Before long, Felix would seek his revenge.

"I will be ready when you come," Merlin said to himself, and sheathed the sword. "Even if I have to spend every night staring out the windows."

As Merlin sought rest for his weary body, Cynara lay awake in her bed, her back propped against the pillows. Estelle sat stiffly on the edge of the mattress and held one of Cynara's unwilling hands.

"Merlin is a better catch than Felix, dearest. If you marry him, Brandon and I will be settled for life, never have to worry about funds again." She paused, viewing the rebellion in Cynara's blue-green gaze. "As you know, your father was an honorable man, but hardly wealthy. We are *poor*, Cynara."

"Mother, are you selling me to the highest bidder only to pay your bills?"

Estelle flinched, her bottom lip trembling. "You would marry Felix to save your brother, so what's the difference? Merlin and Brand are not enemies, and that's more than Felix had to offer your brother. If I recall correctly, Brand detests Felix."

"Felix didn't mind about that." Cynara combed her fingers through her damp hair. "Merlin might be a *murderer*, Mother! I feel the war changed him, made him ruthless and cold. You would have me marry a killer?"

Estelle clasped Cynara's hand anew. *"Non . . .* no, my child. Deep in my heart I know that Merlin is not a murderer. Only an utterly vile person would kill his own sire. Merlin loved Ross."

Cynara shoved the pillows aside and slid along the mattress until she was lying down. Estelle tucked the corners of the coverlet around her.

"Love, bah!" Cynara said.

"I, your mother, love you, like Ross loved Merlin," Estelle said.

"It doesn't prove that he's innocent."

"Cynara, I will not force you into anything—"

"But you've already given your permission to this union. Oh, Mother!" Disgusted, Cynara turned away from her parent. "I have no choice, then?"

"In the eyes of the world you are ruined, since you spent the night with him. At least he's willing to do the honorable thing." She paused. "Max thought the world of Merlin, so he cannot be all evil."

"My feelings don't matter, then?" Cynara whispered tonelessly, more to herself than to her mother. "I'm only a pawn in everyone else's scheme." Heartache weighed her down, a leaden numbness from which there seemed to be no escape.

Estelle sighed and patted Cynara's tense shoulder. "As a married lady you will have much greater freedom to carve out your own life. You might never have to see Merlin. When he's in town you can stay in the country, and vice versa."

Cynara squeezed her eyes shut, wishing that her mother would stop talking. "So be it, then." She stiffened her chin. "I'll talk with Merlin tomorrow. If he promises to help Brandon, I shall marry him."

Cynara never had a chance to confront Merlin, who had left Stormywood early the following morning without saying good-bye. According to Bramble, he had an appointment with the archbishop about the special marriage license, and had left at the first light of dawn. Cynara wondered when he'd had the time to set up the appointment.

She didn't see Merlin until the wedding ceremony that took place two nights later.

After Felix's nightly visit, Merlin had fallen into an exhausted slumber. Nightmares had hounded his sleep, and his thigh had pained him—as it did now—but he'd shut his mind against it. He'd slept the entire night, but the following night when he'd returned to Stormywood, he'd kept vigil. His eyes were gritty and his head pounded with a headache for the lack of sleep as he watched Cynara enter the chapel with Mrs. Hawthorne. The two women were leaning on each other as if seeking strength one from the other.

Merlin's breath caught in his throat at Cynara's loveliness. The pale golden hair hung in rich waves down her back, caught back at the ears by glittering combs. He was grateful that she wasn't wearing the wedding dress she'd worn at Black Raven. This time she wore a simple shimmering ice-blue gown trimmed with lace. Her eyes were dark with distrust, but she met his gaze unflinchingly. The expression speared his heart, and he hated the fact that she cared naught for him.

An alluring scent enveloped her, reminding him of a meadow of spring flowers. He took her hand. The skin on her fingers was so soft, so pliant, but he sensed the steel under the softness. His bride was no simpering miss. His gaze swept over the rounded expanse of her shoulders revealed by the low neckline, and the shadowy cleft between her full breasts. A fierce desire overcame him. He vowed he would one day caress those soft mounds and taste the sweetness of her rosy lips. He would press her lithe body against his in passion, as he'd dreamed of doing ever since he grew from boy to man. But he could wait—wait until those mistrustful eyes looked at him with a desire matching his own.

"I'm glad you came to your senses," he murmured, and winced as her face grew even paler than it already was.

"I wanted to speak with you before the ceremony, Merlin. There won't be a wedding unless you comply with one condition."

Merlin drew her aside while they were waiting for the chaplain to arrive. "Condition?"

"You must promise to help Brandon get out of Newgate. When that's accomplished, I wish you to discover who really stole that diamond necklace and why."

He smiled faintly. "How can you be so sure Brandon didn't really steal the jewelry?"

"My brother is not a thief. You know him; you ought to know that he never steals."

"You already pointed out to me that I don't have any power in London. Who would listen to an accused murderer, eh?"

Cynara tore her hand from his grip. "So let me return to Felix. The thought of marrying you is most tasteless."

He crossed his arms over his chest, and his eyebrows met in a scowl above his eyes. "You'd rather believe Felix's promises than mine? If I'm not mistaken, he *blackmailed* you into marrying him."

Cynara gasped in shock. "How did you find out?"

"Servants listen in wherever they can, and they aren't loath to part with information if the price is right."

"Tildy!" Cynara's eyes narrowed. "I shall deal with her later."

"Your mother is eager for this union. I promised to take care of her."

"I don't know what you told Mother, but she convinced me I had to comply, or be forever ruined."

"Mrs. Hawthorne's a practical person, and you could learn something from her." He pulled her closer to the altar, where the chaplain was ready to perform the ceremony. "Come now. Let's get this over with."

"She badgered me into this. How much did you have to pay her—an amount great enough to see her comfortable for the rest of her days?"

"More than enough. The papers are already drawn up. We have both signed them." His lips parted in an indulgent smile as if she were a recalcitrant child.

"I take it you won't lift a finger to save Brand, as Felix might have done."

"I can try, but I assure you, no one will be able to help Brand if he's guilty. Anyway, Brand's a fool, and if he gets out of this scrape, he'll fall into another. You know that as well as I." He gripped her arm and forced her to look at him. "At least I'm not giving you golden promises—like Felix."

Silence hummed between them, and Cynara's hands trembled. "I know you won't do a thing to help him. I can only hope that you will join him in prison ere long—when they find evidence that you killed your father."

He shrugged indifferently, provoking a hotter wave

of anger to swell in Cynara's chest. "You might have to wait a long time for such relief," he said as his grip hardened. "Listen to me! If Max had been here to advise you, whom would he have told you to choose? Me or Felix?"

Cynara knew that Max would have told her to marry Merlin. There was no way out, not if Brand would have a chance at freedom. And there was her mother, who liked her domestic comforts, to consider.

"Come, Cynara. The chaplain is waiting. You can't back out, and you know it."

"I won't forgive you for this," she replied, and stalked toward the clergyman.

The chapel was dimly lit by two branches of candles, throwing off a flickering light on the gray stone walls that had been erected in 1610. The year had been carved on a frieze above the altar, and a faint odor of incense and wax filled the interior. Bramble, the butler, and Gideon Swift were the only witnesses besides Mrs. Hawthorne. Estelle's muffled sobs disturbed the stillness.

Cynara threw a glance at her mother, a sudden flare of pure, blinding wrath going off inside her. Mother had been prepared to offer her up to this dark, silent man like a side of meat.

Merlin stood beside her in front of the chaplain who began the service. She took a long look at the man who would soon be her husband. She couldn't deny that he was a fine figure in his black cutaway coat and pristine neckcloth. His hair waved over his collar, hair the color of a raven's wing. She could detect not a single sign of softness in those hard shoulders or his proud carriage. Even his hands were hard, cool, demanding, yet curiously sensitive. His was not the pudgy, impatient grasp of Felix, and Cynara was grateful for that, if nothing else.

She stared morosely at the chaplain, and cringed as Merlin said his vows in a firm voice. Her legs weakened as she realized that within a minute, this man would have total power over her life. But he had taken total power the moment he hoisted her into his arms in the Black Raven chapel.

"Well, Miss Cynara, what is your answer?" The chaplain's quiet voice penetrated her thoughts. For one awful moment she thought she was going to faint, but her mother's increasing sobs made her straighten her back. No one was going to witness her weakness. That moment she vowed to never let Merlin—or anyone else—dictate her life. Married, she would have more power to do as she wished. She glanced at Merlin, and his left eyebrow rose a fraction.

"I do," she whispered, her voice wavering slightly. Then she lifted her face to his, and closed her eyes in loathing as Merlin gathered her into his arms and pressed his lips to hers in a chaste kiss. His strength swept her away momentarily, and her resolution faltered. His lips made a soft, stirring imprint on her own, leaving her breathless to a degree.

"If you don't mind me saying so, Mrs. Seymour, welcome to Stormywood," Bramble said on the steps of the chapel. His rotund frame beamed, and Cynara gave him a pale smile.

"Thank you, Bramble." She glanced at Gideon Swift, who was twirling his hat between his hands, and shifting his weight from foot to foot.

"This is truly a blessin'," he said at last. "Why, I see

happier times ahead." He darted off as Merlin gave a laugh.

"Old romantic fool. He believes he can predict the future," he said, and offered his arm to Mrs. Hawthorne. His enigmatic gaze rested on Cynara, and she wondered if she'd seen a fleeting softness in those dark eyes. No, they were as cold and implacable as ever.

The servants had been ordered to meet them with torches despite their aversion to their master, the "murder suspect." Bramble had demanded that they serve a midnight supper to celebrate the wedding, and now they were there to escort the newlyweds to the house. The feast consisted of lobster patties, crab meat, tiny triangular cucumber sandwiches, sweets, and syllabubs. Bramble uncorked bottles of champagne, and the servants raised a toast to their new mistress and darted fearful glances at Merlin.

The food tasted like sawdust in Cynara's mouth, but she plastered a brave smile on her face for the benefit of the servants. She noticed that Merlin hadn't touched any of the food, and he set the champagne glass on the table after participating in that one toast.

Cynara dreaded the night to come. Her things would be moved from the guest room to the master suite, and only one door would then separate her from her husband. A chill traveled up her spine. If only he'd been Max.

As the servants returned to the kitchen quarters, an uneasy silence settled in the room. Only Mrs. Hawthorne's sighs pierced the quietude.

"I must retire," she said at last. "It has been a long, trying day." She rose, giving Cynara a searching glance. "Do you need my assistance? Merlin has sent for the rest of your things from Bluewater, and Tildy is in your room."

He's already taking over my life, Cynara thought. "I don't need anything, Mother." *Not from you,* she mused. "Good night." Feeling entrapped, she stepped out on the moonlit terrace. The night was serene and balmy, in sharp contrast to her tumultuous thoughts.

"A night made for lovers, don't you agree?" Merlin drawled behind her. The irony in his voice stung her.

"You don't know what the word *lover* means." She lifted her eyes to his as he stood beside her.

"And you do?" Without waiting for her reply, he continued. "My heart is not wholly devoid of romantic feelings." His teeth gleamed white all of a sudden, forcing a tiny crack in her invisible armor. "I can think of things that lovers do in the nights of summer." He touched her cascading hair. "This, for instance." He grabbed a handful of her hair and pulled her closer. Her instinct was to jerk away, but she knew he would only pursue her until he got what he wanted.

As he gripped her shoulders and pulled her close to his hard body, she remained stiff. She knew that he would kiss her and her revenge would be to remain cold and unresponsive. She closed her eyes, bracing herself against the attack. It never came. He only trailed his long fingers along her cheekbone, then caressed the tender spot just below her ear.

She shivered in response, anticipation flaring to life inside her. She steeled herself against the softness of his touch. He dropped his hand abruptly.

"I know you wish I had been Max, and believe me, I would gladly have raised my glass in a toast at your wedding." His voice grew rough, uncertain. "Max was dearer to me than a real brother could be, and if he could have made you happy— I would have exchanged my life for his on that dismal day in Waterloo."

She read the truth of the statement in his voice, and wondered what had turned his life into such a dreary abyss that he'd rather be dead. His father's death perhaps. The suspicion of murder.

"I loved Max," she said simply, playing with the fan that was hanging from a cord around her wrist. "I *trusted* him. Our friendship was comfortable, and would always be there, even as man and wife."

"I know; he was a great person." Merlin stared into the darkness. His voice was so low, she could hardly hear it. "He loved you passionately—and he trusted me. He . . . he would have wanted me to watch over you."

"And you hastened to obey," she said sarcastically, "running roughshod over my feelings in the process."

He stood very still, avoiding her eyes. An owl winged through the night, casting a fleeting shadow on the ground. His eyes misted over as he remembered Max's blood-streaked gray, face. He glanced at Cynara and ached inside. *I have always loved you.* He would probably never utter those words aloud. In a way, he'd betrayed Max in the end by loving the woman whom Max had loved to distraction.

Merlin tried to shrug off the icy coldness in his limbs. Ever since Waterloo, his life was tumbling to ruins. Everything he touched crumbled, and his very presence created terror in the people he most loved. A curse had settled on him, and he had no idea how to break the spell before he destroyed everything. Every day he died a little more. If only Father were alive.

Cynara startled him out of his thoughts. "By marrying me you have spoiled any chance of meeting the woman who would love you wholeheartedly."

She sounded so earnest that sorrow tightened around his heart. Cynara would be his in name only.

"And you have ruined my chances to marry a man whom I could love," she said so softly he could barely hear her words. But they burned into his brain like a red-hot branding iron. He stared into the night, and listened to her light steps echoing along the terrace. She was retiring without him, and tomorrow their farce of wedded "bliss" would begin.

As he turned his head, he saw her pale gown flash around the corner of the house. Was she going to stroll in the garden? She shouldn't be walking unprotected at night, what with Felix lurking and searching for the perfect moment to instigate mischief.

The doors to his study were open onto the terrace, and he hurried inside to retrieve one of his swords from the wall above the fireplace. He buckled it around his hips, and felt for the knife in its sheath in the waistband of his breeches.

Keeping his distance, he followed Cynara. He would make sure she was safe.

A night bird shrilled among the bushes, and bats flitted among the trees. Cynara drank in the still-sun-warm scent of flowering roses. The garden held a dreamy atmosphere, the air drenched with perfume. She strolled past the birdbath and the sundial mounted on a marble pedestal. A ring of roses guarded it, and surrounding the roses was a bricked path. She wished she could see the color burst of the perennial borders on each side, but now there was only the stark contrast of silver and shadow.

An owl hooted, startling her. She sat down on a wrought iron bench right below the hedge at the very end of the flower garden. The moon painted the old mansion in shimmering white, and the lighted windows glowed golden in contrast.

A dark figure was coming toward her, and she recognized the slight limp in her husband's stride. He hesitated by the sundial, seemingly studying it. Why was he following her? With a sigh she rose and skirted the hedge, turning the corner and coming upon the copse. She'd seen a pond from her window earlier in the day, and she would explore it. Sleep was the furthest thing from her mind. A strange restlessness gnawed at her as she stepped in among the trees.

She came to a clearing just before the pond, and gasped as a tall shadow swept across her path. Hands grabbed her from all sides, and more shadows loomed around her.

"Cynara, come with me," came Felix's voice from the darkness among the trees. " 'Tis not too late."

"Felix!" She blurted out his name in surprise, and the hands holding her captive slackened their grip. "What are you doing here?"

"Did you expect me to stand by and do nothing when Merlin abducted you?" His voice scorned her.

She glanced back the way she'd come, yearning for a chance to escape. "I married him tonight."

"I watched you come out of the chapel, and I saw no happiness on your face."

Cynara took a tentative step back with a shiver of fear. Felix's voice held a brittle edge of anger.

"You let him marry you without protest," Felix went on. "How could you! Brandon will never be free now. Merlin won't lift a finger to help him."

"I have a feeling Brandon would not agree with you, dear cousin Felix," Merlin's voice echoed across the clearing.

Cynara tried to see him, but he was hidden among the trees. Twigs snapped and leaves rustled around her as the men shifted positions. "Merlin?" she croaked.

"Wife, go back to the house," he demanded. "Felix, come out and fight like a man. Don't hide in the shadows." He stepped into the moonlit clearing, and Cynara saw steel glinting in both his hands.

Three men stepped out on the opposite side, Felix first. He told the other two to stand back. "I have come for revenge," he said, his sword singing against steel as he pulled it out of its scabbard.

"Revenge? Skulking in the shadows? I wouldn't have fainted in fear had you challenged me to my face in broad daylight," Merlin chided.

"Step up and fight like a man, then," Felix demanded, and flexed his sword arm. Moonlight bounced off the steel, and fear constricted Cynara's throat as she watched. She had not obeyed Merlin's demand that she return to the house. In horror, she watched the men come together, steel clashing. Over her. If Max had been alive, this would never have happened, she thought.

The swords danced a deadly dance as the men grunted with exertion and their feet thrashed the tall grass and bushes of the clearing. Merlin parried a lightning-fast jab, and sidestepped a lunge that would have pierced his heart. With a downward slash he ripped Felix's coat arm, drawing blood. Felix swore, delivering a series of thrusts as his other arm hung limp with obvious pain.

Like wraiths they whirled around, Merlin with quick, tall gracefulness, and Felix with bull-like power. Steel jangled and grated in an ever-faster combat. Merlin executed a glissade, and with a quick twist of blade wrenched the sword from Felix's hand. It spun through the air to land ten feet away.

Felix swore, sliding sideways to evade the deadly tip of Merlin's sword, and dashed after his weapon. Merlin waited, chest heaving with the exertion. He rotated his shoulder and put himself in the en garde position.

Just as Felix started to move toward him, a shot shattered the silence, deafening their ears. Everything happened so quickly that Cynara could only gape in surprise. Felix toppled to the ground and lay still.

Merlin dropped his sword and ran forward, closely followed by Felix's henchmen. Merlin touched Felix's lifeless form with his boot, then hurried in among the trees. The sounds of running footsteps crashing through the undergrowth disturbed the silence. Merlin swore as he stumbled and fell.

Cynara stood as if frozen, watching as he returned, limping. "I couldn't see who it was before he got away," he said, panting heavily. "How is Felix?"

The two men warded him off with their swords. "Stay away from him," one of them threatened, and Cynara recognized the voice of Muggins, the head groom at Black Raven. "He's badly wounded." As Merlin watched, they lifted Felix between them and staggered with their burden out of the clearing.

Cynara joined Merlin, and he gripped her arm as

she began to follow the men. "Wait!" He was still holding her as they came out of the clearing and found a coach parked on the lane skirting the pond. Cynara knew since childhood that this particular lane connected with a gate at the south end of the estate.

"Don't come no closer," one of the men demanded. "We don't trust ye. Most likely, ye hired someone to shoot our master."

Merlin gave a dry laugh. "You must be mad. I had no idea that you were hiding in the copse in the first place."

Muggins jumped into the carriage after dragging Felix's unconscious form onto the seat. The other man climbed onto the box and turned the carriage toward the gate. Muggins stuck his head out the window and shouted, "If the master dies, you'll be blamed. I'll see to that."

Cynara heard Merlin's breath hiss between his teeth. He stood tense beside her, his grip hurting her arm. Without another word he pulled her back through the thicket toward the house. "I must go after them."

As they neared the flower garden, they heard shouts and running steps.

Gideon Swift was armed with a rifle. A nightcap with a tassel flapped on his head. The butler was waddling behind, laboring with an old blunderbuss.

"Anyone here?" Swift cried out. "Come out, you varmint." He stopped uncertainly at the edge of the copse, waiting for Bramble to arrive. The butler was panting loudly.

"Most likely a poacher, Sergeant Swift," he wheezed. " 'Twouldn't be the first time. We won't catch no hide nor hair of them." They caught their breath in silence. "Better return to the house."

"Hello! Anyone there? Mr. Merlin?" Swift called out once again, more agitated now, and Cynara opened her mouth to reveal their presence. But before she could yell, Merlin's grip tightened around her and his mouth clamped over hers with such force that she couldn't breathe. She stiffened in shock, but slowly melted as his kiss deepened to explore the softness of her mouth. She fought to get away, pounding his chest with her fist, but he only cradled her closer, tasting, probing, drawing a reluctant response from her very soul. The sky spun above, and her legs gave way, but he scooped her up against him, holding her tightly.

Bramble's voice grumbled as the two men passed very close to where Merlin and Cynara stood. "Why call Mr. Merlin? He's busy with other things, seeing as it's his wedding night. He wouldn't be out here chasing thieves."

The two men returned to the house. "I envy him." Swift's chuckle drifted in the night. "A lovely morsel is Mrs. Cynara Seymour."

Merlin let go of her abruptly, and Cynara's face flamed with anger and—something else. Her heart raced so fast, she could not find her voice to berate him.

Merlin gave her one long, hard look. "It was the only way I could think of to silence you in time. We don't want it known that we fought in the copse—not until I learn who shot Felix." Leaving her in a daze, he strode into the house.

Chapter 4

Blushing, Cynara remembered the hard, disturbing pressure of Merlin's lips on hers as she followed him into the house. His kiss had come so unexpectedly that she had not had the chance to object. There was no denying the warm thrill that had coursed through her at his touch. She sensed he was as aware of her as she was of him; his glances said as much, and the way he seemed to understand her feelings, her thoughts.

She entered her old bedroom, only to discover that all her things had been moved. Snoring in a chair by the open window, Tildy evidently had been waiting for her to come up. She awakened with a start as Cynara closed the door.

"Mistress Cy!" Tildy exclaimed, and heaved herself from the chair and shook out her voluminous apron. "Pardon me, but it seems that I took forty winks."

"It's rather late," Cynara replied. "Where are my things?"

"Aye, I was instructed to tell ye, yer belongings have been moved to the master suite." Tildy paused, studying Cynara closely. "Starting tonight, ye're to sleep in the room next to Mr. Merlin."

Cynara had forgotten that fact, and her hand flew to her throat in an effort to suppress the moan of dismay issuing from her lips. "Now? 'Tis too soon." She gripped the back of an armchair as if to steady herself. How could she fall asleep knowing that only a thin wall separated her from him? At any time he could march into her room and climb into bed with her.

"That's what's expected of ye, Mistress Cy. Yer his wife now, an' ye have certain duties."

Cynara knew very well at which duties Tildy was hinting, and a wave of fear rolled through her. Was he going to invade her bed—her body. . . . She cut off that thought abruptly before she could conjure up mental images of Merlin embracing her. It was almost impossible to forget his kiss, his penetrating eyes, but she steeled herself.

"I take it you can show the way to my new bedchamber?" She walked to the door, her back as stiff as if she were about to face her execution.

Tildy followed her. "O' course. I moved yer things, Mistress Cy. The room is ever so el'gant."

Tildy was right. The chamber was spacious, ceiling lofty with ornate plaster moldings adorning the perimeter of the room. The walls were sectioned with green striped silk panels, and the woodwork was painted cream. A pale green carpet with a blue and gold border complimented the graceful Chippendale furniture. Cynara's glance automatically went to the four-poster whose bedhangings were of the same striped silk as the walls. Would Merlin come to her bed? It was his right, but he had said nothing about his plans . . . other than he was riding over to Black Raven. But later, what would happen when he returned? Cynara impatiently pushed aside the thought, and viewed the escritoire with its formal cream stationery and the goose quill lying beside the inkstand. Sighing deeply, she glanced at the bed once again. Under any other circumstances she would have liked its elegant lines, but now tension gathered inside her, and she feared what the future would hold. Stormywood was the last place she had expected to spend her wedding night. Merlin was not the bridegroom she had envisioned. Life changed from day to day—yes—from breath to breath.

"I would say Mr. Merlin is a generous man," Tildy commented, stroking the fine silk of the bed hangings. "This is so diff'rent from Black Raven, where ever'-thing's crumblin' and dusty."

Cynara nodded. "Yes, Black Raven is in sad disrepair since Max's father died. Felix has no feelings for the estate; he has no plans to refurbish the place." Unease filling her, she wondered how Felix had fared after the shot that had felled him. He might no longer be alive. No, he must have survived; he had only been wounded.

Though she ought to have been relieved that he could not hurt her while prostrate with a wound, she could feel only trepidation.

Something about Felix made her doubt that he could ever die like a regular person. A bullet could perhaps not penetrate his thick hide. . . . Cynara shivered and muttered a prayer. The room was cold all of a sudden, and she wrapped her arms around her middle. She would breathe easier when Felix returned to America. After all, there's where he wanted to live; he had told her so only three days earlier. He would let the ancient seat of the Raven earldom fall into complete decay. He'd planned to take her with him to Virginia, where he had inherited the tobacco plantation from his mother.

Was it her duty to enquire after Felix's health, or pretend she knew nothing about the duel? She was now Merlin's wife, and if Felix was his enemy, then Felix was her enemy as well. However much she wished her life to be different, her loyalty lay with Merlin since their wedding ceremony.

"What's yer thinkin'?" Tildy asked as she spread out Cynara's best nightgown on the bed. "Ye'd better hurry and get ready. Ye don't want to make yer husband wait—bound t' make him ill-tempered."

"I'm relieved that Felix is not in that bedchamber." Cynara threw an apprehensive glance at the door leading to Merlin's room.

Tildy helped Cynara out of the gown and loosened the stays. "Aye, an' ye should be. Yer better off with Mr. Merlin."

Fifteen minutes later Tildy had slipped the filmy confection of white silk and lace over Cynara's head and also brushed out her blond curls. Apprehension built in Cynara's heart as Tildy bobbed and wished her mistress good night. After giving a wink of encouragement, the maid closed the door behind her.

Cynara sat perfectly still on the edge of the mattress. Would he come later, or would he ignore her since theirs was a marriage of convenience? She could never be sure about Merlin's intentions, though she suspected he was a passionate man who would demand her obedience to marital duty.

She curled up in bed and pulled the coverlet over her. Tired after the long day, she finally dozed, only to awaken sometime later as she heard movement in the adjoining room.

Suspense gnawing at her, she tiptoed to the connecting door and pressed her ear against it. She heard sounds, like boots falling to the floor. Merlin was talking in a muffled tones, and she recognized Gideon Swift's rough voice. What were they talking about? She held her breath so as not to miss a word, but their voices were barely discernible through the thick oak panels. She did understand the words *Black Raven* and *nightly callers, secret*—and what was the next word? *Murder?* Yes, that was it, and then Merlin uttered an oath. Perhaps they were talking about the duel and Swift was supposed to keep it a secret.

She wondered again if Felix had survived. For Merlin's sake, Cynara hoped that he had, because if he hadn't, Merlin might be accused of another murder.

Murder. As a frisson of fear touched Cynara, she walked quietly back to her bed and crawled under the cover. Was she married to a murderer? If the authorities proved that Merlin had killed his father, she would be ruined forever. And Merlin—he would be executed. Her name would be linked to scandal for the rest of her life, and she would be excluded from society. It would be difficult to live completely cut off from everything and everybody she had known. She shivered although the night was warm.

She had left the bed hangings open. Eerie moonlight streamed through the tall windows, giving the bedchamber an unreal quality. An owl hooted plaintively, and Cynara felt lonely and exposed, as if her life were

perching on the dangerous precipice of a ravine with
no bottom in sight.

She knew nothing about Merlin except that he'd
always been aloof and secretive, and that evidently
hadn't changed. Turning her head toward his door,
she listened for more sounds, but all was quiet. Gideon
Swift had just left and closed the door behind him. It
was as if she could sense Merlin's very breath beyond
the connecting door. The polished brass knob winked
in the moonlight, and she wished she had the key to
the lock. It was on the other side. She heard Merlin's
bed creak as he settled for the night.

She tried to sleep, but jagged images flew unchecked
through her mind. If she were to get any rest, she
would have to learn the fate of Felix. She pulled on her
filmy wrap and returned to the door. Taking a deep
breath, she knocked.

After what seemed an eternity, he asked her to
enter.

The master bedroom smelled masculine, of leather
and shaving soap. It was different from anything she
was used to. "Merlin?" Her voice trembled, and she
loathed her sudden weakness.

"Yes?"

She saw him outlined, sitting on the edge of the bed
wearing nothing but trousers. The room was full of
shadows and sharp moonlight. "How is Felix?"

She heard Merlin exhale, a slow hiss of exasperation. "He's dead."

"*Dead?* It can't be true!" She gripped the facing of
her wrap and twisted the fabric. "What shall we do?"

He got up and stood in front of her. In a shaft of
light she noticed his gaze roving hungrily over her

body, and she knew the lacy wrap and nightdress clung to her form in a most abandoned manner. Feeling exposed, she pulled the wrap closed at her neck.

His gaze drifted away, and his shoulders slumped tiredly. "We must wait and see what happens next. I feel this is somehow one of Felix's tricks. As revenge, he would dearly see me hang for his murder. But would he go as far as dying just to avenge himself? I doubt it—but dead he is. I saw him."

Cold worry filled Cynara's limbs. "Who shot him?"

"I haven't the faintest idea." He rubbed his chin in thought. "I'm sure I will find out in due time. Let's get some rest now." He held out his hand toward her, and his voice held an edge of derision. "Have you come to join me in my bed?"

She shook her head numbly and stumbled toward her room. His mirthless chuckle made her cringe.

"Good night, Cynara."

Too rattled to speak, she closed the door behind her and fled to her bed. She stiffened as she heard his soft steps nearing her room. Was he about to enter? Drawing the cover with trembling fingers up to her chin, she waited. There came a light scratching sound against the door, and then there was silence.

After holding her breath for what seemed five minutes, something scraped in the lock, and a soft click reached her ears. He had turned the key . . . he didn't want her any more than she wanted him. He was afraid that she would intrude into his domain. . . . Filled with sudden outrage and inexplicable disappointment, she stared at his door until her eyes grew gritty. Sleepiness finally overcame her, and she sank into a blessed, calm void.

* * *

The next morning she awakened to a commotion outside her windows. Yawning, she slid out of bed and looked down on the drive. A mud-spattered carriage that she didn't recognize stood on the gravel. The horse whickered and stomped nervously as someone she couldn't see from her window was arguing with Bramble on the front steps.

She pulled the bell cord, and within a minute Tildy appeared, carrying a breakfast tray. "Slept late, then?" she asked with a teasing smile on her plump face. "Must have been some good—"

"Hush, Tildy," Cynara admonished the servant. "Who's visiting so early in the morning?"

"Early?" Tildy scoffed. " 'Tis nigh eleven o'clock. I thought I let ye sleep late, since ye were awfully tired last night."

"Eleven!" Cynara exclaimed with a gasp. She viewed herself in the mirror, noticing her tangled hair and the sleep-heavy eyes. "What in the world will the staff think of me? Their mistress sleeping most of the day away." She sank down on the chair before the dressing table and accepted a steaming cup from Tildy.

The maid started brushing out her mistress's hair as Cynara sipped her morning coffee. "Who's the visitor, then?"

"Don't rightly know. Some official-looking gent. He's with the master in the study now."

An urgency filled Cynara, and she dressed in haste, choosing a demure dress of pale green muslin. Tildy arranged her hair in the simplest of chignons and attached a lacy cap over it. After finishing her coffee and sugared buns in a hurry, Cynara flung a white gauzy shawl over her shoulders and ran downstairs. Estelle was reading in the morning room at the back of the house, and she gave Cynara a languid glance as her daughter stormed inside. "What's the hurry?"

"Mother, have you met Merlin's visitor?" she asked.

Estelle shrugged. "No, of course not. I don't converse with men of business. He must be Merlin's solicitor, or some such dreadful official."

Cynara left the room to hover uncertainly in the hallway. She should remain calm and sit with her mother, but a premonition of disaster bothered her.

Suddenly the door to the study opened and Merlin came out. He looked haggard and pale under the tan. There was a look of defeat on his face, and an unfamiliar feeling of warmth filled Cynara. She had to grip the banister of the curving staircase to steady herself. "Who's visiting?" she whispered.

He lifted his dark eyes to hers, and she read the pain before a shuttered look came over his face. There was no emotion in his voice as he spoke. "Ah! There you are, my dear. I was going to fetch you. Please come to my study and answer some questions," he said.

"Who's with you?" she repeated as she passed him on her way to the study.

"Squire Albert Henry. He's the local magistrate and a friend of Felix's."

"Is he here about your father's death?" Her chest tightened in apprehension as if she were the one who had perpetrated a crime, not Merlin.

"No—Felix's." Merlin said nothing else as he closed the door.

Cynara pulled her shawl closer as she met the sharp gaze of the squire. He was of stocky build, and as he raised his arm in a greeting, she noticed the bulging muscles under his brown riding coat. The dark eyebrows met over the jutting nose, and bristly brown hair grew in a peak on his forehead besides sprouting out of his ears.

"My congratulations on the nuptials," he greeted her pleasantly in a gruff voice.

She only inclined her head, waiting tensely for his next words.

"I'm the bringer of sad news, Mrs. Seymour. Last night Felix Seymour, the Earl of Raven, drew his last breath—after telling me that Mr. Merlin here shot him in cold blood. As it is, duels are illegal, but here in the country we might turn a blind eye to settling disputes with swords. But when a man is shot in the back, now, that's a matter that cannot be ignored." He took a deep breath, placing his hands behind his back. His gaze bored into Cynara.

"I must ask you, Mrs. Seymour, where was your husband last night?" He cleared his throat. "I'm to believe it was your—ahem—wedding night, and thereby a rather delicate subject to discuss."

Embarrassment surged through Cynara, staining her cheeks red. She glanced at Merlin, noticing the whiplike tension in him. He was as pale as a ghost, and his eyes were dark with pain. He tried to give her a smile, but his lips remained stiff. What had he told the squire? Why hadn't he warned her before they entered the study? Perhaps he wanted to test her.

She hesitated only momentarily. "Why, my husband was with . . . me . . . in my bedchamber the entire night." From the corner of her eye she noticed that Merlin's stance was slightly more relaxed.

"Hmm," the squire said, rubbing his chin. "Now then, how do you explain the shot that the butler heard?"

"I haven't spoken to Bramble yet this morning," Cynara said breathlessly. She hid her trembling hands in the folds of her skirt. "He might have thought there were poachers on the premises."

"Yes, that he says. I just discussed the matter with him." The squire paused. "So you didn't see or hear anything unusual?"

Cynara shook her head, her throat too dry to speak.

The squire's eyes bored into her once more. "Well, well. What am I to believe? *Who* am I to believe? The earl's dying words, or Mr. Merlin here?"

Cynara cleared her throat. "Felix—the earl, held a grudge against Merlin and might have wanted to implicate him."

"Hmm, yes. A grudge over you perhaps? I've heard that you were supposed to marry the earl, not Mr. Merlin." He barked out a question. "Are you protecting your husband?"

Cynara felt herself sway backward as she lied. "No."

If he'd asked her one more question, she might have broken down, but the squire went to the door. "If you are lying, Mrs. Seymour, you might be arrested for aiding and abetting a criminal."

She straightened her back and took a long, shuddering breath. "I have no reason to lie."

The squire muttered something, his hand on the doorknob. "I shall discuss the matter further with my superior, Lord Barton, the justice of the peace of the Black Raven district." He took a deep breath. "Mr. Seymour, since the earl is dead, you're now the new earl of Raven. The solicitors will be in touch with you, I'm sure." He gave Merlin an appraising stare. "Not an easy task to manage the Black Raven estate, but I'm sure you'll find a way to pull it out of its present decline—that is, if you're found innocent of murdering your predecessor."

He seemed to remember something else, and reached into his pocket. "Oh, by the way," he said, and pulled out a folded parchment. "This is Felix's last will and testament, and he requested that—in the case of his demise—his body be returned to America and buried with his parents. I shall arrange all the formalities."

"But that's highly irregular," Merlin protested. "The earls are always buried in the Black Raven vault."

The squire shrugged. "Felix felt more American than English, I know that much." He waved the paper. "You can read about it yourself, but Felix requested that a plaque with his name and dates will be installed in the Black Raven crypt instead of the casket."

"Well, we can't deny a dead man his last wish," Merlin murmured. "I shall organize a memorial service."

"That's what Felix would have liked, something quiet and dignified." The squire left the paper on Merlin's desk. "Everything else was bequeathed to the relatives in America. Not that Felix was a wealthy man, but whatever there was will be sent overseas." He bowed to Cynara and crossed the room once more.

Bramble, who'd obviously been standing outside, held the door for Squire Henry, and Merlin saw him off.

To compose her thoughts, Cynara strolled out on the terrace that lined the entire back part of the house. The morning was peaceful, golden, the silence pierced only by the shrill calls of the swallows swooping through the air.

Despite the warmth, an icy chill had gathered inside her, and she trembled as she sank down on the low stone balustrade. A monarch butterfly fluttered past, and the warm scent of roses that grew in borders below the terrace filled her nostrils. She heard Merlin's hurried step, but she refused to look at him as he joined her.

"Why did you lie?" His voice sounded uncertain, incredulous. When she didn't reply immediately, he pressed her. "Well? Wouldn't you like to be rid of me?"

Cynara took a deep breath. "I have to honor my new responsibility as your wife." She looked up at him, noticing the intensity of his gaze. It made her weak inside, as if his presence were too much to endure. He moved slowly toward her.

He spoke in a hoarse whisper. "You lied to protect your new name—the Seymour name?"

She nodded. "Isn't it enough that you're accused of murdering your father? At this time, no more scandal should touch the Seymours. Besides, if you're arrested and locked up, you won't have the chance to prove your innocence. I know you didn't shoot Felix, but no one else would believe you due to the cloud of suspicion already hanging over your head."

She blinked away a tear as the burden of her hasty marriage weighed her down. Only that morning did she fully understand the implications of her union to Merlin—a possible murderer. She stepped some distance away from him.

He followed her. "Whether I will be found guilty or not, you will always be provided for," he said softly. He was standing so close that she could hear his rapid breathing. "I've already had the papers drawn up that will provide security for you no matter what happens to me."

Cynara whirled around, urgent words hovering on her lips, but when she looked at his tense face, she couldn't utter them. *Are you guilty?* The question echoed in her mind. *Did you kill your father?* "You must be living under a terrible strain," she said instead.

He pulled his fingers through his black hair that gleamed with blue lights in the sunshine. Tired lines dug deeply between his eyebrows. "It will end soon. I'm investigating possible clues to my father's death, leads that I don't want to bore you with now." He sighed and shot her a quick glance. In the golden sunshine she was lovelier than he could remember from last night. The memory of her soft lips set him trembling with an emotion so strong, he could barely check it. The sweet curves of those rosy lips were drooping now, and he wished he could find a way to make her smile. Somehow it seemed more important than Felix's death at the moment. All that mattered was her, her feelings, and her thoughts. He wished he knew what to say. *He* would not be able to make her laugh; she would always look at him with loathing and suspicion, yet now her face only mirrored worry.

"Everything has changed from last night," he said.

"I'm now the Earl of Raven, a title I never desired. It means we'll have to move to Black Raven just as soon as it can be arranged." He studied her pale face, noticing the firm set of her chin and her proud bearing. For a moment he forgot her delicate features and her shining blond curls and saw only strength, determination. He had married a woman of strong character. If only he could make her his friend, then maybe . . .

"I'm prepared to perform my new duty as mistress of Black Raven," she said.

Duty, he thought. That was all she was prepared to offer. "I'm grateful for your support—more than I can say. I must first arrange for Felix's funeral." He longed to touch her, find the warmth of her hand strengthening him, but he could not reach out.

"Yes."

He broached another subject that had been tormenting him. "Another thing . . . I put the key back on your side of the door between our bedrooms. Last night I thought you might be worrying that I would— er, molest you, so I locked the door from my side." *I wanted so much to hold you in my arms.* "From now on, it's your choice to lock the door each night or—not."

"I never intend to offer my—body willingly to you. Never." Cynara's chin rose a fraction and an odd tension hung between them, so thick it was suffocating. What thoughts moved behind those deep, dark eyes? she wondered.

"It's your choice."

She watched him turn abruptly and stroll into the house. There lay so many unspoken words between them, a staggering barrier that would perhaps never be surmounted.

Chapter 5

"Is the dreadful news about Felix true?" Estelle demanded as soon as Cynara stepped into the morning room. The older woman paced, heaving several deep sighs. "Was he really mortally wounded here in the copse?"

"Yes, that's what the servants say. I have no idea what he was doing here." Cynara averted her gaze to prevent her mother from sensing her falsehoods. "Some poacher might have mistaken him for a deer and shot him."

Estelle stopped in front of Cynara and took her daughter's firm, capable hands in her own frail ones. "You have been through so much. Does his death upset you?"

"Mother, stop this charade! I never wished Felix dead, but it would be a lie to pretend that I liked him."

"We shall of course wear black for some time. It wouldn't do to desecrate his memory, even though he was an unpleasant and unreliable man."

Cynara gave a mirthless smile. "Black suits my frame of mind perfectly." She sank down on a sofa

and viewed her mother's embroidery with a listless eye.
"I'm the new Countess of Raven now, Mother. How
would you like to live at Black Raven?"

Estelle shuddered visibly. "That drafty old stone
heap! It never gets warm, not even in the summer."
She sighed in defeat. "I suppose you need me."

Cynara shrugged. "No . . . you can stay here or live
at Bluewater until Brand is free." Still, she wished her
mother's support, however feeble it might be.

With a moan, Estelle sank down beside her. She
pulled a hand across her eyes. "Oh, Brand. What will
happen to him now with this new upheaval? Merlin
won't have the time to— It was the darkest day of my
life when Brand was thrown into prison. Who will help
my dearest son?"

"I will try to help him somehow," Cynara said with
determination. "If Merlin can't act, I shall travel to
London shortly and find someone to help me. This
situation is unendurable."

"What can you do, Cynara? You have no power."
Estelle pushed a pillow under her head and leaned
back against the carved oak frame of the sofa. "I had
hoped we could live here together in comfort, in peace,
but I see now, it's not to be." She pressed a lacy
handkerchief to her eyes.

Cynara rose and looked out over the well-ordered
flower patches that blazed with color. "We must find
a way to turn this new situation to our advantage, not
let us be defeated by it."

Estelle moaned. "You speak just like your father,
but, despite his determination, he never got up from
under the debts that crushed us for more than two

decades. Bluewater ate up all the funds, when there were any. How will we go on without Brand?"

Cynara was silent, refusing to look at the gloomy picture that her mother had outlined. "Bluewater is one of the loveliest estates in the county. Brand will one day bring his bride there, and new Hawthornes will live and prosper there."

Estelle gave her daughter a tired glance. "Your conviction is commendable, but—"

Cynara hurried toward the door. "We will prevail. Haven't we always? Now we must get ourselves ready for Felix's memorial service. In the face of the world we must stand as a united family."

"I thought you didn't like your moody new husband, and would choose to shun his company and his name," Estelle said peevishly.

"Mother!" Cynara pinned Estelle with a steely eye. "Dignity is all we have left, don't you see? Unless Merlin can prove his innocence, we will be banned from society forever. The gossips would like to see us broken with despair, but I refuse to give them that, no matter how dire our situation seems at the moment."

Straightening her back in determination, Cynara left the room. She must hold on to the conviction that the problems could be solved, or she might just break under the burden.

It rained during the morning of Felix's memorial service two days later. His casket had been removed from the estate for shipment to America, but mourners had gathered to see the plaque attached to the wall of the vault. The sky was leaden and a fog swirled along the ground. Rain rattled in the leaves, and the birds were silent. The family vault at the edge of Gairlock Woods at Black Raven had been opened for the occasion. It was located on a slope, and below spread an emerald valley with stables, smithy, granary, and barns belonging to the castle. At a distance huddled the cottages of the Black Raven village, the pointed church tower soaring in its mist.

A marble angel whose head was covered with green moss guarded the wrought iron gates to the Raven family vault. The gates creaked forlornly in a sudden gust of wind. Cynara listened with only half an ear to the vicar's words as Felix's plaque was fitted into the slot in the thick wall. All the earls of Raven and their families had their last rest here, and Cynara shuddered at the thought of once . . .

"My dear." Merlin's warm breath caressed her ear, and he held her elbow protectively. "It's time to go. Do you need some rest? I will ask the housekeeper to bring you a cup of tea in your room."

Cynara shook her head and slipped out of his grip as she left the crypt, following the dark-clad attendees. The mourners were distant relatives and friends, since most of Felix's family was living overseas.

"I don't want to rest. This afternoon I will take a tour of the castle to see what damage time has wrought upon its venerable walls." She knew the only way to keep from brooding was to occupy herself with domestic chores. Besides, she loved the old castle and hated to see it go to ruin.

From her vantage point by the tombs, she could see the Black Raven castle that had stood high on its craggy cliff for four centuries. It had once been a keep with a tall surrounding wall with slits for arrow shooting and a parapet, a gatehouse with walls six feet thick, and a moat. Not much remained of the stone wall, and moss grew on the tumbledown gatehouse. The moat had been filled in with soil, and the only wall existing today was the one surrounding the rose garden to the east side of the castle. The south side plunged one hundred feet straight into the sea. Outcrops of black rocks gave the castle grounds a slightly sinister air, and acted as a barrier to the almost vertical drop to the narrow beach below. Ivy straggled up the walls of the castle, softening the stark grayness. Crowing loudly, ravens circled around one of the crenelated towers where they had built an untidy nest. The whole castle had a run-down, if still proud and noble look. From this vantage point Cynara felt strangely touched. Black Raven was in her care now, a formidable legacy.

She glanced at the servants who were lined up outside the chapel. There was Mrs. Averell, the forbidding housekeeper with silver-streaked hair and a pursed mouth. Mrs. Black, the cook, and her adolescent son, Bobby. Footmen and maids refused to meet her gaze, and the butler had left his post after Felix's demise. Muggins, the stable groom who'd brought Felix Seymour back to Black Raven after the duel, stood uneasily to one side. Cynara's blood chilled as she glanced into his cold, calculating eyes. He had blamed Merlin for Felix's death.

The shot that had killed Felix had come from the opposite side of the copse. However, it was evident that most of the staff resented the sudden change of master, though Merlin looked the noble aristocrat with his double-breasted black frock coat and beaver hat with its black crepe band. He was serious and composed, and Cynara could detect a trace of compassion as he surveyed the line of servants.

He addressed them. "I understand the difficulties you have gone through here at Black Raven, and I will endeavor to lighten your burden. If you have any complaints or questions, don't hesitate to bring them to my attention. I plan to make the estate as prosperous as it once was, but it will be a long, difficult battle, and I need your support."

The servants bowed and curtseyed, but no one spoke. Only Bramble, whom Merlin had brought to Black Raven, smiled and nodded. The others must think they got a murderer to rule them, Cynara thought. And perhaps they are right.

The gathering after the funeral was a somber affair. The ladies, whom Cynara barely knew, were whispering among themselves as their eyes assessed the plates of scones, sandwiches, and cold meats that the footmen offered. The men were standing apart from the ladies, discussing politics.

Cynara spoke only when addressed, and she would not be drawn into any gossip. Some mourners were from neighboring estates, and Cynara recognized Lady Barton and Squire Henry's wife. She suspected they hadn't come to mourn Felix's passing, but to gawk at Merlin—the notorious murderer. If only for her own peace of mind, she longed to discover what had happened on that night when Ross Seymour, Merlin's father, had died.

Estelle pressed a handkerchief to her eyes, but Cynara could see no tears. The older woman was evidently listening to the gossip. "If I stay here much longer, I will certainly say something I might regret," Cynara whispered to her mother. "Please excuse me to the other guests. Tell them I have a debilitating headache." As she crossed the room, she glanced toward the men and caught Merlin's gaze. He was standing slightly to the side, excluded from the male group. There was a tension to his fingers that held the glass of port, and the strain had etched the lines deeper between his eyebrows.

The air crackled between them as their eyes met, and Cynara's breath caught in surprise. Everything receded except his dark gaze. The chattering voices became a distant rumble, the chinking of teacups and spoons sounded like faraway wind chimes. All that existed was their awareness of each other—two flames drawn together in the chilly gloom, two spirits uniting when all else was separation.

Inhaling deeply, Cynara tore her gaze from him and left the room. Bramble was in the hallway talking to two footmen. The rotund butler rubbed his white-gloved hands and exuded bonhomie when he saw Cynara. "If you don't mind me saying so, Lady Raven, this castle is pure magic. There are more stairs, passageways, and winding corridors than I can count. And the walls are at least four foot thick. I never thought I would work for a peer of the realm." He beamed, his round face creasing kindly.

Cynara smiled. "I'm glad it pleases you, Bramble. I will take a tour of the rooms this afternoon to see what repairs will be needed."

"Splendid, milady. This castle needs a firm hand like yours."

Somehow she couldn't face returning to the tea salon after she'd refreshed herself. Aimlessly she strolled along the corridor where the master suite was located. Like Stormywood, her bedroom was attached to that of Merlin, only a door separating them. Whereas Stormywood was a cheerful and warm house, Black Raven had a bleakness that no bright bed hangings or curtains could dismiss. It stemmed from the very rock of which the castle had been built. Cynara mentally made a note to change the frayed red satin in her bedroom at the first possible opportunity. She would find colorful tapestries to cheer up the walls, as they must have done in the fourteenth century.

The space was more cramped at Black Raven even though the castle was much larger than Stormywood. Renovations had happened over the centuries, and guest chambers had been built on all floors. The corridors that skirted the main walls of the keep were narrow and silent with small windows at shoulder height. The stone floors were spread with colorful carpets, but nothing could hide the severity of the architecture or the cold stone.

Several centuries earlier Black Raven had been an invincible fortress against invaders from the sea since the castle rose out of the black rocks like a colossal beast with the waters hissing and spitting against its feet. A crumbling parapet ran the perimeter of the square building, connecting the four towers at the corners. The doors leading to the parapet had been barred since the walk wasn't safe any longer. That would have to be repaired, Cynara thought.

Cynara pressed her face to one of the tiny windows and stared out over Lyme Bay. The fog was lifting, a

weak sun permeating the milky mist. The turbulent
water was a cold bluish-green. She could not get
enough of the view. All her life at Bluewater she'd seen
the sea shift color and shape in the bay. No day
seemed like any other.

She went into one of the unused bedrooms, where
dust lay thick on the old rustic furniture from the
period of Queen Elizabeth. The tester above the bed
was in shreds, the colors indistinguishable. The air
smelled of decay and mold.

She went to other chambers like it, finding the decay
overwhelming. Swatting a dusty pillow, she mused
that it was unforgivable that the Seymours had let the
proud castle lose its dignity to deterioration.

Rooms on the next level were in the same sad shape
except for the one that had been cleaned for her mother.
Still, the curtains had their fair amount of holes and the
carpet was suspiciously threadbare. Cynara pulled her
fingers along the frieze that had turned gray with age-
old grime. They came away dark with dust. Frowning at
the neglect, Cynara glanced at her mother's things that
were still in trunks or spilling over the coverlet on the
bed. Estelle had decided not to visit until Cynara had
settled down at Black Raven.

"Mother, you're too worried about Brand to stay
alone at Stormywood and brood, that's why you came
here," Cynara said aloud. The words seemed to hover
in the still air, then dissolve. Cynara listened to the
silence, feeling as if unseen ears had heard her words.

She found a painted miniature of her brother among
the things on the dressing table, and Brand's eyes
smiled at her in encouragement. Overcome by a sudden urgency, she knew she would have to find a way

today to save him. Mother would waste away without Brandon's carefree smile, and the compliments that came so readily to his lips.

Cynara left the bedchamber and opened a door at the opposite end of the corridor. She found it leading to the round tower room. It was shrouded in shadows since the heavy curtains were partly drawn. She started as she recognized the silhouette of a man against the window. He turned as she stepped across the threshold.

"Cynara," Merlin said quietly. "I had a feeling you were exploring."

"Yes . . . when I visited here before my intended wedding to Felix, it never occurred to me to assess the damage of time. It wasn't my place to do so, besides, Felix wanted to return to America right after the nuptials."

"And now it's your place to assess the castle?" His gaze penetrated the gloom, making her feel self-conscious.

She nodded. "Yes, as the Countess of Raven, it is my duty to see that the house is in order."

A rare smile spread across his face, and Cynara stared at him in wonder. He looked so at home among these forbidding walls. Neglect was evident in this room as in the others, but the furniture was polished and books and papers stacked neatly.

"This is the room Max had planned to use as his study, as his father did before him." He paused, turning once again toward the window. "I can almost sense Max's presence here. Can you?"

As if she'd trespassed into a private sanctuary, Cynara glanced uncertainly around the room. "Max is dead, and I'm sure he's resting in peace, not haunting this place." Sorrow filled her momentarily, but she pushed it away.

"I hope so. I have chosen a room downstairs for my study," Merlin went on. "It has an unobscured view of the bay while this chamber faces the West Country. I prefer the brightness of the water."

Cynara silently agreed, but his presence made her more uncomfortable by the minute. His gaze lit upon her again, encompassing her, drawing her to him. There was no explaining the sensation, only that something about him, a hidden part of him, attracted her irresistibly. Silent, she could only watch him as he stepped closer. When she thought he would touch her, he passed her with a mere inch separating their bodies. Her heart began a dull thudding, and a hot sensation spread over her skin. Deeply disturbed by her reactions, she watched him as he sat down by the desk and riffled through the old bills from local craftsmen and merchants.

"I miss Max dearly—always will—but he had no head for business. Our legacy is a mountain of debt that Max left behind. Uncle Sydney left them to him." Merlin silenced, dragging his hands through his hair. His shoulders slumped with fatigue. "Who would have thought I would one day sit at this desk going through Max's papers? Max was so full of life, much too young to die," he murmured.

"Max would not have liked to have a stranger viewing his private papers describing the endless struggles to keep the estate afloat. We will find a way—"

"We? He stared at her tensely, and she couldn't find anything else to say.

"Do you count us as a . . . team?" he continued.

Cynara lowered her gaze. She nodded slowly. "If we are to pull ourselves out of debt, we have to work together."

"I could use my own money—"

"No, something has to be done to bring in funds for the upkeep, for the future. We must find a solution that will support the estate. Somehow the earlier Seymours discovered a way to save Black Raven from utter ruin. I wish I knew what it was."

He rose and stood before her. "There are possible copper deposits on the castle's lands. I shall finance the explorations."

He paused, and inhaled sharply. "I understand why Max loved you so much. You give such strength, such support to those to whom you're loyal." He gripped her arms as if to pull her into his embrace. Then he hesitated as he looked deeply into her eyes. She wished for one wild moment that he would kiss her, then she recalled her forced wedding ceremony, and pulled back. The ardor died on his face as rapidly as it had appeared, and he let go of her. "I cannot expect—"

He broke off abruptly and sat down. "Aside from surveying for copper, I intend to improve the neglected farms on the estate. That's where previous earls got their support—rents and crops. But before I start anything else, I must discover who shot Felix and why. However much I loathed the fellow, the mystery must be solved."

Unease filled Cynara. He was right; they could not go on without knowing the truth.

"Any ideas?" he asked.

"No, I truly didn't know Felix well enough to tell

who his friends were—or enemies, in this case. Some-one wished him dead, and followed him to Stormy-wood, where he took the opportunity to place the blame of Felix's death on you." She paused, thinking. "But why would anyone follow him to Stormywood in the night?"

"That's a question that might never be answered, unless someone here knew of Felix's plans for the duel."

"Do *you* have an enemy whom you shared with Felix?" she continued.

"Not that I know of. Like you, I didn't know what people Felix cultivated in London or elsewhere. He was more absent from Black Raven than he was present."

"He was the sort of man who easily made enemies," Cynara said with a sigh.

"Yes." Merlin stood with a jerk. He turned to Cynara. "I will try to discover who his cronies were in London. Perhaps someone visited Felix here." He paused, holding her gaze. "I wish we could have met under more 'normal' circumstances. But then you would have married Max, not me."

The words hung between them, and Cynara found it difficult to meet that steady gaze that saw so much. "Does it . . . matter?" she asked, her voice faltering.

He looked down at his hands, wiping off patches of dust. "To me it does. I had not thought of marrying a woman who loved another man." He strode to the door.

Cynara filled with a bittersweet warmth that was akin to longing. She took an involuntary step toward him, holding out her hand, but he didn't see it. He stopped by the door, his back toward her.

"Are you coming? I'm returning to the reception," he said.

"I suppose it's rude to stay away." Cynara walked with him, with every step aware of her racing heart and the warmth inside her chest. Without speaking she felt as if he were communicating with her through his silence. Perhaps it was her imagination, but she was mindful of his sorrow and the man behind the tight, disciplined exterior reaching out toward her without as much as a gesture.

"You must miss your mother, and your . . . father greatly," she said, knowing she was stepping on uncertain ground.

He didn't answer, only gave her a long, measuring look. Did he think she believed he'd killed Ross Seymour? His calm, distant face gave nothing away. She had an urge to reassure him, yet she couldn't know for sure if the accusations against him were true. Would the magistrate come someday with his men and take Merlin away? Only if they found solid evidence of his guilt.

"I shall speak with the grooms at the stable later, and find out what happened on the evening when Felix was brought back here," Merlin said, and opened the door to the salon where a few of the mourners still lingered. "There might be clues I didn't notice while I was here."

Cynara found herself praying he would discover something that would put to rest the rumors that he was somehow responsible for Felix's death.

*   *   *

As the shadows lengthened and darkness crept over the moors, woods, and rolling farmland to enfold the castle, Cynara was gathering a few stray glasses from the reception and put them on a tray. It was a chore for the servants, but she couldn't sit and do nothing. The time seemed to stand still, making her more restless by the minute. She glanced out the window of the salon and saw Merlin striding toward the stables that were located among the cluster of farm buildings at the foot of the castle hill.

She needed to vent her worry about Brandon. Now was as good a time as any. Without wasting more time, she rushed to the door, pausing only to fetch one of the cloaks in the closet under the stairs that lined one side of the great hall on the ground floor. She didn't know why, but she wanted to be there, beside him, when he questioned the men.

The stables were in better condition than the interior of the castle. The roof had been put on recently, and the timbered walls looked solid, Merlin thought as he strode toward one of the grooms, who was mending a bridle. The air smelled of leather and tar, and horse, of course.

The fellow barely touched the rim of his cap, and gave Merlin an insolent smile. He remained sitting, bending over his task. Anger shot through Merlin, and he heaved the man upright with a firm grip of the collar.

"Your manners are lacking," he said between

clenched teeth. "It's about time you show some respect for your new employer, or you might have to look for work elsewhere."

"What's wi' ye, guv, goin' to murder me, same as ye did Felix Seymour?" The groom cackled with glee, and jerked his thumb toward the dark cavern of the stable door. "Mr. Muggins is th' man who hires and fires here."

Merlin dropped him abruptly, and the stone bench connected hard with the groom's bony backside. "Your employment is terminated as of this moment," Merlin said with icy wrath. "Though you don't seem to understand, I'm now the Earl of Raven, and I expect my people to at least greet me civilly when I arrive."

The young lout, hair scraggly and beard stubble shading his gaunt face, gave Merlin a shadowy glance. "If ye say so, but me work—"

"Get going. My steward will pay you a week's wages, and I don't want to see you on these premises again." Merlin noticed that his hands were trembling with anger, and he shoved them into his pockets. Now he had to face the more malevolent head groom, Victor Muggins. He had to duck his head before entering the side door of the stables. The pungent, clean smell of horses filled his nose.

"Merlin . . . Merlin," came Cynara's voice from outside. He halted and watched her coming, cloak flapping in the wind and her voice slightly breathless from the exertion. A faint rose color tinted her cheeks, and the sweet vise he knew as love tightened around his chest. Every time he looked into her eyes it was as if the earth fell away beneath his feet. That piercing glance of extraordinary liquid blue-green haunted him night and day, and made him forget for short moments the abyss into which Ross's death and the memories of war had thrown him.

He smiled, delighted to see her. "I thought you had retired to your room for the night. It has been a strenuous day, and the grooms' language might be rough on your ears."

"I was in the clearing that night when Felix died. I have to hear what the men down here say."

Her eyes widened as Muggins ambled through the gloom of the stables, and Merlin caught the soft white hand as she fumbled for a grip on her flailing cloak.

"Evenin', milord," said Muggins, pulling at the rim of his hat. His rough-hewn face held a surly expression, his eyes black beads under heavy lids. He looked suspiciously from one to the other as silence stretched.

Darkness was gathering rapidly, and Merlin glanced once toward the sky, sensing rain in the sullen masses of clouds. "We have some questions for you, Muggins, and I hope you will answer them truthfully."

"Don't be too polite," Cynara whispered. "Remember, he reported you to the magistrate." Merlin squeezed her hand in warning.

"Muggins did his duty reporting the duel to the magistrate when Felix died." Somehow Merlin had to try to win Muggins's confidence. What he needed to discover was if Muggins truly believed that he, Merlin, was responsible for the accident in the copse, or if someone had asked him to place the blame on Merlin. It wasn't as if he could point to any proof, but he vaguely suspected a conspiracy against him personally. Though the idea was farfetched, this could have a connection to his father's death. God knows, Ross had disliked Felix, always saying that Felix had inherited only the bad strains of the Seymour family.

Merlin sighed. He couldn't wholly believe in his father's nebulous deduction that Felix's character had been tainted. What he needed was proof that Felix's death was linked to that of his father. Or any proof at all that would free him of suspicion.

Cynara's sturdy little hand gave him support, and her eyes were dark, questioning pools. If ever he was to win her love, he had to clear his name.

"Well, Muggins, you were at the duel site. What or who makes you imagine that I killed Felix Seymour?"

Chapter 6

"Like you say, I was there; I saw the whole thing," Muggins said defiantly. "Surely one o' your men was lying in ambush with a musket, ready to pop Master Felix one through his chest."

A muscle worked in Merlin's jaw. "I had no idea that Felix had planned to duel with me that evening. He could at least have sent his seconds around and challenged me in the proper way."

Muggins muttered something and looked away. He walked back into the dark stables and Merlin followed, pulling Cynara with him. He had to swallow his pride and curb his wrath if ever he was to discover what Muggins knew. The dislike the head groom exuded hung between them, and a defiant thrust to the chin told Merlin that Muggins would not disclose anything without a struggle.

"Muggins, I would prefer it if you stayed and talked to me until I consider the conversation over. I can understand your reluctance to accept a new master, but I assure you, I will treat you fairly as long as you keep doing a good job. However, I won't tolerate disobedience on your part, or you spreading damaging gossip behind my back." He waited for Muggins's reaction, which took its time in coming. Unlike the other groom, Muggins evidently knew when to keep his mouth shut, but Merlin could feel the animosity growing. The entire staff gave off the same negativity.

Merlin sighed, knowing the first few weeks at Black Raven would be an uphill struggle. He wasn't looking forward to it.

"If you don't mind me saying so, milord, you don't 'xactly have the purest of reputations. If ye killed once, ye can kill again. My missus is frightened of living on the estate after you moved here."

Sadness tightened Merlin's throat as he met the groom's fierce gaze in the semidarkness of the stables. In the eyes of the local people, the cottagers on the estate, he was an evil spirit sent to destroy them all.

"You must tell your wife not to believe in rumors," came Cynara's clear voice. "Then she will sleep soundly at night. There is no evidence whatsoever that your new master killed his father, and I can vouch for him on that night of the duel. He is not responsible for Felix Seymour's death, and you could help us prove that, Mr. Muggins. You must help us discover who was waiting to shoot Felix so that the rumors might die down." She paused. "Do it for your wife's sake, if not for the master," she added, pleading now.

Her concern filled Merlin with gratitude. Her cool hand trembled in his, and he had an urge to rub some warmth into it, but he refrained. She wasn't doing this for him, but for the pride of the family name, which now was hers as well. The knowledge hurt him momentarily, yet also strengthened him.

"Lady Raven is right. You should urge your wife not to listen to gossip," Merlin said.

"Yes, you could instill in anyone who works here a sense of fairness," Cynara said.

Muggins snorted. "My wife's a superstitious old cow, but, milady, you must admit there has been some strange goings-on with the new—master." He tossed his head in Merlin's direction as if Merlin were worth no respect. "The servants know all about Mr. Ross's death."

"Then you must help the master restore his reputation, Muggins," Cynara said firmly. "The law doesn't know everything about the night when Mr. Ross died. And if the law can't judge the master, we shan't either."

"I have me own thoughts on the matter," the groom grumbled.

"If you know something about Felix Seymour that you think we should know, please tell us. Who visited him? Did he have any enemies? Did you witness any quarrels?" Merlin said, ever conscious of Cynara's hand in his.

A shutter fell over Muggins's face, and he picked up a broom leaning against one of the walls. "I know nothing," he said with a shrug. "I only saw to Master Felix's horses in the stables and drove him in the carriage sometimes when the coachman was too drunk to drive."

"You—or the other groom—drove him in the carriage to the duel," Merlin pointed out.

"Yes, because Master Felix's horse was lame."

"And where's the other groom who was with you?"

Muggins shrugged. "I don't know. He's left; he

worked here for only a few weeks." His voice rose an octave. "I don't know anything more about that night of the duel, no more than what I saw. You might as well not ask any more questions."

Merlin paled, but nodded stiffly. "Only one more. Did you or anyone else in the household know that Felix planned to duel that night?"

Muggins shook his head sullenly. "I thought we were going a-visiting."

"With swords and pistols?" Merlin asked sarcastically, and turned toward the door, pulling Cynara with him. He had to leave before he gave the man a facer.

"The man is holding something back," she said as they walked toward the castle.

"I will have to earn his confidence," Merlin said in a tight voice. "This dilemma is more annoying than I can say. How will I find the real killer?" Seeking her comfort, he held her hand against his lips and planted a small kiss on the knuckles. The skin was so soft to the touch. She rebuffed him, pulling her hand away, but not too brusquely. Her gaze had intensified, and the longing to pull her into his arms became so strong, he could barely contain it. "Let's return to . . . *home.*"

He remembered that she'd said she never wanted any part of the intimate side of marriage. Could he live by her side without touching her for the rest of his life? Perhaps he could find a way to convince her that intimate loving could deepen their relationship. The word *never* echoed in his mind, and he wanted to close his ears to it. What if he couldn't wait; what if he weren't strong enough to withstand his own longing and took her against her wishes? No, he couldn't force himself on her, but how could he make her fall in love with him?

Cynara walked beside him, wondering what he was thinking. The encounter with Muggins could have easily snapped Merlin's control, but he seemed to have retreated more firmly within himself. "If no one else will, at least I can vouch for your innocence in the matter with Felix," she said, wanting to soothe the tormented man beside her.

He flashed her a sudden smile that softened his face. "Thank you. I never dreamed of finding such a loyal wife, such a compassionate one." He took a deep breath. "If only you would become my wife in the true meaning of the word."

"I don't wish to," she said, her voice trembling. "Don't force me."

"You might regret those words one day," he argued. "You don't even know what it's like to touch . . . physically."

"I don't want to know," she snapped, and hurried away from him.

"You don't know what you're missing," he cried after her. "Why deprive yourself?"

That night, leaning against the pillows in her bed, Cynara tried without success to focus on the book in her lap. The image of her tall, handsome husband haunted her, and she could hear him now on the other side of the door that separated their rooms. He was cursing at something, and then came the creaking of wood as he lay down in the ancient bed that had served many earls of Raven as their sleeping quarters. That afternoon she'd planned to ask about Brandon, but the subject had flown from her mind when Merlin had taunted her with his hints of marital bliss. Thoughts of Brandon tormented her, but Merlin was closer, too provocative for her peace of mind.

Tomorrow, first thing, she would confront Merlin with Brandon's problem. If he wasn't willing to help, she would travel alone to London. Cynara sipped the hot milk that Tildy had brought to her room only minutes before. It scalded her tongue, and she set it down on the nightstand with an angry thud. Milk or not, she would not find sleep tonight. Too much had happened since dawn, and endless thoughts swirled in her head. She blew out the candles by the bed and slid down on the pillows. At least she ought to make an effort . . .

It appeared that most of the night had passed when she awakened abruptly and sat up in bed. The room was pitch black, and she had difficulty remembering where she was. A moan pierced the night, and her heartbeat increased with fear. Another moan floated eerily through the stone walls, and Cynara fumbled for the tinderbox by her bed. She had soon lighted a branch of candles.

Another moan came, drawn out and closer than before. Cynara scrambled out of bed, holding the coverlet tightly around her. As the fog of sleep slowly lifted from her mind, she realized that the sound was issuing from Merlin's room.

Holding her breath in fear, she leaned her ear against the old wooden door. The bolts of the wrought iron hinge chafed into her head, but she was barely aware of them. Another muffled sound came, and a creaking noise, as if Merlin were thrashing about in bed. Had someone attacked Merlin? she wondered, alarm clogging her throat. On the previous evening she had locked the door with the huge, ancient key on her side, and now she turned it.

Without thinking she flung open the door and ran into Merlin's room. The chamber lay in dense darkness, illuminated only by two thin shafts of moonlight that came through the cracks in the curtains. Another moan sounded from the bed.

She held up her candles to see better. "Merlin?" she called out. "Are you ill?" He seemed to be alone in the room. At least no one had attacked him; only her sleepy mind had imagined such horrors. She stood by the bed, looking down at the dark shape moving restlessly, head rolling from side to side. "What's wrong?" She shook his shoulder uncertainly, wondering how he would react when he recognized her.

"Merlin! Wake up. Are you having a bad dream?" she demanded, shaking him harder.

The moaning ended abruptly, and he jerked upright, staring at her vacantly.

"It's me—Cynara. You were moaning in your sleep," she said lamely, debating whether to leave him or stay. Embarrassment flowed through her, and her hands tightened around her coverlet. It was heavy and dragged on the floor, making her shoulders ache.

"Cynara?" He sounded groggy, and so filled with sadness that compassion clutched her heart.

"I'm here." She patted his shoulder awkwardly, not knowing what to do.

He awakened completely. "I must have had a nightmare," he said, his voice taking on its usual briskness. "I'm sorry I disturbed you."

"Nightmare? Did you dream of Felix?"

He shook his head. His next words were uncertain, painstaking. "No . . . I dreamed about my father. It's a recurring dream where I manage to save him from his sure death in the ravine. Sometimes I see horrifying scenes from the war. . . ."

Cynara sat down on the bed without thinking. She wished she could ask him more, but he seemed reluctant to talk about the past. He lit the candles beside his bed, and they stared at each other. She averted her gaze when she noticed that the part of him above the covers was naked. But in the span of an indrawn breath she had noted the broad, muscular shoulders that told of immense strength. A spatter of freckles covered his bronze skin that seemed as soft as velvet, and dark hair covered his chest and forearms. The symmetry and power of his body held a seductive allure, and Cynara blushed as the attraction mounted between them. His hair curled beguilingly on his neck, and she longed to touch it.

"Why do you care, Cynara?" He dared to caress her fair tresses cascading down her back, and she forced herself to remain seated.

"I . . . it's no crime to feel sympathy for one's fellow beings, now, is there?"

He shook his head. "I guess not. You look very lovely tonight. So lovely, in fact, that I can barely suppress my yearning to hold you in my arms."

His voice sounded strained, and she saw the desperation in his eyes. His face paled under the tan, and perspiration beaded on his forehead. He had a slightly frantic air, as if the nightmare had touched him more deeply than he cared to admit. She leaned forward and touched his muscular forearm impulsively as he bunched the corner of his sheet into his fist.

"The dream is over. It cannot touch you now."

"But it does." His voice was flat, carefully modulated, shielding his despair. "Someone killed my father in cold blood, and I have to live with that knowledge for the rest of my life."

"Once you find the truth, you'll be able to put his death behind you." Her cover slipped from her shoulders, and consumed by compassion, she momentarily forgot what the filmy nightgown might reveal to his haunted eyes. Only when his gaze wouldn't leave her bosom did she notice her disarray. The strings on the empire-cut lace bodice had come untied, revealing a great amount of her skin and the upper part of her breasts. She tried to pull the bodice together, but his hand halted her. For one moment they stared at each other, unable to break the searing tension between them.

His hands were hot on her skin and his eyes mesmerized her. The heady, virile scent he exuded intoxicated her to a point to where dizziness threatened to overcome her. A longing to thread her fingers through his tousled hair surged through her, but she remained still, barely breathing. She ought not be there, yet she couldn't leave. Not while his self-control seemed brittle. Had his control snapped that night Ross Seymour died? To prevent herself from bolting to her room in a fright, she shook off that cold thought.

"You find me repulsive, don't you, Cynara? Merlin with the dark mind; Merlin with the strange eyes . . ."

"No—"

"Don't lie!" he snapped, hanging his head. "You haven't changed since you were fourteen. You're just as opiniated and prickly as you were then."

"You don't know me, Merlin. One thing is certain, I resent this forced marriage, but I don't mope. I intend to make a life for myself here at Black Raven. A freak situation made us man and wife, but I won't let that ruin my life."

"You're strong. I admire you for that." He leaned back against the pillows, his eyes half closed. His dark gaze glittered like jewels behind the dark eyelashes. She sensed his strength returning, the abyss of his memories closing, giving him surer footing.

"Will you tell me about your bad dream? Sometimes it helps."

He sighed, and his voice tightened as he said, "One day perhaps. I can barely think about Father without wanting to scream out loud." Merlin pounded the mattress with his fist. "Father's death was such a waste, and I would give the world to change the day when he died! I miss him more than I can say."

Cynara sensed that if she reached out toward him, she would be able to touch his sorrow like a thick, gluey presence around him. She shook her head to stop her imagination from running rampant. She ought to be angry with him, not sympathetic. Somehow she felt a responsibility to help him solve his problems. Hers seemed so small in comparison until the memory of Brandon's face swam into her mind.

"Merlin, this is perhaps not the right time to press

you for a favor, but you promised to help Brand. With every day that passes, he moves closer to disaster. What are you going to do to help him?"

"I've contacted the Hawthorne solicitor to find out what can be done. Bribes in the right places, perhaps."

Cynara rose and started pacing, her arms tightly crossed under her bosom. "It's not enough. You'll have to go to London—or I will."

His voice hardened. "I must first discover who is handling the case, then proceed from there. It's out of the question that you travel to London on this errand."

Cynara stopped by the bed, glaring down at him. "Nothing is impossible. I realize you might not have Felix's connections, but you could contact every single one of the officials and offer bribes."

"And be thrown in prison for corruption? No, I prefer to handle the matter with a bit more finesse."

"And *time,* which we don't have." Cynara could not calm her agitation. She kept pacing. "You must *do* something—that was your end of the bargain."

"And who will pay the bribes?" he asked cuttingly.

Her pride prevented her from saying "you," but they both knew she had no funds to call her own. "I have a few pieces of jewelry," she said lamely.

He laughed. "A heroic thought, my sweet, but without substance." He patted the edge of the mattress. "Sit down before you wear out the soles of your slippers."

She refused, still thinking of ways she could push the issue of her brother's release.

"Your loyalty is commendable, Cynara. Brandon is a fool for involving your family in this scandal."

"The world is full of fools," she said, and flinched as he grabbed her hand in passing. His touch was warm, inviting.

"So lovely . . ." he whispered. "So hauntingly beautiful, and though you're at my side, you aren't truly mine." A groan issued from deep within him. "May I make you mine tonight?"

Cynara had to strain to hear those last words, and they did something to her insides. Her heart made a somersault, and a heavy warmth filled her limbs. It would be so easy to give in. . . . He was her husband. . . . He was handsome and intriguing. And strong.

He pulled her down on the bed and laid his hand on the bare skin right below her throat, then dragged it slowly downward until it touched the swell of her breasts. Though enchanted by his caress, she couldn't help remembering that those warm hands might have killed Ross Seymour. With a sigh trembling on her lips she slowly pulled away and held the parts of her bodice together. Their gazes hooked and Merlin's lips parted in a bitter smile.

"Suspicion is heavy in your eyes, my dearest. You don't have to be afraid of me." He took hold of her shoulders and tried to pull her to him, but she resisted harder, frightened not only of him, but of her own attraction for him—a man she could never trust until the truth of his past came out.

He must have noticed her hesitation, because he let go of her arms abruptly. "Go back to bed," he said tiredly. "I'm a fool for dreaming that there is something special between us—a rare depth of feeling."

"I wish to believe that you're innocent of all the accusations, but—" She held out her hand toward him in a conciliatory manner, but he only slid down in bed, turning his back toward her.

"You're careful not to mention love," he said. "Love could bridge suspicion."

"True." Her voice lowered. "And—I don't love you."

"Good night, lady wife. My dreams won't disturb you again."

Legs trembling with emotion, she returned to her bedroom, slamming the door behind her. She didn't want to be angry, but she was appalled at the erotic memories of his naked flesh, and anger masked them—for the moment. But how would she wipe away the imprints of his touch, his sudden smile, his kiss in the garden? The images piled up, one stronger than the other.

She pressed herself against the wooden door, wondering what it would be like not to sleep alone. His bed would be nice and warm. . . . *He* would be warm, comforting. With an odd tightness in her chest she turned the key in the lock. There! He wouldn't dare intrude.

Unable to sleep for the remainder of the night, she stepped down to have breakfast with her mother early the next morning. Her eyes were heavy, and her mind sluggish after too much fruitless mulling in the night. Estelle looked rested, dressed in a charcoal-gray mourning gown with a wide skirt and a tight bodice, a lacy scarf over her shoulders and a black cap covering her silver-streaked hair. Tildy had assisted Cynara into a lighter gray dress, stating bluntly that no one ought to mourn that "snake in the grass, Felix Seymour."

The morning outside was as gray as the dress she was wearing, Cynara noticed as she glanced out the window. She stepped into the breakfast parlor that had been installed next to the dining room by some earlier Seymour. The old castle had much of its ancient layout left, but the great hall that took up the entire width of the ground floor had been partitioned in the back into a dining area and three smaller salons, plus a paneled study.

Although a fire burned in the massive fireplace in the great hall, the castle was decidedly chilly. The cozy breakfast parlor was warmer with a fire crackling in the grate. The curtains were sunny checkered yellow, and the white tablecloth was crisply starched, napkins pristine, china polished until it gleamed. At least the housekeeper, Mrs. Averell, made sure that the new mistress would find no fault with the table settings at Black Raven.

To Cynara's annoyance, Merlin was sitting at the head of the table. He was somberly dressed in a gray riding coat with a black armband around his sleeve. He had not taken breakfast with them before this day. Her heartbeat escalated as she remembered what had transpired between them in the night. Tension mounted in the room as their eyes locked in challenge.

"Good morning, darling," Estelle greeted her daughter, and Cynara pressed a kiss to the cool, papery cheek. She sat down at the end of the long table, opposite Merlin, the place of the countess, the mistress of Black Raven. Sometimes her new position in life intimidated her.

"You look tired, Cynara," Estelle commented. She angled a glance at Merlin, whose face gave nothing away as he calmly cut a piece of ham on his plate. "I said the same to your husband. He has dark circles under his eyes."

"I'm perfectly well rested," Cynara lied, waiting for Bramble to fill her coffee cup. The butler unobtrusively placed a plate of pastries beside her, but she wasn't hungry. "In fact, I almost overslept," she added, regretting her exaggeration just as soon as it left her lips.

Merlin shot her a chiding glance, and his lips curved into a knowing smile. "I'm glad you sleep well in your new home."

Estelle looked from Cynara to her son-in-law, evidently sensing the tension between them. Cynara lowered her gaze to her plate, where Bramble had piled a poached egg and a thin slice of ham. She ate listlessly.

Estelle patted her lips with her napkin and spoke. "I'm sure this rattling old place must have a few ghosts. I hear things in the night." She shuddered delicately and sipped her tea.

"As far as I know, no ghosts have been seen, unless Felix decides to haunt us."

Estelle gasped. "Don't mention *that* name. I feel a distinct chill in the air." She pulled her black lace shawl more tightly around her. "The very air seems to sigh and move unexpectedly, as if spirits were floating from room to room."

"Mother, why are you so ghoulish this morning?" Cynara asked.

"This old castle unnerves me, always has." She paused. "I don't know if I should mention this, but last night I thought I heard footsteps in the corridor, heavy, booted footfalls, and then a door slamming."

Merlin gave Cynara a veiled glance, and a blush

started to warm her cheeks. Had her mother heard the slam of their bedroom door?

"Probably one of the servants," Cynara hastened to say. "There's nothing to be afraid of." *Except perhaps the man sitting at the opposite end of the table.* She met his cool gaze squarely. "Did you hear anything untoward?"

His lips quirked upward for a moment, but when he addressed Estelle, his face was wholly devoid of sarcasm. "You have absolutely nothing to fear from— anyone."

He tossed down his napkin and rose. "If you'll excuse me, I have business to tend to."

Just as he was about to leave the room, Mrs. Averell hurried inside, her mobcap askew and a few scraggly gray wisps of hair flying around her face. "Your lordship, you must come immediately. Someone has dug an enormous hole in the rose garden, in the shape of a grave."

Chapter 7

Gasping with shock, Cynara hurried out of the breakfast parlor after Merlin and her mother. A grave? Mrs. Averell must be mistaken.

"I told you there's something strange going on here," Estelle said under her breath to Cynara. "Someone was in the castle last night, and that someone could have killed us in our sleep."

"Don't be ridiculous, Mother. Rein in your imagination. Who would want to kill us?"

She grimaced as her mother's frightened gaze went—involuntarily—to Merlin's forbidding face. "Mother, as far as I know, he was asleep in his bed."

"I don't believe Merlin is capable of killing, but my instincts have been known to be wrong." She clung to Cynara's arm. "I'm frightened."

Cynara felt a decided chill along her spine, but she only placed her arm protectively across her mother's frail shoulders.

The morning was humid with a blustery wind from the sea. Tatters of fog still hovered over the bluish-gray Channel water, and lingered among the rocks along the base of the castle. Cynara pulled her shawl closer as they rounded the corner of the east wall and stepped into the enclosed rose garden. The mossy stone wall had been erected decades earlier to protect the tender blossoms from the raging sea storms. To one side there was the rose arbor, and on the other side someone had installed a vegetable patch where all kinds of herbs grew. Tufts of green sprouted in the neat rows now, and bright green leaves adorned the rosebushes, but it was yet too early for any roses to bloom.

As a sacrilege against the lovely filigree of the tender leaves was the hole, right in the middle of the garden. A birdbath had been tossed aside, the marble pedestal cracked. Bushes had been mangled around the rim of the hole—the grave.

"Who would do such a ghastly thing?" Estelle asked with a whimper. She clutched Cynara's arm harder for support.

Cynara stared grimly at the hole, which although only a foot deep, was as ominous as a real grave. "Who indeed. Haven't we had enough death and misery at Black Raven already?"

Merlin knelt on the ground by the long, narrow cavity, peering down. With a shovel that had been tossed among the roses, he stirred the loose soil at the bottom, but nothing except a few pebbles came to light. Then he hit solid rock.

"It's a mystery why this happened," he said. He scanned the faces of the assembled servants. Three footmen stared at him as did Bramble, the butler, the housekeeper, and Gideon Swift, Merlin's batman. They looked at one another uneasily, perhaps wondering which of them Merlin might blame, Cynara thought.

Merlin said nothing for a long time, only studying the hollow, then the servants. "I don't know who might be interested in digging up the rose arbor, but the real question is *why*. Why in the world would anyone do this? What did he expect to find?" Merlin's gaze wandered from face to face, including Cynara and Estelle. "One of the men at the estate must be responsible, since I find it difficult to believe that a woman would step outdoors in the middle of the night and start digging a grave."

Gideon Swift cleared his throat. "None here would be that strong . . . or that crafty."

Merlin's quelling glance silenced him. Then Merlin addressed the other servants. "You must tell me if you saw or heard anything strange last night."

An entrance to the kitchen—a stone building with a sloping roof that had been added to the castle long before Sydney Seymour's time—was at the end of the vegetable patch. Now the cook, Moira Black, a sturdy Cornish woman, was viewing the scene from the narrow window next to the door. Merlin waved at her, and she stepped out on the brick path that separated the vegetables from the roses. She passed the steep steps that led down to the dungeons below, and waved a ladle in the air.

"Milord, I don't have time to stand here, gawking at the ground," she said belligerently. "I have your dinner to see to." She gave Merlin a fierce stare from her dark eyes. Her hair, what could be seen under the enormous mobcap, was wiry gray, tightly curled.

"Surely, you can spare a minute," Merlin said. "Did

you see anyone last night? Did any beggar come to the kitchen door yesterday, or any tradesmen?"

"They shun this place, since Master Max left nothing but debts. I haven't had a delivery for months," the cook scoffed.

"That will soon change," Merlin said, tight-lipped. "After I've paid the bills, you may order whatever you want for the kitchen. Are you sure you saw no one in the garden?"

Moira Black crossed her plump arms over her crisp white apron. "I'm sure. Muggins came in for a tankard of ale and a chat late in the afternoon, but he does that now and again."

Merlin's shoulders seemed to slump for a moment, then he raised his head. "All of you must keep your eyes open for strangers, or odd behavior among the villagers. I won't tolerate having the Black Raven rose garden mutilated further. In fact, I want to restore it, and everything else, to its former grandeur. Is that understood?"

The servants nodded, viewing him with suspicion.

"And I will need your help. I'm counting on it." Merlin handed the shovel to Gideon Swift, who started shifting the earth back into the hole. "When I find the culprit, he will be punished. Mischief like this won't be accepted." Without another word Merlin returned to the house and disappeared into his study.

"He's a brave man, your husband," Estelle said as she pushed her arm through Cynara's. They followed him inside. Cynara shivered in the cool gloom of the great hall, wondering if she'd ever be able to shake off the unease that had settled in her. She went with Estelle to the morning room, where her mother showed her the latest progress of her embroidery.

Cynara disliked sewing, but, since a lady was expected to enjoy embroidery, she was making a fire screen that depicted a cat sleeping in a basket surrounded by sprigs of autumn leaves. Today she felt too restless to work on it, but she sat down on the sofa and fiddled with the yarn. She glanced at her mother, who had already settled by the fireplace with her embroidery frame. The fire had died down, but the room was pleasantly warm.

"Tell me, Mother, you knew the three Seymour brothers, Merlin's father and uncles. What were they like?" Cynara asked.

Estelle glanced up from her work. "I take it you're interested to know the past of Merlin's family?" When Cynara nodded, she went on.

"Merlin's father, Ross, was the youngest, and also the kindest of the three. He had much compassion in his heart, and he was a respectable man. Besides your father, I believe Ross was the kindest man I've ever known. Perhaps he was a bit weak too." She hesitated only for a second. "Once I almost hoped to marry him."

Cynara gasped. "You fell in love with Ross Seymour?"

Estelle pursed her lips and snipped off a dangling piece of yarn. "Well, it's difficult to say, really. I had no idea what love was, since I was terribly young, and your father was terribly dashing—as was Ross Seymour. Coming here in May of 1789, I had just escaped the Revolution. Everything happened so quickly." Her voice held enormous sadness. "Why did I escape the guillotine when the rest of my family didn't? Father sent me away, hoping to join me here in England later. I was frightened of everything here, and I was lonely. People were so different, so *British*. I missed my family dreadfully, and your father—and Ross— showed me consideration." Her voice brightened. "It was all so romantic. Yes, I believe I loved Ross once. However, he married Merlin's mother, and that was the end of it. They were deeply in love."

Cynara pondered the words, studying her mother. She saw the birdlike, brittle quality, the vague yet infinitely graceful gestures that were so French. She understood the loss her mother had suffered in her life. "You've never told me this before—"

"Mon Dieu, it was so long ago. Things change. I was very happy with your father. He cherished me; he took wonderful care of me, and I him."

"Tell me about the other Seymour brothers."

"Sydney was the eldest, a pompous, loud man. He had none of Ross's kindness. I believe he could be quite ruthless. There were rumors . . ."

"Rumors?"

"That he ill-treated the servants." Estelle gazed into the fireplace. "I think the real decay of the house started before he became the earl, but for a time it looked like he would drag the estate out of debt. Then his concern with estate matters slipped. He started drinking heavily when his wife died. Thank God Maximilian was away most of the time so that he didn't have to witness his father's debauchery. I think loneliness was a heavy burden on Sydney's shoulders. He liked glittering company; he liked to show himself off as a great golden lion. But all the same, he was lonely here at Black Raven, and there were no funds to set up household in London. Drink took his life, and it was a miserable, melancholy life most of the time."

"And George?"

"I never knew George very well, but if I might judge his character by Felix's—like father like son, as they say—George was the greedy Seymour. Being the middle brother, the only careers open to him was to enter the Church or become an army man. I think it was the last thing George wanted, so he emigrated to America." Estelle paused. "He married a plantation heiress there, but I've never met any of his American relatives. The mother abhorred the English climate and would not travel here."

"Felix's parents are both dead, then?"

"Yes, they died shortly after Felix graduated from Oxford. George insisted that Felix have a British education. After all, only the best is expected for the son of a peer."

"Who was Felix's guardian after his parents died?"

"Ross Seymour."

Silence rolled into the room, and Cynara pondered what she'd just learned. "Did they get along?"

"That I don't know. Felix returned to America, and came back here only a few months ago." She slanted a penetrating glance at Cynara. "Evidently came to take his bride back with him across the ocean."

Cynara shuddered. "In a way, I'm grateful to Merlin for stopping that ceremony. Yet, what about Brandon? I would be on my way to America, but Brandon would perhaps be free." Her voice thinned, petering off. Restless, she rose and paced the room. "I have to find a way to help my brother," she said, ending with a wail.

Estelle let her hands lie idle in her lap. She suddenly seemed frail and old. "I have a feeling that I won't see my son ever again."

"Nonsense! There must be a way. I'm sure he didn't steal that necklace, and if we can discover who did, we'll be able to free him."

"How do you propose we go about it?" Estelle glanced at Cynara over her wire-rimmed spectacles that she used when embroidering.

Cynara stared at her mother in determination. "Perhaps I can discover some of Brand's friends. Perhaps they can help me unravel the mystery."

"Wouldn't they already have done so if they truly were Brandon's friends?" Estelle's voice sounded brittle with defeat.

"I don't know. If only I had some funds . . ."

Silence stretched gloomily. Estelle's sighs were the only sounds for the next few minutes.

"You could always beg Merlin for help," she said quietly at last.

"I *have* asked him over and over. He's in no hurry to act." A frightening thought struck her. "Besides, wouldn't he have found a way already if he'd had any intention helping Brand?"

"Not necessarily. Perhaps he's afraid of dredging up the subject thinking that—with his reputation—he might ruin Brand's chances to acquittal. But, Cynara, he's the only chance we have."

"I don't know if I can beg him again. He might think that I'm a pest and drop the subject. I wish I could help Brand. I don't like to be beholden to Merlin."

Estelle tut-tutted. "You became beholden to him

the moment you wed him. The Hawthornes had nothing, and what we have now is solely due to Merlin's generosity. But I don't believe Merlin's an unreasonable man. He will be fair to you as he was fair to me."

Something warm quivered inside Cynara as her mother said those unexpectedly kind words about her son-in-law. Mother had more faith in Merlin than she had.

"I shall talk to him."

"But don't dawdle; Brand might be dying from jail fever this very moment."

Cynara had no opportunity to speak with Merlin until right before bedtime. They were both on the landing leading to their joint bedchambers.

"Did you discover anything new about the hole in the rose garden?" she inquired politely.

"No . . . nothing." He looked distracted as he glanced at Cynara, and she could sense his turbulent thoughts. His black eyes glittered strangely in the candlelight. "The servants really dislike me, don't they?" he asked suddenly.

"You must earn their confidence." They were standing outside Cynara's door, and she had an urge to ask him inside, if only to be out of earshot of nosy servants. "Come," she said, opening the door. "I need to speak with you privately."

He hesitated, but followed her at last. His face mirrored skepticism. "I don't want to make a fool of myself like I did last night," he muttered, and set down his candle on her dressing table.

"We shall only talk." She indicated a chair by the window, glad that Tildy wasn't in the room.

He sat, staring at her from under heavy eyelids. He was so handsome and desirable that she began to ache inside. She clenched her fists in the folds of her skirts to control her churning emotions. "I believe you're a man of strength and understanding," she began. She had to pace, or she might break down and cry in front of him, and that she didn't want to do.

His lips curved sardonically. "It sounds like you're working yourself up to ask a favor."

She stopped in front of him, angry at his chiding tone of voice. "You know I won't give up on Brand. His life is in the balance. Perhaps you could help me discover who his friends are in London, so that I can visit them and question them about the theft."

"You would go to gentlemen's lodgings and discuss your brother's crime?" He threw his head back and laughed. "They would be quick to take advantage of an innocent lady fresh from the country."

She fumed. "Well, perhaps you could inquire for me, then," she said between clenched teeth. "Tomorrow."

Merlin rose, stretching to his full height, and she had to tilt back her head to look at him. She smelled the strong fumes of brandy on his breath. "Cynara, Brandon might truly be guilty this time. He's been in innumerable gambling scrapes in an effort to line his pockets. Poverty has propelled him to do some foolish things."

"He's innocent!" Cynara spat out. "He has never stolen anything, and, even if he has been a reckless gambler since he left school, that doesn't make him a criminal."

"You're right. I wish you would believe my innocence as easily as you believe your brother's."

"We're not talking about you now, Merlin."

His eyes darkened, and something dangerous flickered in their depths. He took her chin in a firm grip, staring down at her speculatively. "Your brother is very important to you, then?" His words slurred together momentarily.

He had been drinking too much, Cynara thought with dismay. "Yes. But right now I'm mainly concerned for my mother's well-being. She isn't strong, and Brandon's dilemma is preying on her mind."

Silence thickened between them, and Cynara wondered what he was thinking. She tried to move away from him, but he stepped closer and cupped her face with his hands. "What are you doing?" she demanded. She wondered if he was about to kiss her, and a sudden fear that she was a helpless animal before a deadly predator consumed her.

"You're different tonight, not yourself," she whispered between stiff lips.

He snorted. "What do you know about me? Nothing, my dear. Nothing! All you do is hold your chin high and look down on me in contempt. Do you think I'm powerless? Do you think you can deny your duty to me and our marriage, and that I will accept your scorn forever?" His face moved ever closer to hers.

"Let me go," she said, yet longed to feel his lips against hers. But his intentions didn't travel in that direction.

Her heart took a strange leap as a sudden smile transformed his face. "What would you be prepared to give me in return if I helped to free Brandon?" His voice was velvety soft, cajoling, and Cynara pushed him hard in the chest. He only laughed. "Well?"

"I married you, as you wanted me to," she said. "What more do you demand from me?" As she looked into his eyes, she knew very well what he wanted. "Will you *force* me to do something I don't want to do?"

"I wouldn't exactly use such strong words if I were you." He pulled her tightly against his body, and she could feel the hard ridges of his muscles and the lean flesh pressing against her. Though she had expected it to repel her, she was oddly exhilarated, as if he had promised her a delicious treat instead of a demand that she could not fulfill.

"You would find that my price for helping Brand wouldn't be such a revolting sacrifice for you," he continued. He traced her cheek with his lips, kissing her earlobe and murmuring endearments in her hair.

Her resistance faltered, but finally anger made her push him hard in the chest. To her surprise, he let her go. The smile lingered on his face.

"I told you I would never consent to any intimacies. You have no right . . ." she began, instantly realizing he *did* have the right. If he so desired, he could force her to comply with his wishes. The moment she had given her marriage vows, she belonged to him body and soul. Gasping as if she hadn't quite realized that before, she turned away from him.

His voice was gruff as he spoke. "Since this isn't a marriage based on love, it is more of a business endeavor. Therefore, my price for making an effort to free your madcap brother is your surrender. You must truly be my wife. Black Raven needs descendants for the line to continue."

Cynara hadn't thought he wanted children. She had never seen any evidence that he was fond of them, but, like her, he was bound by duty—if not to her, to Black Raven. They were both trapped in a situation that could not be changed. Before their personal desires came the welfare of the servants and the cottagers on the estate. So many people depended on them. And she liked children; there was no denying that.

He stroked her cheek as he headed toward his room. "Think about my proposition. If you agree, there's a good chance I can free Brandon, though I'm not sure he deserves it." He stood by the door, his eyes dark and unfathomable. His lips curved sardonically. "You look unusually pale, my dear. Is the proposition so revolting, then?"

Anger seethed in her, and she glared at him. "You take delight in tormenting me. If there were something else I could do—"

"I've given you my offer. Nothing less than total surrender will buy my services." He opened the door to his room and stepped through. "You'd better turn the key behind me, or I might just take what's rightfully mine in the dark of the night—or right now. My patience is at an end."

"Why, you . . . you arrogant *knave!* I thought you were a fair and sensible man, but I can tell that I judged you wrong."

He was about to close the door. "I like to think that you're a sensible woman, Cynara. I wouldn't hurt you, you know." With those words he closed the door firmly behind him, leaving her feeling strangely stirred up and dissatisfied. In frustration, she twitched the faded red drapes across the windows and began pacing

to quiet her mind. His demand was extortion! Just like
Felix had held his promise to free Brand over her if
only she would marry him. Wherever she turned, she
was trapped. This time it was for good.

A knock sounded on the door, and Cynara replied
automatically. Tildy entered, carrying some dresses
over her arm. "I sponged and pressed these," she said,
and hung them in the wardrobe in the corner. Like the
rest of the furniture in the room, it was of heavy carved
oak that had darkened with age and polish.

"I helped Mrs. Hawthorne to bed and I was
alarmed. She's ever so worn out. Though she tried to
hide it, I noticed that she was cryin'."

"Crying?" Cynara asked, and stopped pacing.

"Yes, I believe she's worryin' terribly 'bout your
brother, Mistress Cy. If this goes on much longer,
she'll go to the grave."

Unease settled in Cynara, the weight of her dilemma
crushing her. She slumped on the chair before the
dressing table and silently succumbed to Tildy's minis-
trations. The brushing of her hair was soothing, but
nothing could take away the dread from her heart. She
would have to give in to Merlin's demands, and she
hated him for it. She had hoped— She tore off the
silver bracelet she'd been wearing and flung it into the
jewelry case. What had she hoped? That he would be
her knight, her savior who would always revere and
worship her? As if she cared . . .

"I say the master is very taken with you, Mistress
Cy," Tildy said, holding up one of Cynara's golden
tresses toward the candlelight. "Like spun gold," she
muttered. "Why don't I have such lovely hair?" Then

she chuckled. "No wonder the master is so much in love."

"He's not!" Cynara said heatedly. "He's only playing with me, cat-and-mouse games."

Tildy laughed. "I wouldn't mind such games at all, especially if he ended up in my bed."

"Tildy!" Cynara admonished, rising. She was too agitated to continue her toilette. "You're dismissed for tonight, and you must guard your tongue better. Things have changed; I'm no longer Miss Cynara, but the Countess of Raven with heavy responsibilities."

"My, aren't you prickly tonight! Master Merlin might soothe yer temper. . . ."

"Out!" Cynara wailed, fuming at her maid's laughing eyes. "I can do the rest myself."

"Whatever you want, Mistress Cy. Like you said, you're th' new countess, and you now share your secrets with people like Master Merlin, not with your old maid."

Cynara relented. "I'm sorry, but it's not like you to take someone else's side against me. Besides, I . . . we . . . I don't share any secrets with Merlin." She sank down on her bed. "I'm frightened of my new role."

"Don't be, you'll see, you'll be a splendid countess and wife. Though the servants here at the castle are a sour group, you'll soon charm them. You'll have them eatin' out o' your hand." Tildy patted Cynara's shoulder and left the room.

As soon as Cynara was alone, thoughts, images, began preying on her mind. She saw no other alternative than to obey Merlin if her brother was ever going to get out of Newgate Prison alive. If only she knew enough to handle the matter herself! But she knew nothing about the procedures of law, and she had no connections in London who might help her.

Dear God. Her hands trembled with worry as she slipped the nightgown over her head. She tightened the silken cords at her neck and pulled a shawl over her shoulders. Her hair felt heavy as it hung loosely down her back, pulling at her scalp. A headache had started at her temples, pulsing pain with every heartbeat. It seemed as if every day, every hour, were a lesson. Gone was her innocence, even though she had never had a man in her bed. It was the manipulation, first Felix's, now Merlin's, and her struggles with him that had made her grow up. Everything seemed to be a business deal.

On shaky legs she went to the door that separated her from him. He would probably mock her fear, laugh in her face. Her marriage had turned out so different from her dreams. She had believed she would marry for love, not for the convenience of her family. But she refused to feel sorry for herself. She was sure her mother would not have forced her to marry Merlin, not really, but Estelle could be extremely persuasive, and those large brown eyes had been so sad. She could not have borne to see her mother's dignity crumble in poverty.

Taking a deep breath, she turned the doorknob and stepped into Merlin's bedchamber. The room lay in darkness, but the curtains were parted, bringing the reflection of the moon playing on the restless seawater.

"Merlin?" she whispered, her tongue feeling papery dry against her teeth. Fear was weakening her legs, and a quality of unreality had overcome her, as if she were about to faint.

No answer was coming from the bed, but he was there. She could hear him breathe. She stepped closer, clutching her shawl in desperation. As she crossed a ghostly beam of moonlight spilling on the floor, she held her breath. Did he see her? He would surely start to laugh in triumph now that she'd dared to step into his chamber. Fear stiffened her limbs, yet she was loath to admit her terror. She took another step, but no laughter was forthcoming. One more step brought her to the side of the bed. The bed hangings were not pulled together. She could make out the shape of his head against the pillows.

He wasn't moving at all. She reached out, touching the satiny coverlet, but dared not touch him.

"Merlin," she whispered, hoping desperately that he wouldn't notice her, yet eager to get the ordeal over with.

He didn't reply. Instead, a soft snore issued from his lips. She stared in disbelief. He had fallen asleep! Had he been so sure, then, that she wouldn't dare to confront him that he'd gone to sleep? As she was at the end of her tether, a wave of wrath surged through her. She would indeed show him that she wasn't a coward!

She shook his shoulder. "Merlin! Wake up. I'm here to fulfill my end of the bargain."

His head moved on the pillow, and he drew a deep breath. He heaved himself up on his elbow, staring at her in the gloom. "Cynara?"

"Have you already forgotten our deal?" she asked acidly.

He shook his head, yawning deeply. "No . . . but I didn't think you would be interested."

She stared at him incredulously. "You believe I

don't care enough about my brother to take action—even if it is blackmail on your part? He might be dying just as we speak."

He slid up against the pillows, all the time studying her. She wished she could read his eyes, but it was too dark. Still, that intensity that she always connected with him was there, simmering between them. She inhaled tremulously, wondering what to do next.

"Shall I light the candles?" she wondered.

He chuckled. "Afraid of the dark, are you?"

She didn't deign to answer that taunt. No more did she care if that devilish face was lit by candlelight as he ravished her than she did about the thoughts going through his mind. She was there to perform her duty as the Countess of Raven, the earl's chattel. After all, she was of no more worth than any piece of china in the house. If Merlin decided to use her, then throw her on the floor, there was nothing she could do about it. But if it would bring Brandon home, she was prepared to pay.

Standing by the bed, she slid the shawl off her shoulders, letting it fall to the stone floor. She shivered in the cool air. Expecting him to laugh at her, she untied the cords at her throat, but no sound came from him. She sensed that he was following her every movement with his eyes, and she almost turned and fled.

Thinking how brave her mother must have been to alone escape the French Terror in '89 and face the unfamiliarity of England, she vowed to go through with this ordeal. After all, her mother had finally found happiness with a man. But would she ever be as lucky? Cynara wondered. Hardly with Merlin Seymour.

He chuckled . . . .

Chapter 8

"Don't look as if you're walking to the scaffold,"
Merlin chided her after lighting the candle on the
nightstand. "You're not the first woman to share a bed
with a man." He chuckled. "In fact, there's absolutely
no danger in it, only supreme pleasure if you allow it
to happen."

Cynara shuddered and reluctantly dragged the
nightgown over her head. "I knew you would somehow take advantage of me, to humiliate me," she muttered, her voice prickly with resentment. "You would
find a way."

"I could have forced my way into your bed on the
very first night of our marriage, but I had hoped
. . ." His voice trailed off, and he momentarily averted
his eyes. Cynara could have sworn she saw sadness
flash across his face.

"I had hoped you would come to me voluntarily,"
he explained reluctantly.

"Why should I?" She stood in her silk shift, shivering. She crossed her arms over her breasts, uneasy now
that his gaze had taken on an appreciative, teasing

glint. Not knowing what to do next, she stood as if frozen to the floor.

"Yes, why should you?" He folded the coverlet aside, and she noticed with a gasp that he was naked. Never had she seen a man in the state of undress before, never had she seen such . . . splendor. The symmetry of muscles and hard angles attracted her in a way she couldn't define.

He leaned over the side of the bed and took her hand. "Come. You will be warmer here with me than standing on that cold stone floor."

His grip was soothing and encouraging at the same time, and she let him pull her into bed. But instead of moving over to make room for her, he dragged her until she lay on top of him, her filmy shift the only thing preventing their skins from touching. Her rounded forms yielded easily to the hard planes of his body. He pulled the cover over them both, and his heady, virile scent enveloped her. Her face pressed into the hollow of his throat, and she kept her eyes tightly shut. He must surely hear her heart racing, but so could she hear his. The beat had a frantic quality, and wonder filled her at the thought that she had the power to provoke such excitement in him.

"You're tense as a board," he whispered, and began stroking her back. His gentle touch appeased her, and she relaxed little by little.

You traitor! she rebuked herself. Where had her determination not to let him affect her gone? She found that she enjoyed his touch, enjoyed the feel of him pressed so close. She had been prepared to surrender her body, but not to enjoy any part of him. She had justified her surrender by the conviction that she would feel nothing. This would merely be a business transaction, and she would return to her room, her heart untouched, and her thoughts remote from the action that he demanded from her. But she found, now, that her body would not be immune to the experience of making love. The only hope she had to maintain her dignity was to refuse him access to her heart.

"There, there," he crooned. "Just let the anger go. I promise I won't hurt you in any way. You'll like this."

"Why would you like to take me against my wishes? What do you gain?" she grumbled, resenting every second of the pleasure his stroking elicited.

His slow indrawn breath gave her an impression of pain, and she realized that her words had hurt him. She should have been delighted at scoring this small victory, but somehow the pleasure wasn't there.

Without replying, he eased her down on her side and turned toward her. Gently, he took one of her breasts in his hand and caressed it through the shift. She could not deny the delicious sweetness that radiated through her entire body. As he touched the hardened crest, she thought she would swoon with rapture, but she managed to control herself.

"For such a slender and diminutive body, you have unexpectedly rounded curves. Do you know what such allure does to a poor fellow like me?"

She shook her head mutinously, and he took one of her hands and placed it against his heart. "This." It pounded violently, and his breath sounded ragged. "Havoc to my senses." He held her hand and slid it firmly along his hairy chest to the flat abdomen, and lower still.

Cynara inhaled sharply. To touch the hard, velvety length of him was a shock, a pleasurable surprise. What was she supposed to do now? He leaned into her so that her grip tightened around him, and she could feel him throb with excitement. Disgusted by her own mounting desire, she tried to shut him out of her mind, but it was a futile effort. It was as if he'd invaded her every pore with his scent, his texture, the essence of his enjoyment. To her dismay, she found that she might easily learn to like his intimacy.

She fought to keep her raging sensations at bay.

"You're still so stiff, darling," he whispered, dragging his fingers through her hair.

He wondered what he could do to overcome her resistance. She felt so soft and pliant, her hair like silk, skin like the finest satin, her body a pure seduction of curves. Guilt gnawed at his conscience. He had desired her so much that he'd stooped to blackmail to get her into his bed. Somehow he had hoped she would understand and surrender her hostile heart. He knew he would have to be very gentle to penetrate her pride, to cajole her into the realm of pleasure. Just holding her against him brought him to the brink of no return, and he fought for control.

"If only you knew how much it means to me to have you here in my bed," he murmured, and slid his hand over her flat belly. At the joining of her thighs he found the warm mound that hid her womanly secrets. To her, virgin that she was, the potential pleasure must be a secret, he mused, and tenderly slid one finger between the hot, slick folds that led to her haven of bliss. Oh, yes, he thought, reeling. She was sweet and wet, already needing him but not knowing it yet. She flung herself over on her back and dug her heels into the mattress as he relentlessly caressed the luscious folds of her femininity. A pleasure so intense he wanted to moan out loud filled him until he thought he would come apart from its pressure, but the doubt that he might not be able to satisfy her marred his delight. Damn her resistance—yet, yet, she was sobbing in his ear. *Sobbing!* He stiffened, slowed his caresses, and peered at her face on his pillow. Her hair was a delicious tangle of blond silk, her cheeks tinted a delicate rose and her eyes dark and accusing. Was she hurting? A tear glittered like a diamond on the tip of her eyelashes, and he couldn't stop himself from bending over her and licking it off.

"What's wrong?" he asked.

She only shook her head. Cynara couldn't bear to tell him about the havoc he wreaked with her senses. She couldn't bear to see the triumph on his face if she moaned in ecstasy. She clamped her eyes shut and turned away from him, her back stiff and accusing. "You're using me," she said.

The gentleness seemed to seep out of him, and a steely determination took its place. He didn't answer at first, only started to pull her toward him. "I'm not using you if you like what I'm doing," he said at last, pulling off the shift that was snarled around her and tossing it onto the floor. "It seems to me that you liked every moment of this." His hand slid anew between her thighs, and she fought desperately against the sensations that once again took her by storm.

"No, I don't," she whispered forlornly, and forced herself to think of mundane, boring things as his magician's hands brought torment to every inch of her skin.

He fondled her breasts, bringing both peaks to an unbearable turgidness of pleasure. All she wanted was release from this sweet torture. She bit her lip until she tasted blood, and then she felt sorry for herself.

Every effort to shut him out failed. When he spread her thighs from the back, inserting his hard shaft into her wet folds, she could not help but squirm with ecstasy. Her backside pressed against his loins, she could feel the pounding of his blood to the part that sought entry into her. While squeezing one of her breasts, he seemed to just slide right into her. There was a momentary pain, but it was buried in the swelling, soaring excitement as he filled her inside, drew back, and filled her again. The rhythm was unbearable, each thrust renewed bliss, her whole body pulsing with desire. The sensation was so intimate, so completely uniting with him, and she knew that no matter how many times she would wash herself to erase any traces of him, he would still be there, embedded in the very texture of her womanhood. Forever and ever.

She lost her breath at some point, concentrating only on the escalating enchantment, but just as she thought she was at the brink of something wonderful, he shuddered over and over, pounding into her and moaning as if in the lap of ultimate rapture, then lay still. Only his ragged breath penetrated the stillness. "God, how I longed for this," he whispered hoarsely.

Cynara's only sensation was that of a raging, pulsating loss, a dissatisfaction so deep she wanted to cry. Battered with pleasure, and ravaged with anger, she heaved herself up in bed, struggling defiantly against her tears. *Humiliation.* The word glared in her mind as if written in fire, and she cursed her disobedient body.

He'd sensed her pleasure. He'd won somehow, but what had she lost besides her virginity? Her pride.

She slid off the bed and groped for her nightgown.

"Don't go," came his raspy voice, his breath still ragged. "It was the loveliest time of my life. You don't know how long I've yearned to make love to you." He held her back, his hand warm and reassuring on her arm.

"Don't touch me!" Before she would break down and cry in front of him, she tore away from him and ran into her room. Pressing her nightgown against her mouth to stifle her sobs, she locked the door and hurtled into bed. The sheets were cold and uninviting, and they smelled of soap, not of heady arousal. Oh, *Merlin!* Why did you put me through this? It was the ultimate betrayal because he had known what her reaction would be, hadn't he? He had known that she would enjoy his touch.

The place he had so sweetly occupied between her legs throbbed unfulfilled, and she wondered how long the torture would go on. Her breasts felt unbearably swollen and their peaks so hard and tender, as if they, too, sought a release. She lay trembling for a long time, until sleep finally claimed her. As dawn filtered through the curtains, she dreamed of him, Merlin, the man who had bewitched her senses.

The next morning she debated how to enter the breakfast room without blushing. Would he be there? Would her mother be able to see any telltale signs of what had transpired in the night? Cynara wished the floor would open and swallow her as she stepped over the threshold.

"Good morning, darling," Estelle greeted her.

Cynara drew a sigh of relief as she noticed that Merlin's place was empty. She kissed her mother's cheek and sat down. Bramble bowed and poured coffee from a silver urn into a cup.

As she bit into a piece of toast spread liberally with raspberry jam, Cynara studied her mother. The older woman looked more frail this morning, dark smudges under the eyes marring that flawless if fragile complexion. She was unnaturally pale, and the eyes dark with worry.

"Mother, I have good news," Cynara said. "Merlin has promised to do what he can to help Brand. Before you know it, Brand will be back here with us."

Estelle sighed. "I wish you were right. However, does Merlin have the power—"

"Power?" came from the doorway as Merlin stepped inside. He smiled at Estelle and kissed her cheek. "What are you talking about?" He sauntered to the end of the table, where Cynara was sitting, and she blushed to the roots of her hair. There was a decidedly wicked glint in his eye, and the dark, brooding quality was gone from his face. Pretending everything was normal, she offered her cheek to his lips, and shuddered as he planted a warm, intimate kiss on her mouth instead. It wasn't a shudder of disgust but rather one of pleasure. The throbbing started in the pit of her stomach, and agitation spread through her.

"We were discussing Brandon's dilemma," Estelle said. "Cynara says you've promised to help him." She glanced from Cynara's face to Merlin's, her dark eyes never missing a detail. "I'm very grateful to you, Merlin. You're proving yourself to be as solicitous as was your good father."

Merlin sat down at his place, watching Bramble pouring his coffee. "I would never go back on a promise to my wife, especially since she proved to be so . . . so very persuasive." He shot a glance at Cynara, and she fumed at him across the vast table.

"I know my daughter. When she's determined to do something, she sees it through, no matter how distasteful a chore," Estelle said with pride. She beamed at Cynara, and somehow last night's adventure didn't seem quite as distasteful. It had brought hope to her mother's eyes, and that was ample compensation for the humiliation at Merlin's hands.

"When will you start?" she challenged her husband. He looked so attractive, so very virile this morning, and she found it difficult to resent him. His black curls were brushed flat, but she knew they were prone to become untidy in the slightest breeze. His starched white neckcloth was tied to perfection. It wasn't as if he'd hurt her body, only her pride.

"Just as soon as I've finished my breakfast, Gideon Swift and I will travel to London and see what can be done to free your brother."

Estelle gasped and clasped her hands to her heart in delight. "I'm ever so grateful."

"If you write a note to Brandon, I might be able to carry it past the guards. It's amazing how bribes ease the way for most criminals."

Estelle slanted a glance at her daughter. "I don't know what Cynara told you to make you leave for London in such haste, but she must have pressed home the importance of speed. All sorts of dreadful diseases lurk in the prisons, and Brandon could be a victim anytime."

Cynara met Merlin's glance, seeing the teasing glitter. "Your daughter didn't have to work hard to convince me."

They finished breakfast in silence, and Cynara was eager to leave Merlin's presence, since tension was steadily mounting between them with every moment they stayed close. She refused to look at him, but she knew he was staring at her—to embarrass her, no doubt. She flung down her napkin.

"Before I start organizing a thorough cleaning of the castle, I will take a ride," she said. "It's possible I won't be here when you're ready to leave." He had stood up as she left the table, and now she raised herself on her toes and placed a cool kiss on his cheek. Nothing more than a display of affection for her mother's sake, Cynara told herself. Still, she couldn't deny the current of excitement that rolled through her as he returned her kiss on her lips.

"Godspeed," she said, and left the room before he would utter something that would embarrass her further.

"Take one of the grooms with you on your ride, Cynara."

The morning was humid and balmy. A light fog hung over the bay, but the wind would soon chase it away, and the day would be even warmer. The heavy material of her riding habit chafed against her skin, but it was the usual dress for riding. This habit was of lightweight gray wool with black velvet lapels. The skirt was very wide, and the jacket snug at the waist.

A hat with a curled brim and a black plume that curled over one ear completed the outfit.

Muggins was at the stables, overseeing the lesser grooms as they curried and fed the horses. "Mornin'," he greeted Cynara sourly, and she noticed that he didn't bother to doff his hat.

"I will take a ride, and I expect you to accompany me, Muggins." Cynara's chestnut mare, Swallow, had been brought to Black Raven after the wedding.

"I suppose I must," he muttered, and Cynara gave him a hard glance. She saw that he was sweating profusely, as if he'd been running.

"It is your job, and not something I suggested as a way to torture you," she said firmly. "Many men would be more than happy to find themselves in your position."

She couldn't quite hear his reply, but it sounded like "don't flatter yourself, ma'am." She stared in disbelief at him, noting the insolent smirk on his lips.

"Simply, what I meant, Muggins, is that no other groom would dare—or have any reason—to complain about the request." Head held high, she watched as a groom who could not have been much older than fifteen or sixteen lead Swallow out on the hard-packed yard in front of the stables. The boy had a limp, but he seemed not to be in pain. His clothes were scruffy but clean, and his red hair was brushed neatly, parted on one side. Every inch of his face and forearms were covered with freckles. He gave her a shy smile, and she inquired, "What's your name?"

"Bobby Black, milady," he replied.

"Can you ride?" She let him boost her into the saddle.

"Aye, milady." The boy flushed beet red, and twirled his cap between his hands. "That's what I like to do the most."

She gave Muggins a speculative stare. "Since Mr. Muggins is so busy this morning, you might ride with me, Bobby. We must exercise the horses, and I like the company of someone who enjoys an outing on horseback." She gave the gaping Muggins a small smile. "Don't disturb yourself, Muggins. Bobby will find a horse to ride—all by himself."

"But . . . what will the master say?" Muggins began.

"When he's away, I'm the one giving the orders. Is that understood?"

Muggins glared at her from under the brim of his hat, and he made her think of a fox, the slanted, calculating eyes, long nose, and pointed chin. His eyebrows were bushy and his hair straggling from under the hat. She felt unease in his presence; he had a furtive air, as if needing to conceal something from her at any cost. The sensation unsettled her.

She rode along the path that went around the stables, curved up on the slope past the Raven vault, and continued into Gairlock Woods that stretched inland toward Dartmouth. Farther away from the coast, the landscape turned more hilly, verdant fields that were made into a patchwork quilt by low stone fences crisscrossing every acre. Beyond the hills lay the moor, a gloomy stretch of nothingness. The sunshine reflected in the dewdrops, creating lacy webs of light on the trees. A fine mist danced over the fields. The morning was lovely, Cynara thought with a contented sigh, and inhaled the fragrance of wet grass and moss.

Bobby rode up behind her on the path, keeping a

few paces behind her in deference to her status. She smiled and beckoned him until his horse was alongside Swallow. "A beautiful morning, isn't it?" Cynara began, and elicited a smile.

"Aye."

"Black? Are you related to Moira, the cook?"

"Me mother," he said, blushing again. "She'll be ever so proud when she hears that I got to ride with milady." His brow darkened momentarily, and the merry blue eyes took on a troubled look.

"What's wrong?" Cynara asked.

He fidgeted in the saddle, and Cynara saw a flash of fear cross his face. "Mr. Muggins will be angry with me."

"Why?"

"Because ye chose me in his place, milady."

Cynara understood what the boy meant. "He's not a man who forgives easily, but I won't let him mistreat you."

Bobby nodded. "Thank you."

Cynara knew he was reluctant to speak ill of his foreman, but she couldn't help but be curious about Muggins, who dared to show such defiance to his employer.

"Do you know Mr. Muggins well?" she prodded.

The boy shook his head. "His family doesn't come from here. From Plymouth, they are. Came here during Master Sydney's rule. The earl wot died in that Battle of Waterloo didn't like Mr. Muggins much, I know that."

Cynara smiled. "You're a clever one, Bobby! You know about what happens in the world, don't you?"

Bobby shrugged, coloring. "I don't know. I listen to

the sailors down at the Salcombe harbor, and at the alehouse in the village. They know everything." He paused a moment. "But 'twould be a blessing to know how to write and read," he said more to himself than to her.

Cynara had a sudden urge to help. She had everything, whereas people like Bobby scraped by on what they could find. Still, he and his mother were lucky to hold a position at a place like Black Raven, albeit a castle burdened by debt. Its inhabitants had yet to suffer starvation, which was a common occurrence among the poor cottagers who had only the vegetable patch by their cottages and perhaps a pig or two to fend away utter destitution.

"Perhaps . . . I could help." She hesitated, not wanting to promise something that might not happen. But in the Black Raven village there must be many young people who could neither read nor write. "Let's go on." She flicked the reins, and Swallow fell into a trot.

They returned to the woods, and the green foliage filtered the sunlight, creating a muted greenish light under the trees. The woods were filled with serene stillness, and Cynara felt an ever-heightening freedom of spirit. They arrived in a clearing, and the only sound was the horses' hooves against moss and year-old leaves.

Suddenly she recalled the duel that had been fought in a similar copse, and she marveled at the thought that Merlin would place her wish to free Brandon before trying to solve his own, much more dire problems. Had she been selfish to ask his help? No, if Brandon were freed, he would without a doubt help Merlin to clear his name. If such a thing was possible . . .

"Look out!" shouted Bobby, and Cynara was vaguely aware of a dark form darting out in front of Swallow. She cried out as the mare reared up, but managed to stay in the saddle. She glanced after the figure, but all she could see was something insubstantial—like the corner of a flapping gray cloak. Then there was nothing.

"What was that?" she cried to Bobby as she struggled to calm her horse.

He rode up, taking Swallow's rein and holding tight. "You're a good horsewoman. A less skilled rider would have fallen off. The mare might have bolted."

"Who was that?"

"Crazy Jean, the village idiot. He looked like a big, swooping bird with that gray cloak of his. Most likely, we startled him from his sleep in some hollow."

"He frightened the mare terribly with his move."

"Jean is a strange one, always has been."

A thin, eerie wail suddenly broke the stillness. Words floated toward them, thinning as Jean ran away. "Death has been visiting Black Raven, and will again. The souls will not rest until the secret is revealed."

Silence descended thick with foreboding in the clearing, and Cynara shivered. She exchanged an apprehensive glance with Bobby. He only shrugged.

"Ol' Jean thinks he can predict the future, the silly fool. Don't ye pay any attention to him, milady."

With a determined nod, Cynara steered her mount toward the path leading back to Black Raven. Even if he was considered the village idiot, Jean's prediction had cast a pall on the day. Now there was no sign of anything or anyone in the forest. Only a few branches creaked, as if stirred by a gust of wind. She could have sworn Jean had darted across the path to frighten her horse. But why? There was no reason for anyone to run in front of cantering horses in the woods.

The morning ride had been ruined by the scare, and Cynara was content heading Swallow toward the stables. "Whatever Jean was doing in the woods, I'm glad my mare doesn't easily panic," she said to Bobby.

Her happy mood gone, she returned to the house. There was no time to brood about what had happened. She would have to start working on the transformation of the castle. Yet, she could have sworn that Jean had known they were coming along the path.

Chapter 9

Cynara forgot all about the strange man in the woods as she immersed herself in the enormous task of refurbishing the castle. Mildewed and tattered curtains and wall hangings were burned, rugs beat until all dust was gone, floors scrubbed, and windows cleaned. A week after Merlin had left for London, she spent one late evening planning what had to be done to restore the glow to the great hall. She was discussing with Bramble the best way of removing spiderwebs in the ancient ceiling beams. It would be a feat of courage, since the ceiling was twenty feet above the floor.

In the midst of their conference, Estelle hurried into the room, dressed in layers of gauzy nightgown and trailing cashmere shawls. Cynara knew instantly that something had happened to upset her mother, because Estelle would never show herself outside her bedroom unless properly dressed. Her face was deathly pale, and her brown eyes were enlarged with distress.

"Mother!" Cynara put aside the samples of materials she carried in her arms, and rushed to Estelle's side just in time to save the older woman from crumpling to the floor in a faint. "What's wrong? Where's Tildy?" She helped her mother to lie down on an ancient settle with red velvet cushions.

Tildy, whose maid services Cynara shared with her mother, came running, carrying a vinaigrette bottle, which she proceeded to hold under Estelle's nose. The restorative had a reviving effect on Estelle.

"I was truly frightened," Estelle whispered between stiff lips. "I had just fallen asleep, when I was awakened by a terrible noise. It sounded like something crashing down." Estelle fluttered her hand in agitation as if the memory were too much to bear. "I sat up in bed, my heart pounding so hard, I thought it would stop. It was very painful." She clutched Cynara's arm. "There was *a man* standing by the bed."

Estelle seemed to be on the verge of losing consciousness again, but the vinegar brought her around.

"A man! Did you recognize him?" Cynara demanded.

Estelle shook her head. "I was so distressed, I dared not take a good look at him. He wore a voluminous gray cloak and a hat pulled low over his brow, shading most of his face." She silenced, her eyes widening as she evidently was reliving the scene. "He seemed young, though, and I remember that he was rather tall. I screamed, and then he was gone without a sound, as if he'd been a ghost."

Cynara and Tildy exchanged worried glances. "Are you sure you didn't dream it?" Cynara asked, knowing that the answer would be negative.

"He was right there, staring at me," Estelle said, her voice breaking.

"Could it have been one of the servants?" Cynara

felt a rivulet of fear. She recalled the figure in the gray cloak in the woods. Could it have been the same man? But Jean had been old and bowlegged.

"His cloak was much too elegant for a servant," Estelle said, finally sitting up. "I declare, this castle is full of evil. I felt it the moment we moved here."

Cynara sighed, hating to admit that there was some truth to those words. She had sensed it herself. Perhaps it was the negative attitude of the servants.

"Please call Mrs. Averell," Cynara begged Bramble, who'd been standing at one end of the settle. The butler complied, and Cynara waited impatiently for the housekeeper to arrive. She chafed her mother's icy hands, and Tildy wrapped the shawls closer around the frail shoulders. Estelle was still shaking, but was much calmer now. Cynara sent Tildy for a glass of brandy.

"Mother, you'll be fine now. I'm here to take care of you, and Brand will join us soon."

"I want to go back to Stormywood," Estelle said, her lips drooping. "I fear for my life here—not to mention yours." She gripped Cynara's hand. "You must come with me until Merlin returns."

"I understand your alarm, but I don't see who would want to harm us. We're surrounded by servants here, so I don't see how we would be in any danger."

"The man entered my bedroom! The servants are lazy and indifferent. They wouldn't care if the castle was invaded by an *army* of thieves."

Mrs. Averell entered, her face set in lines of disapproval. "I was in the middle of executing your orders concerning the linen closet, milady. What's amiss?" she asked, clasping her hands on her stomach. The black bombazine gown crackled with her every movement. Her eyes were cold and suspicious as she stared at Cynara.

Cynara drew herself up and met the chilly gaze squarely. "Mrs. Averell, you must know just about everything that transpires in this house. Did the chimney sweeps arrive? Did someone visit any of the servants today? Any relatives? Friends?"

The housekeeper shook her head. "No. No visitors."

"Was something delivered? Did someone come to the kitchen entrance?"

"No."

Silence fell, a sullen—almost insolent—silence.

"From now on I want you to keep all doors locked, and let only the people you recognize into the castle," Cynara said.

Mrs. Averell snorted ever so softly. "Why, if I may ask? This isn't London, full of thieves and murderers," she said.

"It's my command, and that's enough reason," Cynara said. "I'm sure you don't like strange men to enter the castle any more than I do."

Mrs. Averell pursed her lips and tilted her chin up. "I'm sure that would never happen here."

Cynara had no desire to start an argument, so she dismissed the housekeeper. She asked Bramble, the truly loyal servant in a household of apparent enemies, to ask all the footmen if they'd seen anything unusual. "Ask them to search the castle from top to bottom, including the dungeons."

The narrow passages were ominously dark as Cynara helped her mother back to bed. Tildy promised to sleep in Estelle's room during the night, and Cynara vowed that she would check all the doors herself before seeking her rest. Filled with misgivings after this latest event, she hurried along the dark corridors to the brightly lit great hall below. Her heart raced with fear, but she was determined not to let her imagination get the best of her. It was likely that her mother had dreamt about the figure by the bed, but why? And if she hadn't, who had entered the castle, and why had he gone into Estelle's room?

A thought struck Cynara, but she pushed it away instantly. Yet the suspicion lingered: What if someone were purposely frightening the ladies at Black Raven? The event in the woods could have ended with the horse bolting. I could have fallen and broken my neck, Cynara thought in dismay. She fought against the ever-tightening circle of black thoughts and asked Bramble to accompany her as she checked the doors.

"I would feel better if the master were here," Bramble said, waddling behind her along the passage to the kitchen. "I suspect there will be mounting problems with the staff."

"But why?" Cynara wanted to know. "What has he done to set them against him?"

"These country people are superstitious. They probably think he murdered his father, and is bringing the evil here."

"You don't believe such rumors?"

"I've known the master since he was a wee lad, milady. No one knows better how much he loved old Master Seymour. Master Merlin wouldn't kill a fly." Bramble spoke with such conviction that Cynara felt greatly comforted.

"And if you don't mind me saying so, milady, the servants resent the extra work you're asking them to do, what with the renovations starting."

"If they had lifted a finger in the first place to keep the castle clean, they wouldn't have to work so hard now." Cynara knew that firmness was the only method that would bring the servants around.

"I agree, but they don't like you much for it." Bramble blushed to the top of his bald head as they stepped into the dimly lit kitchen. He wrung his hands in despair. "Oh, I'm sorry, milady. I had no right speaking out of turn."

Cynara laughed. "Don't worry, Bramble. If anyone, I know I can trust you implicitly, and I want you to always be honest with me."

Bramble nodded and swallowed convulsively as he made sure the door was tightly bolted. They returned to the great hall, which was shadowy with the massive carved furniture resembling crouching men in the flickering candlelight. As they stepped next to the staircase that covered most of the west wall of the foyer, the huge oaken front door slammed shut. Cynara could have sworn she saw a flash of gray cloth. It must mean that the man had been in the castle the whole time. . . .

"What was that?" Bramble ambled to the door, wrenched it open, and stared into the pitch darkness. Two of the footmen came running down the stairs.

"We've searched every room, milady," they explained. "No one there."

"Go after Bramble, he needs your help," she demanded, standing in the door opening through which the butler had disappeared. The night was pitch black, not a sign of moon or stars. A cool, salty breeze blew in from the sea.

She watched the men being swallowed by the night, then came a shout and a groan. Beside herself with worry, she stepped out on the front steps and tried to see through the blackness.

Bramble returned, leaning heavily on one of the footmen. He was clutching his shoulder as if in pain.

"What happened?" Cynara asked, helping the footmen settle the rotund butler in a giant carved chair beside the door.

"He hit me with something, probably a stone. I'm lucky he got only my shoulder," Bramble said, wheezing. His face was streaming with perspiration, and Cynara—for the second time that night—administered brandy to a victim of the gray-cloaked intruder.

Mother had been right, there had been a strange man in the castle.

Just as Bramble had recovered his composure, the door rattled. The footman, who'd been careful to bolt it, asked the person to identify himself.

"Open up! It's your master."

The footman drew the heavy bolts aside and admitted Merlin. His hair looked windblown, as if he'd lost his hat, and he was wearing a mud-spattered black cloak. Sensations warred inside her; one was suspicion about his early return, the other relief at seeing him safe and sound, a relief that urged her to rush into his arms. But the most sober side of her decided caution was the best way in which to handle his sudden return.

His dark eyes challenged her, invited her, but he made no move to sweep her into his arms. He only planted a cool kiss on her fingertips. "It was difficult to ride in the dark. No moon to light the way. The wind is increasing, and before this night is over we will be drenched in rain."

"Where's Gideon Swift?" Cynara asked. His touch had sent her heart galloping, and she was as drawn to him as ever. The magnetism that had always been his seemed magnified tonight.

"I left him with the carriage at Dartmouth, but I could not wait to return home to my bride," he said for everyone to hear. His face split in a warm grin.

One of the footmen chuckled, and Cynara blushed. She wished there were no mystery about him, no mystery about his father's death. If she could have trusted him implicitly, then she might have gladly thrown herself into his arms. The way things were, she balked at his show of affection. If he thought she would surrender after one night of lovemaking . . . but oh, it felt so good to see him, as if he'd been gone for a year rather than a week.

"We had an unwelcome visitor tonight. Mother found him standing by her bed, and only ten minutes ago he hit Bramble on the shoulder, almost killing him. The stranger wore a gray cloak."

His face darkened in worry. "Unacceptable goings-on! I see that I returned in the nick of time. We must investigate the strange events at the castle just as soon as may be. Perhaps the local constabulary will help us." He carelessly tossed cloak and gloves to one of the footmen. "Perhaps it was a thief. Did the servants catch him?"

She shook her head mutely. "According to the servants, no strangers entered the house. I have made sure all the doors are secure."

"Have you recovered, old fellow?" he asked Bramble, and when the butler nodded, he added, "You must go to your room and rest now, and don't overtax yourself tomorrow." He concentrated once more on Cynara. He took her arm and led her toward the enormous fireplace at the east wall of the great hall, where a fire chased off the chill in the air. "I had hoped my wife would meet me—the weary traveler—with a glass of brandy."

"You don't seem overly concerned that an intruder entered the castle this evening," she said.

"I am, of course, but what can I do at this hour? I won't be able to catch up with him in the darkness. Most likely it was some bold vagrant who wanted to steal food or a bauble." He tried to embrace her, but she pushed him away.

"Mother might have been seriously injured; she almost died with fright, and as for Bramble—"

His eyes blazed. "What do you want me to do? What *can* I do?"

"Not much at this point, but I wish you would understand my concern. I won't be able to sleep tonight."

"Believe me, I understand. There's nothing but worries in my life at the moment. What I need is some rest and peace, not more problems to contend with." He paused, staring into the fire. "Aren't you going to ask me how my trip to London went?"

Cynara brightened. "Yes, I almost forgot. What can you do for Brandon? How is he?"

"He asked for you, and he's still healthy, if a bit gaunt. He wants to see you in Newgate before the trial."

"Trial? When?"

"It's to be in Surrey, in Kingston, where the crime occurred. That's when I'll make the rescue effort, on the way out of London. At least they decided not to try his case at the Old Bailey. From there it would be impossible to free Brand." He sighed. "God knows, for Brandon I might get into deeper trouble than I'm already in. If I'm caught, I'll end up in Newgate, probably get to share a dungeon with your brother."

Feeling a stab of guilt, Cynara glanced at him speculatively. "The rescue mission sounds like a dangerous idea."

"It is, but when one is desperate, there's no other choice. If only to earn your approval, I'm desperate to settle this matter once and for all." He took a step closer to her, a small smile playing on his lips. He looked as if he were about to embrace her, then evidently changed his mind. "When shall we go to London together?"

"Just as soon as may be." Merlin's closeness disturbed her more than she liked. He had been gone only a week, but she had to admit—to herself, if not to him—that she'd missed him. His presence gave her constant support. He was always ready to deal with any domestic problem that occurred, and that made her feel safe. Even though an intruder had been in the castle, she was no longer afraid because Merlin had come home.

Flustered by her delight at seeing him, she thought of different subjects to broach, but when she looked into his dark eyes, she couldn't recall anything that had happened during the week. All she could think of was his embrace, his lips on hers.

"Are you about to retire to your bedchamber?" he asked.

"Yes . . . alone," she replied. "Nothing has changed in my attitude toward you." *But it had.* Not that she would ever let him know that.

"How disappointing," he said, and strolled to an old carved chair upholstered with faded gold brocade. He pulled it up to the fire and sat down. "When you go up, please ask Bramble to bring me a bottle of brandy."

"You sent Bramble to rest after his blow, but I'll bring you one." Regretting that their chat was over, Cynara left the room. She returned a few minutes later, finding that he'd fallen asleep in the chair, his long legs stretched out before him. She stifled a desire to stare at his handsome face that looked so different while relaxed in sleep. It was as if sleep had laid a veil of softness over the harsh angles of his features.

She set down the brandy bottle and glass, and debated whether to spread a blanket over him or not. When he awakened, he would be stiff and cold. Vacillating, she didn't notice when he opened his eyes. She cried out in surprise as he lashed out his arms and pulled her down on his lap.

"What are you doing?" she demanded, struggling to get away from his tight embrace.

"I was floating in a dream where you featured prominently, and then your presence awakened me." His eyes teased her. "I thought I was entitled to a warmer welcome from you than the formal one I received as I arrived."

She glared at him, not because she was angry, but because he had the advantage of strength. How could she gracefully extricate herself from his embrace without fighting? If he thought she was ready to surrender herself again—as she had that one time for Brand's sake—he was truly mistaken. "Let me go."

"Not until you've given me a kiss."

"Hrmph! I have no desire to dilly-dally in your arms. This chair is extremely uncomfortable."

He chuckled. "We can always move to a more comfortable spot—my bed."

She pushed in vain against his hard chest, but he didn't budge an inch. "Just because I gave myself once, due to blackmail, doesn't mean I will repeat the offer."

"Very well, if you have to be stubborn for the purpose of shielding your pride, then so be it. Nevertheless, you on my lap is an opportunity . . ." Before she could protest, he had captured her mouth with his. The kiss deepened before she could shy away. He tasted so *good,* his kiss so arousing, she would like to melt into his arms and never get up again. He prompted that sweetness in her heart when nothing else did. It wasn't their lips touching, their tongues tasting, it was their hearts communicating, entwining. Shocked by the intimate discovery, Cynara tried to struggle away, but her resistance soon faded. His kiss held such reverence, such tenderness that it killed her instinct to fight. His tongue was velvety soft against hers, intimate, probing, seeking solace in her. And somehow she sensed that her kiss satisfied him deeply, just as it satisfied her. An eternity flowed by as she grew to know him once again. Her body had no difficulty with pride. It opened up like a flower to life-giving sunlight, warmth swooping through her as he deepened the kiss, demanding more. And she responded. How could she not when he obliterated every ounce of resistance within her?

"Dear God, what is it? What do you have, Cynara, that intoxicates me like nothing else does?" Merlin murmured as he lifted his head to gaze at her. *"What* are you, my beloved? A witch who has enchanted me? It seems that I've always searched for you, and now—now that I have you here in my arms, I know you're still not mine because I don't have your love. I know I trampled your pride that night before I left," he whispered. "But we both learned something, didn't we?"

Cynara stared at him in wonder. Never had she heard him speak such tender words before. He was the bewitcher, his words weaving a spell on her heart, so tangible that she could almost see it. Suddenly she felt as if they'd always known each other. Always. The immensity of the thought frightened her, and she struggled out of his embrace.

He let her go. "Is there a way I can make you understand?"

"What?" she asked abruptly, smoothing down her dress as she stood beside the chair. She pretended indifference.

"That something has always connected us, something that we can't exactly see but that we know is there."

She knew what he meant; he was merely putting words to her own thoughts. They shared something that could not be explained, and they shared marriage vows. Those could not be broken, and now she had no desire to break them, not since that night. . . .

Somehow she was bound to this dark, handsome man who lit fires beneath her skin in a way she had never before experienced. Yet it was too early to admit her awakening feelings for him. "A sensation that we're connected by an invisible cord doesn't change the fact that we have a marriage of convenience, does it?"

"It depends how long you struggle to maintain it convenient."

"Don't put the burden solely on me, Merlin."

Just as she was about to leave the room, he said, "Don't go just yet. I have a present for you."

"A present?" she echoed.

He hauled a small package from his pocket and handed it to her. She saw that it was a velvet-covered box, and when she opened the lid, the glitter of diamonds dazzled her. It was a set of gold earrings shaped into drops, each studded by a flawless diamond.

"They are like the teardrops you shed when we made love for the first time. When you wear them, they will make you remember."

A deep blush covered her face. "I don't know if I care to recall that night." She pushed the lid shut and handed back the box. "I see no reason to commemorate the event."

Something dark and painful flickered in his eyes, but he took the box without comment and slipped it back into his pocket.

She regretted her cruel action. "I . . . didn't mean to hurt you," she said lamely. "The earrings are lovely, but I'd rather forget *that* night." *Liar!* she told herself.

His lips curved mirthlessly. "Your wish is my command. Get ready for London tomorrow morning. I will personally escort you there." Not giving her another glance, he tilted his head against the back of the chair and closed his eyes.

"Aren't you going to sleep in your bed?" she asked, unsure what to do or say. She hated to leave him with this ever-widening rift between them. After all, he had gone to see Brandon.

"I didn't think you cared." He stared to her through slitted eyes, and Cynara shuddered at the indifference that had replaced his ardor.

Without another word she turned on her heel and left the room. Had she been wrong not to accept his gift? The earrings had been lovely, but . . . surely, that night was nothing but a memory of utter humiliation. There had been another feeling growing in her, a tremendous yearning, a *need* to discover what the release of the erotic tension that assaulted her every moment she spent in his presence was like. He evidently knew and found it momentous enough to celebrate it with a gift of diamonds.

She undressed with Tildy's help, and when the maid left, Cynara heard Merlin enter his bedchamber. Tensely, she listened to his footsteps, and a longing for him began to spread through her. But there was more than a wall between them now. Still, she had paid for his help to contact Brandon, so why the guilt? Besides the yearning in her heart to be with him, guilt was her constant companion. She had never dreamt that she would find Merlin as fascinating as she now did.

Pressing her ear to the door, she listened to more sounds of him, but the house was filled with a hushed silence. Was he listening for sounds of her? She glanced at the old door handle, tracing its cold contours with a finger, wondering if he was touching the old steel like she was? Just as she liked to pretend that it was true, she heard the old wooden bed creak faintly as he turned on the mattress. He was asleep!

Disgusted by her own foolish longings, she crossed the room to her own bed. The sheets were cold even if Tildy had placed a hot brick under the goosedown quilt. Tossing and turning unhappily, Cynara finally fell asleep. But even as her body rested, she could find no peace.

Chapter 10

Cynara had never had the pleasure of a Season in London, since the Hawthornes had been too poor to pay for a lavish come-out ball and the exorbitant expense of a new fashionable wardrobe for their daughter. No other relative had had the wherewithal to sponsor her. Cynara hadn't exactly missed London and the Season—she did not even know what to miss, since she had visited the capital only twice in her life.

And now she was in London with Merlin. She was looking out the window as the carriage rolled the length of Piccadilly. The cacophony of sounds fascinated her as a tide of humanity converged on the streets. Hawkers offered their wares with high-pitched voices, the flower sellers shouting louder than anyone. Drays and wagons lumbered over the cobblestones, and a pack of dogs was chasing pigeons.

Merlin had been quiet most of the day, speaking with her only when he had some comment about the journey. They were going to stay at the town house that had belonged to Ross Seymour and now belonged to Merlin.

It was a tall, narrow building on Albemarle Street in fashionable Mayfair. The façade was simple and elegant, the front door flanked by two pillars, the tall windows adorned by a frieze of leafy plaster garlands. As the carriage stopped, a plump woman with gray hair and a pale complexion opened the door. A large mobcap covered most of her head, shading tiny, squirrellike eyes. There was a defensive air about her.

She made a curtsy, staring curiously at Cynara.

"This is Ethel Swan," Merlin explained, "Father's old housekeeper. She now lives permanently in London and takes care of the town house."

"I've made sandwiches, Master Merlin, and I'll put the kettle on," Mrs. Swan said.

Cynara smiled at the woman and stretched her stiff legs. It had been a long four-day journey, but it was over. She wished Tildy had accompanied her, but the maid had been left behind to watch over Estelle. Gideon Swift, who had traveled with them, sitting on the box with the driver, carried in their luggage. A light drizzle had begun, and London smelled of wet soot and other malodorous things that Cynara could not name. The sky was a sullen gray, and twilight was falling rapidly.

"Come in, get away from the rain," Mrs. Swan said kindly. When she took Cynara's cloak in the hallway, Cynara thanked her with a smile.

"Isn't there someone here to perform the duties of butler?" she asked, looking around the dimly lit hallway. The floor was checkered white and black Carrara marble. An oak banister curved gracefully upward, leading to the corridor above. The walls were paneled, and portraits of Seymour forefathers hung in a dignified row. By the front door was an ornate girandole mirror and a Chippendale chair.

"Since we're not entertaining, that is—not officially in residence—there is no staff besides Mrs. Swan, a cleaning girl, and a deaf footman," Merlin explained. "As we're in mourning, I saw no reason to open up the house."

He entered a salon through the double doors on the left, and Cynara noticed that all the furniture was shrouded in Holland covers. She followed him, admiring the graceful walls of panels painted cream, divided by ornate plaster swags. The marble mantelpiece held porcelain figurines and an ormolu clock.

"Your father was a successful man. If it had been his responsibility, he would have found a way to restore Black Raven," Cynara said to Merlin. "How come the other Seymour brothers had no such talents?"

Her husband glanced at her, and she felt that curious attraction flaring hot between them. Her breath caught in her throat. Every day seemed to heighten her awareness of him, and his appeal as well. Merlin was a patient man, she thought. He had not pressured her to resume their intimacy since that night in the great hall at Black Raven when she'd refused his gift of diamonds.

"Father took what little he inherited from his father and invested it in land around London. As you must know, the city has grown rapidly, spreading out east and west. The property rapidly increased in value and Father could buy more. That's how he made his fortune." Merlin paused. "I don't think the other Seymour brothers had a head for business. They didn't see the opportunities like Father did." He paused again, pushing aside the golden drapes in front of the windows. "I think Sydney—Max's father—made his best efforts to keep Black Raven from ruin, but it was a constant struggle."

"Perhaps we'll succeed where he failed," Cynara said more to herself than to Merlin.

An intent expression on his face, Merlin said, *"We? I thought you wanted nothing more to do with me, Cynara."*

She blushed, and averted her face. He saw too much, read too much. "We're married whether we like it or not, and we'll probably spend the rest of our days at Black Raven."

His face lightened in a smile. "Perhaps, but I had hoped to show you London someday. When our mourning period is over, I shall give you a belated Season. You deserve that after what you went through with Felix and at our forced wedding ceremony."

He was so thoughtful of her comfort, taking her by surprise every time he showed that tender side that seemed to be boundlessly generous. "I would like that."

"We won't be meeting many acquaintances here, since the Season is over. Most of the gentry has moved to the country by now."

"Anyway, I'm not sure that anyone would acknowledge us as things stand. Perhaps when you've cleared your name . . ." She noticed his face tensing, and she was relieved when the housekeeper returned.

Mrs. Swan showed her the bedrooms on the next floor, and Cynara was grateful that two beds had been made up. Evidently Merlin had informed the housekeeper of their separate sleeping arrangement—which was the common habit of married couples of their class. The two chambers did not have a connecting door, and Cynara drew a sigh of relief. At least here she wouldn't have worry about locking her door. At Black Raven it actually made her feel increasingly guilty as she turned the key in the lock every night—as if she owed Merlin something. But she had paid in full for his help with Brandon. . . .

"What are you brooding about?" Merlin asked, leaning against the doorframe of her room.

She blushed guiltily. "This is a lovely room." The chamber was elegant, graceful, like the rest of the house. High ceilings with plaster moldings, delicate flower-sprigged wallpaper in blue and gold, and a French door that led to a tiny balcony with a wrought iron railing. The balcony looked down on the backyard, where borders of flowers were bursting into bloom. The yard was surrounded by a tall brick wall.

"I'm glad you approve." He went to the French door and opened it to the London evening. Sounds and scents that were unfamiliar to her assaulted her senses, the clatter of iron-shod wheels, shouts, and laughter. Over the entire city hovered a hum of humanity, of movement.

"When shall we visit my brother?" she asked, worried now that something would occur to stop them when they were so close to Brandon.

"Tomorrow. I must find out what day they expect to bring him in front of the magistrates in Kingston."

Cynara stroked the soft velvet of the curtain. "Even if we manage to rescue him, he will always remain a wanted man."

"Not if he can prove that he was innocent of the theft. Like me, he'll have to discover who wanted him blamed for a crime he didn't commit."

Cynara stared at Merlin, listening to his words thoughtfully. "You believe that someone prearranged to have you found guilty of murder? Well, perhaps, but who? There are similarities between your case and Brandon's. If both of you are innocent, why would anyone have gone to such trouble to set you up?"

He pushed his hand through his hair. "I don't know! If I did, I wouldn't be in this predicament now. But the crimes Brandon and I stand accused of are different." His face lit up with a sudden grin. "So you believe I'm innocent, then?"

She gave him a searching glance. "I would like to believe it."

His eyes softened as he said, "You don't know how happy that makes me. I would be in Newgate if the detectives had found some evidence that I murdered my father. Rumors will not make a case against me."

"You must work at clearing your name."

He laughed mirthlessly. "As if I am not! This minute I have my own people working to discover every detail of what went on the evening of my father's death. And I'm trying to locate a certain man who might help me, but so far the clues have led nowhere."

His face slowly darkened with worry, and Cynara had an urge to caress away his distress, but she held her emotions tightly in check. He paced for a while, then stopped before her.

"Now that I have you, I have everything to live for," he said quietly.

Cynara thought he would pull her into his arms, but

he only brushed by her and left the room. "If you need anything, knock on my door."

Early the following morning they entered the square, ugly building that was Newgate Prison on Newgate Street. The stench of this poorer area of London made Cynara reel. She clamped a handkerchief against her nose, but it gave little protection. The doors clanged behind them as the guards let them in, and Merlin spoke with the turnkeys in the guardhouse of the prison. One of them stepped out, a man who was unusually well dressed for his occupation. Perhaps he was the governor of the prison. Cynara noticed that Merlin handed him a purse of coins. That would explain the prosperity of the man—if all the visitors were as generous as Merlin. Evidently, they'd better be if they wanted to see the prisoners. The guard inspected the basket of food that they had brought for Brandon, took a plate of cold meats and a bottle of ale from it, then made a gesture that Merlin could bring the rest. He handed the ale and the plate to another guard.

A rough-looking fellow with keys jangling from his belt led them down a dark, evil-smelling corridor. A babbling voice came from somewhere behind the thick walls, and someone emitted a muted scream. Cynara shuddered, her hands suddenly clammy with fear. The very air in the prison was filled with agony. It had a hushed, waiting quality.

" 'Ere we are, then," the guard said, halting before a door that was fortified with iron bars. "Yer brother 'as better quarters than most since th' guv 'ere"—he pointed at Merlin—" 'as been so kind as to pay for th' young thief's occupancy."

"My brother is no thief," Cynara said coldly, and stepped into the cell.

A faint light came from a tiny barred window high in the stone wall. Gloomy twilight reigned in the cell, and Cynara could barely make out the male form stretched out on the cot. "Brand?"

He moved as she said his name, sitting up hesitantly. By now Merlin had entered, and the door was locked behind them. Merlin brought forth a bundle of candles from his coat pocket and managed to strike a light with the tinderbox.

"Cynara? Am I dreaming?" said Brandon Hawthorne as the cell lit up with mellow candlelight. He rose uncertainly and took two steps toward her, chains jangling. Her heart ached as she viewed his gaunt, dirty face, but there was no mistaking the jaunty grin that he gave her.

They embraced, and hope flared in Cynara's chest. At least her brother was alive, and obviously well enough to walk.

Brandon rubbed his stubbled chin, and viewed his stained clothes. "I'm not exactly dressed for the company of a lady," he said ruefully. His blond hair—so like her own—hung in matted tangles, a trim long overdue. The blue eyes looked tired and tinged with despair.

Sister and brother stared at each other for a long time. Brandon kissed her cheek. "I didn't do it, you know," he said at last. "Someone placed the jewelry among my things. That someone wanted me to take the blame."

She patted his shoulder, only then noticing how truly soiled his clothes were. His former elegance was now nothing but a memory. "I know. You would never stoop to stealing."

Brandon offered Cynara the only chair in the cell, but she declined. She didn't want to touch anything if she could help it. The straw on the pallet looked unappetizing, and the walls were positively slimy.

Merlin glanced from one to the other. "How about some decent food, old fellow?" Without waiting for an answer, he pulled out fresh fruit, cheese, newly baked bread, two bottles of ale, and a cake from the basket they had brought with them.

Brandon looked at the delicacies with longing in his eyes and sat down. "Never really appreciated food before like I do now. Weeks in prison do wonders for a fellow's character," he said with a flippancy that wasn't totally heartfelt.

Cynara could not hold back her tears, but she averted her face so that her brother wouldn't notice. Merlin did. He placed his arm around her shoulders.

Brandon ate with gusto. "It must have cost to grease the turnkeys' palms," he said between bites.

"Don't mention it," Merlin said. "When you get away from here, I will put you to back-breaking work at Black Raven." His eyes twinkled in challenge.

"That old stone heap! Better tear it down and start over," Brandon said carelessly, and finished off a bottle of ale.

Merlin turned to Cynara. "Didn't I tell you? Your brother is a scrapegrace—no sense of heritage at all." He said to Brandon, "Black Raven's roots are so deep in history that you couldn't even imagine it if you tried."

"Imagine all those centuries of accumulated dust," Brandon said with a chuckle. "All the more reason to tear it down."

Merlin scowled and Brandon laughed. He had eaten almost all the food they had brought.

"You'd better be careful what you say, brother, or Merlin might change his mind about helping you escape."

Brandon grew serious, staring intently at Merlin. "You would really do that for me?"

Merlin's dark eyes were inscrutable as he glanced at Cynara. "Actually, I'm doing it for your sister. It's a way to get myself into her good graces."

Brandon smiled wickedly. "You devil!"

Cynara blushed and wished her brother wouldn't give her such a teasing glance.

"I thought it was a marriage of convenience, not one of love," her cruel brother continued. He bit into the seedcake, unperturbed.

Merlin cleared his throat, and Cynara could not believe it when she noticed a faint blush staining his cheeks. She was just as embarrassed at Brandon's careless remark. "It's none of your business, Brand."

"I wish I could have been at the wedding." He brushed off his fingers. "The cake was excellent. Must be Moira Black's specialty, if I'm not mistaken."

Merlin leaned on the wobbly table where Brandon was sitting. "I have a plan, and I want you to listen carefully. I've found out from reliable sources that you will be brought before the magistrates in Kingston, Surrey, on Tuesday next."

"I wonder why they delayed my trial for so long."

"Some . . . er, bribes in the right pockets," Merlin murmured.

Cynara gaped. "You had already started working on Brandon's release before—before the wedding?" Fuming, she gave him an outraged stare. "Oh, you— you tricked me!"

Merlin's lips curved into a smile. "The wheels of the law move tediously slow, especially when the crime involves a gentleman."

Cynara glared. "Of all the treacherous—*you tricked me*—" she repeated.

"Don't fly into a pelter, sis. Merlin visited me the second day I was here." Brandon glanced speculatively from one to the other. "Not that I understand what you're talking about, but whatever it is, it must be something explosive."

Merlin pulled his hands through his hair in distraction. "A private matter, Brand," he said. "Now, to get back to the issue at hand. The coach that will take you down to Surrey will be going this route." He pulled out a piece of paper from his pocket, and Cynara noticed that he'd drawn a map.

"When the wagon they'll use to transfer you arrives at Black Friar's Bridge, I will overtake the guards and swing you up on my horse." He stabbed the exact spot. "I'm hoping that the bridge will be too crowded to make pursuit possible. At the other end, at Albion Place, Gideon Swift will be awaiting our arrival with a horse for you."

Brandon held up his shackled hands and jangled the chains around his ankles. "I'll be in irons."

"Hopefully your legs will be unshackled. If not,

we'll have to deal with that problem later. If worse comes to worst, you can always lie across the horse like a sack of hay." Merlin chuckled. "Ah! That might be the best way to remain unnoticed—we'll cover you up with some old sacks. They will quite fit your new style of dress."

As Brandon groaned in despair, Merlin flicked the soiled cravat around the younger man's neck. "We can't let your mother see you like this. Once we clear London, we'll stop at an inn for a bath and a change of clothes. I will provide everything you need."

"Why the kindness?" Brandon asked suspiciously. "I will forever be in your debt."

"Suits me fine," said Merlin.

"Wouldn't it be easier to bribe the judge to acquit me?" Brandon said after thinking about Merlin's proposition.

"The judge that will hear your case is the only honest judge on the bench. A bribe offer to him would put *me* in a cell as well." Merlin put the empty ale bottles in the basket and folded the napkin over the top. "Do you agree to the plan?"

"Agree?" Brandon slapped Merlin's back with renewed vigor. "Not only do I agree, I approve heartily. Thank you."

Merlin shot Cynara an unreadable glance. "Don't thank me, thank your sister. She made me do this."

Cynara gasped with outrage. "I did not! You had already started. Of all the unfair—"

Brandon hugged his sister, muffling her angry words with his shoulder. "All will be well, sis, you just wait and see."

"Once you're free, Brand, you must think of

Mother. She's worried about you. No more wild scrapes and adventures," Cynara admonished him. "It's about time you settled down and took over the management of Bluewater."

Brandon made a mock salute. "Yes, general. I will be a pattern of propriety."

She punched him lightly. "Always the jester, aren't you?"

Chains clanging against the stone floor, he followed them to the door. "Till the day after tomorrow, then," he said as Merlin pounded on the stout door. The panel across the grille flew aside, and the turnkey glared at them with a bleary eye, pinning Brandon last.

"Are ye ready t' leave, mate?" The warder chuckled at his own joke as he let Merlin and Cynara out. Brandon snorted in disgust, but blew a kiss at Cynara as she turned to wave.

The air outside the steel-studded prison door with its spiked gate seemed like ambrosia after the foul-smelling dungeons. The smells improved as their carriage neared the cleaner neighborhood of Mayfair and Albemarle Street. Cynara would have liked to visit some London shops, but since she was in mourning, there was nothing she needed to buy. Due to Felix's death, and the fact that he was Merlin's cousin, charcoal and light gray would be her colors for the next six months. Besides, she was too wound up to truly enjoy the London visit. What if the effort to bolt Brandon from prison failed? What would happen then? The thought hadn't occurred to her before. All she had wanted was to help Brandon somehow. If the plan collapsed and Merlin was captured, it would be her fault. . . .

She stared in horror at Merlin as the thought took root. How would she be able to live with herself if things went awry? Impulsively she placed a hand on Merlin's arm. "Are you sure the plan is safe?"

Tenderness flickered momentarily in his eyes, and she felt curiously weak. "I have no fears of failure. Bribes in the right pockets work wonders, and the turnkeys who will be escorting Brandon are willing to close their eyes momentarily. That's all we need."

"Did you have to use a lot of your money?"

He shrugged. "What does it matter?"

"It matters to me. I cannot really repay you." Tension mounted between them, and she wondered what was going through his mind. "Besides, I resent that you lured me into your bed on the pretext of saving Brandon. I don't know if I'll ever forgive you for that."

He sighed in exasperation. "It was the only way I could think of that would bring you to me. I had to break your resistance to show you that making love could be a beautiful experience."

She fumed. "Nevertheless, it was underhanded."

"I'm sorry."

She glared at him in silence.

He lowered his gaze and placed his gloved hand over hers on the bench beside him. "You are my wife. I'd do anything for you. Everything I have is yours, including myself. All I want from you is your heart."

Tears burned suddenly in her throat. If only he hadn't asked for that! It was the only thing she couldn't give, not now, not when he had connived her into his bed. "You cannot buy my love," she said, pulling away her hand. "No matter how much money you lavish on me and my family, you cannot make me love you."

He sounded tense. "I've always known there was an attraction between us. You can't deny that."

"There is something, I agree to that. But I don't call it love." She could barely find her breath because the air was filled with tension and unspoken questions. She started, and moved aside as he dragged his hand the length of her thigh.

"What do you call it, Cynara?"

She knew it was pure physical attraction, but she couldn't, she *wouldn't* let him hear her utter those words. She shook her head.

"Let me tell you." His hand found a place on her thigh again. "There's a part of you that responds readily to me, but you fight to suppress it." He paused. "There's no need. Let yourself enjoy life. I'm not here to make you miserable; I plan to give you a happy life—as far as it is in my power to do so."

He sounded sincere, and tears clutched at her throat once more. "That is, if you have a life to share. If you cannot clear your name of suspicion, we will forever be barred from our peers. Or do you want us to forever live like recluses?" She glanced at him, noticing his face twisting as if in pain. The expression gave way to the usual implacable mask, and he smiled. There was no happiness in his smile.

"We shall see. I cannot promise you anything—least of all our peers' approval."

"You will have to prove your innocence."

He sighed. "When the real murderer reveals himself, I shall be free."

"You'll wait until someone reveals himself?" she

asked in disbelief. "Then we'll have to wait forever."

"When I discover the reason behind my father's death, I will certainly learn who murdered him." Merlin's voice had grown cold and distant. The intimacy that had sprung up between them earlier was gone.

He continued. "The more time that passes since Father's death, the more difficult it'll be to discover the identity of the murderer. For all I know, he might be crossing the ocean right now. I'm afraid it might be too late to catch him."

Cynara gasped. "Which will mean you'll never be free?"

Merlin looked pale and tired all of a sudden. He shook his head. "You might never dance in a ballroom among your peers."

"No wonder you were so eager to wed me," she said in disgust. "No one else would have had you."

Chapter 11

They shared a strained dinner at the formal table in the dining room of the Albemarle house. The summer twilight was full of blue lights, illuminated by stars that appeared one after the other on the sky's deep blue cloth. Golden halos encircled the candle flames, softening Merlin's hard features. He ate in silence, and Cynara could barely taste the delicacies that Mrs. Swan and the maid, Alice, had served. The housekeeper had ordered the food, cold meats, jellied tongue, cured ham, and peas from a hotel that catered to the aristocracy in the Mayfair area. She had baked the fragrant rolls and iced cakes herself.

Cynara sensed the mounting tension, wondering if Merlin was as worried as she was about the rescue effort about to unfold in two days. Had he thought of everything? How would they get through tomorrow?

But most of all was she aware of Merlin, his long fingers holding the wineglass, his dark eyes that never left her for long, the width of his strong shoulders. If only he weren't so very attractive . . . It would be easier to withstand his amorous overtures if she weren't so drawn to him.

If only he had rotten teeth, elephantsize ears, hands as large as hams, bowed legs, and a twisted back. Then it would have been easier to ignore him. Instead, he had perfectly formed hands and teeth, neat ears, and a physique that would elicit an admiring glance from the most critical viewer.

"What are you thinking about, dearest?" he said, his gentle tones mocking her.

She glanced at her plate to conceal her guilty look. "Nothing of importance," she said, and pretended to find the slice of ham on her plate interesting.

"You are very restive this evening," he added after an uncomfortable silence.

Cynara wished the housekeeper would return with the syllabub so that he would have to change the subject, but Mrs. Swan remained absent.

"I was thinking that Max and Brandon were cut of the same cloth. Brandon is wild and pleasure-loving, yet honest to a fault, and loyal. Max was the same way." He paused, drinking some more wine. "I would have died for Max if necessary. He would have done the same for me. Do you feel that way about your brother?"

Cynara stared at him in surprise. Merlin spoke so earnestly, as if he were genuinely interested in knowing the depths of her soul. "The thought never occurred to me, but yes, I believe I would go to extremes to help my brother. Brand would do the same for me."

Merlin nodded. "I know. You're loyal to a fault." He pushed aside his plate. "When we were children,

Max would sometimes take the blame for some 'crime' that I perpetrated, and vice versa."

Cynara smiled in recognition. "Brandon sometimes protected me likewise. Only two years separate us in age—Brandon the elder—and we've always been close."

Mrs. Swan entered, carrying the sullabub. Nimbly, she cut two slices and served them with a curtsy. She poured more wine in Cynara's glass. She eyed Merlin uneasily. "Will there be anything else, milord?"

"That'll be all, Mrs. Swan. Thank you."

The housekeeper left. Cynara's head began to reel from all the wine she had drunk during dinner. She had forgotten to count the glasses, knowing she shouldn't drink more than two. The world had taken on a fuzzy, rosy glow. She relaxed, apprehension less pronounced now that they were talking about Brandon and not themselves.

"Brand has never been in such a dire scrape before," she said. "But I could tell he was in good spirits when we visited him."

"Brand *thrives* on adventure. He probably looks forward to the escape." Merlin smiled ruefully. "I can't say I do, but it has to be done."

"You had already planned on helping Brand before—" she began accusingly.

Merlin pushed away from the table and stood, holding out his hand toward her. "Please don't dwell on that any longer. A desperate situation takes desperate measures to solve. You would never have come to me willingly, would you?"

She didn't take his hand. "You know very well that I wouldn't. You have a lot of gall, Merlin."

He only laughed, and gripped her reluctant hand. "Come, let's see if the tea tray is in the drawing room. I asked Mrs. Swan to place it there and leave us alone."

Cynara followed him reluctantly. The wine had made her legs wobbly. It was as if she were walking on cotton, with her head in the clouds, supported only by the teetering stem of her throat.

"Come here," he said, placing his arm around her shoulders. "You seem a bit unsteady."

Just as soon as he supported her, she relaxed, the wavering sensation gone.

The double doors of the drawing room were open, letting in a light breeze. Only candlelight illuminated the room, making it more intimate as the shadows shortened the high ceiling and the soaring walls. The evening was balmy, clean-smelling for London. The night had that quality of spring when the very air seemed exuberant with life. Strains of music wafted in through the doors, the lilting cadence of a waltz.

"Would you care to dance?" Merlin asked. "Even though we cannot go to the ball next door, at least we can join in the festivities."

He placed his arm around her back and gripped the other. She could not resist him as he swung her around and around in time to the music. She discovered that he—despite his limp—was an excellent dancer. His forceful movements literally swept her off her feet, and she felt light as goosedown in his arms. His eyes glittered warmly in the candlelight, and she could not look away. He swept her around the room, never knocking against any of the furniture.

When the music ended, Merlin laughed. "I don't

think I've ever enjoyed a dance more! I didn't have to make polite conversation to a pimply debutante, and the dowagers with their hawk eyes weren't here to stare at me and calculate how good a catch I would be—or not be—for their daughters and granddaughters."

"How unfair," Cynara chided him, "when the only purpose of the balls is for the young ladies to find suitable husbands."

"You don't have that problem, do you, my dear?" Still holding her hand, he slowly pulled her into his arms and looked down on her face. His tender expression made her tremble with longing. She wished she could return that look in his eyes, but she was more aware of the proximity of his body. He emanated heat and strength, and her hands went involuntarily to his shoulders. It would be so easy to cling, to let him sweep her off her feet. . . .

His face came closer, his lips so very near to her own. When the music started again, he took her waist with both hands and whirled her around. She was floating on clouds as delicious and light as whipped cream. When the waltz ended, she was disappointed.

"A true lady should accept only two dances with any partner," she said dreamily, seeing only his sensual lips.

"An *unmarried* lady, that is," he corrected her. "I for one wouldn't mind dancing with my wife all night if she allows me that privilege."

"Most gentlemen have no desire to dance with their boring old wives."

"You're not boring, and will never be, not as long as that bewitching curve remains on your lips." He lowered his head and traced the outline of her mouth with his tongue.

Excitement skittered through her, and the urge to reject him melted away. His mouth was warm and sweet-tasting, his tongue a skillful seducer that easily ignited her desire. She admitted now her desire hadn't been far away from the surface all evening. An exquisite torment flared through her, a yearning to tear away everything that separated them, and give herself freely. She wanted the intimacy; she *needed* it, as if it could fill a void that had plagued her since that first time when he'd made her his.

She sighed, leaning into him. His kiss was more intoxicating than the wine had been. She could not get enough of his probing tongue teasing her into a vortex of luscious pleasure.

He slowly lifted his head and gazed at her in wonder. His hand was infinitely tender as he released the chignon at the nape of her neck and caressed her hair.

"We shouldn't—" she began.

"We should," he insisted. "It's the only thing we should do right now."

As the music started again, he swept her up in his arms, carried her up the stairs to her bedchamber, and deposited her on the bed. She protested feebly, but the longing inside would not be quenched unless— She didn't even want to continue with that train of thought. She wondered what went through his head at that moment.

After divesting his coat and lighting the candles by the bed, Merlin stretched out beside her, holding her around the waist with one arm and propping his head with the other. He looked down at her face, her blond

curls spread like a halo around her on the pillow. She
looked pale and frightened, yet he could sense the
awakening of her sensuality. It stood like an alluring
"come-hither" scent around her, a sign of which he
was sure she was unaware.

"My frightened fawn of a wife," he whispered, and
stroked the long, slender column of her throat. Her
lips quivered endearingly, and he had to bend down
and kiss her yet again. She opened exquisitely at his
touch, and he felt himself drowning in his own desire.
If only he could make her *truly* his. What he wanted
was not just a night of pleasure that would be clouded
by the knowledge that he didn't possess her love. Yet
if her body responded so readily, wouldn't her heart
soon follow suit?

He held on to that thought as he tasted the sweetness of her mouth. He wasn't sure she knew how pleasurable her touch was when she dragged her hand up
and down his spine. Did she know she was doing it?

He lifted his head and gazed at her face. She seemed
lost in a daze of enchantment. Her breasts looked full
and inviting under the tight gray bodice of her gown.
He sneaked his hand under her back and unfastened
the row of tiny buttons that held the dress together.
When she didn't resist, his blood started pounding
hard in anticipation. He gently eased the bodice down
over her shoulders, then the lace-trimmed straps of her
shift. The creamy skin was as shimmering as mother-
of-pearl, and he traced it with his tongue, eager to
touch every part of her. She responded by moving
restlessly under him. He reached the shadowed valley
between her breasts, and it was his undoing. There was
no going back now, he thought hazily as he kneaded

one full breast, taking the swollen rosy nipple into his mouth. Oh, my God . . . was she in the clutches of equal torment?

Cynara could not bear the sweet agony as he sucked on her breast. Such delicious waves radiated to every part of her body that she wanted to moan out loud. He knew exactly what to do to give her maximum sweet torture, she thought during one of the few moments she listened to her mind. How could she maintain her dignity . . . ?

"Just let it happen to you, relax," he murmured in her ear. His breath tickled her, and she wanted to giggle, but what came out was a moan of pleasure as he pulled his hand along her body and came to rest on the mound between her legs. Her caressed her through all the layers of her clothes, and the sensation was more arousing than if he'd touched her bare skin—the mere *suggestion* of what pleasure was to come.

She squirmed with urgency. He couldn't get her clothes off fast enough, and she helped him drag off the gown, petticoats, stays, and shift. All she was wearing now were her stockings, held up only by lacy garters. Oh, such burning in her skin, such longing that had spread like wildfire through every part of her.

She watched him take off his clothes, admiring every part as it was revealed, the broad, tanned shoulders, the muscular arms with such smooth skin, the whorls of black hair on his chest, and then—then he took off the rest. His hips were taut and narrow, flanks long and molded with fine muscular symmetry. He was beautiful, she thought, a man the famed painter Michelangelo could have used as a model.

With a little movement he lay down. She noticed the

white, crescent-shaped scar on his thigh, and touched it gingerly.

"That's the gift some French soldier gave me at Waterloo," he said wryly.

"Does it hurt?"

He shook his head. "No, only sometimes when it's wet and cold outside. It did give me a slight limp—I hope it doesn't put you off."

"No . . ." she said, not quite daring to tell him how attractive she found him.

He sighed and pulled her close. His skin was smooth and hot, his heart pounding against hers, matching the pounding that had started between her legs as his skin brushed against hers. He held her breasts, first one, then the other reverently, making the peaks tighten unbearably. Could he sense how much she yearned for his touch? She was utterly shameless, she thought as she flung one of her legs over his thigh, rubbing herself against that jutting proof of his desire. It felt like the most natural thing to do, even if it didn't assuage her need, only acerbated it. She slid wetly against him, over and over, drowning in sensations, knowing that he could easily take her. That's what she needed now.

"Ahh . . ." he moaned against her, trembling momentarily.

His hands were all over her, ending on her breasts. As she pressed closer to him, he seemed ready to explode, and he roughly held her away from himself, taking some deep breaths. "What are you doing?" he demanded wryly. "Do you want to push me over the brink of madness?"

She shied away, embarrassed now at her wanton behavior.

"Sorry . . . I didn't mean to insult you," he whispered, pulling her close once more. "I loved every moment of it, but I can barely hold back." He wound his arms around her and cradled her against him. Groaning softly, he spread her legs wide with one heel, slid between her thighs, and penetrated her deeply.

She cried out at the sheer beauty of the full sensation of him inside her. When he began moving against her, she thought she would dissolve with the pleasure. All her concentration went to that exquisite union, and before she knew what was happening, she was climbing, climbing, ever higher to a point where all was suspended in a breathless, infinitely sweet moment of bliss. Then she plunged—with him—into the sea, rolling among crashing waves of ecstasy. He cried out her name, and to Cynara that was the most intimate moment of all.

Their breathing ragged, they slowly returned to the awareness of their surroundings. The balmy wind from the open windows caressed them as they lay tired but content among the rumpled sheets.

A warm glow filled Cynara, and she had never felt like this before, replete and beautiful, ripe and full. At last she had discovered the secret that lay beyond intense desire, and it had surprised her, yet, instinctively she had known how it would be, as if she'd always known it. Wonderful.

Merlin gently stroked her hair. "This time you weren't disappointed, were you?" he whispered. "This time you weren't afraid."

She shook her head but dared not look at him. His words brought a blush to her cheeks, and she turned her head on the pillow so that he couldn't see her.

She heard him sigh, wondering what was going through his mind. His fingers closed around her chin, and he brought her head back around so that she had to look into his eyes. Then he kissed her deeply, passionately. Her resistance melted all over again.

The following day Merlin was gone from the town house on Albemarle Street. Elusive as always when Cynara wanted to talk about what had happened to her on the previous night, he'd left nothing but remembered pleasure behind. Just as his hands had touched every part of her body, he had somehow massaged her heart, making it more pliable. And he'd left an indentation on the pillow beside her. The glow was still alive within her, but in the sharp morning light, doubts gnawed on her mind. His skilled lovemaking had been undermining her resistance, and she found herself more attracted to him with every day that passed. Yet he seemed to always slip through her fingers when she wanted to understand him, search his soul.

With a sigh she slid out of bed. There was no way to wholly understand the dark man who was her husband. It would take her a lifetime to comprehend him.

She rang for Alice and ordered a bath. As she was wallowing in the sudsy water of the hip bath, she wondered where Merlin had gone—leaving her to her tormented thoughts without as much as a reassurance that he had adored their night together. *Adored.* What was wrong with her? She ought not think about Merlin in those terms. She would never fall in love with him . . . or would she?

Those disturbing thoughts were interrupted as Alice

entered with freshly ironed petticoats over her arm. Cynara dressed and Alice arranged her hair clumsily into a chignon. Feeling refreshed, Cynara went downstairs to face the world. She met Mrs. Swan in the hallway. The housekeeper was carrying a tray of polished silver, and Cynara held the door to the dining room. The older woman smiled gratefully. "You look lovely this morning, Lady Raven."

"Thank you. Do you know where my husband went?"

Something cold came into the housekeeper's eyes. "I don't know, milady, but he spoke briefly with Mr. Brown, my brother, before leaving." She placed the tray on the gleaming mahogany table and began arranging the silver tureens and plates on the sideboard.

"Oh, I didn't know your brother was here."

Mrs. Swan threw her an assessing glance, as if wondering how much she could divulge without offending the wife of her employer. "Mr. Brown used to be the butler here, but after the . . . er, accident—"

"Accident?" Cynara's curiosity sprang to life.

"Well . . . the accident with Master Merlin's—Lord Raven's—father." The housekeeper heaved a deep sigh. "You see, my brother believes that the rumors are true, that Lord Raven was in fact involved in his father's death. My brother could not go on working here, so he left."

Cynara gasped in distress. "What made Mr. Brown believe—" She couldn't finish the sentence.

Mrs. Swan paled, showing reluctance to speak about it. But on Cynara's insistence, she said, "I don't know what to think about that night of the . . . er, accident. But my brother insists he saw Lord Raven

crawling under Mr. Ross's carriage in the mews and
working on something with tools. When the carriage
went over the side of the ravine, they suspected that
someone had tampered with the coupling where the
shafts attach to the coach. The bolts had broken clean
off, as if sawed through. The horses must have panicked and hurled straight into the gully."

"Why would anyone want to hurt Ross Seymour?"

The housekeeper wrinkled her brow. "That's a
question I've asked myself many times. If you don't
mind me saying so, Mr. Ross was the finest man alive.
Master Merlin takes after him, and I have difficulty
believing he would hurt anyone, but what was he
doing under his father's carriage the same day Mr.
Ross died in that accident? My brother swears it was
Merlin. He moved furtive like, as if worrying that
someone would see him."

Cynara's spirits plummeted. What had Merlin been
doing? Would she ever be able to trust him? "It happened in the middle of the day?"

"No, it was dusk outside."

"It could have been anyone." Somehow Cynara
wanted desperately to push the blame away from Merlin.

"Aye, it could have been, but my brother recognized
the special gray velvet cloak that Master Merlin—
Lord Raven—always used to wear. And then there
was that limp . . ." Her voiced trailed off, and Cynara
experienced a sinking feeling of dread in her stomach.
Had she made love to a murderer last night? The
thought made her clammy with apprehension. She had
been so eager to believe his innocence.

"Are you not afraid to work here, like your

brother?" She stared at the housekeeper as if trying to see the truth about Merlin in those squirrellike eyes, but Mrs. Swan gave nothing away.

"I told my brother I won't judge Master Merlin until the authorities discover what really happened. Innocent until proven guilty."

Cynara noticed the blush rising on the older woman's face. "That is generous of you. But you suspect he's guilty."

Steps echoed across the floor. Cynara had been so intent on the conversation that she hadn't heard the front door close. "Guilty of what?" came Merlin's calm voice behind her.

She whirled around, a tremor of trepidation going through her. He had that cool, distant look about him, and it was easy to believe that this dark, reserved man was hiding something. It certainly was impossible to penetrate his mind.

"Well?" He quirked an eyebrow, and when no one replied, he added, "Guilty of murder?" When Cynara wouldn't meet his glance, he chuckled mirthlessly.

"I see that you're ready to believe the worst of me, wife."

Desperation clawed at her. She stared at him with an acute longing that he would profess his innocence. "Well, are you guilty?"

He said nothing, only turned on his heel and left the room. She knew what Ross Seymour must have felt as he was teetering on the edge of the abyss. Terror and helplessness.

Chapter 12

Cynara spent the rest of the day in tension-filled silence. She went from one room to the next in the town house, too restless to visit the stores in Bond Street even if Alice might have accompanied her there. It felt too frivolous an occupation while her brother's fate was undecided. What if the escape failed? If Merlin were caught . . . Cynara wrung her hands, wondering how to bridge the gap that had opened between her and her husband that morning. If he believed she had no faith in him— The thought was oddly disturbing. She did have faith in him, but how could she trust him wholeheartedly when she didn't know the whole truth about him?

She looked out the window in the salon by the front entrance. A carriage had stopped across the street, and she viewed a young couple coming out of the house, laughing and holding hands. There was no mistaking the love that glowed on their faces. Disconcerted, Cynara turned her gaze to two chimney sweeps with sooty faces and bristly brushes on their shoulders. Even they were laughing.

She moved away abruptly, feeling just as worried and caged in as Brandon at Newgate.

That night she shared a strained dinner with Merlin in the formal dining room. The expanse of the long table made conversation almost impossible, and Merlin seemed closed into himself. He paid scant attention to her, and it hurt more than if he'd ranted and raved. He must be angry with her for listening to Mrs. Swan's suspicions. In truth, she didn't know what to believe. She had discovered that Merlin could be infinitely tender when he chose to be, just as he could fight when provoked. The duel with Felix had proved that.

She started as Merlin spoke. "Tomorrow I will endeavor to free Brandon, but I want you to be long gone from here. You must rise at dawn and take the carriage back to Black Raven. Gideon Swift and Alice will escort you, so you'll be perfectly safe."

"I'm not concerned about my own safety," she argued. "But why all the way to Black Raven? I would worry about what happens to the rescue mission. Perhaps I can be of help."

He pounded his fist into the table and she jumped with fear. "Under no circumstances are you going to accompany me to Black Friars Bridge! I have bribed the guards to leave Brand's footlinks off, and Swift will leave a fast horse for him in Albion Place. While you're traveling in the carriage, we must travel by horse. I want you safe and out of harm's way. If something goes wrong and you are present, you might end up in prison."

Cynara resented his outburst of temper. "But you alone . . . against the guards?" she asked doubtfully.

Even if she didn't want to admit it, she was afraid for him. What if he failed?

"Speed and surprise will be my strategy."

"I'm sure I could help. Take Gideon Swift with you at least."

His brow darkened. "There's nothing you can do except be in the way. You must do as I ask."

Cynara remained silent, knowing it was useless to argue.

"I know that stubborn thrust of your chin," he said menacingly. "You must obey, however much you resent it. I don't want your safety jeopardized. He finished his dinner of chicken pie, roast woodcock, stewed mushrooms, cauliflower, and roast potatoes, and pushed the plate away.

Cynara said nothing, only placed her fork on the plate. Mrs. Swan entered and served the pudding, then left the couple alone.

Tension was rising steadily, and Cynara could no longer stand Merlin's penetrating stares. She stood, glaring at him. "I'm plagued by a headache, and shall retire to my bedchamber—unless you have further orders to give me."

He laughed, but his eyes were as serious as ever. "I demand that you sleep well, especially since we had so little rest last night."

She blushed to the roots of her hair. "I slept just fine, but you must have had a sleepless night, since you left so early. I woke once at dawn, and you had departed."

His lips curved upward. "Did you miss me?"

"I did not!" She hurried out of the room, cursing

him under her breath. "And don't bother to try my door. It will be locked!"

The next morning Alice warned Cynara as they sat in the carriage that would bring them back to Black Raven. "Ye can't do it, Lady Raven. The master's gave us strict orders to travel straight to Devon."

"I promised nothing," Cynara said, fidgeting on her seat. "Besides, we're not going to Newgate Street—we're going to Black Friars Bridge." She glanced outside, wondering how much longer it would be before they arrived at the bridge. Fear crawled through her, but she set her jaw and straightened her back. Her eyes were gritty for the lack of sleep on the previous night. The tension had been building inside her to a point when she thought she would burst. If only this were over, and Brandon safe! "I will watch from a safe distance to make sure that Brandon gets away. Once he does, we shall make all haste to Devon."

"Wot if Lord Raven fails?" Alice asked gloomily.

Cynara gave the tall, gangly girl an quick glance. The maid's face was long, her expression lugubrious. "He must not fail!" Tight-lipped and pale, Cynara stared out the window, every minute more agitated, as it seemed to take forever for the carriage to reach their destination.

"Besides, Merlin is a former military man, Tildy. He will know how to free Brandon even if there are guards."

Alice muttered something that Cynara could not hear, and didn't want to hear if the words contained more doubts about Merlin's mission. The carriage—

driven by Gideon Swift, who had protested against her plans—came to a halt at last at Chatham Place at the north end of the bridge. When Cynara leaned out the window, she could see the glittering brown water of the Thames. People were milling in both directions on the bridge, horses pulling creaking wagons, mongrels zigzagging around legs, children crying. Cynara craned her neck to see if Merlin had arrived, but she couldn't find his tall form, nor were there any barred prison wagons on the street.

"Where is he? Is he late?" she said more to herself than to anyone else.

"Ye don't know th' master's plans? 'E might be dressed differently. I would be if I plotted t' abduct a Newgate prisoner in broad daylight."

Cynara agreed and stared at the men walking along the street. There were mostly laborers and artisans pushing carts and wheelbarrows. Unease traveled along Cynara's spine as she noticed that a rough-looking man was staring openly at her. She drew back, wondering if he had plans to rob her in the coach.

"This is no place t' stand idle," Alice said with a faint sniff. "Afore ye know it, ye might be molested, an' then wot would I tell Milord Raven. 'E would 'ave me drawn and quartered for that."

"Balderdash," Cynara scolded, though she knew that Alice was right about the possibility of strangers ill-treating them. "We won't remain long. My brother's wagon is bound to arrive soon. He has to be at the Kingston court on time."

Alice muttered and took off her heavy clog, clutching it in her hand to use as a weapon if necessary. "It can be none too soon for me," she said, keeping an eye on the ruffian who seemed to be moving stealthily closer every minute.

"There he is!" Cynara cried out as a stout wagon lumbered across Chatham Place. Two guards on foot flanked the wagon, but they, and the driver, were the only barrier between Brandon and freedom. "But where is Merlin?" she added, scanning the road worriedly. There was no commotion, no horses. She leaned out and ordered Gideon Swift to follow her brother's wagon.

Her heart pounded with fear as Swift finally obeyed, after arguing that they'd better stay out of it or face Merlin's wrath. But since Merlin wasn't there . . . What if they couldn't free Brand? What would she do then?

"Oh, milady, this is dangerous," Alice whispered, wringing her hands. "I niver expected that something like this would 'appen on the journey. No one told me about it."

"If you're frightened, you can get off right here and return to Albemarle Street. I won't force you into anything." Leaning out the window, Cynara peered ahead, wondering how they would get past the throng on the bridge once they had rescued Brandon.

"No . . . milady, Lord Raven's orders are law to me."

Cynara gave Alice a speculating glance. "I thought you shared Mrs. Swan's suspicions about the master. You don't believe he murdered his father?" Her abrupt voice made Alice flinch, but she needed to hear that someone was on Merlin's side.

"I don't know, milady. The master 'as always been kind t' me."

Cynara nodded. "He is kind to the servants, isn't he?" It wasn't really a question, only a confirmation of her own experience in the matter.

The sound of the coach wheels changed as they entered the wooden bridge, and Cynara leaned out the window once more. The prison wagon was now quite close. Gideon Swift didn't let any other vehicles in between the two coaches. At least this would enable him to act when the time was right, she thought. But where was Merlin? She glanced back toward Chatham Place, but there was no sign of him. Drumming her fingers nervously against the window frame, she wished she could have seen Brandon inside the wagon, but the windows were barred and dark. Besides the two guards flanking the wagon, there was the driver whose muscular arms and shoulders looked quite capable of curbing any attack. He would be a tireless fighter. She prayed fervently that it wouldn't come to fighting, since Merlin alone wouldn't have a chance.

Suddenly a shout rended the air, and the traffic on the bridge halted momentarily. Cynara craned her neck to see better, and drew in a sharp breath when she recognized Merlin on a big horse. Though he had his hat pulled low over his eyebrows and a black half-mask on his face, there was no mistaking his stubborn jaw. A gray cloak swirled around him.

Just as she was about to order Swift to stop, the old man reined in. Alice whimpered, and, transfixed, stared out the opposite window. She looked so pale that Cynara felt a stab of compassion.

"Oh," Alice wailed. "The master is aiming a pistol at the driver!"

Torn between a desire to get down and assist Merlin, and fear of his anger, Cynara watched in fascination. The guards dropped their muskets onto the bridge, and gaped as Merlin swung himself down and whipped another pistol from the waistband of his breeches.

A moan of surprise went through the crowd as the door to the wagon was kicked open from inside. Out jumped another guard, aiming a cudgel at Merlin's head. He ducked, but the other guards were instantly upon him. Brandon, whose legs were unshackled, got out, watching helplessly as Merlin struggled. His wrists were still manacled, making it impossible for him to fight. One of Merlin's pistols fell onto the wooden path.

A roar went up from the crowd, and a burly hawker pushed Brandon back toward the wagon. "An 'xcaped prisoner!" he shouted, and barred Brandon's way.

Cynara had to act. It was clear that the guard inside the wagon had taken Merlin by surprise, and he would be overpowered if she didn't go to his aid. She grabbed the stout walking stick that she had brought from Albemarle Street and stepped out of the coach. She heard Alice scream behind her in fear, but she never hesitated. In a blink she reached Brandon's side and started pummeling the hawker with the walking stick. As the guards momentarily backed off from the onslaught of Merlin's flying fist, he saw her. His eyes widened in surprise, then blazed with fury. Still, she didn't care, and she managed to hold the hawker at bay long enough for Brandon to reach Merlin's horse.

"No . . . not there!" she cried as he put his wrists over the pommel of the saddle and tried to heave himself up on the stallion, which was now skittish with fear. "Get in the coach."

Her battle with the hawker had momentarily pushed back the crowd a fraction, and as the snort of a horse blasted her ears, she was just quick enough to step aside as Gideon Swift took the opportunity to inch the coach past the prison wagon. Merlin's stallion neighed in fear and reared. The crowd moved aside with a collective gasp. As the horse pawed the air, Brandon fell to the ground.

Everything was happening so rapidly, it made Cynara reel. At the corner of her vision she noticed that the driver of the prison wagon had jumped down, sword drawn. He managed to push aside Merlin's second pistol, and it clattered onto the bridge and exploded with a puff of smoke and a roar.

"Ahhh!" screamed Brandon, rolling on the ground. Cynara saw a red stain spreading on his sleeve just above the elbow, and she kneeled by him, at once oblivious of anything but her brother's agony.

The fight escalated behind her, and she glanced up as she was pushed aside by two burly men. Merlin was fighting desperately with a sword in one hand and a dagger in the other. Cynara knew he didn't want to injure any of the guards, but his situation was getting more desperate every second. She prayed they wouldn't recognize him. If they did, Bow Street would send out detectives to arrest him.

"Help me get your brother to the coach," came Gideon Swift's gruff voice in her ear. "Alice was useless; she took off runnin'." Without a moment's delay, they dragged Brandon through the mob that was now wholly intent on the fight between Merlin and the guards.

Drenched with cold sweat, Brandon heaved himself into the coach without as much as a groan. His face was pasty as he jerked his head in Merlin's direction. "Help him, sis. Make a diversion so that he can get onto his horse."

Cynara gave the fighting men a frantic glance. The mob had grown, the bridge congesting at both ends. She slammed the coach door. "Go on, Gideon! I'll come back with Merlin."

The old man set his jaw and gave her a glare. Then he flicked the reins and the horses pulled the coach off the bridge on the south side. Cynara feared that she was too late to help Merlin, but he should not get caught! If he were caught, the rescue effort would had been for naught. . . . She wouldn't exchange one man's life for another. Pushing through the crowd, she made sure to quiet the stallion that was now pressing against the prison wagon. Patting his neck soothingly, she viewed the fight with trepidation. She thought her legs would buckle any second if this nightmare wasn't over soon. As one of the guards, fighting off a swift parry by Merlin's sword, came close enough for her to touch him, she pushed her walking stick between his knees and wrenched sideways. He toppled to the ground with a shout of anger.

Merlin delivered a punch to the other guard's jaw. The man fell without a sound, but now angry spectators were swarming around Merlin, and the driver found his sword that Merlin had managed to knock to the ground. Cynara thought the moment was lost. She got one flash of inspiration, an idea she would never have considered had the situation not been desperate. A lady would never show her ankles, let alone her *legs* in public, but she must ride to safety. Grim with determination, she hitched up her skirts and pushed one foot into the stirrup. Fear giving her strength she didn't know she had, she boosted herself into the saddle and swung the other leg over the horse. Never before had she used a man's saddle, but this was not the time to ponder the delicacy of the situation. Knees poking out for all to see, she urged the horse on. She was afraid that he would bolt, but he inched through the crowd, all the while snorting and rolling his eyes.

"Bootiful legs," someone growled, and slapped her ankle.

She blushed, and dug her knees into the horse's flank. He danced, getting more nervous with every breath. The crowd slowly dispersed in the horse's path, and she reached Merlin, who was fighting the driver and one of the spectators desperately. Neighing wildly and tossing its head, the massive stallion pushed between the men. If she didn't manage to get him away from the throng, he would bolt through it, trampling God knows how many bystanders.

Merlin looked up, his face glistening with sweat. He was panting hard, and the mask over his eyes sat slightly askew. Without wasting more time, he swung himself up behind her and gripped the reins. As soon as the horse recognized his authority, it stopped dancing sideways and broke into a canter. The crowd had parted, and within seconds they had gained the south side of the bridge.

"Where's the carriage?" Merlin shouted in her ear. She could barely hear him, since a roar had gone up among the onlookers. The sound of rapid hoofbeats reached her ears. She looked over her shoulder and saw four mounted men bearing down on them.

"I don't know where the coach is, but Brandon is in it. He's wounded and cannot ride the horse you said Gideon would bring for him." She wondered if Merlin was still angry with her for meddling, but this was not the time to start an argument. "I could ride in his place."

"I see we are pursued," said Merlin grimly. "We'll ride together on this mount for now. I couldn't let you get behind and captured by the law."

"Who says I would get behind?" she scoffed, but she didn't argue more as Merlin pulled the horse in among warehouses in Southwark. There was an acrid smell in the air, perhaps stemming from one of the many breweries. She had never been in the area before, but she barely noticed her surroundings as Merlin pulled the horse to a halt behind a stack of barrels. They waited in tense silence, and sure enough, half a minute later the horsemen thundered past. Merlin's heart hammered against her back, and she felt oddly relieved that she was there with him, not in the coach worrying about him.

"Now we must find Brandon." He listened intently for a while before ordering the stallion to move on. "We gained some time, but I think the pursuers won't give up that easily."

"Was it lawmen?" She wondered how they could have caught up with them so fast. How would they have found out about Merlin's plans?

"No, I doubt they were lawmen. But there's no doubt that they were after us," he said bleakly.

Chapter 13

"You should be whipped for disobedience," Merlin said as he lifted her down from the horse. They had found the coach carrying Brandon at the Elephant and Castle in Walworth parish. There was no sign of the pursuers who might still be looking for them in Southwark.

"I couldn't bear to be excluded," she defended herself. She placed a hand on his arm. "Say that you forgive me."

He gave her a dark glance. "I suppose your sudden appearance tipped the scale of the fight in my favor," he admitted reluctantly. "But it was foolish to endanger your life, and Alice's."

"Alice left us on the bridge. She probably returned to Albemarle Street. I'll ride with Brandon in the coach and look after him."

"I hope his wound isn't serious." Merlin spoke with Gideon Swift, and Cynara joined her brother inside the coach. Obviously in pain, he grimaced at her and saluted her with a brandy bottle.

"I had to dull the pain with something," Brandon

said. "Swift sawed off my manacles and bandaged my arm, but bungled the job, if you ask me. Said it was only a flesh wound." He laughed mirthlessly. "I don't think I could have endured him digging pincers into my arm in search of a bullet."

Cynara shuddered and viewed the makeshift bandage.

"A more ham-fisted fellow I have yet to meet," Brandon said in an effort to be lighthearted.

"Shh, you don't have to pretend with me."

Merlin stuck his head through the open window. "We'll take back roads to Basingstoke, and there we'll spend the night. I'll ride beside the carriage."

They had traveled for hours, it seemed, when the sound of hooves thundered behind on the hard-packed road. Dusk was falling as a shot rang out after them. Cynara feared for their lives. The carriage jolted faster along the road, jarring every bone in her body. Brandon was moaning in agony every time his wounded arm was rattled. His face was pale and covered with perspiration, his eyes dark with pain.

"Don't worry, we'll get away from them," Cynara said without much conviction. She glanced out the window, but all she could see was the hedge bordering the road. Well out of London now, she wondered who their pursuers were; if they weren't the law, who were they?

As if reading her mind, Brandon said, "I don't know who they are, but the villains are after *me,* that's certain now. Perhaps it's Lady Fidalia's men. She isn't content having her jewelry back. She wants my head on a platter."

Cynara clutched Brandon's hand. "But you're innocent, you told me so."

"That I am, sis." He heaved a deep sigh. "And I shall prove it once we've fooled our pursuers and this wound heals."

Merlin rode up after having scouted the terrain ahead, a wooded area of Hampshire. He said something to Gideon Swift, the driver of the carriage, then looked through the window. His face expressed grim determination. "We're going to stop shortly, and when we do, you must jump down and hide. I shall ride on, acting as a bait. Then Swift will take you toward Devon on another road, and we shall meet again in Basingstoke. By then our pursuers will be gone—I hope."

"It's dangerous for you, old fellow," said Brandon.

"I'm in no more danger than you are at this moment," Merlin said, trying to stay level with the window as the frantic horse threatened to bolt. "Just do as I say, and you'll be safe. With you wounded, Brand, we cannot overpower them and discover their identity."

"Ambush . . ." Brandon said weakly, but Merlin had already hurried off, the hoofbeats growing weaker with every second that passed.

"We must do as he says," Cynara maintained as Brandon tried to get up from the carriage seat. "This once I'm certain Merlin is right."

Brandon studied her intently. "No other times?"

Cynara lowered her gaze. "I have little experience in the matter. We haven't been married for very long."

He placed his hand over hers. "I was surprised that

you married Merlin. You never professed any interest in him before."

"Circumstances changed drastically when Felix died."

Brandon's face reddened. "Bloody Felix! I couldn't believe my ears when I heard about your impending marriage to him. How could you even consider it?"

There wasn't time to explain as the carriage lurched to the side, then turned sharply around a building. The horses neighed, but the coach plunged through a thicket of low bushes, then was still. A second later Gideon Swift stuck his head through the window.

"Hurry now, milady. Th' villains are right behind us." He waved a musket, and the handle of a knife protruded out of the waistband of his breeches. "C'mon, then!"

Brandon eased himself off the seat, his bloodstained left arm hanging limply at his side. He clutched a pistol that Merlin had given him at the onset of the journey and swayed momentarily, but then found enough strength to jump down. Cynara was right behind him, and they followed Merlin's old retainer into the building that shielded their coach. It was a barn partly filled with year-old hay. Swift urged them to hide behind some rotting crates, then took a stand by the door, aiming his musket toward the road.

"They will find us," Cynara whispered, tense now that the very silence seemed threatening. Suddenly she realized that Merlin's presence would have calmed her.

"Merlin will lead them away somehow."

"They must see the coach as they ride by."

"Not necessarily. Shh, here they come." Brandon

stiffened, leveling his pistol toward the door. "Put your head down."

Cynara didn't listen to him; she heard only the sound of approaching hoofbeats. There were four men, each carrying a musket. She wanted to close her eyes to shut out the fearsome group, but she could not stop staring. They were wearing voluminous cloaks and hats, and since twilight was gathering, it was impossible to see their faces.

"Who are they? What do they want?" Cynara whispered.

"Shhh, they have slowed down. Perhaps they've noticed the carriage."

They waited until the silence grew unbearable, then a shot came farther down the road. *Merlin,* Cynara thought, her heartbeat thudding like a mad thing in the cage of her chest. What if he were hurt . . .

"There! They are off again. Merlin won't have any difficulty leading them onto a side road. As a former military man, he's canny as a fox." As the sounds of the horses faded, Brandon sank down in the hay beside her. His sleeve was drenched with blood, and he looked utterly exhausted. "There was a spot of trouble on Black Friars Bridge, what with the extra guard in the prison wagon. I thought Merlin surely would lose that battle." He moaned in agony.

"We must find help for you just as soon as may be," Cynara said. "A doctor must look at that wound before you bleed to death." She wrapped the soaked bandage tighter.

Brandon managed a weak smile. "I'm not finished off yet. Before I turn up my toes I must discover who planted the jewelry among my things. I never knew that my desire for revenge could be so consuming."

Gideon Swift urged them back to the coach. " 'Twill be dark ere long; we'd better make haste to Basingstoke."

"Merlin will get there first, I'll warrant," Brandon said, settling on the coach seat.

"You have great confidence in him," Cynara said, and arranged a folded cloak under his head. She examined the makeshift bandage once more, but there was nothing she could do to it.

"Merlin is one of the sharpest men I know. I'm glad you married him."

A possible murderer? she wanted to say, but remained silent.

Night had fallen outside, and the only light guiding them was the silver glow of the moon. Apprehension filled Cynara when she thought she heard distant hoofbeats, but she relaxed when the sound faded. Perhaps it had been a trick of her overwrought mind. However much she tried, she could not shut off the niggling worry that something might happen to Merlin. Why should she care? He'd done nothing but aggravate her existence. . . .

They reached the inn at Basingstoke an hour later. A light breeze fluttered in the trees, and washing flapped on a line behind the building. Before allowing Cynara to enter the inn, Gideon Swift surveyed the taproom. It looked empty except for two old men drinking ale.

"You shall have a chamber, milady. Then I will find a doctor for the young sir." Swift consulted with the innkeeper, and a pert maid with curly black hair and a fine figure led Cynara up the stairs to the rooms above. The chamber was small, the furniture shabby, but everything was clean, as if recently scrubbed. With a weary sigh Cynara sank down on the bed that was narrow compared to the one she slept in at Black Raven. She wished she had Tildy with her, but the maid at the inn would have to unfasten her gown at the back. After washing her face in a porcelain bowl, she straightened her hair and went to the room across the landing, where she could hear Brandon arguing.

She entered and found her brother pinching the cheek of the dark-haired maid who was in the process of cutting off his sleeve. Brandon looked more animated than Cynara could recall, and the maid's blue eyes were sparkling wickedly.

"I can see that you're well taken care of," Cynara said ruefully. "The injury can't be as dire as I feared."

"A mere scratch, sis," said Brandon with a wink. "Swift has gone to fetch the doctor, and until then I should manage to survive, especially with such a dedicated nurse as Millie here."

Cynara was loathe to leave the room since she worried about Brandon's wound—no matter what he said. "When do you think Merlin will arrive? He should have had plenty of time to deceive the villains."

"Like his namesake the legendary magician, Merlin tends to come and go when it pleases him." Brandon paled as Millie unwound the bandage. "Begad! Be careful, wench."

"Don't go faintin' on me now," said the maid, and pushed him back against the pillows.

He croaked, "Get me a bottle of brandy, sis. This woman is intent on torturing me to death."

Cynara left the bedchamber and stepped down into the taproom. She glanced around the room, but saw only the party of old men, which had now grown to include four more. They were chatting and smoking chalk pipes, only throwing her a cursory glance as she passed their table.

"A bottle of brandy to be sent up to Mr. Hawthorne's room," she said to the innkeeper as he was wiping one of the tabletops.

"Ye look like ye could use a drop yerself, milady," he said.

"Has my husband, Lord Raven, arrived?" she asked.

" 'Aven't seen 'im. 'E usually stays 'ere every time 'e travels to London. A fine, generous gent 'e is," the proprietor said with a smile.

Unbidden pride surged through her. "I'll return to my brother's room to await the doctor. Don't forget the brandy."

By the time the doctor had stitched Brandon's wound and assured Cynara that it wasn't fatal, she was prepared to fall asleep—standing up if need be. It was almost midnight, and after imbibing half of the brandy bottle, her brother was fast asleep. He looked pale but peaceful, and the wound had stopped bleeding.

"You should find some rest, milady," the rotund doctor said, and peered at her closely. "You look a bit peaked, if you don't mind me saying so. Do you need a sedative?"

She shook her head. "No . . . I'd like to be alert if my brother needs me in the night."

The doctor chuckled. "Nay, he'll sleep all night after

drinking all that liquor. You need your rest, milady. I shall ask one of the maids to sit with him tonight."

"He would like that," Cynara said dryly. After making sure the blankets were securely tucked around Brandon, she left his room. She was so tired, she could barely walk. The floor seemed to undulate under her.

Where was Merlin? Hours had passed since they had separated on the road. She threw a glance down the stairs and recognized Gideon Swift's bent figure. He was nursing a tankard of ale at the table closest to the stairs. Always vigilant, Cynara thought fondly. The old man was an unexpected ally and totally dedicated to Merlin.

She went to her room, kicked off her shoes, and released her hair from the constraint of pins and ribbons. Worry had seeped away, being replaced by weariness. Sighing, she brushed her hair and massaged her scalp. Then she realized she would not be able to unbutton her dress. She twisted and bent to reach the buttons in the middle of her back, but found that she would have to sleep in her dress. Sighing, she rolled down her stockings and folded them. As she struggled with the clasp of the simple gold chain around her neck, the door creaked behind her. Gasping, she whirled around. She hadn't known what to expect, but relief washed over her when she recognized her husband. He looked tired and disheveled.

"Merlin!"

His lips quirked upward. "Are you happy to see me, lady wife?"

A blush spread across her cheeks, but she couldn't hide the relief in her voice. "You're safe. What happened on the road."

"Not much—a lot of riding across fields and bumpy lanes." He entered and closed the door behind him, turning the key in the lock.

"The men?" She fought to unfasten the chain.

"They are set on course to Wiltshire. Hopefully, they won't realize their mistake until they reach Stonehenge." He circled around her. "Come here. I'll help you." His warm fingers touched her neck, and a delicious shiver traveled down her spine. He deftly unfastened the clasp and placed the chain on the stand by the washbasin.

Then he started on the buttons, the intimacy creating gooseflesh on her back. Long, sensitive fingers sliding down her back, warm, vulnerable lips touching the tender skin at the nape of her neck.

"Stop it, Merlin," she demanded, trying to tear herself from his seductive presence. His very touch cast a spell on her, unabling her to think clearly.

"Why should I?" he murmured. "You're as eager to explore the realm of love as I am." His lips skimmed her bare shoulder, and she weakened. It would be so easy . . .

"No!" she moaned. "Don't—" She forced herself to remember that she didn't trust him. There might be a devious side to him that didn't balk at killing. How could he live with himself if he'd murdered in cold blood? She knew she wouldn't be able to; anyone with a conscience wouldn't. She managed to drag herself away and held the bodice closely against her chest. Once no part of him touched her, she could face him coolly. Yet, her heartbeat . . . she knew no way to slow it down.

"Why are you fighting?" he asked, crossing his arms over his chest. His face darkened in a glower.

"I'm frightened," she whispered.

"Frightened? Of me?"

She looked away. "I'm afraid of the influence you have over me."

He shifted uncomfortably. "I'm your husband."

She nodded. "But you cannot force me to love you."

He chuckled then, and took a step toward her. "I don't have power over your feelings, but neither do you." He lifted her chin, and she had to look at him. His eyes were dark, searching. A tender light glowed within him, soothing her, still making her more confused. His touch on her face once again made her senses reel and her willpower weaken.

"Don't," she whispered, but he did not obey.

As soon as their lips touched, Cynara knew it was too late to protest. As she drowned in the sweet intoxication of their kiss, he effortlessly peeled away the layers of clothing that separated their bodies. She trembled with pleasure as he pressed her close, his skin as smooth and soft as velvet, his muscles as hard and strong as granite. How could she resist such virile allure? Cynara asked herself, almost swooning as he took one hard nipple into his mouth.

He carried her to the narrow bed. "This wasn't fashioned for lovers," he muttered as he eased her down on the mattress.

It was crowded as he stretched out beside her, but Cynara could not complain, since her mouth was occupied otherwise. She explored the strong neck, tasting every inch of him. Her hands wandered over the smooth flesh that enticed her so until she encountered the hard part of him that sought union with her. She longed to give him enjoyment just as he had given her.

Merlin sighed in pleasure as her hands traveled in feverish passion all over his body. If only she were as unrestrained outside the bedroom, he thought. In daylight she always stared at him with eyes tinged with suspicion and dread, eyes like a sullen sea right before a storm.

Her caress brought him to a point to where there was nothing but the building desire between them. She seemed to be on fire beneath him, skin warm and pliant, legs curling around his in a most enchanting way. Love burned so bright within him that it was almost painful. He wanted her so much, but he also needed to be loved. By her.

"Say that you love me, Cynara," he urged in the moment when desire became an unbearable need.

She moaned something, and he looked into her dear face, yearning for the tenderness that should be there. Her cheeks were delicately flushed, her delicious mouth half open, her eyes cloudy with passion. They were all signs of the storm raging through her body, but it would soon be over, and then daylight would come. . . .

As if he'd never loved a woman before, he entered her urgently, the union bringing a sensation of new wonder and delight. She moved restlessly under him, pushing up her hips, getting even closer as she sought to fulfill her consuming hunger. For this moment she was his completely, and he was hers—forever.

The sweet softness of her brought him to a hot,

searing wave that took him effortlessly into a sea of rapture.

Cynara could not get enough of his bewitching hands on every curve and valley of her body, nor could the teasing tip of his tongue on her throbbing nipples bring her solace. The final union with him first brought contentment, then satisfaction as she rode with him into the engulfing, enchanted crests of release.

Afterward, Cynara felt closer to Merlin than ever before. It was as if when they made love, he took another part of her into himself—or she *gave* him bits and pieces that no one else had ever glimpsed before. Not even her. He was teaching her the ways of love, but he was evidently discovering it together with her, not just guiding her through a maze he'd walked through many times.

"Is it different to make love with someone you . . . well, care about?" she asked timidly as he took her hand and squeezed.

"For me it is," he said quietly. "For me it's a frightening yet infinitely inspiring experience." He paused as if reluctant to go on. "I don't know how it would be for you—to make love with someone you truly love, I mean."

It couldn't be better than this. Cynara didn't know what to say. She didn't really know what consuming love was, except that what she had just shared with Merlin felt right.

"How was it for you?" he continued.

"Sweet and wonderful," she said without hesitation. "Earthshaking."

He patted her stomach tenderly and chuckled. "A good way to embark on a life of love." He cradled her close, their heads resting together on the pillow. It was warm in the room, but he pulled the sheet up over their naked bodies and snuggled his face against her hair. "Now sleep."

Cynara didn't need much prompting. In his arms, nothing could frighten her. A gentle patter of rain against the window lulled her to sleep. For once since the moment she had married Merlin she was in complete peace. She refused to think about their uncertain future.

Chapter 14

Merlin was rudely awakened as a taloned hand dug into his shoulder. The room was pitch black and he couldn't remember where he was. Cynara's sweet body was pressed against him, and the night would have been perfect if it hadn't been for the fingers and the wheezy voice in his ear.

"Captain, wake up! Captain . . . looks like the men have found us. We must hurry away."

"What? Who?" Merlin eased out of bed gingerly so as not to disturb Cynara. Had the law discovered their whereabouts? Were they all going to hang for this mad escape? Damn Brandon for involving everyone he knew in his scrapes! Merlin stumbled on his breeches in the dark and, hopping on one leg, then the other, pulled them on. Cynara was stirring in bed, yawning. Merlin led Gideon Swift out of the room and closed the door gently. No need to disturb his wife.

The old man had set down a candle by the door, and Merlin glanced at his servant, whose eyes were red-rimmed and bleary. "What's going on?"

"The four men are down in the yard, questioning

the landlord. I've already alerted Master Brandon, and he jumped out the window. He's even now waiting in the carriage, musket at the ready."

Merlin pinched his lips in anger. "I'll be damned if I'll let these unknown men menace us! Who are they if they aren't lawmen? This time we'll try to catch them. At least we have the element of surprise on our side."

Swift nodded. "They probably think that we're asleep in our beds and an easy target."

Merlin patted the old man's shoulder. "Thank you for keeping watch. Without you I would be crippled."

Swift grumbled something and gave Merlin the candle. "What about the lady wife?"

"We'll leave her in her bed for now. I'll lock the door and put the key in my pocket." He tiptoed into the chamber. "I'll finish dressing, get my extra pair of pistols, and we'll ambush them outside. I'll jump through the window in Brand's room."

Merlin pulled on the rest of his clothes hurriedly and tucked two pistols that he'd brought in from the saddlebags on the previous evening. He stuffed the pouches of bullets and black powder into his pockets. After making sure that Cynara was sleeping peacefully, he went out and locked the door quietly. He prayed she wouldn't be frightened if she woke up and found him gone. The hallway was dark, but he made it safely into Brandon's room. From there it was easy to climb over the windowsill and jump into a wagon of hay that was parked below.

"Psst." Gideon Swift was waving at him from the side of a barn, and Merlin ran across the yard, keeping to the shadows.

"There. Look!" the old man continued, and Merlin

obeyed. Four mounted men were talking and gesticulating to the landlord in front of the inn. They had just finished, and were about to alight.

"Bloody hell," Merlin swore under his breath, and started as a twig broke behind him. Whirling around, he came eye to eye with the musket barrel, and Brandon's pale face behind it.

"You should be in bed, old boy," Merlin said to the younger man. "You're whiter than a ghost."

"It's the deuced brandy. Gave me a splitting headache, and now my arm's hurting like the devil." He grinned. "But I wouldn't miss this for all the bullet wounds in hell."

They crept forward in the shelter of the inn wall until they could see the men clearly. Merlin didn't recognize a single one of them, even if one man slightly resembled Muggins, the head groom at Black Raven. It couldn't be, or could it? He was the same height, and showed a bleak gauntness that always reminded Merlin of a skeleton.

The landlord went inside, and holding the reins of their horses, the four men discussed something in low voices. Probably a plan to stab us all in our sleep, Merlin thought grimly. He waved at Swift and Brandon, who were right behind him.

"Now!" he cried, and charged into the yard, pistols drawn. The four men stared at him in surprise. Merlin wished he could have seen their faces clearly, but the earlier moonlight had been obscured by rain clouds. All he saw were their outlines, and the blur of faces. But he could read their expressions by the way they carried themselves. Now they were crouching low, ready to spring at first opportunity. They drew their swords, but too late.

"Weapons on the ground, hands in the air, or I will shoot," Merlin said, taking aim at the tallest, Mugginslike person. Gideon Swift was right beside him, but from the corner of his eye he noticed that Brandon had stayed behind, concealing his presence, yet aiming to shoot at first rebellion. A good precaution, he thought.

Before Merlin could gather the men's weapons, one of them fired, missing widely. The horses panicked, and rushed in front of Merlin, all but one, which turned in the opposite direction. Too late did Merlin perceive that one of the men had held on to the saddle and thrown himself up on the mount. Within seconds he had galloped down the road, beyond their reach.

The others held up their arms, and Gideon Swift kicked aside their weapons. He found more pistols in their pockets, and a dagger in the top of one boot. Unarmed, the men grumbled that they wanted to be released.

"We 'aven't done no 'arm," one of them said.

"You will be free the moment you tell me who hired you to follow me and my wife," Merlin said, pushing the barrel of his pistol into the midriff of the man closest to him. "Just make it easy for yourselves and tell me the truth."

"We bain't followin' ye, whoever ye are," another stranger said sullenly.

"But you were paid well to ride into Hampshire in the middle of the night, weren't you? And armed too."

"Aye, ye can say we're doin' a night's work." The man chuckled at his own joke, but Merlin wasn't amused. He aimed his pistol at the man's boot and squeezed the trigger. A shot ripped the air, and the man took a wild step back. He gasped as dust settled on the ground.

"Ye could 'ave shot me toes orf," he complained.

"I will right now if you don't tell me the truth," Merlin said angrily. He grabbed the front of the man's coat and shoved him up against the wall. "Well?"

"We was 'ired by a nob who called 'isself Merlin Seymour—the' man on th' 'orse wot just left."

Merlin's jaw fell. "Merlin Seymour? But that's my name, and I'm the last member of the family."

The ruffian spit on the ground. "Then ye 'ave a double. 'E the one wot just left—left us to face th' danger. Scum!"

Merlin mangled the man's lapels again. "What did he want you to do?"

The man shrugged. "I don't know. We were just told to watch th' inn, and when ye left in th' mornin' we were to keep a watch on ye—find out where ye were 'eadin'."

Merlin's jaw set grimly. "Not murdering us in our beds, then?"

The man shook his head sullenly. "Later—away from civilization like."

"I see." He let the man go. "We don't need an escort, so you might as well leave."

"Ye aren't goin' to call in the law?"

How could I, Merlin thought, *with a fugitive from Newgate Prison right around the corner of the house.* He shook his head, and the ruffians bent down in a hurry to hoist their weapons, but Gideon Swift growled ominously, aiming his musket at the nearest villain. The men ran across the yard and disappeared among the trees.

"Why did you let them go?" Brandon asked as he staggered out of the shadows.

Merlin shook his head as he pondered the fact that someone had used *his* name when hiring the thugs. "The law would be more interested in capturing you than them. The question is, why would anyone be interested in my or Cynara's movements?"

"Perhaps they were interested in mine," Brandon said. "Someone might have learned of your plans to bolt me from prison."

Gideon Swift had gathered the weapons and carried them toward their coach. "Who except the bribed guards would know about your escape, Master Brandon?" he said in passing.

Merlin and Brandon exchanged glances. "Yes, you have a point. Who indeed? Someone must have told the man calling himself Merlin Seymour about the escape plan. Perhaps the same guards, after lining their pockets with another bribe."

Brandon scratched his head. "Who knew about the plan?"

Staring at the place where the roughs had disappeared, Merlin thought for a moment. "Mrs. Swan, the housekeeper at Albemarle Street, Alice—the maid, Cynara and myself, and Gideon, of course. Your mother doesn't know, unless she overheard our plans." He added, "It might be possible that someone overheard us speaking about it."

"Is Mrs. Swan loyal?"

Merlin nodded. "I know she's discreet. She wouldn't gossip about the family. Besides, she was in my father's employ for twenty years, and he trusted her to look after the London house and all its valuables. He never once had reason to mistrust her. I feel the same way."

Grinning, Brandon slapped Merlin's back. "Then it must be you who slipped, old fellow."

Merlin scowled and muttered an oath under his breath as he walked toward the door. "I will remember that remark. Perhaps I should take you back to Newgate."

Brandon laughed and followed Merlin. In the light from a branch of candles in the taproom, he looked pale and drawn. Merlin supported him as he lost his balance for a moment. "Silly old fool," he scolded. "Go back upstairs while I speak with the landlord."

The proprietor had heard the shots and had a worried look on his face. He wore a green-striped nightcap and a voluminous white nightshirt tucked haphazardly into his breeches. Merlin watched Brandon climb the steps, then he addressed the landlord, "What did the men want from you?"

The proprietor rubbed his nose once. "Confirmation that ye were 'ere, Lord Raven. Nothin' else. I said ye were, since they were aimin' pistols at me 'ead. I don't know why ye 'ad to shoot in the middle o' the night. I watched ye through the winder. Gives my 'ostelry a bad reputation, it does."

Merlin's face went rigid with anger. "It was my life or theirs. Besides, no one lost any blood." He turned on his heel and went back upstairs. *But who wanted them dead?* The villains had admitted they were hired to kill.

After unlocking the door to Cynara's bedchamber,

he stepped inside. She was standing by the window, wrapped in only a sheet. Her eyes were dark and huge with worry.

"Why did you lock the door?" she demanded, eyes flaring with anger. "I was beside myself when I heard the shots."

He smiled, but his eyes remained wary. "Were you worrying about me?"

Her eyelashes shielded her eyes, and a stab of dread went through him. She still didn't trust him. But could he blame her? He had yet to discover who really killed his father. Until he did, doubt would cloud her eyes. Still, he sensed that her resistance was wavering. Each time she surrendered herself to him in bed she wavered a bit more. Perhaps love would grow in place of suspicion. Too noble a hope, or what?

"Come here." He pulled her into his arms, perceiving the tension radiating from her body. Gently massaging her neck, he told her about the men in the yard. "I don't know why Muggins—if it was him—would use my name when hiring thugs."

"If it was him riding away, he will never tell you the truth. That man is hard, and implacable too. His allegiance is not with you, Merlin."

Merlin sighed. "Then with whom? He works at Black Raven. I might have to let him go if his disposition doesn't change."

"I have a premonition of danger," Cynara said, her voice muffled by his shoulder. "Someone wants to hurt us—wants to destroy us."

"I shall fire Muggins tomorrow," Merlin said with suppressed wrath. He hated the thought of anyone in his employ frightening Cynara, and if Muggins made her uneasy, he must go.

"Merlin, don't act rashly. You don't know for sure if Muggins was here tonight. It could have been any-one, a stranger, an enemy of Brandon's, an enemy of your father's."

They exchanged uneasy glances. "What if Ross kept a secret from you, something that someone would be willing to kill for," Cynara said.

Merlin smiled and planted a tender kiss on her fore-head. "You sound like you wish to find someone else but me to take the blame for Father's death. Does that mean you believe I'm innocent?"

She stiffened in his arms, then pulled slowly away from him. "I don't know, but I would like to know for sure that you're innocent. Any solid proof will do."

He sensed that it pained her to utter those words. In her heart she wanted to believe him; as much was obvious. A glimmer of hope flickered in his chest. That hope inspired him for the first time to speak to her about Ross's death. Perhaps the day was coming soon when his men who were searching for the missing driver would find him. Catching the murderer had seemed more impossible with every day that passed since that fatal night, but there must be some clue to the where-abouts of the witness *somewhere*. He must find it.

Cynara took his hand. She sat down on the mattress and pulled him down beside her. "Please tell me what happened the night of your father's death."

She had read his thoughts. Merlin stared at her long and hard, noticing the candid yet apprehensive light in her eyes. Taking a deep breath, he plunged into the story. He was certain her face would mirror mistrust and disbelief before long.

"You've heard that my father and I had gone to White's Club that night. It's true, we went, and we'd been quarreling earlier. Father wanted me to leave the army life and settle down at Stormywood." He paused, looking down at his hands. They were trembling. "After Max died, I was overcome by grief, and the wound in my thigh wouldn't heal. Max was as dear as a brother to me. He took something vital away from my life, and I couldn't find anyone to replace him—until I found you." He smiled at her, that by-now-familiar tenderness curling around his heart.

"I was a bit—wild—" he continued, "mad, if you will. I wanted to go on fighting any war that would have me—as a mercenary. A kind of revenge for the loss of Max. I wanted to kill soldiers. Father was trying to make me see the folly of my life before I went the same way as Max." Merlin hung his head. "He was right, of course. I was crazy to think that more deaths would make Max's easier to bear."

"That night at White's, we'd been drinking quite heavily and Father kept arguing. He said he wanted to dandle a grandchild on his knee before it was too late."

"I'm sorry," Cynara said as Merlin's voice cracked with emotion. "Was someone else there that night—from Devon, I mean, someone who knew your father?"

"He knew most of the gentlemen at the clubs, since he spent part of his time in London. As far as I know, he had no enemies, especially not in Devon." Merlin took her hand and traced the delicate blue veins along her wrist. "I wish you could have met my father. You would have liked him. He was the gentlest and most loyal person."

"I did meet him some years ago at Black Raven, but I never even spoke to him."

"Your father and mine were once rivals over your mother's hand, I believe. Not that they were enemies, mind you, but I think Father always had a tender spot for Estelle Hawthorne." *I'm glad she didn't marry Father, because then you would be my sister,* he thought.

"Father stalked out of White's in a rage when I wouldn't promise to stop fighting. I stormed after him, but I couldn't catch up with the carriage as it sped away." Merlin didn't know how to spell out the next words. He had not spoken to anyone about that night for a long time, only to the magistrates at Bow Street. They had always been set on finding him guilty.

"I called for my curricle, since we'd taken separate transportation to the club. I figured that Father was on his way to Stormywood, so I headed out that way. With the new expert driver, Father's coach had been traveling fast. It took me more than an hour to catch up with him in my lighter carriage. He had traveled through Richmond, and was coming out on the country roads. There were some copses of lime trees and beech, separated by gorges. The ravine wasn't that deep, but the slopes went almost vertically to the stream bed below. I don't know exactly what was happening as I watched the carriage lurch sideways. The horses seemed to literally leap over the side of the ravine. It turned out that one of the horses had been shot in the stomach. It panicked and hurtled to its death—Father without the chance to save himself."

Merlin could barely control his voice. "He was crushed in the carriage."

Silence, as brittle as glass, crept into the room.

"But you were not on that *exact* spot at that moment," Cynara whispered.

"The bullet that killed the nag came from one of my Manton dueling pistols. The authorities later found it thrown into the hedge by the road close to the accident." Merlin rose, unable to remain still. "Someone had my pistol, and shot to kill. Perhaps he aimed at Father, but hit the horse."

"But who would know your father would travel that road that night?"

Merlin stared at her unseeingly. "He must have followed us. Someone on horseback could easily have traveled across the fields and never been seen. Riding cross-country will often save time, and he must have ridden on ahead to ambush my father."

"But why didn't the magistrates put you on trial if your pistol was used?"

Merlin glanced at her again, a numbing despair spreading through him. "My groom was with me and swore that I was nowhere in a position to shoot my father. The groom was later found dead in his room at Stormywood."

Cynara's eyes were incredulous. "Aren't you afraid for *your* life? Who says you aren't next on the killer's list?"

"If the man wanted me dead, he would have killed me by now. He wanted me to be blamed for Father's death, don't you see?"

She stared at him narrowly. "Or perhaps there is no

enemy. You *did* kill your father; you killed your groom to prevent him from speaking the truth."

Aghast, Merlin stared at her accusing eyes. "I cannot deny the logic."

"I really wish I knew what to believe," she said, now sad.

"Well, since I'm alive and not beheaded for murder, I might still be a threat to that unknown enemy. But I also have a chance to clear my name. I think that tonight I saw a glimpse of my enemy's existence. All I have to do now is find out how Muggins fits in—if indeed it was he riding off." He stared into space, and his voice was barely audible. "Some fact connected to Brandon's escape seems to have changed everything. The enemy wants us dead now."

Cynara gasped in fright. "We'll have to be very cautious."

"We're evidently caught in a cat-and-mouse game. Time is of the essence. We must catch the villain before he tries again, and I must solve Father's murder."

Cynara leaned against him comfortingly. "I'll be the first to cheer when you're free of suspicion."

He wanted desperately for her to believe him. "Does that mean you—?"

"Then we won't have to live under a cloud any longer. We could hold our heads up in society."

His newfound hope that she truly loved him crumbled. "Family pride means more to you than my innocence?"

She shook her head. "No, but justice should be done, don't you agree?"

He laughed mirthlessly. "Yes, justice must be done."

Cynara knew that she'd said the wrong words, and desperately wanted to retrieve them. But it was too late.

Chapter 15

The following evening they arrived at the Devon coast. After crossing the border from Dorset, they kept to the country roads until they reached Dartmouth, located northwest of Stormywood. Just in case Black Raven and Bluewater were watched, Brandon would hide out at Stormywood for a day or two. He would have to remain in hiding until the mystery of the jewelry theft had been resolved. Though it might take a long time to get acquitted, Brandon was remarkably cheerful about his predicament.

"Don't worry, sis," he said to Cynara when she urged him to be careful. "I shall be invisible." He shook hands with Merlin when they reached the copse where Felix had been shot. "I'll hide here until you tell me it's safe to enter the house. I can't thank you enough for what you've done for me."

Merlin pumped his hand. "I might need your help sooner than you think."

Leading his mount, Brandon disappeared among the trees like a wraith. Streaks of moonlight patterned the garden with silver as Cynara followed Merlin to the mansion. Gideon Swift had already driven the carriage and horses to the stables. They were not observed as they arrived at the silent house.

"In Basingstoke I sent a messenger to your mother, Cynara. Since she must be eager to see your brother, she should be here by now." He took her hand and held her back as she was about to climb the front steps. "Be careful. We don't know who awaits us inside."

"The men in the night?" she asked with a shiver of apprehension. "Or the man who used your name?"

He nodded grimly, sidling up to the door. After glancing through the window, he waved at her to join him, and she obeyed. The house lay in brooding silence, but with only a skeleton staff, what could one expect? She wondered if her mother had arrived. If she had, was she in danger here? Cynara didn't want to follow that thought to the end.

The lawns shimmered eerily in the moonlight, and Cynara wondered if she and Merlin were fully visible against the house façade. What if their pursuers were even now hiding at the fringe of the forest that surrounded the estate? A sharp gust of wind blew through, the leaves rattling on the trees. Cynara scanned the woods, but there was no one in sight.

Merlin pulled her around the corner of the house. They entered through the kitchen entrance after he'd located the key on the edge of a jutting stone in the wall. "We always keep a spare key here, just in case we're locked out," he explained. "Someone is usually here all the time, but . . ." He pulled her inside without finishing the sentence. She sensed his tension, and it heightened her own worry.

Red embers glowed in the fireplace, and the water

kettle was still hot, she noticed as she held her hand over it.

"Do you want something to eat or drink?" Merlin asked, but she shook her head. Fear tormented her, and food was the last thing on her mind.

"I want to see if Mother is safe," she whispered.

"She'll be in the blue guest room," he said. "Guests are always settled there, since it's the nicest chamber."

Merlin first, then Cynara went into the shadowy hallway, listening intently. Silence hung heavy and sullen everywhere. The carpet on the stairs muffled their steps, and Cynara's heart hammered with trepidation as she entered the corridor above. Not a sound anywhere. The moon cut a swath of light through the tall window at the end, and she easily found the door to the blue guest room.

Pistol at the ready, Merlin was right behind her when she knocked, then entered. The room was dark, but there was a movement in the bed.

"Mother? It's me, Cynara. We've come with—"

"Darling? Is that really you?" came Estelle's sleepy voice. She fumbled with the tinderbox and managed to light the candles by the bed.

Merlin waited discreetly outside while Cynara entered. "We brought Brand, Mother. He's even now hiding in the woods, waiting to join you here."

Estelle clasped her hands reverently together. "Brand here?" Intense joy brightened her face, and Cynara was happy that they'd managed to free her brother, no matter to what danger.

Estelle slid out of bed and pulled on her dressing gown and slippers. Her head was already covered with a voluminous cap. "Where is he? Is he unhurt? I have to see him at once."

"You must wait until we bring him here. But we'll be back in a few minutes."

"We?"

"Merlin is waiting outside this door."

"Why all this furtiveness?" Estelle asked suspiciously as Cynara stuck her head into the corridor before letting the older woman pass.

So as not to upset her mother unduly about the men who had followed them from London, Cynara softened the truth. "Brand is a wanted man now. We don't know who's snooping around. That's all."

Estelle laughed. "Ha! What stranger would snoop around this godforsaken place in the middle of the forest. Only the servants, and reluctantly. Since Ross's death they are loathe to work here, and I don't blame them."

Estelle silenced as she recognized Merlin. "Oh, hello." She took his arm as he left his position by the door. "I hear that a thank-you is in order. Young man, you don't know how happy I am that Brandon is free at last!"

"He's eager to see you, no doubt," Merlin said dryly. "You must wait in the breakfast parlor at the back, and I will bring him to you."

Estelle seemed about to protest, but she changed her mind. "No candlelight, eh?" she said finally.

Merlin shook his head. "No lights. The fewer people who know about Brandon's whereabouts, the better. He must move around at night and sleep during the day."

"We shall soon clear him of any suspicion," Estelle

said with a conviction that Cynara could not feel. For Brandon's sake, she prayed that her mother was right.

She waited with Estelle in the breakfast parlor, and within ten minutes there was a tap on the door.

Brandon entered, disheveled, tired, and dirty. But the grin was pure delight as he swung his mother around. Estelle sobbed with relief, repeating his name over and over. Merlin and Cynara exchanged amused glances. She could not describe the sensation of relief, the warm new softness in her heart as she gazed into Merlin's eyes. She tried to swallow, but there was a catch in her throat. Although many problems still separated them, the window to the future had brightened somehow. Was this sweetness in her heart love? It must be.

Brandon set Estelle down, and laughed. "Mother, you're a veritable watering pot." He took the handkerchief from her and dabbed at her cheeks.

"Mon Dieu, I never thought I would see you again." She took his hand and led him to one of the sofas as if he'd turned into a young boy again.

Merlin drew the heavy drapes across the windows and allowed Brandon to light one branch of candles on the table.

"Now, let me look at you," Estelle said, studying Brandon's face until he squirmed. She clucked. "So thin, so thin; we must do something about that."

Cynara sat down beside Brandon. The three Hawthornes were sitting side by side while Merlin sat in a chair opposite them.

"Tell us everything that happened that night you were accused of stealing the jewelry. By the way, where is the loot now?" Merlin asked.

"At Bow Street, I presume," Brandon said. He sighed, suddenly deep in thought. "I had planned to make a round of the clubs with my cronies, Lord Ebersham and Whitely Dinmore. As you know, I went to school with them and never had any occasion to doubt their honesty. We've always been the best of friends."

"As far as I know, they have an impeccable reputation," Merlin said. "Can you recall every detail of that evening?"

Brandon shrugged, throwing an embarrassed glance at his mother. "I was well over the oar, if you must know. The events were somewhat of a . . . er, blur. We had homemade punch at my lodgings. If you must know, I'm quite a dab at mixing liquors—"

"Get on with it, Brand. We all know that your punch is exceedingly strong," Cynara said.

"At around ten o'clock we went around to White's for a meal, but I can't for the world remember what we ate."

"What happened after that?" Merlin sounded so calm, when Cynara wanted to shake her brother for babbling about unimportant details.

"Card games. I won a godly sum at Brooks's, then we continued to Watier's, where I lost all that I'd won—in one hand." He shot another guilty glance at his mother.

Estelle pursed her lips, and her cheeks looked paler than before, but she didn't flinch. Even though she had a soft spot for Brandon, she'd never closed her eyes to his wild ways. Cynara admired her courage. Would Brandon's ordeal subdue his lively spirit in the future? she wondered.

"Then we went to a gathering at an estate in Surrey, at Kingston, I believe. So many guests were present that their faces were all a blur to me. It was about dawn when I returned to my lodgings." Brandon made a significant pause. "Someone accompanied me. A . . . well, eh, a bird of paradise."

Estelle gasped and fluttered her handkerchief in front of her face as if the room had grown too hot and stuffy.

Brandon fidgeted on the sofa. "Mother, are you sure you want to hear the rest?"

Estelle straightened her back. "I admit I'm shocked, but it is not unexpected under the circumstances. I knew there was a woman involved in this scandal."

"The woman left some hours later. Then I had a rude awakening as the police—two Bow Street Runners—pushed their way into my lodgings. My valet could not keep them out. They barged into my bedroom and began riffling through my evening clothes." He chuckled ruefully. "I was angry, I admit. I yelled at them to stop, all the while clutching my pounding head. Yes, I thought my poor head would split that morning. You must understand how utterly puzzled I was when one of the policemen hauled out a diamond and ruby necklace from my pocket."

"They maintained you'd stolen it," Estelle said in a toneless voice.

Brandon nodded. "They accused me of removing the necklace from Lady Fidalia's neck at the gathering in Surrey and bolting with it. The truth must be that the—er, woman—nameless street woman—put the necklace into my pocket when I'd fallen asleep. I don't even know where to find her again. It's clear that someone took Lady Fidalia's necklace and put it in my pocket so that I might get blamed for the theft. The diamonds are worth ten thousand pounds—great stones they were."

Rubbing his cheek, Merlin muttered something under his breath. "Fidalia. She's a gambler, widowed, and has a tarnished reputation. Her lovers have been innumerous over the years." He snapped his fingers. "Even Felix visited her scented boudoir for a time."

"You seem to know a great deal about Lady Fidalia, Merlin," Estelle said dryly.

Merlin gave her a cool glance. "I have ears and eyes in my head," he said. "But why would she want to implicate you, Brandon?"

"Perhaps she thought I really had stolen the necklace," Brandon said. "I know for a fact that Lady Fidalia is desperate for funds, and perhaps the necklace was her only asset."

"Or she pretended to be heartbroken while slipping it into your pocket herself," Cynara pointed out.

"I don't see what she would have to gain by it," Brandon said. "Even if the loss of the necklace doesn't put her in the workhouse, she wouldn't *give* it away, surely."

"No . . . ." Merlin said, "but perhaps someone paid her to *give* it away. Anyhow, the trollop you met in London probably put the necklace in your pocket at your lodgings. That's the most logical explanation. If we could locate her, we would find the answers we need."

Brandon snorted. "That would be like searching for a needle in a haystack. You know how many, eh . . . females loiter on the street corners."

"Is that where you, er . . . invited . . . ?" Merlin asked with a discreet sideways glance at Estelle.

Brandon nodded. "She stood about half a mile from my doorstep—ready for the taking." At last Brandon blushed to the roots of his hair. "Really, Merlin! No more such talk in the company of ladies."

Estelle sat pinch-lipped beside him, and Cynara lowered her gaze to the floor in embarrassment.

"Very well," Merlin said, unperturbed. "I'm sorry if I offended your sensibilities, ladies. However, if ever we are to get to the solution of this puzzle, we must probe every clue."

"Perhaps Lady Fidalia has answers for us," he added. "I shall endeavor to discover her whereabouts, and then Cynara and I could pay her a visit."

"I'm sure she was in London for the duration of the Season," Brandon said. "She's bringing out a shady niece of hers—balls, routs, levees, musical evenings— the entire whirl of entertainment."

"Then perhaps we'll find her in London." Merlin shot a glance at Cynara. "Would you like to accompany me? I'm sure the lady would be more inclined to speak with you than with me."

Cynara nodded. "If it'll help Brandon, I'm willing."

"I wish you wouldn't speak to such a *fast* woman," Estelle interjected. "Any contact with her will corrupt you, daughter."

"You must keep in mind that I'm married now, Mother," Cynara said, blushing delicately. "However, I doubt Lady Fidalia will help us in this matter. If anything, she'll demand to know Brand's whereabouts."

Silence rolled into the room, bringing gloom. They

were all locked into private thoughts, and no solution to Brandon's dilemma seemed available.

Estelle broke the silence. She took Brandon's hand in hers. "Do you recall what the necklace looked like—exactly?"

Brandon thought for a moment. "As far as I know, it was a handsome enough article. When the police arrested me, I had to get up naturally—despite my headache—and then I studied the necklace. I told them I'd never seen it before. The diamonds were octagonal cross-cut, seven large ones encircled by a ring of smaller ones. A ruby pendant hung at the center, an unusual teardrop-shaped faceted ruby of the deepest red. The ring attaching the ruby to the diamonds was held in the beak of an exquisite bird in flight, made of tiny diamonds. Excellent craftsmanship, if you ask me."

"*La Hirondelle!*" cried Estelle, and she clutched Brandon's arm convulsively. "Did it have a small ruby on its chest?"

Everyone was now staring at Brandon, willing him to remember. "Yes . . . I believe it did, but I'm not quite sure."

Estelle's breath grew raspy. "Only one such pendant was made, many years ago for my great-grandmother in France. *Hirondelle* means swallow. It symbolizes the sacrifice my great-grandfather made in the war against Spain during Louis XIV's reign. Ever loyal to the king and his country, my ancient relative sold his estate to help finance the war. It tore him apart, and Louis awarded him with a necklace such as you describe. The tiny ruby in the swallow's chest represented the heart that bled, and in the process of its suffering it grew as large as the pendant ruby. It was a sorrow too deep to bear, but Louis understood the ultimate sacrifice of his minion. The necklace, and matching bracelet and earrings, have always belonged to the Mournay family. You see, the Mournay estate in Gascogne was the home of a great flock of swallows.''

"You're a Mournay, Mother." Brandon supported his parent, whose voice had grown thinner every minute. "Mother, it cannot be *that* necklace. It was lost during the Revolution. You told us so yourself."

Estelle nodded. "That's true. Everything—the riches my grandfather amassed—all disappeared in the tumult of the Revolution. When I arrived in England, I had nothing."

"It could be that Lady Fidalia bought the necklace from someone in France after the Revolution," Merlin said thoughtfully. "Surely the jewelry wasn't destroyed, just confiscated and sold to finance the new government."

Silence fell again, but then Estelle straightened. "I just *know* it was *La Hirondelle*. But why would it appear in Brandon's pocket after so many years?"

"That's a coincidence I cannot explain," Merlin said. "Somehow the thought of the necklace resurfacing—if it is the swallow necklace—makes me uneasy."

"Perhaps there's more than just theft involved here," Cynara said, her voice laced with apprehension.

Chapter 16

In the early morning hours, right after dawn had brought its first milky light, Merlin, Cynara, and Estelle set out toward Black Raven. Brandon was sleeping the sleep of the utterly exhausted in a guest room at Stormywood, Gideon Swift watching over him.

Cynara was so tired she thought she would collapse before they arrived at Black Raven. Estelle sat ramrod straight on the seat across from her, nervous tension keeping her eyes wide open. "This isn't over yet," she whispered. "My baby Brandon . . . he'll be a hunted man."

"Brand is hardly a baby, Mother," Cynara said dryly. "Not a word to anyone about this, not to anyone! Not even to Tildy." Cynara knew her mother had difficulty keeping a secret for any length of time. "Brand's safety depends on our discretion."

Estelle nodded like a wooden doll. "Not a word shall pass my lips."

Merlin was drowsing in his corner, and Cynara experienced that unfamiliar soft pang in her heart once more. He looked young and defenseless in his sleep, not the least forbidding. One of the grooms from Stormywood was driving the coach, never once suspecting what their errand had been at Merlin's estate. The staff thought they'd just returned from London, where they'd supposedly been shopping.

The first cottages of the Black Raven village appeared as the hedge-lined road widened into High Willow. At one end stood the old inn, the Duck and Swallow, a cross-timbered building with a thatched roof whose cellar served as local detention house. At the other end, the humble stone church with its pointed tower and its mossy, listing tombstones.

They had planned to travel directly to Black Raven, but the carriage slowed down in front of the inn. Merlin stirred, instantly alert. "What's amiss?"

Just as soon as the vehicle had halted, he jumped down and spoke to the driver. Then he stuck his head through the open window. "One of the horses has gone lame. We must put another one in its place. While we wait, would you like a cup of coffee or tea?"

"Yes, coffee, please," Cynara said with alacrity. "It will help me stay awake."

Estelle nodded dreamily, looking pale and wraith-like in the morning light. "Coffee, *merci.*" As Merlin went into the taproom, Estelle leaned forward and clutched Cynara's hand. "I can't stop thinking about Brandon. I worry so about him. Do you think he'll be safe at Stormywood?"

"He knows the danger. I'm sure he'll be careful, Mother. If he's caught, he won't get another chance to discover the truth about the necklace."

They brooded in silence until Merlin returned with a maid carrying a tray. Steam wafted from the coffee, and Cynara accepted her cup with eagerness. She sipped gingerly so as not to scald herself, and Merlin smiled at her above the maid's head. Seeing the tenderness in his eyes, she swallowed convulsively, scalding her throat nevertheless. She could not deny the response in her heart, a response that was growing stronger every day.

Merlin left to speak with the driver, and Cynara drank her coffee in silence. The daylight had grown brighter, a golden sunlight painting the landscape. A glinting mist hung under the trees in the distance.

She admired a pot of flowering geraniums outside the inn door, but was startled out of her reverie by a growling laugh. A shadow had fallen across the door opening of the coach, and a humpbacked old man who seemed faintly familiar stared at her. His eyes were red-rimmed and watery, his skin leathery, and his nose was bulbous. Gray wisps of hair protruded from under a dirty stocking cap. Cynara noticed that he was holding a bottle in one hand, and he swayed on his feet.

Estelle gasped and moved away from the leering face with its rotting teeth.

The man was staring straight at Cynara. He saluted her unsteadily. "Lady of death," he said in an accent that Cynara placed as French. "Mark my words, your marriage to Merlin Seymour has already cost lives. *Oui,* you're guilty of those deaths, milady. You've made a terrible mistake, and now more blood will flow."

"What are you talking about?" Cynara demanded angrily. "You have no right—"

"More blood shall be shed because of you," he growled ominously, and staggered aside, almost falling. Merlin had arrived and was holding the old man's arm in a hard grip.

"Was he molesting you?" he asked, his lips tight.

Cynara was too dazed to reply, but Estelle nodded. "He was talking a madman's gibberish."

The old man wrenched away, running in a surprisingly sprightly fashion around the corner of the inn. Merlin pursued him, but the innkeeper standing on the doorstep called out after him. "He's harmless, milord. He's a lunatic Frenchie sailor who comes and goes like a sea fog around these parts. Been in this country since the Revolution, he says."

Merlin returned reluctantly. "He frightened the ladies, Mr. Cobb. Do you know his name?"

"He calls himself Jean, that's all I know. A drunken old sod, nothing else. He reads everyone's fortune, whether they want it or not."

Merlin frowned, but he let the incident pass. "Very well. If the horses are ready, let's continue to the castle."

The equipage rattled over the cobblestone yard.

"I believe I saw the man once before," Cynara said to no one in particular.

"Where?" Estelle demanded. "I don't want you to get involved with unsavory characters."

"He was in a copse in Gairlock Woods," Cynara explained. "I was out riding one morning with Bobby Black, the stable lad, and the old man darted across the trail, frightening the horses."

"I shall have the men at the estate keep a lookout for the vagrant," Merlin said, frowning. "I don't want you to be frightened."

Cynara smiled. "Thank you for your concern, Merlin, but a drunken old man doesn't intimidate me."

"Well, anything out of the ordinary should . . . especially since the staff at Black Raven and the people of the village are hostile toward us."

"Toward you," Cynara corrected him, instantly regretting the words when she saw the hurt in his eyes.

A hush descended in the carriage, and Cynara wished they were back at the castle, where she could close herself in her bedroom and think through everything that had happened. So much had taken place since they left Black Raven, and she was tired, so tired, yet relieved that her brother was out of prison at last. *I'm sorry,* she whispered silently to Merlin, but she could not utter the words aloud.

Mrs. Averell, the housekeeper, greeted them sourly in the hallway. She ignored Merlin and stared disapprovingly at Bramble who, obviously in a flutter, was waddling from one side of the foyer to the other.

"Good morning, Bramble," Cynara greeted him, but he was too distracted to notice. He watched the footmen unload the luggage, and, after taking her cloak, he evidently could not contain himself longer.

"Dear me, dear me!" he exclaimed, wringing his hands.

"What's wrong?" Merlin asked, another frown gathering between his eyes.

"Oh, dear me. Someone has dug more holes in the garden, milord. We've kept a guard stationed there at night, as you commanded, but twice he'd been knocked senseless and the holes have been dug. I ordered more guards, but the men are too frightened to venture out at night." He stopped in front of Merlin.

" 'Tis the man dressed in the gray cloak, milord. Last night I stood hidden behind the dungeon door, watching the rose garden, when the fellow appeared. Even though it was dark I could see in the light from his lantern that he wore a gray cloak—the same as the stranger who broke in. I threatened him with a musket, but he took off running, and I—er, don't run fast—"

"Poor Bramble," Estelle said, clutching a hand to her forehead. "I'm not sure I can take more excitement."

Cynara flashed a warning glance at her mother so that she wouldn't reveal more. The secret about Brandon might easily slip out if Estelle grew absentminded. "You're tired, Mother. Perhaps you should lie down and rest. I shall call Tildy."

It wasn't necessary, as the maid appeared at the top of the stairs. "Aw, am I glad to see ye," she called out cheerfully. "The household has been topsy-turvy since ye've been gone. People a-faintin' and a-screamin' only because o' some holes in the garden."

"You weren't the tiniest bit afraid, then, Tildy?" chided Merlin, and handed Bramble hat and cloak.

"Not a bit." Tildy tossed her curls and led Estelle upstairs.

Cynara was tired, but not too tired to go outside and view the destruction of the rose garden. Wind gusted from the sea, whipping her hair into disarray. "Whoever is doing this is out to thoroughly annoy us," she said thoughtfully.

"Only that, I wonder?" Merlin stood beside her, staring broodingly at the hollow at his feet. "These are all different shapes, not like the first coffinlike cavity."

"Either the digger is looking for something, or is out to destroy us as he destroys our garden," Cynara said.

"Destroy?" Merlin gave her a skeptical look. "Indeed a strong word, but you're right. Perhaps someone wants us away from here."

"But you're the new earl. Black Raven would be lost to the Seymour family if you were—gone."

"You talk like 'gone' means dead," Merlin said with a hint of derision. "You should not have such pessimistic thoughts, dear wife."

"Time and time again we've witnessed the staff's hostility toward you."

"That's true, but why would they want to see me gone from Black Raven? I have treated them fairly."

"They might consider it a bad omen to—" Cynara lowered her gaze.

"To have a murderer rule them," Merlin filled in, his voice flat.

"I didn't mean that," she said miserably, though the exact phrase had been on her tongue. "I'm tired, and my thoughts are muddled."

Abruptly, Merlin turned on his heel. "I shouldn't keep you from your rest. You have nothing to fear. I shall personally guard the rose garden tonight to see if the intruder returns."

"I wager he won't now that we're back."

Merlin gave her a quick, penetrating glance. "You have a point. Still, I would dearly lay my hands on the scoundrel."

On a cool note they separated in the hallway, Cynara on her way to her room to freshen up and rest, and Merlin turning toward his study.

Cynara slept almost all day. The late afternoon sun

gilded the sea when she rose from her sleep. Weighed down with listlessness, she eagerly drank the coffee that Tildy had carried from the kitchen. She ate the steaming omelette and the buttered bread, and felt better. She glanced out again, this time toward the rock-strewn land around the castle. Catching a glimpse of Merlin, she longed to speak with him, to close the gap that had sprung up between them. He strode purposefully toward the stables, dressed in riding boots and jacket.

"I shall take a ride to clear my brain," she explained after refusing to wear the high-waisted muslin gown that Tildy had pulled from the armoire. "Bring out my habit."

Half an hour later she was walking toward the stables, crop in hand. The plume of her hat danced in the breeze, and the wide skirts whipped around her legs. The air was brazing, and her spirits lifted miraculously.

Bobby Black was the only person in the stables. He was sweeping out one of the boxes. He bowed deeply and gave her a shy smile.

"Did the master go for a ride?" Cynara asked, and when the boy replied with a nod, she continued. "Did you see in what direction he went?"

"Rode off along the coast, toward Gairlock Woods." He hesitated. "When he discovered that Mr. Muggins had left the estate about the same time as you went to London, he went pale with anger."

Apprehension leapt through her at his words. Then it must have been Muggins pursuing them on the road. "I'm going after Lord Seymour. Would you please accompany me, Bobby?"

"Of course," the boy said, and blushed. "Mr. Muggins told me to obey your orders while he was gone, milady."

"Did he now?" Cynara commented grimly. "Did he say when he was coming back?"

"I told the master that I didn't think Mr. Muggins was coming back. He took all his things with him. But I have no idea where he went as he left on the road to Dartmouth."

"I had the impression that Mr. Muggins wasn't very fond of me or the master." She surprised herself by gossiping with a servant, but any information that might explain Muggins's reason for leaving would be helpful.

"Mr. Muggins kept mostly to hisself. He had no friends, only drinking companions." Pinching his lips together as if regretting the gossip about his erstwhile superior, Bobby loped off to saddle the horses.

Cynara viewed the stables, noticing the decay and the slipshod upkeep. Every surface was grimy, and the saddles, besides other leather equipment, needed urgent polishing. When Bobby came back, she said, "Mr. Muggins didn't care much about his work, did he?"

Bobby looked to the ground. "No . . . Mr. Muggins took to the bottle, milady," he grumbled, "all the fault of the bottle." He glanced at her quickly. "I do all I can to keep the boxes clean and the horses fed and curried. You shall find no fault with the horses, milady."

"Of course not," Cynara said with a kind smile. "Swallow is positively glowing."

The sky above Lyme Bay had a light orange tint as

the sun slowly dipped its chin below the horizon. It would soon be dark, so she'd better content herself with a short ride. Bobby was staying at a respectful distance behind her, but she reined in on the path along the ridge and waited for him to join her—which he did reluctantly. He held her in great awe.

"You've heard about the holes in the garden, haven't you, Bobby?" Cynara asked. "Do you know anything about them?"

Bobby shook his head, a frown marring his young face. "I don't know who would do such a blood— blasted thing, milady." He scratched his head, tilting his grimy hat toward the back of his head. "And I haven't seen any strangers around the village."

"Do you go there often?" Cynara asked, guiding her mare around a clump of gorse. Bobby's mother, the cook, lived at the castle, and Bobby was always in the kitchen when not working at the stables.

"Sometimes I have to run an errand for Mum. I know everyone in the village, since most of them are working at the castle anyhow, or on the grounds."

Cynara nodded thoughtfully. "Have you ever spoken with Jean, the mad Frenchman?"

"Aye, everyone knows him. He's was already here when I was born. Part of the village, he is. A harmless old fool who earns a few shillings doing odd jobs, like mending nets and tarring boats. He must have been a sailor at one time, before drink claimed him."

"He's a fortune-teller," she said. "He told me about my future, a dire one at that."

Bobby stared at her sideways, as if too shy to look her squarely in the eye. "Fortune-teller? Aye, it's one of his usual habits."

"Really? What are his other habits?"

"Aw, he climbs the inn roof sometimes when he's drunk and wails French songs while holding on to the weather vane. Sometimes he falls asleep in my aunt's hen house. He used to have a donkey called Trotter, and one night he fell asleep in the cart that was still attached to Trotter's harness. When Jean woke up, he found himself at the outskirts of Sidmouth." Bobby chuckled. "He sold Trotter after that."

So intent were they on their conversation that they barely noticed entering Gairlock Woods. Dusk, and a sudden chill, settled under the trees, and Swallow snorted as if unhappy with the change of scenery.

"He's never told you your fortune, then?" Cynara continued.

"Naw, only the Gypsies tell fortunes around here. Twice a year they camp in a valley a few miles west, on Lord Barton's property." He smiled guiltily. "They once told me I would have an important job."

Cynara was so close, she could pat his arm. "I don't doubt that for a moment. In fact, I shall teach you to read and write, and you shall be allowed access to the library at Black Raven. I'll see what I can do to set up a village school."

His eyes lit up, and his freckles seemed to glow. "Thank you, milady! I know my letters—the vicar taught me—but I would dearly like to learn how to write."

"I shall teach you, and the others on the estate. You tell them to be prepared." Cynara contemplated how full her days would be with refurbishing the castle and teaching the children. If only there weren't such a menacing cloud hanging over her head. Would she ever be free of it? Would Merlin ever be free of suspicion?

"Milady, it's growing too dark to ride in the forest," Bobby said. "We should turn around before the horses stumble and break their legs."

Cynara shivered and wheeled Swallow around. "You're right."

They rode back toward Black Raven in silence, Bobby taking his respectful stance two yards behind her. Only the wing beats of a lonely dove disturbed the silence at first, but then the faint sound of hoofbeats cut the still air. The noise came closer, twigs breaking, leaves rustling, as the speed of the hooves accelerated. The horse was behind them at first, then it veered off onto another path that also led to Black Raven.

Her heart hammering with fear, Cynara stared as the dark rider hurled past. Then she let out a breath of relief. "It's Lord Raven," she said. "Why is he in such a hurry? Didn't he notice us?"

Eager to discover the answers to those questions, she steered Swallow through the brambles to the other path and followed Merlin at a brisk clip. Due to the ever-gathering darkness, she didn't want to push Swallow too hard, but she burned to discover what Merlin was about. Still, her swift horse left Bobby far behind.

When she arrived back at the stables, there was no sign of Merlin. Panting from the exercise, Cynara slid off her horse and led it toward the dark opening of the stables. "Merlin?" she called out, but there was no answer. She waited silently for a while, listening for sounds of Bobby's horse. The only thing she could hear was the faint crashing of the waves, then the rustling of the wind in the treetops.

"Merlin?" she called out again toward the quiet cavern of the stables, but absolute stillness reigned. Where were the rest of the horses? Apprehensive now as silence pressed around her like a live being, she strained to see the shape of Bobby returning. Nothing.

"Bobby? Where are you?" Her words echoed forlornly, then they were shredded by the tempestuous wind.

Swallow stomped impatiently, the only living thing besides herself. The brown eyes looked accusingly at her as if urging her to stop this strange new game. Cynara patted the mare's sweaty neck.

She waited for what seemed an eternity, then stepped into the timbered building and lighted an oil lamp that was hanging on a hook by the door. Nervous about the darkness pressing around her, she hurriedly unfastened the girth strap and slid the saddle off the horse. Where was Bobby? Had something happened to him in the dark? She should have waited for him instead of hurtling after Merlin on the uneven path. And where did Merlin go in such a hurry?

As her eyes gradually adjusted to the darkness inside, she hung the saddle over the side of nearest box stall. To her surprise, she discovered that Merlin's horse was inside, staring at her in utter silence. It was still wearing its saddle and harness. "Merlin?" Consternated, she looked around the box, but there was no sign of him. Why had he been in such a hurry that he hadn't had the time to care for his horse? Perhaps he was planning to ride out again.

She wiped down Swallow's damp hide and led her to another box. A faint sound outside startled her, but she gritted her teeth and continued with her chore.

Fear wasn't going to get the best of her. Surely there was nothing to be afraid of. She thought she heard voices, one of them Merlin's.

"Anyone there?" she called out, her voice strangely weak and breathless. It wasn't more than a whisper.

No reply. Her hands clammy now, she led Swallow into the box next to Merlin's horse and closed the wooden gate. She had to get out. Another sound reached her ears, that of shuffling steps. Frightened in earnest, she ran toward the door opening, stumbling over something soft that she hadn't noticed before. She halted and peered at the floor. The lamp inside the door sent a pale glimmer of light around the walls, and she recognized the male form stretched out in the hay.

"Merlin!" she cried out, touching his clammy forehead. Was he dead? She placed her fingers against his throat, sighing in relief when she found a steady pulse. "What happened?" she continued, shaking his shoulders. He didn't move.

She had a sudden premonition of danger, and looked up. A shadow flashed before her eyes, a sweep of soft cloth brushed by her cheek, then pain shot through her head.

Chapter 17

A cold wind whipped across Cynara's face, and slowly memory returned to her aching head. Her hand trembled as she pressed it against the area above her left ear, from which the white-hot pain emanated. She moved slightly, wondering where she was. Then the pungent scent of grass and moist earth reached her nose, and she knew she was outside somewhere. Gasping as renewed pain pierced her head, she hoisted herself onto her elbow and studied her surroundings. It was very dark, masses of clouds moving across the sky. Stray raindrops splashed her face as she discovered that she was lying in the rose garden. The lumps under her back were from the diggings among the roses.

Gasping in fear, she rose on unsteady legs. She sensed that she was alone, and she was grateful that the villain who'd hit her had left her alive.

Walking gingerly so as not to jar her head more, she moved toward the gate. Due to it slapping against the stone wall in the brisk wind, she knew where it was located.

Then she remembered Merlin. Something dreadful had happened to him. She grappled with the gate, stepped outside on the overgrown moat, and stared toward the stables in the distance.

Horror filling her, she watched as flames licked the roof of the stables. The whole building was on fire. Even as she ran down the hill toward the burning edifice, loud popping sounds shot through the night as the windows exploded. Forgetting about her aching head, she bolted faster, thinking only of Merlin and the trapped horses.

Voices rode toward her on the wind, dismembered sounds that seemed to come from the wind itself. Someone else must have seen the fire.

To her relief, she found that the part where she'd found Merlin wasn't completely covered in flames. The other end was, and the horses were dangerously close to it. She could hear them scream in terror.

"Help!" she called out, her voice drowning in the roar of the fire. "Help!" The heat scalded her face and seared her lungs, but she defied terror and rushed to the door, which was, she found, locked. The iron key sizzled in her hand as she tried to turn it. She cried out in agony. Sobbing, she tore off her jacket and wound it around the key before she could grasp it again. Her worries slightly appeased, she found that the door swung open quite easily. The wood creaked, and smoke billowed through the opening. The fire roared with renewed vigor as air streamed into the building.

"My lady Raven!" Someone was shouting her name, but she was intent only on rescuing Merlin. From the light of the fire at the other end of the building she could see his prostrate form in the hay.

Tiny flames were already licking at the straw, and she knew it was only a matter of seconds before it would be a blazing inferno.

"Milady!" The voice was coming closer as she pressed her jacket over her nose and mouth and darted into the stables. She was vaguely aware of the sound, recognizing it as Bobby's. Realizing she couldn't drag Merlin outside without taking her jacket from her face, she tried to plan ahead. The horses' screams were filling her ears, and her eyes watered so much, she thought she would go blind. Without hesitating any longer, she dropped the jacket to the ground and grabbed Merlin's legs. He was so heavy, and the smoke was making it impossible to breathe.

To her infinite relief, she made out Bobby's gangly form beside her. He was coughing incessantly, but he understood what she was about to do and gripped Merlin's shoulders. With a strength she didn't know she had, Cynara lifted his legs. He sagged as Bobby began dragging him across the floor.

Cynara's legs buckled, but she gritted her teeth and strove to keep up with the frantic youth pulling at Merlin's shoulders. Inch by inch they got closer to the door. . . .

A mighty crash roared through the building as one of the beams came down, sprinkling sparks everywhere. When she thought her lungs would burst, and she would faint from the intense heat, Cynara gulped in a breath of fresh air. It cooled off her tortured lungs and cleared her reeling mind.

Still Bobby was dragging Merlin across the ground, as far away from the fire as possible. Cynara's heart tightened with despair as she heard the horses' screams escalate. She couldn't stand the thought of Swallow perishing in the flames.

Coughing wildly, she dropped Merlin's legs and ran back inside. The stables were now completely filled with smoke, and flames roared above her and around her. Instinctively, she moved toward the boxes where the horses' wheezing could be heard. Burning her hands terribly, she pulled the bolt on the first box, and Merlin's stallion leapt at her in panic. She staggered aside just in time to prevent being trampled. Her mare was silent now, and Cynara wondered if she had come too late. Her lungs were searing with pain, and only the fear of the fire made her pull aside the gate to Swallow's box. The mare came out, stumbling drunkenly toward the door opening. She seemed disoriented, and Cynara slapped her over the rump several times before the mare found her way out. With a heartbreaking whinny, the horse bolted for freedom.

Cynara could barely move, only slowly dragging herself toward the exit. Fire crackled and roared, intent on swallowing her. If she didn't get another breath, she would die, she knew that. Crawling, she made herself move forward. The air was slightly cooler against the hard earth floor, but she couldn't breathe. Unable to give up now, she pushed herself another inch forward, then another.

Groans, and another crash came from behind as more timbers collapsed.

Cynara had to give up, but just as she crumpled in a heap on the floor, someone dragged her outside and held her upright. She vaguely recognized Bobby's fiery mop of hair as his arms encircled her and squeezed her abdomen, forcing her to expel a breath. She had never tasted anything as delicious as when fresh, cool air streamed into her seared lungs at last. Sputtering and coughing, she kneeled on the ground, head hanging, breathing ever deeper breaths until she could find a measure of relief.

Her burned hands pounding in agony, she crawled on her elbows to Merlin's side as the building behind her gave a immense groan. The crash reverberated throughout the night as the roof beams collapsed in an enormous shower of sparks.

Gritty-eyed and utterly exhausted, Cynara looked at Merlin's sooty face so close to her own. "Is he dead?" she croaked as Bobby kneeled beside her.

"No, but he needs attention. I shall fetch the doctor."

Voices crowded in from all sides. Cynara had no idea how long the servants had been there. Everywhere people milled around, carrying buckets of water. When the beams crashed, they stopped. The stables would be a complete loss.

Dully, she stared at Merlin, shaking his shoulder. She had no more strength than a kitten. People pressed around her, and she recognized her mother's shrill voice and Tildy's. Something cool was held against her face, and she closed her eyes in gratitude. Pain kept shooting through her head and up her arms, and every breath was painful.

"There, there, my pet," came Estelle's tear-filled voice in her ear. "How could you go into the burning building, daughter? You could have died. *Died!*"

"Merlin?" Cynara croaked, and fell down beside him. She didn't have the strength to remain on her knees any longer. "Swallow?" she whispered, then a swirling mass of darkness closed in on her.

When Cynara awakened again, it was already late morning. Every inch of her seemed to be on fire, and she doubted that she had really escaped the raging inferno in the stables. Immovable in bed, she relived every terrifying moment of the previous evening. What had happened to Merlin?

Her eyes flew wide in worry, and she was instantly aware of her mother's concerned face. The older woman looked pale, her lips drooping. "You're awake at last," Estelle said, placing a cool hand on Cynara's forehead. "It's a miracle that you're still alive. The doctor said you were extremely foolish."

"Merlin?" was the only word Cynara could manage to press forth.

Estelle spoke grudgingly. "He'll survive. His voice isn't any better than yours, but at least he has no burns on his hands. He came away from the ordeal with a bump on his head and a raspy voice." She sighed. "Not that I understand what he was doing in the burning stables."

Cynara knew it hadn't been his choice, but she didn't say anything. She was so tired. Her hands throbbed dully, and she viewed the white bandages covering them in dismay.

"Aye, you should look dismayed. The skin was burned off your palms, and we had an awful time cleaning the soot from the wounds. Thank God, Mrs. Black is somewhat of a healing woman, and she had an herbal ointment that we could spread on your hands."

Cynara nodded, wondering if she would ever find strength to stand on her legs again. She closed her eyes and drifted off, only to wake some hours later with a burning thirst. Tildy was keeping vigil now, and Cynara noticed the late afternoon sunlight gilding the walls.

"How are ye?" Tildy held up Cynara's head and propped her up on a heap of pillows. "Here. Drink this." She held a glass of cool lemonade against Cynara's lips, and Cynara discovered that she could drink quite easily. The liquid soothed her aching throat.

"Ye look better, Mistress Cy, but ye have a slight fever. Not that I'm surprised after the ordeal ye went through. Everyone is talkin' 'bout yer daring, savin' the master an' all. Ye must be very fond o' him to have bothered," she added with a chuckle.

Cynara smiled grimly. "I would have done the same if it had been *you,*" she whispered. It hurt to speak, so she had to stop.

"I'm flattered," Tildy said with a twinkle. She held out a vase of wild roses that she'd picked and let Cynara smell the intoxicating sweetness. "This is very different than the stench o' fire." She set the vase on the table by the bed.

"How is Bobby?" Cynara managed to ask.

"Got away wi' a few bruises is all. A sprightly young lad wi' his head where it should be—on top of things. He said the horses bolted all the way to th' Gairlock Woods. But they are unhurt except for a few burns."

Cynara closed her eyes again, as if her eyelids were

too heavy to keep open. "How's Merlin?" she asked at last.

"Improved, but still in bed. He had a nasty bruise on his head, but he isn't talkin' about it. He won't tell anyone who gave him a whack on th' head, but that lump tells me that someun' did. He has no idea who set fire to th' stables, but flatly refuses to accept that it might have been an accident."

He doesn't want the servants to worry, Cynara thought. "I would like to . . . see him," she croaked.

Tildy wagged her fingers. "So ye shall, when ye're well enough to get up."

Cynara went back to sleep after drinking some broth. She couldn't stand anything warm on her tongue, so Tildy chilled everything she ate or drank. She woke several times during the night, always finding Tildy or her mother at her bedside. It rained outside, great sheets of water swishing against the windows. She was in pain, but she bravely pushed her thoughts to other things, always finding that she was too exhausted to stay awake any duration of time.

Two days later her wounds weren't quite as painful, and Mrs. Black, who rebandaged her hands every morning, assured her the burns were healing nicely. Cynara sat up in bed, watching the cook wind the wide white strips around her hands. Her voice had gotten steadily better, and her throat wasn't as sore as it had once been.

"Your son was a hero that night," she explained to Mrs. Black. "If it hadn't been for him, I would have been dead now."

"He told me you'd ridden back to Black Raven in a haste after seeing the master on the path. Bobby's horse stumbled over a root and sprained her fetlock. He had to leave her tethered to a tree and return to the estate on foot."

"It was fortunate, or he might have been trapped in the stables, since he works there." Cynara voice trembled slightly. "I owe him my life."

"And the master owes you his." Mrs. Black patted the bandages. "You'll need help to eat for a while until these burns are completely healed."

"It makes me feel so helpless."

Mrs. Black held a glass of water to Cynara's lips. "It'll make you appreciate your hands even more."

The next day Cynara was too restless to stay in bed. Estelle entered to feed her the breakfast that Tildy had carried up earlier. "Have you heard anything from Brandon, Mother?" Cynara asked instantly, and sat down by the table in front of the windows.

Estelle nodded. "When he heard what had happened, he rode over here in the dead of night and came into my room. I've never had a worse shock. He put his hand over my mouth to prevent me from screaming, which in this instance was the right thing to do. I was prepared to call every servant in the castle with my wail."

"If I'm not mistaken, my brother is growing restless," Cynara said.

Estelle agreed to that. *"D'accord.* He will do something stupid, you mark my words."

Cynara chewed a piece of toast. "Has he found out who stole the jewelry?"

"No, he's working on something that Merlin asked him to do. What, I don't know. Brandon doesn't confide in me like he used to. However, he returned to Stormywood before dawn."

Cynara fidgeted in her seat, chafing against the constraints of her debilitation. "I must speak with him, or Merlin."

They hadn't heard the door opening. "You want to speak with me, dear wife?" came Merlin's scratchy voice from the opposite end of the room.

Cynara flinched in surprise. She had never dreamed her reaction would be that strong when she saw him again. Her heart raced out of control, and she blushed to the roots of her hair.

Estelle cleared her throat. "I will go to my room. Send Tildy if you need me, Cynara."

As Cynara could not take her eyes away from Merlin's bruised face, Estelle left the room and closed the door softly behind her.

Cynara rose, clutching the edge of the table. "You . . . you look terrible," she said. And he really did with a bruise spreading from the hairline to his cheek, eyebrows singed, and hair much shorter than usual.

He smiled wryly. "Gideon Swift isn't very handy with his scissors. They slipped in his hand and he ended cutting off most of my hair."

Cynara's hand flew to her own face, knowing it didn't look much better than his. "I . . . you shouldn't see me like this."

He strolled closer, bearing as proud and assured as ever. His eyes were soft as he gazed down on her face. "You always look enchanting, no matter what." He'd had his hands behind his back, and now he pulled the left hand forward with a single rose. "I'm afraid there aren't many roses left in the rose garden, but this one is perfection, just like you."

She lowered her gaze then, her blush deepening. There was no use denying it, he was laying bare her heart with his kindness. "Thank you," she whispered, accepting the rose with her clumsy, bandaged hand. She buried her nose in its fragrant petals.

He took her shoulders, forcing her to look at him.

"If it weren't for you, I would be dead," he said hoarsely, and to Cynara's surprise, tears glittered in his eyes. "You endangered your own life to rescue me. No man—except perhaps Max—would have been that brave."

She didn't resist when he pulled her into his embrace. Her face flattened against his white crisp shirt, and she murmured, "I had no other choice. I could not stand by and watch you die in the flames. I was worried sick."

"Does that mean that you . . . er, love me . . . just a little?" His words were so soft, she could barely make them out.

"I think I do . . . I wish I could tell you for sure." She touched the area of her heart. "I know I would have missed you terribly if you'd died in that fire." Embarrassed, she lowered her gaze but didn't move away from his embrace. Perhaps she loved him, if the tightening in her chest and a racing heartbeat every time she saw him was any indication. Yes . . . no. She didn't know him well enough. She couldn't bear the thought that she might one day be a fool if it turned out that Merlin had murdered his father.

"Oh, darling Cynara, there's no haste." His arms tensed around her. "But I had so hoped . . ."

"I'm confused," she said, pushing away. "I still don't know for certain if you're a murderer or not, Merlin." She gave him a penetrating stare. "I *like* you so much, and respect you, but love—? I don't see how I can give you all of me while you're suspected of murder." She didn't add that her heart didn't care about legal matters. It went its own way, and now it was reaching out blindly toward the proud man in front of her. Tears burned on the inside of her eyelids. She wanted desperately to follow its lead, to trust, but . . .

He changed the subject, turned brisk and matter-of-fact. "Did you see anyone at the stables when you returned from your ride?"

She shook her head. "After I saw you, someone came and knocked me down. I woke up in the rose garden."

He looked aghast. "Not in one of the—er, holes?"

"No. Close to the gate. The man—or woman—who hit me wore a cloak. I remember that it swept against my face before I fainted."

"Why kill me and not you?" Merlin said, rubbing his chin. "Someone was trying to get rid of me in a fire that might look like an accident."

"But who? The servants?" Cynara frowned, as puzzled as ever. There was no logical explanation to the strange occurrences at Black Raven.

"No . . . why would they have to *kill* me to make my life miserable?" he commented in an effort at joking. "All they would have to do to rid themselves of me is to ignore their jobs—like most of them do already— and I would pack and move back to Stormywood. I like things tidy and in good repair." A muscle worked in his jaw, and his eyes blazed. "But they don't know how stubborn I can be."

Cynara smiled at that. "I admire your determination." She pointed at her breakfast tray. "Would you like some tea? Mother didn't touch hers."

He settled at her table, and somehow the scene looked so right, Cynara thought as she joined him. She sat down and waited as he filled his cup with hot tea from the pot, then refilled hers. She would have liked to serve him, but her hands were still too painful to take much pressure. As she watched him stir sugar in his tea, she said, "Tell me, what were you doing in Gairlock Woods? You rode as if followed by the devil himself."

"I went over to Stormywood with some papers concerning my father's death," he said, once again more subdued. "Brandon insisted on seeing them. Looks like he's bent on helping me clear my name. He's working on some ideas he had about finding Father's missing driver."

Warmth flooded Cynara's heart. "Brand always had a strong sense of loyalty. He wants to repay your kindness toward him, but what can he do? He has to remain in hiding until the matter of the necklace is resolved."

Merlin shrugged. "I will help him. Since I still am a free man—however long that may last if they don't find the real killer—I must make the most of it."

"What are you going to do?" Cynara sipped her tea and studied him intently.

"I shall visit the lady to whom the necklace belonged, Lady Fidalia. It will be interesting to hear how she got hold of your mother's family heirlooms."

Cynara thought hard. "I know it sounds preposterous, but do you think all these events are linked together, your father's death, the theft, the destruction of Black Raven?"

He furrowed his brow. "It doesn't seem to fit at all, but Black Raven has always been tied to the Seymours, and Estelle has always been close to the family even if she married a Hawthorne."

"It gets more confusing every day." Cynara sighed. "What's next for us, I wonder. Will the villain burn Black Raven next? I'm frightened."

Merlin moved to her side of the table and, kneeling, placed his arm around her shoulders. "I have ordered the men to patrol the grounds at all hours. They are armed with muskets and pistols. No stranger will be allowed in the castle without my approval."

His words soothed her, and she knew she could trust him to protect her. *She could trust him with her life.* She gasped as that realization struck her like a blow. It wasn't possible that he'd done away with his own father. . . . She gazed at him with new clarity. She read the concern in his eyes, and knew then that he could not be a murderer. He cared too much about life. It was as if the suspicion that had poisoned her mind had fallen away and let her see the truth.

"Oh, Merlin . . ." she whispered, leaning into him. An urge to say something about it came over her, but before she could open her mouth to speak, his lips captured hers. Swept away by urgency, they embraced. Merlin rose, pulling her with him. Every part of her pressed against him, her thin wrap only a flimsy barrier against the body that she had come to love. His strength seeped into her through his paisley-patterned dressing gown, and one fingertip that had escaped the burns followed the contours of his back through the slippery satin. Every ridge of muscle, every inch of supple skin, his every movement, had grown dear to her.

"Darling," he whispered against her hair. "If you had perished in the flames, I would not have been able to go on." He lifted her into his arms and carried her to the bed.

She wanted to warn him that someone might arrive and catch them in this intimate embrace, but no words came across her lips. She wanted him as badly as he wanted her. His breath came fast against her neck, then he raised his face to her, gazing deeply into her eyes. So much love glowed within his dark gaze that she was once again embarrassed. How could her feelings ever match his? And still . . . an exquisite warm sensation filled her to every inch.

"I love you," he whispered before claiming her mouth. The kiss deepened until her senses whirled, floating free, liberating her from any caution. She eagerly untied the sash holding his dressing gown together and slid her arms around his naked body. His hand was already caressing the inside of her leg, moving aside any lacy material that stood in his way. His touch was tender yet arousing, demanding, the higher up he moved. Just as she thought he would touch the place that had begun its sweet throb between her legs, he stopped. She wanted to cry out with frustration, but instead, she watched hypnotically as he untied her wrap at the neck and parted it to reveal her breasts. His gaze darkened even more as he viewed her nakedness. Heat brushed through her, and she felt strangely exposed and vulnerable.

"You are so lovely, my dainty porcelain figurine," he said with a chuckle. His hands were hot on her flesh, and she pressed against him, wanting more.

He could not get enough of her, no matter how many times he viewed her delicate shape, her rounded breasts. He took one rosy nipple in his mouth and sucked gently. A fierce bittersweet longing swept through him. It was bitter because it desperately needed quenching, but the mingling sweetness wanted to prolong the rapture as long as possible. He bunched up her gown and gently parted her legs. The wetness gave her longing away, and he knew she was striving as hard as he was to find release. Happiness soared through him as he knew he could give it to her.

"I want you," she whispered. "Please don't wait, please . . . now!" Her eyes, dark pools of pleasure, flew wide as he pushed himself into her, gently as first, then pounded relentlessly until she moaned and arched against him.

"Merlin . . ." she cried out breathlessly as a swift release came to her, then another. She was swimming through wave after wave, and she had never known such completeness, such wonder. Such force took her as he held up her hips and, standing on his knees among the tangled sheets, pushed into her with such a frenzy that she thought she had become an integral part of him. When he let out a long groan of rapture, she knew she belonged wholly to him.

They hugged each other desperately, as if this were

the last embrace ever, and every kiss exchanged was honey-sweet and lingering. Peace arrived at last, a full, glowing sort of peace.

Cynara drifted into sleep, Merlin's arm a welcome weight over her stomach. She would like to go to sleep next to him every night.

She had no idea how long they'd slept, perhaps only a few minutes, when she awakened to his moans. He was tossing in bed, his face pulled into a dark frown, as if he were in terrible pain. Perspiration glistened on his skin, and his hair was plastered to his forehead as if he'd been involved in intense labor.

She hoisted herself up on her elbow and poked him gently with her bandaged hand. "Merlin!" When he didn't awaken, she called louder. "Merlin, wake up."

"Wha—where am I?" he croaked, and his eyes were dark with anguish as he tried to focus on her.

Cynara wondered what he was seeing in his mind. "You're having nightmares."

He jerked upright, shoving her away, then slumped on the edge of the mattress. He dragged his hands tiredly through his hair. "Damn, and double damn!" he swore under his breath.

"What did you dream?" she asked, stroking his back with her unhurt fingertip. "Tell me."

"The war was a terror that returns to me like a sucking black . . . vortex. If I'm pulled into its middle, I fear I will never get out again. I'll be filled . . . with madness." He sounded more tortured with every word, and Cynara got up on her knees to embrace him and hold him tight. She leaned her head against his.

"Don't worry, the dreams will go away with time."

"I . . . see them walking in a row, all those dead

French soldiers. Thousands of them. Instead of faces, they have skulls. They stare . . . at me accusingly," he went on, every word evidently a small torment.

"Yes, tell me more," she urged. "Tell me everything."

His shoulders that had been tense as wooden boards relaxed slightly, and he leaned into her, seeking her strength. "In the middle of that vortex is hell, continuous cannonades, blinding orange light from explosions. I'm deafened, I'm frightened stiff. No one is going to save me from there. Black smoke, soot, mud, blood. It's war . . . forever."

"You won't fall into that hole. It's only in your imagination. It isn't real."

He seemed to snap out of his somnolent state of mind and stared at her. "These are real memories, Cynara. For years I saw nothing but death and destruction. I was part of it all. It hurts to know that I'm capable of killing someone."

"Killing?" She instantly thought about Ross Seymour, but she pushed that thought away.

"You become an animal, without compassion and reason. The only instinct left is survival." He sighed and wiped the perspiration from his face. "It's difficult to live afterward. You've visited hell, and always struggle to leave it—ever after."

She kissed his cheek and pulled him down beside her in bed. "Let's rest some more. I believe the dreams will cease in time. You will push those memories into a sealed compartment."

He nodded slowly. "I look toward the living, and that strengthens me. Life goes on, thank God. You're helping me to heal, Cynara. The love I feel for you is slowly pushing away the dark memories."

He seemed slightly frantic, as if his world had just been shattered into tiny fragments. Obviously, he had difficulty putting it back together. He nuzzled her throat as if sensing her worry. "I'll be myself in a moment."

They lay silent, and within minutes Merlin had fallen asleep. Cynara lay awake, staring at the ceiling. Not only did Merlin have the ever-mounting problems of an invisible enemy, but he had the terror of the war that was still going on inside him even if it ended one year ago.

He slept deeply, and evidently without dreams, for an hour, then awakened as if nothing had happened. When he discovered her beside him, he proceeded to take advantage of the situation and seduce her.

Gone was the troubled man, and in his place emerged a happy, joking lover. As their ecstasy subsided, they came back to reality. The morning sunlight had made the room even brighter and sent golden rays to warm their bodies among the tangled sheets.

"My God," Merlin moaned. "I really needed that." He slapped her bare bottom lightly. "I'm king of the world now."

Cynara laughed. "You're smug, aren't you?"

Growling, Merlin drummed his chest with his fists as he stood on the floor by the bed and gazed down on her. "Successful mating makes any male proud," he said, then tweaked her nose. "You look delicious, darling, so delicious, in fact, that I would like to eat you."

She flapped her bandaged hands. "Help! I can't protect myself."

As he was ready to overcome her with a mock attack, a knock sounded on the door. He stiffened and whispered, "My God! What if it's Estelle?"

Cynara giggled, and managed to pull her rumpled nightgown and wrap together. She rose and smoothed down the folds as Merlin scrambled madly for his dressing gown. "I'm sorry that this interlude is over," he said in an exaggerated whisper as he tiptoed toward his room, "but I shall return someday and ravish you again."

Cynara could not suppress a laugh as he closed the door behind him.

Tildy stepped inside. She viewed Merlin's closed door, then Cynara's glowing cheeks. "I see that I should have timed my arrival better," she said with a cocky smile. She bustled about the room as Cynara guiltily patted down her disarrayed curls.

"Don't be impudent, Tildy. You may help me dress. I'm going downstairs today."

"I need t' speak with the master, but let th' blokes wait, I say."

Cynara viewed her maid. "What are you talking about?" Tildy kept her lips pinched together as she helped Cynara dress, then brush out her tangled hair. In record time they were finished, and then Merlin sauntered through his door, dressed in faultless linen, burgundy waistcoat, gray trousers that fit him snugly, and a superbly cut black coat.

"Ah! Good morning," he greeted Cynara as if it were the first time he'd set eyes on her that day.

"My lord Raven," Tildy began with a curtsy. "I'm sorry t' disturb ye, but there are two gentlemen from Lunnon downstairs insistin' on speakin' with ye." She made a face. "Police, if ye arsks me. They've been kickin' their heels in your study half an hour or more."

Merlin and Cynara exchanged apprehensive glances. *Brandon,* Cynara said to herself, and she knew the same thought was going through Merlin's mind.

Merlin swore under his breath and stalked out of the room. Tildy raised her eyebrows and glanced at Cynara. Then she shrugged her plump shoulders and followed Merlin out. Cynara had to know the men's errand, so she accompanied her maid down.

The strangers, the younger tall and slim, the older of medium height with a considerable paunch, were twirling their tall beaver hats in their hands while staring in awe at the portraits lining the walls of the study.

"Good morning," the rotund man said. He patted the thin strands of brown hair on his head. "I'm Sergeant Rigby Todd of Bow Street, and this is Constable Hoskins."

Bow Street Runners. The top police detectives in London, Cynara thought, terrified.

"How can I help you," Merlin asked coolly. Cynara admired his control.

"Lady Raven's brother, Brandon Hawthorne, while escorted to Surrey, escaped from his jailers. We have reason to believe that he had help from someone outside." Sergeant Todd's voice turned insinuating. "Perhaps from a *relative.*"

Merlin crossed his arms over his chest. "You must be out of your mind. Who would have helped Mr. Hawthorne?"

The two runners shifted uncomfortably. Mr. Todd's lips worked, and he was evidently boosting himself to speak the next words.

"Perhaps *you* were involved, Lord Raven. After all, you were in London at the time of Mr. Hawthorne's escape. Someone witnessed a man who looked remarkably like you, and a woman who looked like Lady Raven, on the scene of the escape."

Merlin didn't move a muscle. "I have no idea what you're talking about. Why are you here?"

Under bushy eyebrows, Mr. Todd's eyes were round and watery blue. Now they took on an indignant cast. "Why, to find Mr. Hawthorne, of course."

Chapter 18

"Well, he certainly isn't here," Merlin said at his haughtiest. "We haven't seen Mr. Hawthorne since he was incarcerated, but if you believe he stole the necklace from Lady Fidalia, you're sorely mistaken. Mr. Hawthorne is not a thief."

"Be that as it may," said Sergeant Todd, and twirled his hat more quickly. "Nevertheless, we will stay in the area, at the Duck and Willow in the village, until Mr. Hawthorne turns up. He's bound to pay his mother and sister a visit in the not too distant future."

Cynara's heart raced, and she worried that the men could read the guilt on her face. She averted her gaze, sensing that the tall Hoskins was staring at her most intently.

"Mr. Hawthorne's escape is an indication of his guilt. An innocent man would face the jury, milord."

Merlin's voice grew icy. "Is Mr. Hawthorne's escape the only reason you're here, Sergeant Todd?"

Twin spots of red flared on Todd's cheeks. "Well, seeing as there's a mystery surrounding Mr. Ross Seymour's death and that of your cousin, Felix Seymour, we thought we combine the investigations. You're connected to some strange goings-on, Lord Raven, and we shall get to the bottom of it—seeing as you might be a murderer."

Cynara thought Merlin would explode, but he only pinched his lips together. She admired his control.

"We're only doing our work, y'see, Lord Raven, and you cannot stop us." Sergeant Todd's eyes filled momentarily with triumph. "If you don't mind me saying so, I have a reputation for getting fast results to my investigations."

Suddenly Merlin's stiff shoulders relaxed and he forced out a smile. "Actually, you could not have come at a more opportune moment. Someone in the vicinity is bent on destroying this estate." He told them about the fire in the stables and the holes in the rose garden. "If you could give me some speedy results on that mystery, I will reward you with a handsome bonus."

The two runners preened, and Constable Hoskins's long, thin lips parted in a pale smile. His face had the look of a bloodhound with its cavernous cheeks and drooping eyelids. A man who didn't miss much, Cynara thought. Sergeant Todd was the talker, while Hoskins was perhaps the real brain behind the team.

"You must have a glass of ale in my study," Merlin went on. "I'm sure you will find the Duck and Willow comfortable, but you can spend as much time here as you want."

"We shall be staying at the inn, thank you," said the sergeant. "However, I hope you won't deny us the grounds around here. We must search for clues." He eyed Merlin speculatively. "In fact, we would like to start with questioning the servants, if you don't mind."

Merlin only nodded, but Cynara felt a frisson of fear. Thank God they hadn't brought Brand to Black Raven. But how safe would he be at Stormywood if the investigation moved that far? He would have to be warned somehow.

Accompanied by Merlin, the men departed. Cynara knew she would find no peace while they lingered at the castle. How long would she be able to shield Brandon? Never before had she been involved in anything illegal, and shielding an escaped prisoner was certainly unlawful. If she and Merlin were ever to free Brandon of all suspicion, time was of the essence.

Easily tired, she spent the rest of the day resting in her room. Anyway, she had no desire to go downstairs and view the destruction of the stables. Besides, the Bow Street Runners might be snooping around the grounds. She couldn't ride off to Stormywood in the middle of the day without an excuse.

At one point she glanced out one of her windows and noticed that Constable Hoskins was staring thoughtfully out at Lyme Bay. He was standing right above one of the coves, the one closest to the castle. A steep narrow path led down among the rocks to the half-moon-shaped stretch of beach below. Hardly anyone ever went down there because of the treacherous tide. One moment it was possible to walk across the coarse sand to the next cove, but at high tide everything was covered with water. Woe to anyone who was stranded at the next cove from there, since there was no path up onto the ridge. Entrapped by jagged cliffs, one would meet the raging sea. . . .

Cynara shivered and returned to her bed. She slept fitfully, and the following morning Merlin knocked on her door and asked if he could share breakfast with her.

She was pleased that he sought her company. After Tildy had brought a tray and they were comfortably stirring their coffee cups, Merlin said softly, "I had a terribly busy day yesterday, or I would have sought your company at night." Then he turned brisk. "After we spoke with the runners downstairs, I went down to the stables—or what was left of them—with Sergeant Todd."

"It must have been a terrifying sight."

Merlin nodded. "Yes, mostly charred timbers and crushed bricks. Even the trees around the building had been charred. Anyway, I wanted Todd to question Bobby, who confirmed that Muggins had left us for good. Bobby was down there, doing his best to clean up with the gardeners' help. It seems he's the only groom left at the stables. The rest have abandoned us—taking the spare horses."

"You dismissed one of them for rudeness, and perhaps they all took umbrage to that and left."

"A well-paying job at the castle? Hardly." A muscle worked in Merlin's jaw. "I don't like it one bit. There's something very strange going on."

After sipping coffee and taking a bite of her buttered toast, Cynara said, "Is this connected to the men who followed us to Basingstoke?"

Merlin rubbed his chin. "I don't know, but I suspect it is." He took a deep breath. "One of the reasons I came directly here this morning is to tell you that Lady Fidalia is a house guest at the Barton estate, the Hollows, on the north side of Modbury. You do know the Bartons? Lord Barton is a member of the House.''

"Yes, of course I know them, but not very well. Barton went to school with Father. We've been invited there before, but my parents never established a friendship with them."

Merlin chuckled. "Too disreputable? Barton is somewhat a gamester and a libertine. Evidently fit company for Lady Fidalia."

"Are you planning to visit?" Cynara finished her toast and coffee.

"Yes, this morning. Would you like to accompany me?" He finished the last of his coffee. "A social call merely, but if we by any chance can bring the conversation around to the *Hirondelle* necklace, so much the better."

A shiver of apprehension shot through Cynara. "I don't like this one bit, but I appreciate your efforts to help Brandon."

Merlin gave her a long, tender look. "He's your brother, lady wife. Anything connected to you is important to me. Besides, Brandon is doing a little errand for me." Merlin rose, stepping closer to her.

"What's that?" Brimming with curiosity, Cynara looked up at him.

"He's been very helpful. He has discovered the whereabouts of Father's driver. You know, the one who survived the accident and disappeared. The police have been searching for him in vain. I think he has a lot to tell us once we catch up with him."

"I hope you're right." She blushed as his face lit up.

"So you do really care," he whispered, and pulled her up from her chair. "I'm delighted. And now, the other reason I came to you this morning." He pulled her into his arms, holding her so close she could feel every part of his body.

Her heart fluttered wildly against her ribs. His presence never failed to excite her. She looked into his dark eyes as he lowered his head to kiss her. She read a mixture of tenderness and wistful longing in the obsidian depths. With a moan she closed her eyes and offered her mouth to him. He tasted of coffee and sweet raspberry jam. But he also tasted of excitement and passion as his tongue moved forcefully against hers. She wanted him. As long as she lived she would always want him. He never failed to arouse her deepest desire.

"Darling . . . shall we draw the curtains and go back to bed?" he asked her, pausing in the intimate kiss to gaze into her eyes.

"What if—?" She tried to move away, but he recaptured her lips. Despite her protests, he continued to wear down her resistance. She prayed that she hadn't judged wrong when she decided to trust him; she prayed that he was innocent, because she knew she was falling deeply in love with her handsome husband. She would be heartbroken if she found out that her intuition had been wrong, but for now she would have to trust wholly—or go mad.

"Come . . ." he whispered, clasping her hand. "I know you want this as much as I do."

She hesitated, still a little frightened of the powerful passion he evoked. "I don't know . . ."

Disbelief in his eye, he stared at her. "You know you want me. Tell me that you love me as much as I love you."

She resented the demand in his voice, and pulled back. "How high-handed! You cannot force me to do—or say—anything."

"*Force* you? You're lying, Cynara. Why deny our love?"

"I don't," she whispered. "I don't deny it, but I'm too worried about Brandon to loll in bed this morning. We have to *do* something, fast.

"You're right, darling. However much I want you for myself, I must put our problems first. He clasped her waist and pulled her with him. "Let's travel to the Bartons' house now, before I ravish you. Perhaps that will shed some light on Brandon's dilemma."

Her heart torn in two directions, Cynara wanted to stop him and confess her deep love, and let him "ravish" her. What was wrong with her? Some days she trusted him and loved him; other days were clouded with suspicion.

Her newfound love was a fragile thing that might shatter. Maybe he would tire of her if she didn't comply with his wishes. Merlin moved toward the stairs even as she slowed, deep in thought.

"Merlin!" she called out urgently. "I do—"

"Do hurry up, darling. We must take this opportunity to speak with Lady Fidalia."

Love . . . you, she whispered. She held out a pleading hand, but he was already halfway down the staircase. He waited for her at the bottom of the steps. Reaching out to her, he said, "Why are you dawdling?"

Cynara glanced at him, noticing his businesslike stance, and she lost her courage to confess her tender feelings. "I was merely woolgathering." She gave him her bandaged hand.

He held it lightly and kissed her cheek. "Come, let's dig into Lady Fidalia's secrets."

The Hollows, the Bartons' place, lay in a narrow valley surrounded by tall elms. Outcrops of rocks dotted the rolling hills that marched on each side of the estate, and the sloping sides were verdant, fertile fields. The tall grass swayed gently in the breeze, and birds sang in the trees as the Black Raven coach passed on the lane.

"Lovely, isn't it?" Merlin said as the carriage swung onto the poplar-lined drive. "This time of year is the best."

Cynara nodded. "It's so different from Black Raven with its dark rocks and raging sea."

"Would you rather live here?"

She shook her head. "No . . . Black Raven is like a ferocious beast. There's a certain beauty in that wind-beaten castle."

"I'm glad you like it. I've always loved Black Raven, but never thought I would be master there."

Do you love it enough to kill? Did you somehow plan Felix's death? Those thoughts came unbidden to her mind, but she suppressed her traitorous suspicion angrily. Though she would trust him with her life, those were questions she wanted explained if ever the cloud hanging over the Seymour name—and their love—was to lift.

"Here we are, then," he said as the carriage pulled up by the front steps. He alighted and helped Cynara down. She was wearing charcoal-gray taffeta with a matching pelisse in deference to Felix's demise, but she wished she could have worn a lighter dress in the summer sun. Fluttering her fan and adjusting her simple gray pokebonnet, she entered the cool hallway as a footman held the door for her. The butler was striding toward them.

"Lord and Lady Raven," he greeted them.

"Good morning, Godfrey. Please announce us," Merlin said pleasantly.

The butler led them to a salon that was predominantly decorated in gray and yellow tones. Two landscapes hung on the walls, the ornate gilded frames overpowering the paintings. The gray and yellow striped sofa looked inviting, and Cynara sat down. Lady Barton arrived ten minutes later. She was a tiny, birdlike woman with brown curly hair and clear gray eyes. Due to her slim, youthful figure, she looked much younger than her years. Full of questions, her gaze flickered from Cynara to Merlin.

"Lord and Lady Raven. A surprise indeed, but welcome to the Hollows." Her eyebrows shot up as Merlin spoke.

"I know my sordid reputation has prevented any social calls to Black Raven by the local gentry, but you must not judge my wife harshly, Lady Barton."

The lady fluttered her hands in indecision and sat down beside Cynara. Merlin took a chair on the other side of the table and watched them silently.

Lady Barton held Cynara's hands between her own. "You're always welcome here, child. One day soon I must travel to Black Raven and see the ongoing refurbishments. I've heard about them, of course, since no secrets are kept in this part of the world."

Cynara smiled. "We've only just started. The whole

castle needs an overhaul. However, there have been events that have prevented the renovations." Cynara pointed at her bandages.

"Oh, yes, my dear, I heard about the fire. How ghastly it must have been for you."

"It was, more than you can imagine." Cynara looked at Merlin's battered face, but he made no expression. She continued. "In fact, we came here to see one of your house guests on a matter of some urgency. I'm alluding to Lady Fidalia. Is she still here?"

"Oh, yes, but I think she's getting ready for a ride. I shall ask her to come down though." Lady Barton went out, and returned five minutes later with Lady Fidalia. "I shall leave you to your business," Lady Barton said to Merlin, "but I do hope you will stay for lunch."

Standing, Merlin bowed. "Thank you, but it would be more convenient at another time."

"Of course." Lady Barton smiled at Cynara. "I'm delighted that you could come, child." After making the introductions, she left the room, and Cynara was aware only of the majestic woman who had accused Brand of stealing her jewelry. Lady Fidalia was almost as tall as Merlin. She had a buxom figure, her full breasts straining against the scarlet riding jacket that hugged her torso. Her face was dominated by a hooked nose, and her heavy coils of black hair was braided and tucked under a curly-brimmed hat with a swaying red plume.

"Have we met before?" she asked haughtily, and slapped the leather crop against the heavy material of her black skirt.

"No . . . I don't think so, unless we attended the

same functions in London," Merlin said pleasantly. "Please sit down. We have a small matter to discuss with you."

Lady Fidalia sat down on a hard-backed chair, sweeping her skirt around her. "What can I do for you?"

Merlin sat also, staring at her intently as he said, "Lady Raven's brother is Brandon Hawthorne. An acquaintance of yours, I believe?"

Lady Fidalia's eyes narrowed suspiciously. "I've played cards once or twice with him, and, no offense intended, he's a mediocre gambler." She turned her haughty stare at Cynara. "Your brother—as you must know—is a rather wild young man."

Cynara bristled at such outspokenness, but she remained silent.

"It appears that Mr. Hawthorne—according to you—is more than a gambler. A thief, in fact," Merlin went on. His voice brooked no nonsense, and Lady Fidalia moved slightly on her chair and shifted her gaze away from him.

"Mr. Hawthorne stole a very valuable necklace from me." She paused. "I thought Mr. Hawthorne was a charming young man—if a bit too wild. When he stooped to stealing, however . . ." She gave Merlin a cautious glance.

"How can you be so absolutely sure that he was the one who stole the necklace?"

Lady Fidalia laughed mirthlessly. "Surely, the sole fact that it was found in his pocket is incriminating enough."

Merlin went on relentlessly. "How do you know where it was found?"

The lady's eyes widened in disbelief. "From the authorities, of course!"

Merlin silenced, rubbing his chin. Cynara sensed that Lady Fidalia would not give away more than she had to. A gambler at heart who knew how to keep control of her expressions. Now she only looked slightly bemused. "How exactly did you lose it, Lady Fidalia?"

"It disappeared from my jewelry case at the Suttons, where I was a house guest. Their estate is located in Kingston, if you must know. Your brother was seen coming out of my bedchamber while I was in the middle of a card game downstairs."

"I see. While in prison, my brother described the necklace once to me. Mrs. Hawthorne, my mother, recognized it as one of her French family heirlooms. The necklace, *l' Hirondelle,* was given to her great-grandfather by Louis XIV. Could you please tell us how you came to be the owner of an heirloom like that?"

"I won it . . . at a card game." She slapped her crop once against her thigh, and her face reddened with indignation. "No crime, surely? Besides, I don't understand why you have to interrogate me when it is I who has been wronged." She gave Cynara a hard glance. "I understand your concern about your brother, but that doesn't change the fact that he committed a crime."

"Did you win the necklace from a Frenchman?" Cynara continued.

Lady Fidalia shook her head, her lips pinched shut in mutiny. She rose, straightening her skirts. "Now, if you please, I have another engagement—with my horse."

Merlin rose and bowed. "Of course. I only wish you would divulge from whom you won the necklace. It's important to Mrs. Hawthorne to discover who confiscated the family heirloom. It rightfully belongs to her, not to English . . . er, gamblers."

Lady Fidalia thrust up her chin. "I have no idea what road the necklace traveled before it ended up on the gambling tables. It probably changed many hands on the way. I would have liked to keep it." She fingered her throat absentmindedly. "With its great value, it would be very helpful now . . ." She changed subject abruptly. "I heard that Mr. Hawthorne escaped. Once he is captured and tried, Lady Raven, Bow Street will return the diamonds to me. And it is about time!" Without another word she turned on her heel and left the room, slamming the door.

Merlin and Cynara exchanged exasperated glances.

"Did you get the impression that she *needed* the necklace?" Cynara asked.

Merlin nodded. "Like most gamblers, she's probably rich one day and poor the next. Perhaps she has a debt to pay, and would need the necklace to cover it."

"Is she all alone in the world?"

"She's a widow, and ever since her husband, who was thirty years her senior, died, she has moved with the fast set in London."

The butler ushered them outside, and as Cynara shaded her eyes against the sun that beat against the façade of the mansion, she saw Lady Fidalia's scarlet coat sway like an exotic flower along the path to the stables. The lady's stride was angry, and the crop swung back and forth in her hand. Cynara wished she'd discovered something of interest during the interview, but the result had been disappointing. Sighing, she let Merlin hand her into the carriage.

They traveled through the countryside toward Black Raven. The sun streaked every tree and grass with gold, and wildflowers dotted the ditches with blue, red, and yellow. The scent of sun-drenched earth filled the coach as the lane wound around a newly plowed field.

"While riding through this idyll, it's difficult to believe that strange things ever happen at Black Raven," Cynara said dreamily. "I wish it would always be like this."

Merlin's dark eyes softened, and he leaned closer to her on the seat and touched her cheek. "You deserve better than a forced marriage and the horrors at Black Raven."

She glanced shyly at him. "Mother says I'm very like my father. The best part I inherited from him is his loyalty. He could have died for his family."

His fingers traced her face and curled into her hair. "Would you die for yours, then? Would you die for me?" He murmured the words in her ear, and she found it difficult to breathe. His touch always obliterated her reason, and she squirmed in her seat. "I don't . . . know. However, I would always want to protect the Seymour name, and you carry that name. And I've always loved Black Raven."

"Just as Black Raven tries to break us, it also ties us together. It's strange that an old castle has such an influence on its inhabitants." He pressed his lips gently against hers, and white-hot desire flared through her. She wished now that she would dare to tell him how much she'd grown to love him, but she felt shy under his probing stare. She returned his kiss, a kiss that was making her warm and vibrant all over. The thought that he'd gone to this length—interviewing Lady Fidalia to save her brother—made tenderness flow sweetly through her. Merlin was a better man than she had ever dreamed.

He was smiling when he lifted his face to look at her. "I knew I had found the most glorious wife possible the night I wedded you." He chuckled teasingly. "I don't think you agreed with me at the time, but now . . . ?"

She pushed him lightly in the chest. "When I hear that arrogant overtone, I'm determined to deny any feeling but physical attraction between us."

The carriage pulled onto the shady lane that skirted Gairlock Woods. Right at that spot the valley spread out like a glittering jewel at their feet, and Cynara impulsively asked the driver to halt. Her heart racing, she needed to get away from Merlin's presence to compose herself. Could she tell him about her feelings, or would he only tease her? At this point she couldn't take any chiding on his part, not when it concerned her most tender secret. Once the truth came out, she would be at his mercy.

She fanned herself as she stood at the edge of the trees, staring at the valley. "It's so lovely," she said as she found that Merlin had joined her.

"Yes. There isn't a lovelier place on earth. I know that under the hills lie rich veins of copper, and perhaps tin. Ore will be the salvation of Black Raven. Just as soon as we've discovered who wants to ruin the Seymours, I'll start prospecting."

"I admire your determination," Cynara said. She

looked down the long, curling ribbon of sandy lane behind her, and saw movement on the side of the road, a horse and rider. She wondered if someone was trying to catch up with them from the Hollows. The rider seemed to be in a hurry, as the horse kicked up great billows of dust.

The coach was shielded by the trees, so the rider could not know their presence.

"Look, Merlin. Who's that?"

They stared in silence until the red riding jacket was clearly visible a quarter of a mile down the road.

"By thunder, it's Lady Fidalia!" Merlin said. "Did she forget to tell us something, I wonder."

They waited for her arrival, but to their surprise she stopped abruptly beside the road. The mount, a high-spirited gray, danced around, but the lady had no difficulty controlling the animal. Her head turned toward the woods. She called out, but Merlin and Cynara could not make out the words. Surprised, they watched two men coming out from the trees. Both of them were swathed in cloaks, and beaver hats concealed their faces. But there was no mistaking the bent old form of the village madman, Jean.

"It's the Frenchman!" Cynara exclaimed. "The one who threatened me outside the inn at the village of Black Raven."

Merlin swore under his breath and took a rapid step toward the group.

"Wait!" Cynara said. "Let's see what happens before you get involved."

Lady Fidalia seemed to argue with the taller man. When he lifted his hat and scratched his head, Cynara recognized the missing head groom at Black Raven, Mr. Muggins.

"Blast and confound!" Merlin had evidently recognized him as well. With an angry growl he set off toward the group at a run. They didn't notice him as Lady Fidalia slid off her horse and started pounding the taller man in the chest.

Merlin shouted at them as Muggins slapped the lady across the face and tossed her up in the saddle. He then slapped the rump of the great horse which pranced around until setting course for the Hollows. The men saw Merlin running down the lane, and they leapt through the thicket.

Cynara hurried after Merlin, but her long skirts hampered her movements. She saw him sprint across the ditch and follow the men in among the trees. When she arrived at the spot where he had disappeared, she had to stop, her heart pounding with fear. What if the two men ambushed Merlin and hurt him? She was certain now that they were linked to the mysteries at Black Raven, but she could not imagine how.

Angry and frustrated, she kicked a pebble on the lane, but the gesture didn't lessen the fear and anxiety inside. She walked up and down the road, once in a while glancing toward the Hollows to see if Lady Fidalia would return. The lane remained empty, but the driver had left the carriage and came hobbling toward her.

"Where's the master?" he asked, and Cynara shook her head, pointing toward the trees.

"I wish I knew. The forest is large, and it's easy to lose one's way."

"Not Master Merlin, milady. He knows every inch of these grounds."

His words didn't console her. "So do the other men."

"Who, milady?"

"Muggins and the Frenchman, Jean."

The coachman stared at her in surprise. "Muggins, milady? He's been gone for days, and his family says he's not coming back." His voice lowered. "Did you know he left a wife and a small son behind?"

"No . . . I didn't know!" Cynara wrung her hands in agitation. "No man in his right mind would leave a young family," she said.

"Muggins always had grand plans, milady."

They waited in silence, both looking toward the woods. Half an hour passed before Merlin returned, and by then Cynara was beside herself with worry. When he burst through the trees, twigs sticking untidily from his hair and his coat ripped in several places, she threw herself into his arms.

"I was so worried," she sobbed against him.

"Damned rascals!" he spat out angrily. His wrath disappeared and his eyes warmed as he looked into her tear-streaked face. He dabbed at her tears with the back of his hand. "It looks like you care a bit about me after all."

She hesitantly pulled away, remembering that the coachman was watching. "Did you find them?"

Merlin shook his head, his tenderness gone in a flash. "They must have had a hiding place nearby, because I would have outrun them if they'd stayed on the forest path." A muscle worked in his jaw, and Cynara noticed that he was struggling to control his anger. "Muggins has a lot to answer to once I track him down." He took her hand. "Come, let's go back to Black Raven. I want to send men out into the woods to search for Muggins and Jean."

"Perhaps we should tell the Bow Street Runners," Cynara suggested.

"We might, but remember that they suspect only me of a crime, not my stable groom."

"I'm frightened, Merlin. I sense danger is closing around us more every day."

He pulled her close, then lifted her into the carriage. "I will protect you with my life," he said.

And I shall protect you, Cynara thought.

Chapter 19

That night Cynara could not sleep. She tossed in her bed, staring at the shadows in the corners of her room as if they would move in and suffocate her if she dared to close her eyes. She was reassured by the thought that Merlin had sent men into Gairlock Woods to search for Muggins and Jean. Hopefully they would not return empty-handed, but what if they did? Would Muggins continue to torment the habitants of the castle? And why? What reason did he have for terrorizing the Seymours?

Fragmented thoughts swirled in her head, parting her further from sleep. She wished that Merlin was beside her in her bed, but he'd claimed exhaustion and gone up to his chamber early. She would have truly welcomed his presence, and she wished she'd told him so.

Suddenly she sat upright in bed, listening intently. A creaking sound reached her ears, like boots moving stealthily in the corridor outside. Her heart hammering, she waited breathlessly. Had she only imagined the noise? The old castle walls sometimes sighed and creaked as if inhabited by long-dead spirits. Cold drafts sometimes swept past without any evident reason. Cynara had never been afraid of ghosts, but tonight her scalp prickled.

She eased herself out of bed when the sound came again and went automatically toward the door that separated her room from Merlin's. To her relief, it opened on silent hinges. Despite the darkness, she more or less knew the location of all the furniture. Soundlessly, she made her way to the bed. She could hear Merlin breathe, and that soothed her fears. Gently, she shook his shoulder, but he was already rolling over and lifting his head.

"Cynara? I just woke up," he said.

"Thank God! Did you hear the footsteps outside?"

"No. Steps, you say?" He moved about in bed, and before long he'd lit a candle on the nightstand.

"Yes, I thought I heard someone walking outside my door." She viewed his rumpled hair, and the shadows under his eyes. He hadn't slept much. Suddenly she knew that he'd kept vigil, probably suspecting that an attack would come at night. Beside him on the mattress lay an unsheathed sword and two loaded pistols.

She gasped in surprise. "Your weapons . . . you don't trust the guards to keep watch," she said, staring at the weapons.

"You don't either, do you?" he retorted, getting out of bed. He was still dressed in dark breeches and a white shirt. "I shall investigate." He dragged on his boots, slid one of the pistols into his waistband, and hefted the sword. By the door he whispered. "You stay here."

She obeyed even though she feared for his safety. Yet, she knew she would only be in the way if it came to fighting. Easing into Merlin's bed, she waited for him to return. Tension made her body ache, and her eyes were gritty for the lack of sleep. Unblinkingly, she stared at the door. Everything was quiet outside, and she wondered if the sounds had been generated in her imagination.

Her fears mounted as time trickled by without any sign of Merlin. Finally, she got up, tiptoed to the door, and put her ear against it. She heard nothing, not even the usual sounds of the castle.

Biting her lip in concentration, she eased the door open, praying it wouldn't creak. Tendrils of cold air floated along the floor, chilling her feet. She peered into the corridor, but saw nothing except a candle glowing in one of the wall sconces. Silence pressed down on her, and she sensed evil all around her, but that must be pure imagination. Despite the strange goings-on, Black Raven had never given her anything but feelings of belonging and comfort.

"Merlin?" she whispered. The faint sound echoed hollowly along the dim corridor, but he did not appear. She had gone out of the room and taken some uncertain steps along the flagstones, when he finally returned. He motioned her to go back inside, and she obeyed. The bedroom was much warmer, but she still shivered in her thin nightgown. He closed and locked the door and put his weapons on the chest of drawers that also held his hairbrush and a stack of starched neckcloths.

"No sign of anything strange," he said, and kicked off his boots. "I took a tour of the castle, and the guards are all alert. No one has seen anything untoward."

"I'm sorry," she said. "I was sure I heard something."

He held her shoulders, his hands warm and reassuring. "I don't blame you for being on edge. Everyone is at this point. I looked in on your mother, and Tildy was still awake. She looked exhausted, so I told her to go up to her room in the servants quarters. Then I placed a guard outside Estelle's room."

Cynara curled her arms around his waist and pressed herself against him. Her hands were still painful, but she didn't care. She only wished she could have touched him without bandages. "You're the kindest, most thoughtful man I've ever met," she whispered, and knew that she really meant it. "A lesser man would have railed and ranted at me for disturbing his sleep."

He held her tightly, his breath escalating against her hair. "Are you not going to fight me any longer?" he asked softly. "Fight my love?"

She shook her head. "No, for once I'm not going to fight."

He chuckled then, and slid his hands the entire length of her back. The erotic caress sent flares of desire to every part of her body. Shyly, she lifted her face to his, and saw his eyes glittering in the candlelight. The tenderness found a response within her, and she thought her heart would break with the sweetness of her love.

Moaning, she clung to him, and he kissed her fiercely. Molten desire coursed through her as his tongue mated with hers, and she pushed her hips against him.

He gave a groan, and as he slid the lacy material of her nightgown from her shoulders, she could feel the stiff proof of his desire against her. An urgent need to tear away everything that separated them overcame her, and she fumbled with his shirt. He smiled as she struggled unsuccessfully, and pushed her gently aside. Deftly, he discarded his shirt and his breeches, and stood before her as splendid as God had created him. She ran her hands over his chest, reveling in the tautness of his muscles and his evident strength.

"My darling," he whispered, and slid down her nightgown over her hips. It tumbled to the floor, and she stepped out of it. Nakedness meeting nakedness was almost too much for her senses, and when Merlin lifted her up and carried her to the bed, Cynara sighed with pleasure.

"Yes, oh, yes," she said, digging her bandaged fingers into his massive shoulders.

He eased her down on the mattress and stretched out beside her. Cradling one full breast in his hand, he leaned over her and trailed kisses along her throat, over the soft flesh of her breast to the turgid nipple. It throbbed as his tongue flicked over it repeatedly, and Cynara's heartbeat accelerated until she thought she would explode if he didn't stop the delicious torment of her senses soon.

"Merlin . . ." she urged, but his tongue only traveled farther down, flicking across her stomach and down on her thighs. When he spread her legs, she gasped because she knew what was about to happen. Shivers of excitement coursed through her as he gently kissed her, and as his caresses grew more heated and his muscles tightened in an ever-mounting passion, she pulled him up, twining her legs around him as his shaft thrust into her slick softness. Their union was the culmination of all her longings, a moment of exquisite understanding between her and Merlin. For once she was free of her prejudice and could meet him without reservation.

Merlin strained against the ecstasy that threatened to explode within him. All he could think of was her softness, her yielding body pressed so tightly against his, he thought he could step right into her and become her. Her enchantment flowed straight into him, and it heightened the pleasure more with every move as he brought them both to the pinnacles of bliss. Cynara had become tuned to him, and this time—this time . . . he groaned as he exploded in a mind-shattering release . . . this time there were no barriers between them. Effortlessly, they flowed into each other as if bodies mattered no more, only the soaring love between them.

Cynara cried out over and over as the wave crested, sweeping her into an overwhelming pleasure that went on and on. "I love you," she whispered against his mouth as the pounding of her heart slowly subsided, and his tight hold on her eased gradually. "I love you so much, Merlin."

Silence brought peace into the room, and all that mattered was the revelation of their love, the celebration that at last they had truly united as they should have before the chaplain at the wedding ceremony— had the situation been different.

"I'm the most fortunate man in the world. Never

did I dare to dream that you would become mine, heart and soul," Merlin said, his voice gruff with emotion. He eased her head onto his shoulder and swept the sheet over their bodies. "Is it really true that you love me?" he asked at last, as if afraid that what he'd just heard was a lie.

"I do love you," she said, smiling. "How could you doubt it now?"

"But nothing has been resolved," he pointed out. "Suspicion is still hanging over my head."

She caressed the wide span of his chest. "I know, but right now I don't care to think about the past. You're innocent in my eyes. Someone as tender as you can't have murdered his father. However, until evidence of that fact surfaces, some small doubt might haunt me at unguarded moments. I've seen how kind and helpful you can be, how much you *care* about others, and that trait finally broke my resistance."

He laughed, a loud, happy sound. "You had to give in at last. I knew my love would wear down your resistance."

"Don't start teasing me," she threatened, "or I will take back every word I said."

"It's too late now," he said, his dark eyes twinkling in the candlelight. He played with one of her curls, tickling her nose. "Too late, my darling."

"Oh, you," she cried out, pinching his nose. She tried to slide out of bed, but he held her fast, then covered her mouth with his. She slowly relaxed in his arms, deeply savoring the intimacy they shared. Her senses started humming with a faint desire that soon flared into a raging fire. Before she could protest, he had dragged her back into the throes of passion, and all she was aware of was the ready response of her body to his.

It was almost dawn as Cynara sat up abruptly in bed. The room was cold, and she got up and picked up her nightgown that she could see in a pool of gray light on the floor. She slipped it on and touched Merlin's sleeping face. He felt warm and comfortable. He'd had a peaceful night, unmarred by nightmares. Not knowing what had awakened her, she snuggled up against him in bed and pulled the bedcovers up over them both. Just as she drifted off to sleep, she heard a high-pitched scream.

She bolted out of bed, her heartbeat battering her ribs. Her throat went dry with fear.

Merlin had heard the sound too, and was scrambling out of bed.

The scream came again, and Cynara rushed toward the door. "Mother!" Without thinking about the danger, she ran down the corridor, hearing Merlin calling out after her. She didn't heed him, only yearned to protect her mother from whatever horror had made her scream. She ran up the winding stairs to the next floor. Estelle's room was exactly above her own bedchamber.

Dawn's milky light penetrated the narrow windows high in the walls, and she had no difficulty seeing where she was going. The door to her mother's bedroom was ajar, and she pushed it open without a thought to any danger. But as she stepped inside, she hoisted a heavy candlestick that was standing on the chest of drawers beside the door. The velvet drapes let in only a thin sliver of brightness, but the light from the windows in the corridor partly penetrated the darkness in the room.

Cynara saw a shape on the floor. There was no one else inside, and silence reigned. She knelt beside the form, dropping the candlestick when she recognized her mother's shape. The huge mobcap she always wore at night was askew, and her nightgown twisted around her. There were no signs of struggle, but Estelle's head was propped against the wall, a wall that had a slight protruding angle that hadn't been there before.

"Mother!" Cynara cried, shaking the thin shoulders. She groped for the bottle of smelling salts that Estelle usually kept by the bed, and held them under her mother's nose.

Estelle revived, shaking her head in an effort to clear her mind. "Wha—what happened?" she said.

"You tell me, Mother. You are on the floor. I found you in a dead faint."

Estelle gasped and clasped her hand to her throat. "Oh, dear! Some man came into my room and hit me. I thought I had seen a ghost; the man looked like a Seymour, like Sydney looked in younger days . . . I can't think straight now." She kneaded her forehead, and looked so pale and bemused that Cynara feared for her mother's health.

Pulling Estelle up, Cynara said, "Come, Mother, you must get back into bed."

"I don't want to stay in here," Estelle wailed. "Don't leave me alone." She clung to Cynara, who stared frantically toward the corridor. Where was Merlin?

"Mother, I'll have to go and fetch help. I can't carry

you away from here, and you're too weak to walk."
She held the smelling salts under Estelle's nose, praying that Merlin would arrive. When he didn't, she
swept the coverlet around Estelle's shoulders and
pushed her mother into a chair. She glanced toward
the corridor, and, in the brightening light, she noticed
that there was something on the floor outside the door.
She hadn't seen the shape before, since it had been too
dark. It was a man lying on his side.

She patted Estelle's shoulder gently and went to
take a closer look at the fallen man. Her heart thundered with fear, and her legs were wobbly, insubstantial. She kneeled beside him and instantly recognized
one of the footmen—evidently the guard that Merlin
had placed there. He had no weapon, but the villain
who'd scared Estelle might have taken it. *Where was
Merlin?* She stared down the corridor, but there was
no sign of him. The man stirred, groaning as he turned
on his back. He blinked twice, staring uncomprehendingly at Cynara.

"Bloody . . . hell . . . what? What happened?" He
rubbed his head gingerly. "Someone knocked me a
good one; my head is still ringing."

Estelle had begun to sob hysterically, but Cynara
remained kneeling beside the footman yet a moment.
"Did you see who attacked you?"

The servant staggered to his feet and leaned against
the stone wall, clutching his head. "No . . . but the man
wore a gray cloak that reached from neck to ankle. His
hat was pulled low. Seemed familiar though."

"Could it have been Muggins from the stables?"

His eyes widened in surprise. "Muggins, milady?
No, this man wasn't that tall."

"Did he speak?" Cynara moved toward the bed-room, where Estelle was crying her name.

"No . . . not even a blo-blasted curse." He glanced down sheepishly. "Sorry, milady."

She nodded briskly. "Go bring Lord Raven here, please. It's urgent. You'll find him in his bedchamber."

As the footman hurried down the passage, Cynara returned to her mother's side. Estelle had calmed slightly and was blowing her nose.

"It was the most dreadful experience," she wailed as she pulled the handkerchief away. "I shall not sleep here another night. This is the second time I've been attacked."

Cynara rubbed Estelle's hands, then she lighted a candle. "What exactly did you see?"

"A man fully dressed in outer garments, cloak and hat, came in. I stumbled out of bed, and he pushed me hard in the chest, and I fell and hit my head." Once again tears began to flow freely down the thin face. "Then I fainted and didn't know what had happened until you appeared."

Cynara didn't say anything about the strange angle of the wall where she'd found Estelle. She could even see the crack now, and it was shaped like a door. *A door!* A hidden stairway most likely. That's why she had heard steps in the night. They hadn't come from the corridor outside but from the secret passageway that went through one of her bedroom walls. With a shiver of apprehension she wondered if the intruder still waited behind that door, listening to their every word. She placed a protecting arm across Estelle's shoulders, and said, "Come, let's go to my room. You can sleep in my bed for now. I shall summon Tildy, but let's leave this part of the house first."

Estelle didn't protest. On shaky legs she stood, holding on to the bedpost as Cynara swept a dressing gown around her and then a shawl over her thin shoulders.

"Are you cold, Mother? You're shaking."

Estelle nodded. "I believe it's the shock. A cup of tea would help greatly."

Throwing a last glance at the crack in the wall, Cynara led her mother hurriedly from the room. They reached her bedchamber without mishap, and as Cynara tucked her mother into bed, she said, "I shall fetch Tildy immediately. You don't have to be afraid here." She watched as her mother closed her eyes in relief. Cynara went out into the corridor, then looked into Merlin's room. He wasn't there, nor were the weapons, and there was no sign of the footman.

Frowning in consternation, Cynara ran to the landing by the stairs, and there she met the footman.

"There's no sign of the master," he said, shifting uncomfortably from one foot to the other. "I've looked everywhere, milady."

"Very well, fetch Bramble and ask him to help you search, but first see that Tildy watches Mrs. Hawthorne in my bedroom. Perhaps Lord Raven went outside for some reason." A twinge of fear clutched her at the thought. Why would he have gone out? Where had he gone? He'd been following her to Estelle's room, or hadn't he?

The footman left and she was hesitating on the stairs. Should she return to Merlin's room and wait for him there, or should she investigate the secret door in

Estelle's room? Aimless waiting would drive her to distraction, so she decided to search for him herself.

She toured the castle, looking into every room, even in the wardrobes. Silence and emptiness met her eyes everywhere. Merlin wasn't in the house. Misgiving crawled through her, making her stiff and cold. What now? she wondered as she stood on the landing, watching a bright candle burn. She had to act alone as long as he was gone.

She decided to return to her mother's bedchamber and examine the secret door. She climbed the steps, her heartbeat escalating with anxiety. She wasn't sure she had the courage to explore the secret passageway alone. Yet, if she didn't make haste, the door might be hidden and she would not know how to open it again.

When she arrived at the bedroom, she glanced cautiously around the corner of the door. No one was there, but she could clearly see the crack in the wall now that the sun had risen above the horizon.

Her hands were trembling as she lighted a branch of candles and stepped closer to the wall. Glad that she had the heavy brass candlestick for protection, she swallowed convulsively as she touched the cold stone wall. Her mouth was dry with fear.

She calculated that the door was about six inches thick, granite set in a wooden frame with mortar—to match the existing walls. She knew this was common in old castles. Passageways had been built so that the masters would have a way out if the enemy penetrated the stronghold during the battles of the Middle Ages. She wasn't sure if it had ever been used, but she knew that many battles had been fought at Black Raven in the past centuries.

Her hands trembling, she pulled the door toward her. An old tapestry that had partly concealed the door swung aside completely, and Cynara shone the candlelight into the dark opening. No one was there, thank God. Taking a step forward, she was instantly aware of the stairs that had been hewn into the thick wall. They made a steep drop with nothing to hold on to but the rock wall on each side. It was too narrow—suffocatingly so—barely holding the width of one person. At the bottom there was nothing but darkness.

The air was musty, and dust swirled around the candles. The faint salty aroma must be coming from the sea, she thought as she took one step down. She shone the light closer to the steps so as not to stumble.

There were footprints in the dust, prints of men's heavy boots, several kinds. Drawing in her breath sharply, she stared in consternation at the prints, wondering if Muggins had made them, and if not he, then who?

She listened intently for sounds, but silence lay like a heavy blanket in the passage. The candles trembled, and she was shaking so much she could barely move. The flames flickered crazily in a draft coming from the depths of the castle.

She forced herself to take another step down, all the while praying, "Dear God, please protect me . . . I'm so frightened."

Without daring to think another thought, she took a series of steps down, and the blackness was now complete save for the candles. As far as she could tell, there were no other cracks that outlined doorways in the walls. She remembered Estelle's first encounter with the man in the gray cloak in her bedroom, and realized that the man had perhaps tried to scare Estelle out of the room so that he could use the concealed door.

Something that the intruder wanted was down at the end of those steps, she was sure of that now. But what was so important that he kept "haunting" the castle over and over. Had he also made the attempts on Merlin's life?

Her bandaged hands scraped against the stone, and she took more steps down. It was too late to turn back now. If the answer lay at the bottom of the stairs, she wanted to know.

Wind suddenly moaned softly in a cavern, and she found that there were no more steps. She had reached a wooden platform of sorts. She held the candles stretched out before her, but the light blinded her and she could see nothing. Therefore, she set down the candelabrum on the floor and stepped away from it. Some dark shapes took form, but she couldn't tell what they represented. The smell of the sea was stronger there, and she heard the faint whining sound of the wind pushing through a crack in the stones somewhere.

She stood perfectly still, listening tensely. She sensed that she was alone, because there was no movement, no sighs, nothing but cold stone. Relief made her weak, but what if someone would come while she was alone down here? Nobody knew where she'd gone.

She noticed that short wooden stairs led to the floor. Leaving her candles, she went down. Flagstones rang out under her steps, and she knew then instinctively where she was—in the dungeons under the castle. The draft was distinct now, a cold wind directly from the sea. She followed it, finding that this new passage was much wider than the one cut into the stone wall above.

On both sides she noticed doors leading to the cells where criminals of old had been locked up. What misery they must have lived through, Cynara thought, already chilled to the bone by the wind. What would it be like down here on cold winter nights? At the other end of the passage was another door.

She returned to pick up the candelabrum, then continued her exploration. The corridor suddenly widened, and she found that she was in the wine cellar. Beyond it, past an arched door opening, was the potato and carrot storage bins. From there, stairs led up to the kitchen. She'd been down there before, but never explored the section of the cells.

She decided to return to the stairs by which she'd descended and see if she could discover the mechanism that opened the hidden door. Just as she passed one of the wine racks that reached from floor to vaulted stone ceiling, she sensed the draft strengthening again.

Frowning in consternation, she stared past the wine racks, and found that a very narrow aperture reached up, into the blackness above. She went closer and discovered that the aperture had been completely concealed by the wine bottles. Only the cold draft had given it away. A small wooden door opened as she tried the handle. A slender person like herself could easily fit in the opening, but the rough stones underfoot made it difficult to walk. Lighting her way with the candles, she stepped gingerly as the passage led down at an angle. The sounds of the crashing waves soon reached her ears, and the air was tangy with salt.

Daylight shone faint at first, but grew stronger with every step.

The path ended in a rough-hewn cave, right at the edge of the bay. Water lapped at the sand in the cave, and Cynara realized the cave would be filled at high tide. Seaweed and oysters littered the sandy floor, and Cynara remained standing where she was. She had no desire to step into the water. Rocks of all shapes and forms constituted the walls, and Cynara saw nothing unusual in those. This had been the course ancient Raven ancestors had taken when they fled the castle. A rowboat could easily fit into the cave, and surely it had brought its passengers to a larger ship waiting in the bay.

Whispers from the past wafted around her, and the hair on her neck rose. She sensed that the old secrets this cave was shielding weren't entirely pleasant. If she rounded the jagged rock at the west end of the cave, she knew she would be on the sheltered beach right below the castle.

Since the tide was low, perhaps she should explore the area. No harm in that, surely, especially since there were no signs of any intruders. To tell the truth, she didn't relish the idea of retracing her steps in the musty darkness.

She kept to the perimeter of the cave, thus avoiding immersing her feet in the water. One of the rocks at shoulder height that lent her hand its support felt strangely smooth compared to the others. She clambered over stones slippery with seaweed, and by the time she'd reached the crescent-shaped beach, her slippers were saturated and the edge of her nightgown and wrapper were soggy.

On the beach, the water could not reach her, but the sand was wet and packed tightly into rippling formations. She stared down at it and noticed the boot prints and a wide continuing track as if something had been dragged through the sand.

She rounded some cliffs protruding from above and stared uncomprehendingly before her. There in the sand lay a man, facedown. A voluminous gray cloak was spread around the still form like wings of a bat.

Cynara couldn't stop the scream that erupted from her throat, but as the form didn't move or respond, she tottered toward it. She already knew the man was dead.

Chapter 20

She forced herself to turn the limp form over, and instantly recognized the French madman, Jean. Her heart leapt so hard, she thought she would die with fright. For one irrational moment she had feared the dead man had been Merlin. She screamed once again, then scrambled up the steep path that led to the rose garden.

It was broad daylight, sunshine bathing the landscape by the time she yanked the kitchen door open and rushed inside. Even though it was still early, she found the two Bow Street Runners having breakfast by the kitchen table while Moira Black watched over them like a mother hen. The room was filled with delicious aromas of frying ham and eggs, but Cynara had no time to dwell on that now. Relief flooded her at the sight of the lawmen.

Holding her side where a painful stitch had developed, she blurted out, "Come quickly, there's a dead man in the cove. The Frenchman Jean is lying there in the sand. Hurry!"

She noticed their shocked expressions as she waited

for them to precede her. Constable Hoskins was first, wielding his spindly legs with alacrity. Sergeant Todd drained his coffee cup before following the younger man down the steep path. Cynara was reluctant to accompany them, so she hesitated by the kitchen door.

"Have you seen Lord Raven this morning?" she asked the dazed cook.

"Oh, dearie, oh, dearie," Mrs. Black sighed, and waddled toward the door without answering the question. "This I will have to see for myself," she said, mauling one corner of her white apron. "Poor old Jean, drowned though he was a splendid sailor once."

"Drowned?" Cynara asked, following the older woman. "It looked like he'd been stabbed in the chest." Horror filled her at the memory of his face. The warmth had gone out of the day and she shivered. With Mrs. Black she waited at the top of the path. They could see the two runners down on the beach, examining the body.

Cynara clasped her hands across her middle. "This is awful! One atrocity after another happens at Black Raven, but why? I would give anything to find out the truth."

Mrs. Black clucked her tongue. "Aye, this is frightful. First the stables, now this." She shook her head and muttered something that sounded like "sorcery and evil."

"Have you seen the master this morning?" Cynara asked again.

"No . . . mighty early for anyone to be up yet." Mrs. Black threw her a searching glance. "You really surprised me when you burst through that kitchen door. Never did I suspect you would be about that early."

The confession about the secret passageway was on Cynara's tongue, but she restrained herself. The last thing she wanted was to have the servants walking up and down those stairs in the wall, exclaiming their surprise.

"I . . . I couldn't sleep, that's all." She took a few steps back when the runners struggled up the path with their loathsome burden. The Frenchman could not weigh much, Cynara thought, all skin and bones that he was. She shuddered with revulsion as they placed the corpse on the grass.

Mrs. Black crossed herself and pulled her apron over her face. "Oh, dearie, oh, dearie," she wailed over and over. Other servants flocked to the rose garden, hesitantly at first, but then with more curiosity. Mrs. Averell, the housekeeper, and the footmen stood in a grim circle around the runners and the dead Frenchman. Then Bramble came huffing, closely followed by the footman Cynara had found outside Estelle's room.

"Have you discovered Lord Raven's whereabouts?" Cynara asked as soon as Bramble reached her side. He was out of breath and mopped his brow repeatedly.

"No, milady, I haven't found him anywhere. Looks like he rode off somewhere. His horse is gone."

How strange, Cynara thought. Why hadn't he followed her to Estelle's room first? Apprehension crawled over her skin. Perhaps he'd had an urgent need to ride over to Stormywood. But why? Mayhap he'd received a summons during the time she'd spent in Estelle's room. All these explanations were feasible, but the realization didn't soothe her. Tears gathered in her eyes, but she resolutely pushed her agitation aside. The runners straightened, and their faces were grim.

Cynara stepped up to them, avoiding looking at the corpse. "Can you tell what happened to him? Not drowned, surely?"

"No, not drowned," said Sergeant Todd, and he wiped his hands on a florid handkerchief. "He was stabbed three times in the chest, and then dragged out on the sand. What we don't quite understand is why he was lying on the beach. Why would he go down there?"

"Perhaps the murderer wanted the tide to bring the body out to sea," Cynara suggested, thinking that Jean might have been in the cave or in the dungeons just like herself. Or he might have been the person who'd climbed the stairs in the hidden passage. Estelle had seen a voluminous cloak, and Jean was wearing one. It seemed that that cloak had been seen at various instances—all of them connected to the strange goings-on.

Sergeant Todd pursed his lips and viewed the corpse once again. "You're probably right. We might never discover the reason he went down to the cove."

"He was a drunken sod," said Mrs. Black. "Perhaps he was in one of his stupors last night, and wandered unwittingly down to the beach and saw something that cost his life."

A cold cloud seemed to have settled over the group, and Cynara trembled. She wished that Merlin had been there to support her.

"You can take the Frenchman to the chapel for now," Cynara said. "I shall speak with the vicar this morning and arrange for a speedy funeral."

The runners nodded, and gestured for two sturdy footmen to carry the body away.

"Too many peculiar things have been happening," said Sergeant Todd. "We must work around the clock to solve this mystery before any more murders occur. It looks like there's more involved than what meets the eye."

Cynara's bandaged hands were unsteady, and she hid them in the voluminous folds of her wrapper. Mrs. Averell suddenly placed a concealing cloak around her shoulders, and only then did Cynara realize her state of undress, and she blushed. However, holding her chin high, she resumed the conversation. "Do you think there's a connection between the deaths of Ross Seymour, Felix Seymour, and this one?" she asked.

Todd and Hoskins exchanged glances, and Cynara could read the veiled message that passed between them. "You still think that Lord Raven is involved in all this?" she confronted them, and Todd shifted uneasily.

"There's that possibility, of course," he said, hedging.

Anger flared through her. "You have no proof. I'm absolutely convinced of Lord Raven's innocence." Her gaze swept the assembled servants, challenging them to disagree, but she saw only reluctant respect. Suddenly they appeared to be a united front behind her, and she had no idea when the transformation of their attitude had happened. But, even if they supported her, they might still be suspicious of Merlin.

"We have no proof, that's true, but we shall soon find what we need to apprehend the culprit," Hoskins said calmly, straightening to his full height.

"I was surprised to find you here so early," Cynara said.

"We've been keeping watch to see if smugglers might be involved in the strange goings-on," Hoskins said.

Cynara replied, "Anyone in the village could tell you that the smuggling stopped fifty years ago."

Sergeant Todd looked wounded. "We wouldn't expect the lady of the manor to know anything about such things."

"In a small village like Black Raven it would be impossible to keep anything secret for any length of time."

Todd bristled and gave the servants a sullen glance. "They are remarkably good at keeping secrets when they want to," he said scathingly. He headed toward the castle. "And now, if you don't mind, I would like to speak with Lord Raven. After all, this murder business is hardly a problem for ladies to solve. Where is he? I'm surprised he hasn't come down to witness this."

Fuming, Cynara followed him, but she didn't speak again. She would have to discover where Merlin had gone, but first she had to get dressed and arrange her hair. Placing a hand on the housekeeper's arm, she said, "Thank you for rescuing me, Mrs. Averell." She touched the concealing cloak.

"No more than I would do for any other undressed female," said the housekeeper, then pursed her lips in disapproval. "It's none of my business, of course, but why would a lady step outside clad only in a nightgown and wrap?"

Cynara started climbing the stairs. "That's a mystery that I have no desire to shed light upon," she said with a smile. Inwardly, she shuddered with embarrassment. Before going to her bedchamber, she returned to Estelle's room and made sure the secret door had been pushed to. It was still open, as she'd left it, and she slid a magazine that she found on the table between the wall and the door before closing it. Hopefully, she would be able to open it again if she failed to discover the workings of the mechanism. Reluctantly, the door slid into place, and Cynara studied the stone wall beneath the tapestry, but she could not discover any locks or knobs. Knowing that a maid would soon arrive to straighten the room, she let the tapestry fall into place and returned to her own chamber, where Tildy welcomed her with fresh clothes.

The rest of the day continued in an uproar as the villagers heard about the death. The comings and goings at the castle never seemed to end, and Cynara had to play hostess to nosy ladies from neighboring estates who wanted to hear everything about this latest scandal. Not that they would have bothered to visit otherwise. Had Merlin been behind this death also? their eyes seemed to question her, but she kept a cool smile on her face and a denial on her lips.

She grew more agitated as the day went on, finally realizing she would have to ride over to Stormywood to find out if Merlin was there. His horse was still missing, and it worried Cynara. Usually, he didn't ride more than an hour every morning, but why did he go out riding when Estelle was screaming for help? It was wholly illogical, and new suspicion grew in her chest, where so recently trust had taken its place.

As the afternoon light started to slant toward the

sea, she had Tildy help her dress in her riding habit and then flung a cloak over her shoulders. To Cynara's relief, Estelle had taken a sedative and had slept all day. She should be spared from hearing about this latest calamity as long as possible.

"If I'm not back before dark, inform the master that I've decided to stay at Stormywood overnight."

"I reckon th' master will be gone—for a long time," Tildy said glumly.

Cynara stared hard at her in the hallway. "What do you mean, gone?" she demanded.

"Seein' as he's disappeared. God only knows what might have happened to him—after what happened to th' poor Frenchie." She threw a fearful glance around the foyer. "There are madmen around here."

"Don't be such a doomster," Cynara said. "Go keep watch over my mother, and don't frighten her with such gloomy talk when she wakes up."

Tildy muttered something as Cynara left the castle. She hurried down the slope to the makeshift stables, an old washhouse that now held mounds of hay and four horses. Bobby greeted her pleasantly, and she found that he kept the premises clean and tidy.

"Did you see the master ride out this morning?" Cynara asked as she inspected Swallow. The burns on the mare had been healing nicely, thanks to Bobby's care.

"No," he said, and saddled the horse. "The stallion was gone when I got here, and hasn't been seen since."

"I shall take a ride—alone—in Gairlock Woods," Cynara said. It wouldn't do to inform Bobby of her intention to contact Brandon at Stormywood.

"You be extra careful, milady, seeing as there's a murderer on the loose."

"I promise." Cynara smiled grimly. "I don't think he will attack me in broad daylight, especially since I'm on horseback."

"One can never be too careful, milady." He gave her a boost into the saddle, and she turned Swallow toward the woods. It would be the shortest way to Stormywood, and she would ride as fast as she possibly dared. She had to see Merlin and tell him about the murder and the secret passageway. He would decide whether to inform the authorities or not. She could picture Todd and Hoskins sniffing around the wine cellar, and she felt as if the Raven privacy would be violated. They had nothing but conjecture to brag about anyway, she thought rebelliously. Her fierce need to protect Merlin surprised her, but it was only one facet of her love for him.

Gairlock Woods was silent, only a gentle breeze rippling through the trees. Year-old leaves cushioned Swallow's hooves, and she kept to the path easily even though the setting sun gradually darkened the forest so much that it was hard to distinguish the trampled route. However, the worries about Merlin's disappearance overshadowed any fear of the dark that Cynara might have.

Forty-five minutes later, as darkness had completely fallen, she arrived at Stormywood. The estate was quiet, as if slumbering until human voices and laughter would wake it up. Apprehensive now, Cynara slid off her horse in the shadow of the trees. She could see across the vast expanse of lawn, trying to discern some movement.

Just as she was reassured that no one was about, she saw something walk the perimeter of the hedge that parted the garden from the copse where Felix had been shot. Holding her breath, she stared at the figure, which looked unusually bulky for a person.

Straining her eyes, she tried to recognize the dark shape, and when it lifted its head and shook its long mane, she knew it was a horse, but whose horse? It was ambling along the grass, grazing as if it had no care in the world. The moon climbed over the treetops, bathing the lawn with silver light, and Cynara gasped when she recognized Merlin's stallion, Thunder. Holding the bridle, she dragged Swallow with her to the other horse. They sniffled each other, and Thunder gave a little snort of recognition.

Cynara frowned as she noticed that the saddle and the harness were still on his back, and she touched his flank. He was cool, as if he hadn't been running for several hours. "What happened to your master?" she whispered. "Did you toss him off your back?"

She doubted that, however, since Merlin was an excellent rider and Thunder an obedient stallion, if a bit frisky. She threw a glance at the mansion as if expecting Merlin to come out to meet her, but there were no movements, no sounds. She returned to the woods and tied the two horses to a tree. Then she moved slowly toward the house. She knew Brandon would be there, hidden somewhere, but who else might lurk about?

Gideon Swift had been gone from Black Raven, so Cynara suspected he was keeping her reckless brother company. She skirted the house and looked in through the French doors leading to the study, but she could see nothing there since the curtains were drawn. Avoiding the front entrance, she went around to the kitchen door and tried the knob. It was unlocked, so she stepped inside. Merlin kept a skeleton staff at his estate, but none was in evidence this evening. The fire in the kitchen hearth glowed dimly, and the room was pleasantly warm. Cynara stepped along the corridor leading to the main house, and she almost fainted with shock as she walked straight into a male form.

"Help!" she moaned, and expected everything dreadful except her brother's cheerful voice.

"Sis, what are you doing here, prowling about in the dark?"

"Brand!" Cynara clutched her head to steady her dizziness. "You frightened me."

Brandon pulled her into the kitchen and made her sit down. "I can't exactly light all the candles in the house to divulge my presence here," he said, and poured her a glass of lemonade from an earthenware pitcher. "Drink up."

She obeyed, studying her brother in the faint light of the fire. "I'm glad you haven't been captured yet. If I'm not wrong, you were on your way out, weren't you?"

"A fellow needs his exercise. It's deuced boring to be cooped up here at all hours." He sighed and sat down on a three-legged wooden stool. "What brings you here, sis?"

Her anxiety returned with renewed force. "Have you seen Merlin today? It seems that he has disappeared without telling a soul."

Brandon shook his head. "No . . . Gideon Swift has

kept me company, but there has been no sign or word from your husband."

Fear clutched her heart. "Oh, dear. Where could he have gone? I would have thought he would tell me his plans before dashing off. Besides, his stallion is here, still saddled."

Brandon got up in a rush. "By Jove, he must have been thrown!" He walked toward the door. "I shall look for him."

Cynara rose, still clutching her glass. "Wait! What if you're discovered. Swift must have told you that two Bow Street Runners literally live at Black Raven at the moment. Who knows how far they will venture."   .

She saw the rebellion on his face. "If anything, don't ride out alone," she urged.

He paused, thinking hard. "Very well, we'll send Gideon Swift out on Thunder, and perhaps you and I can ride together. I take it you're not content waiting for word here?"

She shook her head. "I must find him."

"I'll tell Swift right now. Just rest here until I return."

Cynara sat again, tears gathering in her eyes. Something must have happened to Merlin; why else would his horse be loose? Where had he gone in such a hurry?

Brandon came back a few minutes later, followed closely by the old man, Swift, Merlin's most trusted servant. He was carrying a musket, swords, and two pistols that he proceeded to load as she watched. To stop the bullets from rolling out of the barrels, he pushed a piece of rag down each black mouth, then shoved one pistol into his waistband and gave the other to Brandon. There were furrows of grimness on his brow, and Cynara realized the old man was just as worried as she was.

"Now then, tell us what has 'appened at Black Raven," he said, pinning Cynara with his disconcerting brown and blue eyes.

In her anguish about Merlin she had forgotten about the grisly discovery on the beach below Black Raven, and the words tumbled from her lips as she retold that morning's events.

"Something awful is happening, and I think Merlin is caught in the middle. But I haven't the faintest idea as to the purpose of this terror directed at the castle, and the people in it."

"The captain—meanin' the earl—is a clever man. 'E will get to the roots of this soon enough," Gideon Swift said with conviction. "In fact, 'e's probably workin' on it right now."

"I hope so," Cynara said with a sigh. Her body leaden, she followed the men outside. The wind had increased, the trees dancing a ghostly dance to its rhythm. An owl hooted forlornly, making Cynara's neck prickle.

"So, the master 'asn't been seen since this mornin'?" Swift asked, cautiously viewing every part of the garden.

Cynara bowed her head wearily. "No. I tied the horses on the other side of the house, in the woods."

"That was clever, sis. My nag has been in hiding in the woods as well, in a tumbledown cottage. Can't have anyone spot an unfamiliar horse on the grounds—especially not the runners."

"They are determined to capture you, Brand. You be extra careful, do you hear?"

"Yes . . . yes," he replied absentmindedly. "In fact, I believe I've fulfilled my mission."

"Mission?" Cynara clung to his arm as they sneaked from tree to tree until they reached the shelter of the woods.

"Merlin asked me to look into some things for him. It appears that the driver of Ross Seymour's coach on the night he died has been found at last. By me." Excitement tinted his voice, and Cynara could not help but feel a spurt of hope.

"The driver? What does he have to say?"

"He doesn't know that I've discovered his whereabouts. That will be a surprise when Merlin decides to confront him. Preferably, he'll bring the runners with him, and the driver will have to confess that Merlin wasn't involved."

"But why would the coachman hide—not confess the truth?" Cynara was startled as some animal rustled in the bushes beside her.

"Because someone *made him* keep silent, either by money or threat." Brandon chuckled. "I'm glad I was the one to find the driver. It repays my debt to Merlin for saving me from hanging."

They waited in the shadows of the trees while Gideon Swift fetched Brandon's horse.

"Merlin hasn't been idle either," Cynara said, and she explained about the visit with Lady Fidalia. "However, it wasn't the interview that yielded anything, but the meeting she had later with Muggins and the Frenchman, Jean."

Brandon sighed deeply, thinking in silence. He caressed Thunder's soft muzzle, and the horse butted him in the chest. "There has to be a connection between these events. Why would Lady Fidalia know Muggins, of all people? It doesn't make sense. She isn't from these parts, and why would she consort with servants?"

Cynara wound her arm through Brandon's. "Too many questions, too few answers. I have a feeling we know only a small portion of the truth."

Gideon Swift came back, leading a chestnut that seemed calm enough, compared to the more volatile Thunder. "What if I ride down to the village and across to Bluewater to discover if Lord Raven has traveled there? He might be following some clue that might solve your problem, Mr. Brandon."

"Very well, Lady Raven and I will search the woods, even if we'll have problems seeing anything in the dark. Then we'll go over the stretch of path that leads along the sea to Black Raven. See you back here by daybreak."

The two men shook hands as if closing a deal, and Cynara grew cold with apprehension. What if the search wouldn't bring results? What then?

They rode in silence through the woods, scanning every hollow, every bush, for a sign of Merlin. They called his name, but only night birds responded with flapping wings and harsh cries. A rabbit sat on its hind legs in a patch of moonlight, staring tensely before scuttling into a hole in the ground. As they rode out of the woods, Cynara saw Black Raven and the entire village bathed in eerie silver, but there was no movements, no signs of a man making his way home.

"Where is he?" she said forlornly as Brandon rode up beside her.

Brandon spurred his horse on. "I know it's dangerous, but I must go with you into the castle to see if Merlin has returned."

"Without his horse?"

"If Thunder threw him, he might have walked home. Come, sis, let's not dawdle." He clucked his tongue, and the horse set off in a canter. "Besides, it'll give me a chance to pay my respects to Mother."

Chapter 21

Due to a fierce cold eating into his limbs, Merlin slowly awakened. He'd rather stay in a void where no problems existed, but the cold, and a nagging, insistent thought that he would have to get up or die, finally brought him around. Clutching his head as a sharp pain pierced his brain, he swore. Someone had almost cracked his head with a club.

Gingerly, he opened his eyes but could see nothing. Pitch blackness surrounded him, and he reached out, only touching freezing air. Had he gone blind from the blow? He doubted it, but why was is so black and chilly around him?

He eased himself upright, taking one cautious step forward, and his toes connected with stone. He touched the rock, shaken by the slimy, rough surface. Only one place had slippery granite like this—the very deepest dungeons at Black Raven. Even twenty years ago, when he'd played down here with Max, the rocks had been damp and covered with slime. He prayed that he could see something, and after a time, he didn't know how long as he sat on the stone floor, knees drawn to his chin, he noticed a change of light. A grayness softened the blackness, and as time progressed, he recognized the circular opening with its jagged bars. Waves were already whooshing through it as the tide was rising. He knew he was in the cell that had been used over the centuries to get rid of unwanted criminals or enemies. Just lock them up in the dungeon, and the sea would do the rest. At high tide the water would reach the ceiling of the cell and drown the prisoner. The slimy floor was littered with bones.

He viewed the opening grimly. There was no chance of escape. Anyone who risked swimming under the jagged spears shooting deeply into the water would instantly discover the force of the waves as one was either pushed against the sharp teeth of the bars or crushed against the reef underneath.

Over the years the water had weakened the bars, but it was unlikely anyone would survive the reef or the suction of the current. As daylight crept in, he found that he was sitting on a ledge about three feet above the water. The round trapdoor was high in the ceiling above him, a series of rough-hewn steps leading down to the ledge. Any other place or time, he might have enjoyed the sound of the crashing waves, but here they had become his executioner. There had to be a way out, or he would drown.

"Blasted hell!" he swore, clutching his sore head. He made his way up to the top of the steps, remembering how he'd dressed in breeches and shirt, and planned to follow Cynara to Estelle's room. In the corridor, someone had jumped on his back, and another figure had swooped from the side, dealing him a thunderous blow to the head. Then he'd been out—for hours, it

seemed. There had been something vaguely familiar
about the figure that had dealt the blow, but he
couldn't connect the face to the body. The resem-
blance had appeared too incongruous at the time, but
he didn't know why.

He tried to push up the stout trapdoor, but it was
locked. Heaving with all his strength, he prayed that
the bolts might break, but nothing happened. His head
swam dizzily, and he felt nauseated by his efforts.

"Damn! Damn you, whoever you are. Why do you
want to destroy me?" he shouted. His angry voice
echoed eerily around the dungeon, and he screamed
louder, against all hope wishing that someone could
hear him, if not inside, outside. He knew it was futile,
especially since this prison was at the very lowest edge
of the castle wall. He banged on the door until his
knuckles started to bleed.

Damn all to hell! he thought. If no one found him
soon, he would die. The water had already risen by one
foot, and the tide would not slow down because of his
plight.

He kept banging on the door, praying. Even though
Bramble might visit the wine cellars to bring up the
dinner wine, he would be two floors above this rat
hole. Above this cave was another set of cells and a
narrow winding staircase. Then there were more dungeons and the wine cellar. Would Cynara miss him
enough to look for him? Would their love story end
before it had truly begun? She'd given him her heart at
last, but perhaps he wouldn't be there to enjoy her love
any longer. . . . The thought brought savage sorrow to
his heart.

* * *

As dawn started to creep up on them, Cynara and Brandon had made a thorough search of the grounds around Black Raven.

"We must get inside before someone sees us, sis," Brandon said. "I'll hide somewhere in the castle during the day. Merlin might return by nightfall."

"Shh," Cynara said. "Look, there are the runners." She was pointing at two men slowly making their way toward the kitchen. "We don't want them to see you. Who knows how long they've been skulking around here."

Brandon narrowed his eyes, and his lips thinned to a grim line. "How do we cross this part unseen?" He was talking about the long grassy slope that surrounded the castle.

Cynara frowned, staring thoughtfully at the forbidding black cliffs along the perimeter of the drop to the sea. "If we keep to the trees, then scramble down the path to the beach below, I know a secret passage that will take us all the way up to Mother's bedchamber."

Brandon whistled under his breath. "Have you been exploring, sis?"

"Yes, you might say that. I will show you what I found." She gave her brother a searching glance. "You must have explored the castle from top to bottom when you were a boy."

He laughed. "Naturally, but we were frightened of the dungeons and the passages. Max's nanny always told hair-raising stories about ghouls and wandering headless sailors."

Cynara turned her horse toward the cliffs. "A good

way to dissuade boyish pranks, surely." As they reached the cliffs, they slid off their horses and tied them out of sight. Crouching below the rocks, they made their way to the path and scrambled down to the beach below. The water was rising rapidly, and Cynara knew that the cave that held the secret route into the wine cellar would soon be filled with water. She stepped from stone to stone, trying to hold her skirts aloft from the greedy waves—a losing battle, however, as she finally had to step into the water to reach the passage.

"Too bad we don't have any candles with us," she said.

"I do. Since Merlin gave strict orders that I stay hidden at Stormywood without undue light, I took to carrying a candle and tinderbox in my pocket." Brandon pulled out the stump and lit it. It was almost full daylight when they entered the steeply rising path hewn into the rocks. Brandon's candle weakly illuminated the damp rocks, and as they reached the wine cellars, the familiar musty odor reached their nostrils.

"I could spend a week down here without being bored once," Brandon said with a chuckle, and dusted off an ancient bottle. "Begad! This bottle is one hundred years old."

"Stop that nonsense, Brand," Cynara admonished him. "Have you no sense of the danger? Bramble might come down here any minute, and you're joking about the wine."

"Steady on, sis. Would Bramble, that old duck, babble about me?"

"Perhaps not, but we can never be too careful." She

dragged Brandon by the sleeve and made her way back toward the wooden platform she remembered. She wondered if she could find the way, since a warren of paths led to the cells.

"This is like the old times, you know, sis. We used to explore every one of these passages. Did you know there are 'layers' of cells, one on top of the other?"

"No . . . I never had the inclination to study the dungeons at close range."

"The cells haven't been used for ages, of course, but in the Middle Ages they would have been full of villains from every village in a twenty-mile radius."

Cynara shuddered, wondering what memories these ancient walls hid. "Come along, let's hurry. Perhaps Merlin returned in the night."

Brandon was right behind her, muttering to himself. "There's one especially dreadful hole under this castle. There, a prisoner would disappear without a sign, never to be seen again."

"Where did you learn all this?" Cynara asked with a sigh of relief as they reached the platform.

"Max told me. He knew everything about this place. He loved Black Raven, and would have made a good earl." Brandon paused. "Still, I believe that Merlin is just as good. If only we could discover his whereabouts."

"You think he might be . . . be dead?" Cynara could barely breathe for the anguish clutching her chest.

"No, that's ridiculous! This isn't Waterloo, y'know." He stopped on the stairs, listening intently. "What was that? Sounds like someone banging on the wall."

Cynara strained her ear. "I don't hear anything."

"There! Again, someone is hammering against one of the walls. It could be a servant driving in a nail somewhere, with the echo reaching us."

"The walls are too thick to return any sound." She had heard it too, like a muffled beating on a door from far away.

"Shall we investigate?" Brandon asked.

"You shall concentrate on staying hidden. I'm certain this has nothing to do with us. Let's go." She resumed her climbing as the banging faded in the distance. "I do hope that we can open the door upstairs from the inside. I never had the time to discover the locking mechanism, but I pushed a magazine in the crack to prevent the lock from clicking into place."

They reached the top, and Brandon's candle flickered wildly in the draft. Cynara prayed that it wouldn't go out before they had learned how to open the door. She tried to push the door open, but instantly discovered that it was locked.

"Some nosy servant probably removed the magazine in a zealous cleaning session," Brandon said with disgust. "Here, let me shine the candle close to the wall."

They studied every crack and crevice and pushed every knob in the stone, but nothing happened. They were trapped in this suffocating stairway with nowhere to go except down.

Heaving his shoulder against the frame, Brandon pushed with all his might, but the door didn't budge at all. "Blast!" he cursed under his breath. "I can't open this."

"What do we do now?" Cynara wanted to know, and the brother and sister stared at each other in the gloom. "You simply cannot show yourself outside, Brand. Besides, I think the tide is almost at its highest now. It's impossible to reach the beach safely."

"We must wait until nightfall, then," Brandon said with a groan of exasperation.

"This staircase makes me feel as if the walls are about to move in and suffocate me. Let's wait down on the platform."

Brandon brightened. "Mayhap we could sample one of the wine bottles. Bramble wouldn't be any wiser what with racks filled from floor to ceiling."

Cynara sighed, but she didn't say anything. They made their way down the steps again, and when they reached the platform, Brandon extinguished his candle. "We have to save it till later," he said.

They sat down, side by side, staring into the musty blackness. It was as if it had a life of its own as it pressed in around them. Cynara shivered and pulled her knees up to her chin.

Brandon chuckled ghoulishly. "Do you want to hear a ghost story, sis?"

Cynara jabbed him with her elbow. "Don't you *dare*! I shall never forgive you if you force me to listen to one."

"There is that noise again," her brother said thoughtfully. "It sounds closer."

"Would someone be in the wine cellars, do you think?"

"There's no light anywhere. No one would work in the cellars without a candlestick."

They listened in silence as the noise continued, then stopped abruptly.

"What could it be?" Cynara mused.

"It really sounds like someone pounding on a door somewhere." He paused, evidently waiting for another round of bangs.

When they returned, he said, "They seem to be coming from below, not from this level or from upstairs."

"Below? But you said yourself there's nothing but dungeons down below. I doubt that anyone ever goes there. I wager the servants are even more afraid of ghosts than we are."

Brandon hooted with laughter, and Cynara angled a glance full of apprehension toward the wine cellar. "Be quiet, you great looby! What if Bramble is stepping down this very minute to fetch the wine?"

Brandon quieted, but not much. "That old duck probably comes down here to take a swig of brandy or two every so often. I know I would if I were him."

Cynara gave him a shove. "You never change, do you, Brand? You are a scrapegrace, and you will always be."

Brandon shrugged. "Not so bad considering the alternatives—dullard or henpecked husband." He halted abruptly. "There it is again. Egad, I believe someone is truly banging on a door in the deepest dungeons. We must investigate this, sis."

Cynara reluctantly agreed. "It's probably nothing, but if we don't examine it, we will always wonder. It's probably nothing more than a loose shutter banging against the wall somewhere. After all, it is rather windy outside."

"I know the way." Brandon lit his candle again and walked in the opposite direction from the wine cellar.

Cynara had vaguely noticed it before, the door at the far end of the passage. This one was tall and arched at the top. It creaked torturously, as if it hadn't been opened for years. Brandon and Cynara waited tensely to hear if anyone had noticed the groan of wood, but everything was silent, even the pounding.

The air in the murky corridor beyond was rank and humid.

"Are you sure this is a good idea, Brand?" Cynara asked, clinging to his arm. "I don't hear anything now."

"Me neither. Perhaps it was only in my imagination that the sound came from here." They hesitated for a time, and everything was silent.

"I don't like this at all. Let's go back." Cynara shuddered with apprehension. "Sharing a bottle of wine might not be such a bad idea after all. It's getting frightfully cold in here."

A draft moaned through some invisible opening in the stone wall, and Cynara took an involuntary step back. "This is an awful place . . . such sadness, don't you agree?"

"Yes," Brandon said between his teeth. "Let's go back."

They retraced their steps and began to close the door. Then the banging started again, a sound so forlorn and desperate that they halted, hands on the edge of the door.

"Well, seems that we *must* investigate now," Cynara said. "Someone is down there, Brand, but why? And who? Perhaps one of the servants went to clean and got lost."

"Clean?" Brandon angled the light toward the dusty floor. "This floor hasn't seen a mop and water for years." He bent closer. "But look, here are foot-prints."

They studied the prints with interest. "There seems to be three kinds," Cynara said, "all male boots."

They exchanged long glances. "What if one of them belongs to Merlin?" Brandon breathed.

Hope shot through Cynara, and suddenly she yearned to discover who was pounding in the dungeons. "Let's hurry now."

Brandon grabbed her hand, and they hastened along the dank corridor. Soon the banging appeared to be coming from behind them.

"Deuced strange," Brandon said, shining his candle closer to the walls of the passage. "Where is it coming from?" The sound stopped abruptly, and they waited tensely for it to reappear.

"Hello?" Brandon called out. "Anyone there?"

Silence.

Merlin stood with his face pressed to the wooden trapdoor to prevent the water from coming into his nose and mouth. Once the water rose two more inches, he would be drowned. There was no escape. How many desperate prisoners had been standing on this exact spot with their faces against the door, praying, shouting for someone to show some mercy. At least Max had had died in battle. Even Felix's death by a pistol wound had been more dignified than this. . . . The last Earl of Raven would die like a rat.

The water had numbed every part of his body as it gradually immersed him. Several times he'd lost his foothold on the topmost stone step and had to fight his way back, swimming underwater. Once he'd been disoriented and located the trapdoor only at the last moment before his lungs burst. Not many more minutes to get puny gulps of air from the cracks in the wood. Soon the water would take him whole. . . . In a last flurry of strength, he pounded the door.

"Merlin?" Cynara shouted, her voice trembling. She wanted so much to hear his voice that she almost cried. What if he were locked up somewhere, desperately needing her help?

The knocking returned, this time more faint and irregular.

"Is there another floor under here?" Cynara wondered.

Brandon nodded. "Yes, in fact there's the 'death hole,' right at the edge of the water. The tide should have filled it to the brim by now." Brandon hesitated before walking to the door at the end of the corridor. "The cell was used for the most villainous criminals. Drowned like rats, their bones would litter the floor or get swept out to sea on the tide."

The door led to a set of spiraling stone stairs, and Cynara realized that they were in the base of one of the towers. The knocking was coming closer now, but more intermittently.

"There's definitely someone down here," Brandon said as they reached the stone floor. The rank smell had been replaced by the brisk scent of seawater. The candle flame flickered wildly in the draft, but he cupped his hand around it.

The banging came in another staccato burst, then silenced.

"Did it come from the hole?" Cynara demanded, her heart pounding frantically.

"Yes . . . if only I could find the blasted door. It's like a lid in the floor." He crouched and searched every inch of the flagstones.

Cynara stumbled over the protruding metal ring set into the oak, and she exclaimed, "Here it is! Come . . . hurry, Brand." She tugged at the ring, but the lid didn't move. "Merlin, are you there? Merlin?"

She thought she heard a muffled shout, but it could have been the wind buffeting the trapdoor. Water was slowly seeping around the edges.

Brandon pushed her aside. "Hold this!" he demanded, and thrust the candle at her. "The tide is up to the top of the cave. No time to waste." He tore aside the rusty bolts and flung open the lid. Water poured over the top, and Cynara gasped when she saw the hand thrusting up, a head hanging limply forward in the water, strands of dark hair floating around the head.

"Merlin!" Cynara shouted, trembling so much she almost dropped the candle.

Brandon braced his hand on one side of the opening, gripped the collar of Merlin's shirt, and hauled his friend's head above the water. "C'mon, old fellow, help me. I can't pull you out all alone."

Tears coursed down Cynara's cheeks when Merlin showed no sign of reviving. "Is he—dead?" Without waiting for Brandon's reply, she kneeled by the edge of the hole, freezing water soaking through her skirts. She helped to hold Merlin up.

Brandon groaned as he got a grip under Merlin's arms and pulled the man out of the water. As he pressed Merlin's chest, Merlin began to sputter and cough.

"Thank you . . . thank you, God," Cynara whispered, sobbing. She brushed Merlin's wet hair from his icy face and caressed his cheeks.

Merlin's eyes flew open, and he coughed some more, convulsing on the floor. Slowly he regained his breath as Brandon sat beside him, panting after the exertion of pulling the unconscious man out.

"Cynara . . ." Merlin croaked, and held out a chilly hand toward her. "I never thought I'd see you again."

Setting the candle in a crack in the floor, she kneeled beside him and pulled him into her arms. They clung desperately together, and Brandon snorted in disgust as he saved the candle from falling over at the last moment. "Bah!" he muttered. "How cloying."

Cynara had heard the derisive comments and smacked her brother on the arm. "Just be silent. You don't have to look." Euphoric to feel Merlin's arms around her once more, she kissed her husband deeply, and he responded like a man who'd just been given the most glorious gift—another chance. His wet clothes soaked hers, but she didn't notice it much, wishing only that they could toss the wet garments aside and lose themselves in each other. But Merlin was so cold, he trembled violently.

Brandon snorted and slammed the trapdoor shut. Then he stalked toward the exit. "Nothing romantic about this spot," he said with a sigh.

Merlin laughed, burying his face in Cynara's sweet-smelling hair. "Don't be such an old curmudgeon,

Brand," he said, and caressed Cynara's back. Still holding on to her, he laboriously got to his feet. Holding her close, they joined Brandon. "Thank you, old fellow. You saved my life, you know."

Brandon studied Merlin's bloodied knuckles. "You sure made enough noise to awaken the dead. Having nothing more important to do, we investigated the thumping sound," he said airily.

Merlin laughed and slapped Brandon's shoulder. "I'm eternally grateful that you're such a nosy person."

"It was sis, not me."

Cynara protested, but she didn't care who should take the credit for Merlin's rescue. Contentment filled every part of her body, like a layer of soft cotton. Only now did she really understand how keen her anxiety had been. "Let's go upstairs. So many things have happened since we parted, and you have to tell us how you ended up here."

"I know someone attacked me," Merlin explained as they made their way upstairs. "I believe it was Muggins, but he wasn't alone." His voice turned thoughtful. "The strange part is that I could have sworn I knew the other man, but I can't place his identity. All I know is that something is very wrong, and that man is the key to the calamities at Black Raven."

Chapter 22

"You can't come upstairs with us," Cynara said to Brandon as they reached the wooden platform. She explained about the secret passageway to Merlin.

He whistled under his breath. "I knew there was one, but not that it ended in your mother's bedchamber." He studied the narrow stone steps that were partly concealed by a protruding slab of rock.

"We can't get up that way though." Cynara explained about the door, and they thought for a moment.

"I'll go up alone through the wine cellar," Merlin said at last. "Then if no one is around, we'll smuggle you to one of the tower rooms," he said to Brandon. "You have to stay here until dark."

They agreed, so once again brother and sister were sitting side by side on the platform, waiting.

"I'm glad we investigated the pounding. What if we hadn't? We would never have found Merlin," Cynara said with a shudder.

"Yes . . . and you would have grieved for the rest of your life, sis," Brandon chided her. "I'm delighted that you've taken such a liking to your husband, especially since he forced you to the altar."

Cynara appreciated the darkness that shielded her blush. "It has turned out for the best. Besides, I know I will be happy at Black Raven, if only we can discover who wants to harm us."

"I'm so restless. I'm sure something of monumental importance is about to happen," Brandon said, fidgeting.

"Really, Brand, you and your restlessness! You never sit still for more than five minutes, but that doesn't mean you have the gift of looking into the future."

"Mark my words, sis, something is about to happen. My neck is itching, as it always does before a fight."

Cynara shrugged. "Well, I would be relieved to solve the mystery of who's behind these dark deeds."

"You solve the mystery? You leave such dangerous missions to the males, who are here to protect you."

Cynara's snort was most unladylike. "I'm in more danger in your company than alone, Brandon. You draw mischief like nectar draws a bee."

Merlin returned at that moment. "Bickering as always, I hear. Well, if you can tear yourselves from each other's throats, you are now free to sneak upstairs. I set Bramble into the situation, and he's eager to be of assistance. He will see to it that no servants lurk on the stairs or in doorways while we pass."

"He must have had the shock of his life to see you stumbling out of the cellar, soaked from head to toe," Brandon said with a chuckle.

"He was slightly taken aback, yes." Merlin led the

way upstairs once again, and the entire castle seemed to be asleep even though it was in the middle of the day. They saw Bramble waving conpiratorially from behind the door leading to the kitchen, and they made it unseen to the tower room that had been Max's study.

"You can sleep here on the sofa, Brand," said Merlin. "No one ever comes in here, but make sure you lock the door behind us."

Arms entwined, Merlin and Cynara went to their adjoining bedchambers. "Mother will be worried about me by now," she whispered, and stuck her head around the door. Tildy jumped up from a chair and put a finger to her lips. The drawn bed hangings suggested that Estelle was asleep.

"Oh, Milady Cy, I wus thinkin' something dreadful had happened to ye," Tildy whispered after giving Merlin a curtsy and a probing glance.

"I've been involved in a dangerous adventure, but I'm fine," he said lightly.

"Mrs. Hawthorne was ever so distressed at yer disappearance. I finally gave her a sleepin' draught."

"Very well, then, I won't disturb her rest. Please bring a clean dress and petticoats to the master's room."

Tildy went to collect the garments, and Cynara followed Merlin to his chamber. He looked pale and tired, the old bruises from the fire fading, but a recent one discoloring his left temple. She gently traced the area with her hand, finding a slight bump.

"I still have a pounding headache," he said, sitting down on the bed and massaging his neck, "but better that than drowning."

"The question is: Who would want you dead?" Cynara found a towel and dried his hair.

"If I knew that, I would have captured the villain by now."

She undid the buttons of his shirt and breeches. He chuckled, his dark eyes flaring with desire. "Despite my tired, aching head, I have a mind—"

"Don't even think it," Cynara interrupted him as tender warmth filled her chest. She dried his back vigorously. "You must put on some dry clothes and get warm. Though it's summer, you still might get pneumonia."

He didn't protest when she dried off his broad chest, and she pushed him back on the bed and pulled off his boots and breeches. Her burns under the grimy bandages protested, but she kept at her task.

An ache started in her heart when she saw how helpless her handsome husband looked for once. The brush with death had subdued him. The brisk authority had seeped from him, and he reminded her of times past, when they were children. She recalled their first kiss on her fourteenth birthday, and how she'd hated and feared his dark magnetism then. Now, however, she didn't think that his eyes were too secretive or too brooding. Now she saw only the love and sensitivity of which Merlin had such abundance.

She dried his abdomen, and he murmured, "Move farther down, my darling."

She only clucked her tongue and quickly dried his legs. In the top drawer of his highboy she found clean shirts, and in the next, neckcloths. The wardrobe was full of coats and breeches, and she chose something severely cut, dignified gray and "befitting an earl." It wouldn't do to have Merlin look less than what he was as he faced the servants and Bow Street Runners. Despite his discolored face, he was a man who commanded respect.

He tried to stand and pull on his clothes, but he was trembling too much. "I guess I got colder than I thought down there in the water," he said, his teeth chattering.

He held her against him, and Cynara pulled the cover over them both. When his limbs had thawed, she got up and fetched his clothes. Though he protested bitterly, she pulled the breeches over his legs and fastened them.

"Why did you have to get up so soon, Cynara? I could have stayed all day in bed with you."

"I know you could have, but you must talk to the servants. They were very worried about you."

He snorted. "Don't lie to me! I know they don't like me in the least."

"I think they're getting used to the idea of you as master of Black Raven." She slipped a white shirt over his head and ordered him to tie the neckcloth.

He viewed the cravat with loathing, but slid it obediently around his neck.

"You must show yourself downstairs as if nothing has happened. If the enemy lurks about, he'll know that you survived the attack. That might draw him out."

Merlin didn't protest, only kissed her bandaged hands. "You're more than a man deserves," he said, and pulled her close. Wrapping his arms around her waist and pushing his head against her breasts, he hugged her until she grew breathless. The familiar sweet desire that his touch always provoked surged through her, and she could barely find the determination to push him away.

"It's broad daylight, and Tildy will be here any minute."

"She probably peeping through the keyhole," he muttered, his teeth tracing one erect nipple through the material of her gown.

A sharp knock interrupted Merlin's amorous overtures.

"She heard what you said," Cynara said with a laugh, and went to open the door.

"Which only proves my point."

As Merlin finished buttoning his shirt, Cynara was surprised to find her mother, not Tildy, at the door.

"Mother! What are you doing up? We thought you were asleep."

Estelle, dressed in a voluminous dressing gown and lace-trimmed cap, stepped into the room. She gave Merlin a sharp glance, but then tiredness seemed to sap her of all strength. With a sigh she slumped on the chair. "I heard about the Frenchman's death," she said. "It's too dreadful to bear. Why are these atrocities happening at Black Raven? What have we done to deserve them?"

"Death?" Merlin echoed.

"Oh, I forgot to tell you, what with everything else happening." Cynara described what she had found when she stepped onto the beach that morning.

"It's impossible!" Merlin's wrath was explosive. "Who would want that poor madman dead?"

Estelle flapped her hands to get his attention. "I've been thinking about it as I lay sleepless in bed last night. There might be a connection to my family some-how." Her voice trembled now. "If the *Hirondelle* necklace wasn't lost, what about the rest of the family jewels? There was a full parure of sapphires and dia-monds—tiara, necklace, everything. Then there were pearls and rubies."

"Do you suspect they were never in the hands of the new government?" Cynara demanded.

Estelle hunched her shoulders as if the thought were too heavy and troublesome to think through. "Yes . . . yes, that's what I think. What if the jewels were here in England all this time? But who possesses them?"

Merlin stepped briskly across the room and leaned over his mother-in-law. "Think hard, Estelle. Who would know?"

"I don't have many French friends in England since most of them live in London and we haven't spent the Seasons there very often. However, I'm distantly re-lated to the Lagrange family. They owned the neigh-boring estate in Gascogne, but, while we lived in France, they spent most of their time in Paris, so I hardly know them. I do know that they escaped the Terror. I was only a girl then, so I didn't keep up the acquaintance. I do know their address in London."

"Perhaps they have some answers to give us," Mer-lin said. "I suggest you write to them instantly. I will send Bobby to London with the letter, and he must return with a reply. We should have their answer in a few days."

Estelle nodded. "I shall write this instant. What was Jean's last name?"

"Leblanc," Merlin said.

"I shall ask if they know about him." She rose slowly. "Then I shall rest. I'm so tired."

Another knock sounded on the door, and Cynara opened it, finding Bramble on the threshold.

The rotund butler looked uncomfortable. "I know I shouldn't disturb you, but once the servants found out—through Tildy—that you've returned, I could not stop them from blabbing to the runners." He lips worked convulsively. "They are asking to see you, milord."

Merlin frowned. "What for? There's no new development in Brandon Hawthorne's disappearance," he added with a sly wink.

"Ahem . . . yes, I wouldn't know about that, but I believe this is about the Frenchman's death," Bramble said with an innocent air.

Merlin's scowl grew more pronounced. "The Frenchman's death? I had nothing to do with it." Merlin shrugged on his coat, once again a man of purpose. He brushed his hair and stepped into the corridor. "See if you can discover where Gideon Swift is," he said to Bramble.

He smiled roguishly to Cynara. "I'll be back and we can continue where we left off," he whispered, and kissed her cheek.

Tildy entered, laden with garments, but Cynara passed her and headed toward the door. "Not now, Tildy. I have to go down. Wait for me here." She had to hear what the runners had to say to Merlin, who knew nothing about Jean's death. They had already questioned her. After all, she had been the one to discover the body on the beach, not Merlin.

Sergeant Todd and Constable Hoskins met them in

the foyer. They wore solemn expressions, as if what they had to say was a sorrowful burden.

Doffing their hats, they greeted Merlin and Cynara good morning. "I'm glad you have returned, milord," Todd said stiffly. "We were concerned when there were no signs of you yesterday."

Merlin eyed them suspiciously. "Did you think I had bolted with the Raven silver service?" he asked scathingly.

Todd shifted uncomfortably. "No . . . not exactly, milord. However . . ." He gestured to Mrs. Averell to step forward from the shadows under the staircase. Cynara had not noticed her before. She was carrying a cloak over her arm, a gray cloak. Jean's cloak? Cynara gasped, her world starting to spin.

"We have discovered that a man has been seen on the premises clad in this cloak. Every time it has been sighted, some crime has been committed, be it arson or murder."

"That's true," Merlin admitted, "but what does it have to do with me?"

Sergeant Todd held the garment toward Merlin. "Take a closer look, milord. Can you deny that it belongs to you?"

Tension was thick in the air as Merlin slowly fingered the fine gray velvet. "It looks like one that belongs to me."

"It is yours," the sergeant said, unable to hide the triumph in his voice. He turned the collar inside out, and there was an embroidered label bearing Merlin's name.

"So? What does it all mean?" Merlin went on, lines of anger furrowing his forehead.

"It means you were on the beach when we found the dead Frenchman, Jean Leblanc. The cloak was snagged on a rock close to the spot where the dead man was found."

"I didn't see it," Cynara said shrilly.

The law men ignored her. "Where were you last night, milord?"

Merlin and Cynara exchanged glances. She knew that his story of being shut into the dungeons would sound preposterous. She could not stop herself from blurting out, "He was with me, Sergeant."

Silence heavy with accusations fell in the room. "And where were you, milady?"

"In my bedchamber, of course," she said, raising her chin a fraction.

"How come both your horses were gone, then?"

"Better tell them the truth, darling," Merlin said, and cleared his throat. He told them everything except Brandon's part in the dungeon rescue. "Someone must have taken my horse to make it look like I had left, and Lady Raven went out to look for me. That's all that happened. If it hadn't been for my wife, I would be dead now, drowned in the dungeons."

Todd and Hoskins exchanged incredulous glances. "Of all the outlandish stories," Todd said, bristling. "I suggest you tell it to the magistrates." He stretched up to his full height, his corset creaking. "I'm here to arrest you, milord, on suspicion of murder. You killed the Frenchman Jean."

Merlin jaw dropped momentarily, and Cynara cried out. "That's ridiculous! You cannot arrest him."

Todd motioned toward the great hall, where a figure got up from an armchair by the fire. Cynara recognized the local magistrate, Lord Barton's thin body and curling silver hair. He sauntered toward the group and greeted them with a bow.

"I've listened to the questioning, and I cannot describe how it saddens me to arrest you, Lord Raven. But with so much evidence against you, and your wife evidently trying to protect you, I have no other choice but to place you in the detention house in the village." He hastened to smooth over his harsh words as thunderclouds gathered on Merlin's forehead. "For the time being. Only until this unfortunate matter is cleared up, of course." He motioned for Merlin to follow. "Come along now. No fighting, if you please."

"This is ridiculous, Barton, and well you know it."

The other man nodded, his face twisting painfully. "The sooner we clear up the matter, the better. You must account for your every move, you know."

Cynara clung to Merlin's arm and addressed Lord Barton. "You can't do this! It's preposterous. My husband never murdered anyone, you must know that."

"We know no such thing," said Sergeant Todd loftily. He gripped Merlin's other arm. "Now, come along."

"Merlin!" Cynara cried out in despair as they pulled him away.

Merlin looked grim, but as he glanced at Cynara, his expression softened. "Don't worry. I'll be back very soon."

Helplessly, Cynara watched them take him away. The villain would have a free hand now, especially after he had planted the cloak at the scene of the murder. She would have to find a way to help Merlin, she thought, but where to begin?

She thought of demanding Brandon's help, but not during the day. He would be brought to join Merlin in the detention cell, and then she would truly be all alone.

Sighing, she went back upstairs. While she had been in London, the maids had cleaned several of the upper rooms, but Cynara could not set her mind to continue the renovation of the castle. Not now, perhaps not ever if the evil surrounding them all was not dispelled. She paced the corridor outside her bedchamber, unable to shape a plan. Then she dressed, listening to Tildy's gloomy predictions about Merlin, but she kept silent, knowing that the maid might be right.

The midday meal came and went, Cynara eating in stately loneliness in the dining room. It was then the inspiration came to her. If she could open the stone door to the secret passageway in her mother's bedchamber, she might find the courage to further explore the dungeons. Tonight she would make Brandon go with her, and together they might discover what, if anything, was concealed in the damp cells. She shuddered at the thought, but this time she would have to show courage—for Merlin's sake.

After the meal she made sure that Bobby got the important letter destined for the Lagrange family in London. She gave him a purse of coins and told him to choose a good horse. "You must not return without a reply," she admonished him as she waved him off. "Godspeed."

She went to the gun room next to Merlin's study and took one of the Pauly breechloading pistols from a locked cabinet. She stuffed as many cartridges as she could into her pocket—just in case she would come face-to-face with Merlin's enemy. Thank God, Brandon had taught her how to load and shoot both muskets and pistols. Even though hunting was a sport she abhorred, she was now glad she'd learned the basic skill.

She hurried up to Estelle's bedchamber. It was just as well that her mother was using her room now; that way she wouldn't worry about the goings-on in her former bedroom and the dungeons. She might—with another bout of hysterics—prevent Cynara from further exploration.

The chamber lay in deep shadows, and apprehension filled Cynara once more. This time there was no knowing if the villains were in the house already. They had proved that guards at all doors couldn't keep them out.

She had brought with her a simple candlestick that held two candles. Starting, she pushed aside the drapes across the windows, and blazing sunlight filled the room. It instantly made her feel better.

"Now, let's see," she whispered to herself. An urgency filled her as if she were fighting with time. She pulled the tapestry to one side and held it away by shoving a chair up against it.

"There must be a mechanism somewhere." Studying the stone closely and trailing her fingertips over every inch, she searched for something that would open the door. All she could see was the mortar and the rock. Getting down on her knees, she examined the minutest parts of the wall and the abutting floor.

When she was about to give up, she solved the puzzle. In a spot on the floor, just past the tiny crack that outlined the door, she discovered a slightly higher piece of rock. She pushed it down with the palm of her hand, and with a whir the door slowly opened, pushing against her hip. It opened only partly, and she pressed the stone in the floor down once again. The door closed silently. She repeated the maneuver, and the door obeyed. She pulled it wide. The musty air flowed through the opening, and she wrinkled her nose. Nevertheless, she lit the candles, putting some extra stumps into her pocket. She pushed one cartridge into the pistol, and holding it in one hand and the candlestick in the other, she slowly descended the narrow stairs.

She trembled now that absolute silence and darkness was closing in around her. Perhaps she ought to go back. . . . She promised herself to return upstairs instantly if she heard some strange noise in the dungeons. But right now there was no one she could rely on except Brandon. And she couldn't wait until nightfall. Tildy would have refused to step into the dungeons, and Bramble, he would have gotten stuck in the narrow stairway. She smiled at that thought. Yet he could have joined her through the wine cellar. It was too late now, she thought grimly as she stepped onto the platform, then into the drafty passage that led to the bottle storage area.

"One thing is for sure, I'm not going down into the 'death hole,' " she said to herself. She listened with a shiver, wondering if she was alone. A faint tapping sound came from behind her, but who would be in the dungeon part of the cellars? Why not here, where an intrepid thief could steal valuable wine and bring it to the sandy cove through the passage? A ripple of fear went through her. These villains were much worse than thieves. . . .

* * *

Merlin paced the tiny cell in the basement of the Duck and Willow, once again testing the bars across the window. They were rusty, but not weakened enough to break under the pressure of his grip. He fumed with anger, unable to sit still.

Praying, he hoped that the guard had been able to locate the old village vicar. Not that Merlin wanted to ask for the last rites as he'd implied, but he had questions for the vicar, one of the oldest men in the village. Hope rose in his chest as the keys jangled outside and the stout oak door swung open. Reverend Henry Sidbourne stepped inside, his wispy white hair like a halo around his head, and his shoulders stooped as if he'd been burdened with too much sorrow during his lifetime. His eyes, however, were bright and friendly.

"My dear boy, what have you gotten yourself into now?" The vicar shook his head. "Scrapes . . . scrapes. I seem to recall a pair of boys, you and Max, who forever got embroiled in peccadilloes."

Merlin chuckled grimly. "This time it's a bit more serious, I'm afraid. They accuse me of murdering the poor madman Jean."

"I heard about his death," said the vicar, and he sat unbidden on the only chair in the cell. "But it's ridiculous that they would accuse you of his death. What would you gain by it?"

"They're desperate to apprehend someone. They haven't found Brandon Hawthorne, and they haven't discovered any more proof that I'm guilty of Father's death. They haven't found anything, and they are desperate. But they did find my cloak on the beach by the body."

The vicar smiled. "My dear boy." He patted Merlin's arm. "You have great burdens to bear at the moment, but mark my words, the light will rise over the horizon." He paused, giving Merlin a kindly stare.

His words made a burden lift from Merlin's heavy heart, and it seemed he could truly breathe again, as if he hadn't quite managed before.

"What is it you want, my boy?"

Merlin sat on the cot that was right beside the chair. "Tell me everything you know about Jean Leblanc."

"That's a strange request," the vicar said thoughtfully. "But I do recall the time he arrived at Black Raven. It happened twenty-five years ago, during the French Revolution. He was a victim of one of the greatest sea disasters that ever happened in this area." He glanced at Merlin. "Don't you recall hearing about the shipwreck?"

Merlin nodded. "Yes, my nanny told me about it a long time ago."

"You can't see the ship now, but what's left of it is right there among the reefs outside the castle. I believe Jean was the only survivor. I recall his head was bruised and bloodied after the accident. He never talked about it to anyone. Perhaps he didn't even remember. It was about that time he went off his mind."

"Do you know the name of the wreck?"

"Hirondelle."

Merlin flinched as if he'd been slapped. "I'll be damn—ahem—gormed."

"It was a French vessel, possibly a smuggler. The free trade was brisk at that time. They used the cove at

Black Raven, but also others along the coast to Dartmouth."

"This man Jean never told anyone what they were carrying that night?"

The vicar shook his head. "No. He didn't confide in anyone; that's why I think it was a smuggling boat."

Merlin rubbed his chin. "But why didn't he go back to France? Why remain here?"

"It's possible he didn't know he was from France, or something held him here. Shortly after the accident, he took to drink. He would work odd jobs—a good farrier he was—then he would squander the proceeds on ale."

Merlin thought about what the vicar had said. "Mayhap he knew something that the murderer is afraid would become public knowledge."

"Everything is possible. Jean must have known about the shipwreck and what it contained."

Merlin gripped the vicar's arm. "Please do me a favor, Reverend Sidbourne, write down what you just told me about Jean, especially mention the name of the ship, and have the letter sent up to Mrs. Estelle Hawthorne at the castle. This might explain some things to her, even if it doesn't to us."

The vicar rose. "It's a strange request, my boy, but I shall do it, of course. I want to do anything I can to free you." He patted Merlin's shoulder. "Just have faith, and you will be helped."

Merlin thanked the old man, and wished he could have left the cellar with him. With so much at stake, inactivity was more unbearable than any other punishment he could think of. He paced the floor, watching the sun slip down among the treetops. What was Cynara doing right now? Was she worrying about him?

Chapter 23

Cynara's heart pounded with fear. She debated with herself if she should continue her investigation or go for help. The latter road was the safest, and she started retracing her steps toward the secret stairway. The sounds started to change pattern, as if coming closer, a methodical hollow tapping. She halted, barely daring to breathe lest he—or they—would hear her. Hiding behind a crate that separated the wine cellars from the passage to the dungeons, she lifted the pistol. The click as she cocked the hammer sounded as loud as an actual shot.

She swallowed hard and extinguished her candles. Had the sound been heard in the dungeons? She listened until her head started aching with the strain. Making her way slowly toward the platform, she held the pistol pointed at the dark passage. What if she were discovered? Would she dare to shoot? She forced herself to drop that awful thought.

Just as she thought she would reach the platform unnoticed, she heard steps coming toward her. She saw a flickering of candlelight, and the shape of a tall man. He was right by the platform now, staring at the opposite end of the passage.

Cynara pressed close to the wall, praying that he wouldn't see her. Fortunately, she was still wearing dark mourning clothes, blending well in with the rock wall.

Her hand trembled so much around the pistol, she thought she would drop it.

The man slowly moved on, and Cynara could not recognize him due to the hat shielding his face. There was something familiar about his gait, but his identity eluded her. He passed the platform and moved toward the passage leading to the dungeons on the floor below. To Cynara's relief, he disappeared through the door, the light from his candles flickering eerily along the walls.

Cynara waited for several minutes before taking another step. Her heartbeat slowed down, and her hands steadied. Who was the man? If only she had gotten a glimpse of his face, she would have learned his identity. If she knew him, she could go straight to the authorities with his name. He would be apprehended when he came out of the dungeons. . . .

She would have to find out. She knew it was a reckless idea that prompted her to move toward the door through which he'd disappeared, but she wouldn't confront him, only watch from the darkness until the light gave his identity away. Still, she was so frightened that when her toes pushed a pebble across the path, she almost fainted from the shock.

The only light guiding her was the faint glimmer of the man's candle. She followed it, and when it slowed down by the door to the first cell, she also slowed her steps. Barely daring to make another move, she had to force herself to inch forward. She prayed there were no obstacles in her way as she cautiously put one foot in front of the other. She heard him muttering to himself as he studied the walls from top to bottom, holding the candlestick aloft. The closer she got, the better she could see him. Every step was more dangerous than the next, and she could barely breathe for fear that he would hear her.

To her surprise, he suddenly left the cell. Swearing and kicking the door shut behind him, he went to the next cell and started the procedure all over. She had to move toward him since his identity still eluded her. If only she hadn't been alone . . .

Somehow her concentration broke for a moment, and she stepped down hard on something on the floor. It sounded like a brittle piece of wood cracking, and she gasped in terror. The noise waxed enormous in the stillness, giving away her presence as easily as if she'd been shouting her name.

There was a flurry of movement, the candlelight flickering wildly. She turned and ran blindly down the passage toward what she believed to be the door by the platform. The walls seemed to have disappeared. All there was now was a black void, and she was hurtling through it.

It was inevitable that she would stumble. She hit the wall, breaking her fall with her bandaged hands. Crying out in pain, she tumbled to the floor. Then light was shining in her eyes, and she stared up into a face that was hollowed by diabolical shadows. Never in her nightmares had she suspected she would gaze into those murky brown eyes again.

"Hello, Cynara," Felix said, leering.

Brandon was glad the night was overcast. He'd slipped from the tower room unseen and hovered about the corridor that led to Cynara's and Merlin's bedchambers. There had been no sign of them. He debated whether he should visit his mother or not, but decided against it. She might make too many delighted exclamations, thus draw the entire staff. Losing his patience finally, Brandon sought out Bramble in the butler's pantry—first making sure that no one had noticed him.

Bramble, his eyes widening in shock when he recognized Brandon, dragged him into the pantry and locked the door. "Mr. Brandon, you shouldn't take such risks!" The butler told him about the happenings during the day, and Brandon swore under his breath. "I must try to rescue Merlin."

"I think Lady Raven might already harbor the same plan. She has not been here since midday."

Brandon rubbed his chin thoughtfully. "I wonder . . . are you sure she has left the castle?"

"She isn't in her room, but seeing as the master is locked up, she must have gone to see if there's a way to free him. Perhaps she's bargaining with Lord Barton, the magistrate."

"Is her horse gone?"

Bramble pursed his lips. "As a matter of fact, I don't know."

Brandon cursed as worry swept through him. Had

she gone exploring on her own? He pushed away that thought as preposterous. She wouldn't dare go alone, or would she? She had ridden through the forest at night to seek him at Stormywood. "Where's Gideon Swift? I might need his help."

Bramble said he would send Swift out to the make-shift stables to meet Brandon.

"I'll return with the master, and we might have to hide him until this latest scandal blows over," Brandon said.

Bramble clutched his head. "Oh, my, oh, my, what's this house coming to? The master in hiding. Begad, *you* are already in hiding."

"Never mind that. This is the only way we can prove my innocence—and your master's."

Bramble brought a tray of food to the pantry, then he managed to smuggle Brandon out of the house unseen. The hushed night, heavy clouds slowly moving in, promised rain.

Alert after sleeping all day, Brandon moved through the shadows to the square building that held the horses. He got past the guards at the doors without difficulty, and he realized the lazy footmen would be useless against a cunning enemy. Anyone who truly wanted to get into the castle would find a way. He looked inside the stables, instantly recognizing Swallow.

Frowning, he knew without a doubt that Cynara was still somewhere in the castle. Most likely in the dungeons since she hadn't been seen elsewhere . . . Damn her to be so foolish! He was torn whether to go in search of her, or take the time to rescue Merlin from his prison. Two men would overpower any enemy lurking inside the castle, he reasoned. Besides, there wasn't any indication that a stranger was about.

He might have only one chance to rescue Merlin, and he would have to take it.

A movement beside him told him that Gideon Swift had arrived. He was carrying a satchel strapped over his shoulder. Without speaking, the old man pulled him past the stables. At a crouching run they moved up the slope behind the burned-down stables and entered the woods. The horses were tied to a tree, and after jumping into the saddles, the two men chose the forest path that would skirt the Black Raven village.

Gideon Swift spoke when they were out of earshot of the castle guards. "They locked up the master at the inn. There's a cell in the basement there. With any luck, we'll have him free before the turnkey can cry out for mercy."

Brandon nodded grimly. They hid the horses and crept into the village. The revelry at the inn was in full swing. Swift led Brandon toward the back of the building. Hiding behind a bush, they could see the glowing fire of the turnkey's pipe. A puff of fragrant smoke blew past their faces.

Without speaking, Brandon motioned that he would go first, and Swift follow him. Pressed closely to the wall, he moved up behind the guard soundlessly. With a jump he was on the man's back and instantly pushed his hands across the jailer's mouth to stifle any shouts.

Swift stepped forward, pulling out rope from the satchel, and bound the guard. Then he proceeded to push a handkerchief into the man's mouth. Indignation came from the jailer in waves as he sprawled on the ground, kicking, and trying to speak through the gag.

Swift soon found the key ring dangling from the guard's belt, and without further ado he proceeded to unlock the door. There was another, stouter door behind it, but one of the keys fit into that lock.

Merlin's teeth gleamed white in the darkness as they stepped into the cell. "It's about time," he muttered under his breath, and led the way out of the cell. They dragged the guard into the cell and locked the door, leaving the keys dangling in the lock.

Merlin spoke when they reached the horses. "I was worrying that you'd forgotten about me," he said jokingly.

"You can thank me later," Brandon said. "I don't want to worry you, but it looks like Cynara has disappeared."

The two men shared one horse, and Brandon sensed the panic in Merlin. He urged the mount on with his heels.

"What happened?" Merlin demanded through clenched teeth.

"I don't know. I was in hiding all day, and Bramble told me she hasn't been seen since midday."

"Blast and damn! No one has looked for her, then?"

"Bramble thought she'd gone to bargain for your release with Barton, but I discovered that her horse is still at Black Raven."

Merlin pondered that in silence. "The dungeons," he said at last.

Brandon grimaced. "That's what I suspect."

"She's too nosy by half."

They reached the fringe of Gairlook Woods and

rode toward the castle along the coast path. Black Raven was barely visible in the dark, only a few windows lit by candlelight.

"There's a way into the dungeons from the sea," Brandon shouted above the noise of the crashing waves. "Do you know about it?"

Merlin nodded. "I think it was used in the heyday of the smugglers."

They alighted, and left Gideon Swift to see to the horses. From his satchel the old man took two pistols, cartridges, and two knives, and handed them silently to the men. They took the weapons and slid down the path to the beach below. The inner bay was still relatively calm, but the wind was picking up, and stray raindrops splashed their faces.

Closely followed by Brandon, Merlin jumped over the rocks to the cave that hid the secret passageway. He prayed they wouldn't find Cynara hurt—or worse. At least the tide was low, if rising rapidly.

He could barely contain his worry as they made their way up the steep path. More than ever, he realized how much he loved her. Fear tightened his chest so that he could barely breathe. Dear God, don't let me be too late, he prayed.

The path was rough, and only through Brandon's carrying a candle in his pocket did they have light to show the way. They hurried through the wine cellar and through the passage to the wooden platform.

"Do you think she's down by the 'death hole'?" Brandon asked, his voice grim.

"Why should she be, unless the villain got her and put her there? But I suppose we should look there first, especially since the tide is rising."

They found the door that led to the lower dungeons and hurried along that passage. As they stepped down toward the staircase, Brandon stumbled on something on the floor. He bent to pick up the object.

"Look, it's Cynara's slipper!" he cried out.

Frantic, Merlin tore the shoe from his hand and studied it closely. "She wouldn't have dropped this if she hadn't been in a hurry—or been carried."

Cynara glared at Felix, still shocked to find him alive. He had pushed her into a rowboat that had been pulled into the cave at the end of the secret passageway, then jumped in and shoved off with an oar. The sea was choppy in the rising wind, but Felix rowed with unexpected strength, keeping as close to the rocky shore as was safe. Now they were rounding a huge cliff that would lead them to a series of coves past Gairlock Woods. The scent of seaweed and salt was strong, the wind and the intermittent spatter of spray against Cynara's face cold. She shivered and tried to form a plan of escape. Her thoughts flitted like butterflies in her mind, unable to create a coherent picture.

"Wait till everyone hears that you're alive," she snapped. "I'm sure it's illegal to stage your own death."

He laughed. "I'll be long gone by then, my sweet."

She wound her arms around her middle and hunched forward in an effort to conserve warmth. "Anyway, why would you want to pretend you were dead?"

"If only you had married me, I wouldn't have had

to go through this charade," he said, his voice now suppressed with anger.

"What do you mean?"

He snorted. "If you had become my wife, I would have had the legal rights to do whatever I wanted with the treasure. As the Earl of Raven, I had free access to every part of the castle, but I couldn't find the damned casket."

Cynara eyes widened. "But since you're not dead, you *are* the Earl of Raven. What is it that you want from the castle, Felix?"

"I don't want the castle!" he spat out. "It's a dreadful dreary heap of stones, a mammoth millstone. I don't care about the earldom or this cold country. I want to go back to America a wealthy man. The plantation needs funds desperately." The rowboat rocked as he turned it toward shore.

"I don't understand what you're talking about! There are no funds at Black Raven. Without Merlin's fortune—which his father amassed—we would be poor."

"You don't know Black Raven's secret. For twenty-five years the castle has been sitting like a fat dragon on a fortune. How do you think Sydney Seymour kept up appearances during his time as earl? The copper mines are empty, and the farms ramshackle."

"The farms surely brought in more revenues then than now. They still do, and once we've rebuilt the cottages and prospected for more mines, Black Raven will once again be prosperous." Cynara's teeth began to clatter, not as much from the cold sea breeze as from fear. "You mentioned a secret."

"If you'd married me, I would have had control

over the fortune, don't you understand? Your brother
was in prison and would soon rot there, unless he was
sentenced first, and Estelle would have been taken care
of. I promised that. Once your brother was dead, we
could have sold Bluewater and made a tidy little sum
on that sale."

"What are you talking about, Felix? What does
Brandon have to do with this?" She stared at him in
the gloom, noticing the satisfied smile on his face.

"I will win as long as I keep you at my side" was the
only explanation he gave.

No matter how many questions she threw at him, he
only shrugged, concentrating on bringing the rowboat
past a series of rocks to a cove a mile east of Black
Raven. Cynara silenced as the boat ground against
shale. The beach sloped steeply upward, and she
scrambled on hands and knees to reach a rocky platform above. Perhaps there would be a way to escape
up on the ridge. But as she got to her feet on the flat
surface, a voice startled her.

"I didn't know you had invited a lady for supper,
Lord Seymour."

Cynara stared into Muggins's malicious face.
"You!" she exclaimed. "We always wondered why
you disappeared and why you tried to kill us on the
road to Basingstoke. I saw you speaking with Lady
Fidalia on the Gairlock road."

"I keep lofty friends," Muggins said with a snicker.
He turned to Felix. "You haven't told her about the
secret?"

"No . . . why should I? She'll find out soon enough."
Felix studied her intently. Desire, then cunning, then
anger crossed his face. The wrath remained. "I haven't

decided whether to bring her with me to Virginia, or leave her with the others—dead." Without another glance at Cynara, he walked into a cave among the cliffs. "Till I decide, you must watch her day and night," he said to Muggins. "Tie her up if necessary."

Muggins, taking Cynara by the arm, dragged her into the cave. A small fire burned close to the cave's mouth, and soup bubbled in a pot. Felix had already sat down by the fire.

He looked nothing like the sleek, well-fed bridegroom she'd left at the altar. Now he was dressed in ragged clothes, his hair unkempt and dirty. He'd grown thinner, his face all burning eyes and diabolical hollows.

Muggins pushed her down beside Felix and served soup in wooden bowls. It tasted of fish and onions, and Cynara forced it down, not knowing when her next meal would come. Muggins threw her a chunk of hard bread, and she dipped it in the soup.

"No luck, then?" Muggins said to Felix. Cynara noticed the wary glance that the former stable groom gave Felix, as if a wrong word would trigger some kind of explosion.

"Blast and damn!" Felix swore, tossing down his empty bowl. "We've gone over every cell now, and there isn't the slightest sign of the chest."

Cynara listened intently. Chest? There were lots of old chests in the castle, clothes chests, trunks filled with books, and carved tool chests. She almost blurted out a question, but what good would it do except incense Felix further?

"We've looked everywhere, and I don't have any idea what to do next." Felix rose and began to pace.

The cave was wide at the mouth, then, sloping down toward the back, a narrow opening—too slim for humans to pass through—leading farther into the hill.

"We cannot give up now," Muggins said, ladling up more soup for himself. "We'll return at dawn, after a few hours of rest."

Felix kicked a loose rock. "We can't take a break now! They'll be missing Cynara at the castle, and search every part of the area." He chuckled softly. "At least that hothead Merlin isn't there to complicate things. It was a stroke of good luck that the runners found the gray cloak on the beach. Clever idea, Muggins."

"Cloak?" Cynara burst out. *"You* put the cloak there to implicate Merlin for Jean's murder, while you're the murderer."

Felix gave her a slow, appreciative smile and Cynara shuddered with revulsion. "There's nothing wrong with your powers of deduction, my darling. Perhaps I shall take you with me to America after all. I always thought your company was refreshing. I always had a tender spot in my heart for you."

Cynara shrank back, suppressing a frantic urge to bolt out of the cave. She would have to outwit Felix to save herself. "Why did you kill Jean? What threat was an old madman to you?"

"Jean knew about the secret. He was there at the time when it happened, and he wanted a piece of the fortune. He's been blackmailing me since I got the title after Max. He had to die."

"Fortune? You must explain yourself, Felix," she said.

"I don't owe you any explanation, Cynara. You

betrayed me by marrying that failure of a man, Merlin." His voice grew whiny. "I've always hated him, just as I hated your brother. They—including Max— were always so close, shutting me out of everything." He puffed himself up. "I have as much right to Black Raven as Merlin has, even though I'm half American. My father, George, had just as much right to the fortune as any of the other Seymour brothers."

"I'm afraid I don't understand what you're talking about."

Felix shrugged. "It's just as well that you don't know the whole story. Once I've finished with Merlin and your brother, you'll cling to me for support—as will your useless mother."

Cynara seethed, but she controlled her fury. Never had she felt a more urgent need to get away. She had to stay calm, or she might go the same way as Jean.

Merlin pushed Cynara's shoe into his pocket and dragged Brandon with him. "Come, let's examine the 'death hole.' The tide will drown her if we don't get there first."

They stumbled down the slippery stairs, and Brandon held up his candle with the wavering flame. Dampness glistened on the walls, and the hollow sound of water dripping filled the cave forlornly.

"It makes me cold all over to view this place again," Merlin said, and wrenched the bolts of the wooden trapdoor aside. Then they pulled it open and peered into the blackness. "I can't see anything. The water is rather high already."

Brandon kneeled and pushed his candle through the hole, but still they couldn't see much.

"I will have to go down there," Merlin said with a sigh. When Brandon was about to protest, Merlin added, "I know the cell, and you don't." He swung his legs over the side and located the stone steps. Holding on to the edge, he stepped down on the ledge. "Hand me the candle now."

Brandon obeyed, and Merlin studied the slimy cave. "No one here, thank God! Nothing in the water." He thrust the candle back to Brandon. "But where could she be?"

"We must search every part of the dungeons. Then the castle, then the grounds." Brandon voice trembled slightly. "She's a plucky old girl, but this time I have a terrible feeling."

Merlin heaved himself up and slammed the trap-door. "No time to lose. Come on, let's search the next floor."

Night moved on into dawn. Cynara had been bound around the ankles and around her wrists. She was stiff after lying on the rocky ground, and a stone kept eating into her back every time she tried to shift onto her side. If only there was a way to escape, she thought, staring with aching eyes toward the sea. The surging of the waves came with monotonous regularity. Usually it was a great remedy for insomnia, but now it only irritated her. The sea had calmed, and the day was gray with a steady rain.

She moved stiffly under the musty horse blanket that Muggins had thrown over her. Casting a glance over her shoulder, she noticed that the two men were still asleep. Felix had wanted to return to the castle dungeons after supper, but Muggins had dissuaded him, pointing out that the search for Cynara might go on all night. The servants would surely search the dungeons.

"Even if they doubt Merlin Seymour, they still like the mistress of the house," he'd said. "Even the sourly Mrs. Averell has taken a liking to Lady Raven. They're bound to stage a frantic search."

Felix had muttered something and thrown himself onto a heap of blankets. Cynara wondered when they planned to return to Black Raven. Surely not during daylight, she thought, fearing that she might have to stay confined to this cave in the company of her enemies all day. She closed her eyes, her mind running around like a rat in a cage as it sought for a way to escape. As the morning grew lighter, she eased herself into an upright position.

Her hands were still bandaged, now two bundles of filthy rags. The cords were tight around her wrists, partially closing off the circulation. She wished she could untie them, and maybe—if she could unwind the bandages—she might manage to slip out of the ropes.

She chewed on the knot that held the bandage on her left hand together. The new skin on her hands felt itchy and tight. She wondered if the burns had healed completely. Just as she was about to succeed, Muggins stirred, instantly awake. He stared at her suspiciously as she hid her hands under the blanket. Perhaps she would find some time later to work on the knots.

* * *

Merlin and Brandon were tired, dirty, and frantic with worry as they stumbled out of the dungeons at dawn. "Where could she be?" Merlin shouted, kicking open the door at the end of the wine cellars.

"I wish I had a crystal ball," said Brandon wearily. He was closely upon Merlin's heels.

Merlin halted. "You'd better stay down there, old fellow. What if the runners come to breakfast?"

Brandon shrugged. "What about you? They will only incarcerate you again."

A slow smile lit up Merlin's face. "Unless we incarcerate them first. There are plenty of dungeons here, after all."

Brandon laughed and punched Merlin's shoulder. "A splendid idea!" He rubbed his dirty, stubbled chin. "But perhaps we'd better only tie them to the most comfortable chairs in the house with a deck of cards and some brandy. That way, they might not take our 'prank' too badly."

"Hmmm, you have a point there. So it shall be." Merlin steered his steps toward the kitchen. "Let's go and give them the surprise of their life."

Chapter 24

Even though she spent the entire day trying, Cynara could not get the cord off her wrists. The men had gone somewhere, leaving her tied to a rock with ropes around her waist and neck. She could barely move all day, and cried with the pain of her stiffened muscles. By nightfall she was so stiff and full of despair that she was ready to do whatever Felix and Muggins wanted. However, during the long hours of the day she had devised a plan that might work. She had remembered something that might be of utmost importance.

"Still here?" Felix chided as they returned, carrying a sack that contained a dead chicken and ten potatoes. "I take it you are loathe to leave my company." He tittered and patted her thigh. "I like such devotion in a woman."

Cynara wanted to kick him. "Please untie me, Felix. I have something important to tell you."

Muggins took the sack from Felix and set it down, muttering, "Don't get taken in by false promises, Master Felix."

Felix only shrugged and untied the rope around her

neck and waist. Now she had limited movement. Felix watched her try to squirm into a standing position. "I suppose you need to respond to nature's call," he said, and untied all the ropes. "But don't try any tricks." From the top of his boot he hauled out a knife, the sharp tip glinting evilly in the setting sun. "Go down to the beach, but don't try anything, because I'll stand guard right by the boat."

Cynara obeyed, her limbs so stiff that it was almost impossible to move. While she had the opportunity, she had to find a way to escape. She scanned the length of the rocky beach, finding that there was no way out except by boat. Felix was standing beside it now, arms crossed over his chest, and a belligerent scowl on his face.

Sighing, she went behind a large rock, knowing she would have to rely solely on her initial plan.

Two hours later, when they were eating a stew of chicken and potatoes, she brought up the subject. "You're looking for a chest, aren't you, and you haven't found it yet. Well, I might know where it is," she said casually.

The two men stopped eating, staring at her with narrowed eyes.

"Don't listen to her," said Muggins. "She's tryin' to fool us."

Anger blazed in Felix's eyes. "If that's the case, then she knows I show no mercy." His lips curled contemptuously. "And where, pray tell, would the chest be, and how would you know about it?"

"I've explored the dungeons on occasion," she said airily, trying to pretend that their evil faces didn't frighten her. "I could show you the spot—on one condition."

The men glanced at each other and laughed. "There it is—the trick," said Muggins. "I told you not to trust her."

Felix leaned back against a boulder, his hands clasped over his stomach, a satisfied smile on his lips. "There's no harm in listening to her plan. As long as she's in our power, I'm sure we're safe from her machinations."

"I will show you the spot, but only if you let me go free." She held up her hands to silence Muggins's shouted protest. "You can let me go the moment you are ready to leave Black Raven. No one will be the wiser, but I treasure my freedom more than any chest full of secrets."

Felix's chuckle erupted into a gale of laughter. "You are out of your mind, Cynara. You either die or come with me to America." He leaned toward her, his eyes glistening with greed. "However, you can tell us the spot, and thereby shorten your own suffering."

Cynara set down her bowl carefully, though she burned to throw the contents in his face. But such a gesture would only jeopardize her own safety. She would have to keep a cool head, even though her hands trembled and her heart raced with fear.

"I can't recall exactly, but it's in the beach cave outside the secret passageway." Since she suspected they wouldn't let her go with them, she added a lie. "It's down below the rocks, right at the waterline."

Felix shot Muggins an excited glance, but Muggins looked skeptical. "Why would she suddenly remember this?" he commented. "She's lying."

Felix rose with finality. "You can stay here and guard her, and I will go and search the cave. We might as well—while the tide permits."

Muggins shrugged. "If you must," he said grumpily.

"Well, we can't remain here indefinitely. With every day it gets more dangerous. I'm certain they're searching seriously for Cynara by now. We have to find the chest tonight, or give up." He left, carrying a storm lantern in one hand and a pistol in the other.

The wind was whistling among the rocks, and gulls wheeled above the cold blue-green water in search of food. Cynara had never felt lonelier than at that moment.

As an hour passed, Cynara and Muggins stared at each other uneasily, the crashing of the waves the only sound. Tension mounting, Cynara finally couldn't stand the silence.

"What made you choose to serve such a villain as Felix Seymour?" she asked the sullen groom.

He spat on the ground right at her feet. "Who else is there to serve? Master Felix is truly the Earl of Raven—not your husband. I serve the earl, just like I have done all my life." He paused. "Aside from that, I wouldn't mind becoming a rich man, and Master Felix has promised me part of the treasure."

"You're devoted to him after what he's done? You know that he's capable of murder. He's a madman."

Muggins heaved a sigh. "Be that as it may. I cannot change my plans now. Too late."

Cynara silenced, pondering his words. If it hadn't been for his loyalty to Felix, and greed, none of this would have happened. He helped Felix bluff his own death.

The sun dipped into the sea, coloring the water a savage crimson. It reminded Cynara of streaks of blood, and she averted her gaze from the spectacle. A cold wind from the north cajoled its way into every crevice of the cave, and under Cynara's clothes. She trembled, thinking she would never get warm again.

Misgiving came over her when Felix didn't return as promised. What had happened to him? Would she be forever trapped here with Muggins?

She stood, stretching. Her wrists ached where Felix had pulled the cord too tight before he left. To her relief, he hadn't bound her ankles. She could walk around the cave to get the cold out of her bones. She strained her eyes to see any movement on the beach below.

"Don't try anything," Muggins said, aiming a pistol at her. "I won't hesitate to shoot you."

"Look, Felix is coming back. There's the rowboat now."

Muggins craned his neck over the edge. His sullen expression changed to excitement, but the aim of his weapon never wavering, he waited calmly until Felix had reached the cave.

Cynara noticed instantly that Felix was in a terrible mood. Swearing, he flung down the lantern. "I didn't find anything except clams and rotten seaweed," he said accusingly to Cynara. "If you've fooled me, I will wring your neck slowly until it snaps."

Cynara took a step back due to the hatred in his eyes. "I have to go there myself," she said, her voice trembling. "You must let me look at the cave, since I can't remember the exact spot."

Fury darkened Felix's face. "How do you know what's hidden there?"

"I don't, other than it's a chest with a secret. I hope it's located where I think it is, but I can't be sure."

Felix studied her for a moment. "Very well, but if you trick me, I will kill you. Come along now, and no complaints!"

A cold shiver went along her spine. She knew he meant it, and she prayed that the chest would be behind the smooth rock she remembered. Her legs turning into a jellylike substance, she struggled through the shale on the beach, closely followed by the two men wielding pistols.

Merlin and Brandon viewed their handiwork as the two Bow Street Runners were scowling at them from the two armchairs in Merlin's study. Their waists and legs had been tied securely to the chair legs, and their right hands had been tied to their backs. That way they could drink brandy and play cards—with some difficulty—without any chance of untying the knots.

"They look rather angry, don't you think, Merlin?" Brandon said, chuckling.

"You'll hang for this, Mr. Hawthorne," Sergeant Todd spat furiously.

"We have important work to do," said Merlin, "and we don't need your interference. If you'd remained free, you would have locked us up instantly. It came down to the choice between you and us." Merlin walked toward the door. "If you have the sensibility that I think you have, you ought to take advantage of this time of recreation. The brandy is excellent." He bowed. "Gentlemen, enjoy yourselves."

Laughing, Brandon followed Merlin, and they locked the door behind them. "They were so angry, I swear I could smell the sulphur of hell in the air," he said. He slipped the key into his pocket. "It wouldn't do to have the servants find the venerable lawmen tied up," he commented. "And release them."

"No," Merlin said, frowning. "Let's hope we find Cynara before the servants find the lawmen. We must search the dungeons once more."

They looked into every corner and crevice of the musty cells below ground without finding anything but dust and mouse droppings. By the time they had emerged from the wine cellar, they were covered with grime. The sun's last rays slanted red over the sea, reminding them that they hadn't eaten all day. Hungry and thirsty, they hurried to the kitchen, where they partook of a hasty meal brought from the larder by Mrs. Black.

"My son just returned," she said. "He went out to see to the horse, but he'll be back in a few minutes."

Standing by the window, Merlin chewed a cold meat pie hurriedly. "I'm eager to hear what he has to say. By the way, Mrs. Black, please ask one of the footmen to fetch Mrs. Hawthorne. We'll meet your son in the breakfast parlor."

"I take it you haven't found Lady Raven?" the cook said, her round face worried, her hands twisting the white apron.

"No . . ." Merlin's lips tightened, and Brandon thought he looked close to collapse. The man hadn't slept for days.

"I take it none of the servants has found any clues on the grounds?" Merlin asked.

The cook shook her head. "I'm afraid not." Furtively, she wiped a tear from her eye. "I loved the countess," she said hoarsely.

Merlin swung around, slamming the empty plate on the table. "Don't speak of her as if she were dead!" He stalked out of the room.

"Don't take any notice of his temper," Brandon said to Mrs. Black. "He's out of his mind with worry."

"We all are. Your sister is a treasure." Mrs. Black buried her face in her apron and rushed into the scullery.

Hanging his head, Brandon went to reassure his mother, whom he knew would be another person frantic with anguish.

Merlin was standing by the window of the breakfast parlor, staring out to sea. Brandon and Estelle were sitting by the table, holding hands on the white starched tablecloth, as Bobby Black entered.

The boy looked tired, and his face was streaked with dust.

"Well, what message did you bring back?" Merlin asked curtly, holding out his hand. Deep lines of worry slashed from his nose to the corners of his downturned lips.

Bobby handed him an envelope, and Merlin tore it open. A hush had fallen over the room.

Merlin read aloud.

Dear Estelle Mournay Hawthorne,

We never thought we would hear from you again. It has been twenty-seven years since we arrived in England, and we thought you must have died in Cornwall—the last member of the Mournay family—since we haven't heard from you for so long. However, your query came as a shock to us as we realized that all these years, you didn't know that your father sent a ship to England that carried the Mournay fortune. He changed everything into gold, except for a cache of family jewels. After the Revolution, we tried to contact your old solicitors in France, and discovered that all of the Mournays—except you—had been executed in Paris. One of our loyal servants at our ruined château reported shortly after the Terror that the ship that carried the Mournay fortune sank in the Channel. We were sure that you'd found out about it. After what the young groom who visited us from Black Raven said, we deduced that Jean Leblanc was part of the crew that sailed from France on the ship *Hirondelle*. We shall investigate further.

"*Hirondelle?* Estelle said with a gasp. "That was one of Father's ships."

"The vicar, who still remembers the wreck quite well, told me the name."

"But why haven't I heard about it before?" Estelle demanded.

"You probably did hear about the disaster, but perhaps no one mentioned the name of the ship. You must take into consideration that you didn't live at Black Raven, but at Bluewater at the time. Anyway, no one connected the tragedy to you."

"Then how come the *Hirondelle* necklace was found

if Father sent the cache here and it sunk to the bottom of the sea?"

Merlin slammed his fist into the window frame. "Someone got hold of the Mournay fortune, and I intend to discover who before I rest another minute."

Cynara shivered in the sharp breeze, but she trained her eyes toward Black Raven, whose towers could been seen soaring above the cliffs. Many windows were lit with candles, and she felt reassured. People were there, searching for her. What she needed was more time. . . . Sooner or later someone would search the dungeons for her, then the passageways . . . then the caves. Perhaps she could rush up the path on the beach.

"Sitting there plotting like an old statesman, aren't you, Cynara?" Felix shouted angrily over the wind. He maneuvered the rowboat into the lee of the cave by the sliver of beach at Black Raven. "You must find the chest before the tide is up, or you'll be sorry." He pushed her out of the boat, and the hem of her gown and her feet were soaked with water instantly. Her back ached where he'd pushed her. "Don't you believe you can fool me," Felix droned on.

Biting her teeth together to prevent herself from moaning, she scrambled onto the sand. Her eyes had already adjusted to the darkness. As Felix lighted the storm lantern, she knew exactly which spot she had touched once before. The rocks glistened wet and black in the light as Cynara went over to the stone step that led into the secret passageway. Balancing precariously on a boulder, she touched the strangely smooth rock face at shoulder height. "It's behind this slab." What if she were wrong? Still, the plan would give her more time to make her escape. The stone slab seemed too heavy to shift.

Felix muttered something as he stared at the rock thoughtfully. He gave her a dark glance. "If you've lied about this, you shall be punished."

Cynara couldn't answer, as fear made her numb. She watched as the men got to work on the slab. They had tied her hands and feet so that she couldn't run away, and she sat dejectedly on the step leading to the secret passageway. The lantern threw a flickering light around the rough walls. She watched the men slowly wrenching the slab aside, and she was once again stricken by the smoothness of the rock compared to the others in the cave. It could be true that it concealed the treasure. . . .

As darkness deepened due to the lantern's weakening flame, the men managed to push the slab away. Felix scrambled for the lamp, and Cynara prayed that someone would appear to rescue her. Fearing for her life, she didn't dare to scream.

"There certainly is a cavity behind that rock," Felix said excitedly. "Perhaps you weren't lying after all."

Cynara didn't reply. Her curiosity aroused, she stood, craning her neck to see better. Since she was tied, she couldn't join the men on the rocks. Felix had climbed up, leaning halfway into the hollow while Muggins was holding up the lantern at his elbow.

Felix cried out. "There definitely is something here." He eased himself farther into the cavity, and Cynara sat down and tried desperately to pull her feet through the hard noose of the rope, but it wouldn't budge. This would have been the perfect time to escape, while the men had their attention elsewhere.

Felix dragged something out of the cavity, a dusty square box. It seemed heavy as he puffed and groaned under the weight. With Muggins's help, he lifted it to the rocks below, then carried it to the step where Cynara was sitting.

Felix's eyes gleamed with speculation. "I knew it was here somewhere. But that you would know how to find it, Cynara, came as a surprise."

The chest gave a metallic clang as they set it down. Holding the lantern aloft, they set to work on the lock.

"It looks new," Muggins commented. "Not a speck of rust on it."

"Which means that someone has taken care of the chest, even opened it recently. You must know that this was a Seymour secret. The three brothers knew about it," Felix said.

"What are you talking about?" Cynara asked.

Felix looked at her hard. "Sydney, George, and Ross Seymour, of course. They stole this treasure from a sinking French ship twenty-five years ago."

Muggins had managed to destroy the lock with a sharp rock. Using his knife, he pried open the lid. Cynara leaned forward to get a look. She gasped as gold glinted in the light from the lantern.

Felix pulled out a smaller chest and opened the lid. Gems of all colors and shapes glittered under Cynara's dazed eyes.

"It's all here," Felix crowed, "or what's left of it over the years. I'm a rich man!"

Muggins chimed in, "So am I." He indicated

Cynara with his thumb. "What shall we do about her now that she knows the truth?"

"I don't know anything except that this treasure was stolen by the Seymour brothers a long time ago," Cynara protested.

Felix rubbed his chin. "Do we dare to let her live? I had planned to take her back to Virginia without her knowing the truth about this." He glanced at the treasure. "But now she knows about it, and I doubt that she could keep her mouth shut for any length of time. Perhaps we'd better get rid of her—hmmm—another drowning victim, eh?"

"No! That's not fair. I helped you!" Cynara was stiff with fear as she glanced into Felix's cold, calculating stare. Wasn't anyone looking for her? With Merlin locked up at the Duck and Willow, she wasn't sure if anyone was there to help her—unless Brandon was still at Black Raven . . . *God, please help me.*

"I must come with you," Estelle called out after Merlin and Brandon as they, armed with pistols and lanterns, were preparing to go outside.

"It's a cold night, Mother," Brandon said, trying to ignore her pleas. "You'd be safer inside the castle."

"Listen to your son's advice, Estelle," said Merlin, knowing now, as Estelle sailed past him, head held high, where Cynara had gotten the stubborn thrust of her chin.

Estelle flung a shawl across her shoulders. "I shall go mad if I have to sit alone and brood," she said, and stepped outside. Wind whipped her black skirts around her legs, but she didn't seem to notice as she hurried around the corner. "We might as well start in the rose garden," she said.

"No use arguing with her when she's in this frame of mind," Brandon said ruefully.

"I have no intention of arguing," Merlin said. He was close on Estelle's heels. "Women have a remarkable intuition." He prayed that his trust in Estelle's instinct was a sound one.

"We've searched the castle from top to bottom, so there's only the garden left. That is, if Cynara is anywhere on the Black Raven premises," Brandon said. "It's beginning to look as if she has left the estate."

"Balderdash," scoffed Estelle. "She's still here somewhere. She wouldn't go off without letting us know."

The wind was rising by the minute. It moaned along the castle walls and through the cracks in the crumbling stone fence around the garden. Within minutes they had searched the square area without finding any trace of Cynara.

"The nightly digger has given up his pursuit," Estelle said thoughtfully.

"He was evidently digging for the *Hirondelle* treasure," Merlin said. "What now?"

Estelle seemed to be sniffing the air, turning this way, then that way, like a dog.

"Like Brandon said, we've searched every inch of the castle, and the dungeons." Merlin paced impatiently.

"Let's go to the burned-out stables," Estelle said, heading out of the garden at a run.

The men exchanged dubious glances, but had no choice but to follow her.

"I'm so nervous," Merlin said between clenched teeth. "I have this dread in my heart, as if we won't be in time to save her."

Cynara viewed the two villains in front of her, knowing that they intended to kill her.

"A blow to her head, and then the water," Muggins said, smiling evilly.

"Yes . . . sounds like the best solution." Felix touched Cynara's tangled curls. "She's a lovely piece. Sad to destroy her, really."

"Don't be sentimental," Muggins scoffed, bending once again over the chest.

"Let me at least see the entire treasure," Cynara said with a trembling voice. She moved closer to the chest, as if it could save her. All she needed was more time . . . time to escape.

"Well, I guess that's not an unreasonable request since these gems should rightfully adorn your neck."

Confused, Cynara stared at Felix. *"My* neck?"

"Yes. I suppose it won't hurt to know the truth now. You will take the secret with you to the bottom of the sea." Felix placed the open jewelry chest in her lap, shining the lantern at the costly glitter. "These once belonged to the Mournays, your French grandmother, and your great-grandmother, and even farther back than that."

"My mother's heritage?" Cynara asked with a gasp. "She always thought the new government confiscated the riches as they took over the estate in Gascogne."

"Your grandfather must have been a shrewd man,

but he didn't count on the stormy Channel, nor did he count on the villainous Seymour brothers."

"They stole it," Cynara intoned, her voice weakening, "while we Hawthornes were so poor all those years. It should have been our gold, our jewelry."

"You're right there, Cynara." Felix took the cache from her lap. "But it's too late to mourn that fact now," he added. "In the sea you don't need any worldly riches."

He untied her and led her down toward the sea's edge, where the tide was rapidly rising. "You'll go out with the tide at dawn," Felix said kindly, as if offering a gift. Her legs would barely carry her, and such a dread engulfed her that she ached all over. She was too frightened to cry. So this was it; she would die without even saying good-bye to the man she loved, to her family. It seemed an eternity since she'd last seen Merlin.

Cold waves sucked at her dress and plucked at her knees as if eager to grab the rest of her body. She staggered along the rocky bottom, pebbles cutting into her flesh.

"Get up on the sand bank," Felix ordered her, and she obeyed. But as he was still jumping from rock to rock behind her, she took the only chance that would be hers. Bending lightning-fast, she grabbed a fist-size rock and threw it at his head. She screamed as it glanced off the side of his face to slide down his back—harmless. It had served only to provoke his anger more. He gripped her arm painfully, and she cried out.

"Help! Help!" she cried, then his hands closed around her neck.

"Shut up!" he spat out, squeezing.

Her voice died in her throat, and her legs sagged. An excrutiating pain went through her head, and she desperately gasped for air as his strong hands squeezed harder. Red waves swam before her closed eyelids and a roar pounded in her ears. Then all went black.

Chapter 25

Merlin stormed down the path to the beach after seeing the flickering light of a lantern. Estelle had changed her mind halfway to the stables and ordered the two men back toward the beach, and now it looked as if she had been right. The shadows of two men wavered in the cave, then one moved aside, and there—was that a third person?

Rage flared through him as he heard Cynara's cry for help, and he literally flew over the rocks, closely followed by Brandon.

As he stumbled over the last boulder, he found Cynara stretched out in the sand, a man on top with a grip on her throat. Blinded with fury, Merlin kicked out, crunching into Felix's chin. Felix crumpled, his face close by the lantern. Merlin and Brandon swore in unison as they recognized Felix. "That blighter is still alive," Brandon shouted, incredulous. As Merlin kneeled by Cynara, holding up her head, Brandon went in pursuit of Muggins, who was trying to escape with the rowboat.

Plunging through the water, Brandon aimed his pistol at the hull and squeezed the trigger. The shot echoed around the cave, and water started to fill the rowboat with a gurgling sound. As Muggins scrambled out, Brandon caught him, pushing him up against the cave wall with the barrel of his weapon. "Give a hand here," he called out to Merlin.

Cynara moaned and opened her eyes as something wet splashed on her face. Still dazed, she recognized Merlin's worried eyes above her. He was dabbing water on her forehead. "Oh, Merlin," she whispered.

The shot startled her, and she sat up abruptly. Her head spinning, she felt Merlin's lips against her own.

"I love you," he whispered. "Everything will be fine now." Then Brandon was shouting in the background, and suddenly she was lying with her head in her mother's lap.

"What happened?" she croaked, her throat aching terribly.

"Shh, be silent, Cynara. You're safe now."

But Cynara struggled up, watching as Merlin bound Muggins's hands behind his back and forced him from the cave to the spot where she was standing. She took a step toward him and stumbled on Felix's prone body. Gasping in fear, she viewed his face so close to the lantern, and noticed his closed eyes. At least he wouldn't threaten her again. She found a coil of rope in his pocket, and though her hands trembled so much that she could barely tie a knot, she struggled to bind his hands. He had to be made powerless, and as long as he was untied, he was a danger to everyone. She almost fainted with the exertion, but Estelle helped her, and then they watched as the men struggled with Muggins. They forced him across the sand to stand beside the lantern, then they carried the chest across from the cave. The water was now reaching to their knees.

Muggins was staring sullenly at Cynara. "It's all your fault," he growled. "If you hadn't turned Master Felix's head, we would have been rid of you a long time ago."

"Then you wouldn't have found the treasure," Cynara said hoarsely. She squeezed her mother's hand. "Thank God you came in time to save my life."

"I sensed an urgency that wouldn't go away," Estelle explained. "So much has happened. My head is spinning with all the startling events."

Panting with the exertion, the men set the chest on the ground. "This must be the Mournay treasure, then," Brandon said, throwing an angry glance at Felix, who was coming around. He groaned and tried to clutch his head—to no avail.

"You already know about it, then," Cynara said.

"We found out just today," Estelle explained.

Brandon nudged Felix with his wet boot. "You evidently knew all along about the treasure," he accused him. "No wonder I found the *Hirondelle* necklace among my belongings—hanging for theft would be a sure way to get rid of the rightful heir to the Mournay fortune."

Merlin dragged Felix to his feet. "You'll have a lot to explain to the Bow Street Runners in the castle," he said. Aiming his pistol at Felix, he said, "Get going! We'll return for the chest later."

Cynara went up to him. "Don't leave it behind. You and Brandon can carry the chest. Just tie Felix and Muggins together, and I shall make sure they don't go anywhere." She took the pistol from Merlin's hand, and he could tell she meant every word. He chuckled. "I don't think they will get away with you as their guard," he joked.

"I have no intention of letting them escape."

The two villains were tied together, and the young men dragged the chest up the cliffs. Estelle went first, and when she heard that the runners had been tied up in the study, she immediately went to release them.

"I'm terribly sorry about this treatment," she apologized. She ordered one of the gaping footmen to fetch a bottle of the finest French brandy to refill the runners' glasses. The two lawmen had imbibed liberally from the bottle that Merlin had left, but they were yet not drunk enough to lose their authority. They stared with boiling wrath at Merlin and Brandon.

"What's going on?" demanded Sergeant Todd, staring at the dripping villains scowling at them. Todd's mouth opened and closed several times before he could speak again. "You shall be taken into custody, Lord Raven, and this time I shall personally stand guard outside your cell." He sounded uncertain. "Apprehend Lord Raven and Mr. Hawthorne!"

"Don't!" warned Merlin as Hoskins steered his steps toward him, handcuffs in hand. "We're innocent, and the crimes Mr. Hawthorne and I were accused of will be explained in a moment." He pointed at Felix and Muggins. "By these two men."

The villains stared with hatred at the two runners. Merlin pushed Felix into a chair and tied him securely to it. "I suggest you explain everything. As you know, there's no getting away from this room before you confess—everything."

Felix muttered under his breath, and Merlin went to confer quietly with Brandon, who had secured Muggins to another chair. Then Brandon left the room, closing the door carefully behind him.

"Where's he going?" Todd wanted to know. "He's running away again."

Merlin held up his hands. "Trust me, he'll be back in an hour." He sat down on a chair, crossing his left ankle over his right knee. "Just listen to these men, and when Mr. Hawthorne returns, it will all be explained."

The runners sat down reluctantly, staring uneasily at the two sullen villains. Merlin indicated the chest that was right inside the door. "We shall inspect that treasure later, but first"—he pinned his gaze on Felix—"we shall hear their explanation."

Felix was silent, and Muggins hung his head. Tension mounted, and finally Merlin said, "Felix, do you remember a man called Eliah Porter?"

Felix flinched, snapping his eyes open. "Eliah?"

"Yes . . . I wager he knows everything there is to know about you, coz." Merlin turned to the runners. "Eliah Porter is the driver who drove my father's coach on the night he died. He'd been in Father's employ only a month. The strange thing is, he didn't die at the coaching accident. He disappeared. Fortunately, Mr. Hawthorne has been able to locate Porter, and he just left to fetch him here. I'm sure Porter won't be averse to speaking the truth if we promise him his freedom—though he should rightfully hang, due to his involvement in my father's death."

"He won't say a word," Felix shouted, two red spots glowing on his cheeks.

"Like I said, he can choose between the noose or telling the truth. Any sane man would talk—all night if need be."

Muggins suddenly blurted out, "The plan might have worked if only we'd found the treasure earlier."

"Treasure?" asked Todd. He slanted a glance at the chest.

"Perhaps we should start with the chest after all," Merlin said, motioning for Hoskins to help him carry it across the floor.

Cynara watched, her hands cold in her lap as she sat next to her mother on a wooden settee. The aftermath of the events on the beach had her shivering, and the wet skirts clung to her unpleasantly. She knew she ought to go upstairs and change, but she didn't want to miss any of the men's words.

"What was the plan?" Todd insisted as the two men carried the chest to the middle of room. Merlin bent down and opened the lid. He pulled out the cache of jewels and set it on the floor. Beside it, he piled the gold bars that Cynara had glimpsed in the cave. There were about ten of them.

"I believe there used to be many more gold bars," explained Muggins, "but they disappeared over the years to pay for Black Raven's upkeep. The plan was to take the chest and bring it with us to Master Felix's plantation in Virginia."

"Shut up!" Felix demanded, throwing a murderous look at Muggins.

Muggins shrugged. "They'll find out anyway, especially if they have Porter. I knew we should have gotten rid of that man."

Merlin carried the jewelry cache to Estelle and

opened the lid. "The lost Mournay gems, Estelle. They are yours now."

Todd stared with bulging eyes at the costly array of jewels. "Please explain this!"

Merlin paced the room as he told the runners of the ship that Lord Mournay had sent after his daughter, Estelle, as she fled to England. He described how it had stranded outside Black Raven in a raging storm, and that someone had taken the treasure from the ship. "How the treasure came to be in the castle, we don't quite know yet," said Merlin.

"Felix mentioned that your father and his two brothers stole it," Cynara said.

Merlin halted in mid-stride, and turned to Felix. "Is that the truth?"

Felix nodded sullenly. "Yes. . . . When I became the earl after Max's death, Jean, the Frenchman, approached me and told me the whole story. He extorted money from me, and if I refused to pay, he would go to the authorities. It seems that he blackmailed Uncle Sydney all his life."

"But why didn't Jean take the treasure if he knew about it?" Cynara asked.

"He didn't know where it was hidden. Nobody did after Ross's death, until Cynara discovered the spot."

Merlin's eyes softened as he looked at her. "I knew she would bring luck to Black Raven. The very stones of the castle seem to love her. As do I," he added in a softer voice. "Please go on, Felix," he urged, watching as Hoskins pulled the last gold bars from the bottom of the chest.

Felix pinched his lips together, and Merlin shrugged. "We can wait. No matter how long it takes, you'll be stuck to that chair—without food and water."

Hoskins waved something in the air. "Look at this. It's a letter, and it doesn't look that old. It was under the paper lining on the bottom."

Todd snatched it from his assistant and tore open the envelope. He studied the signature at the bottom. "It bears the name of Ross Seymour," he said, handing Merlin the note. "You'd better read it aloud."

Merlin cleared his throat. His hand on the back of a chair had gone white as he clutched the wood so hard, it might break. He looked pale as he read.

To whomever it may concern,

The Seymour brothers are guilty of a crime, a terrible secret that would be carried to the grave unless I speak up now. After Sydney and George died, I planned to go to the authorities and unburden my guilty conscience, but I couldn't ruin Merlin, my son's, name. The Seymours were a proud lot, but I abhorred the day when we became thieves, and, worse, murderers. On the twenty-fifth of May 1789, the French ship l' Hirondelle capsized outside Black Raven. As we rowed out, we didn't have any plans to loot the ship—at first—only to save any survivors. The only sailor alive was the captain. He was trying to salvage a heavy chest as we embarked on the rapidly sinking ship.

We tried to persuade him to leave with us, but he maintained that the chest had to reach its destination. He never told us what destination, but we opened the chest and saw all that gold.

Something evil came over Sydney. He'd been distraught about the Black Raven estate, knowing there weren't enough funds to keep it from ruin. I think he saw his salvation right at that moment. George agreed that we all could benefit from the treasure.

Though I protested, they insisted in taking the chest. The captain fought, and George hit him unconscious with an iron bar. The sailor went down, but we had the gold. My life was ruined at that moment.

Never did I realize how heavy that secret would lie on my shoulders over the years. Still, I couldn't tattle on my brothers . . . could I? We swore a pact of secrecy. One small consolation was that I refused to take any of the loot. That day I decided to make my own fortune by honest means. I can only pray that the next generation of Seymours will be wiser than we were. I wrote all this down so that the truth will be known if what's left of the treasure is ever found. George got his part and moved to the colonies, and set up household with a plantation heiress. Having a conscience of sorts, I think that Sydney couldn't spend more than he needed for the estate's upkeep. His life was miserable after the theft. My heart is heavy, and I beg forgiveness from the Lord, and from the poor people who lost a fortune that night. I wish I could give it back to them, but that would ruin the Seymour name forever.

Ross Seymour.

"This was written one year and six months ago," Merlin said. "I wish Father had told me." Merlin's voice was unsteady. "I'm ashamed of them." Turning to Felix, he added, "And so you should be."

"Father liked gambling and squandered his fortune soon after he married Mama in Virginia," Felix said bitterly. "Until now I didn't know he got his fortune from the *Hirondelle* chest."

"My father paid for your English schools, Felix," Merlin said, frowning. He braced his hands on the armrests of Felix's chair. "George let his two brothers pay for the best of everything for you, Felix. And what do you do? You sneak behind everyone's back to get your busy fingers on the rest of the fortune. You didn't plan to tell us anything, did you?"

"Why should I? You have your father's fortune, and Max is dead. I need the gold and you don't."

"You *killed* for it, just like they did." Merlin gave Felix's chair a shove so that it almost toppled.

Felix eyes shifted to the floor. "I haven't killed anyone."

Merlin laughed harshly. "I think you killed my father. In fact, I shall prove it somehow."

"He as much as confessed to murdering Jean," Cynara said, remembering Felix bragging earlier that nothing could stand in his way. "Jean died because he was extorting money from Felix."

"Then you made it look like *I* killed the poor madman," Merlin snarled. He turned to the runners. "You must see the connection. Everything that happened to Brandon Hawthorne and me is tied to Felix's desire to abscond with the treasure."

Sergeant Todd nodded thoughtfully. "Yes . . . it's possible, of course."

The door opened suddenly, and Brandon stood on the threshold with his hand on another man's shoulder. Eliah Porter was a small, bandy-legged man with untidy black curls and an unkempt beard. His dark eyes shifted suspiciously from person to person in the room.

"He can tell you a thing or two," Brandon said. "When he heard that we've captured Felix Seymour, he was ready to speak his mind, especially since I explained that if he didn't speak, he would find his air intake severed by a noose."

Eliah Porter thumbed his grimy hat and stepped hesitantly into the room. "Who's the runner bloke from Lunnon?" he demanded.

"I am Sergeant Todd," Todd introduced himself. "Speak your mind, man. You will go free if you do."

"I—er—know summit that will put that jack's"—he indicated Felix—" 'ead on the block."

"Good," Todd said. "Speak up."

"Seein' as I'm a good carriage driver, I got employment with Mr. Ross Seymour when 'is old coachman died. I'm from Axminster, but the chance t' make a good livin' servin' a Seymour, well, I couldn't say no, so I moved to these parts." He viewed Felix cautiously. "This sod once came to me and told me I could make a tidy sum, more money in one go than wot I could earn an entire lifetime as a coachman." He laughed dryly. "I didn't 'esitate that time either; I took th' job, it bein' to make Ross Seymour's death look like Mr. Merlin 'ad done it. Wearin' Mr. Merlin's gray cloak, Mr. Felix tampered with Mr. Ross's carriage in

Lunnon, but not enough to make it break, mind you."
He paused, taking a deep, wheezy breath. "That night
Ross Seymour died, I waited on the road until Merlin
Seymour's curricle came into view. Then I shot one of
Mr. Ross's 'orses in the belly and let them run straight
into the ravine. I managed to jump orf at the last
second. Like I said, the axle had been tampered with
earlier—persumably by Mr. Merlin—as the 'ouse-
keeper at the Albemarle Street house in Lunnon testi-
fied."

"But *why* did Mr. Felix Seymour pay you to kill Mr.
Ross?" Todd wanted to know.

"They 'ad been arguin' about a necklace that Mr.
Ross 'ad in 'is possession. I watched them through the
window at Stormywood one night." He heaved a long
sigh. "Ahh, ye should 'ave seen the sparklers! A 'uge
teardrop ruby 'anging from the end. Felix Seymour
was tryin' to get the old gent to tell 'im the 'idin' place
of some other jewels—that's all I 'eard. Mr. Ross
swore 'e would go to the law with some secret if Master Felix kept pryin' into the past." He shrugged. "Not
that I know what the secret was."

Merlin kicked the chest. "This was it." He turned to
Felix. "So you tried to force Father to divulge the
truth, and when he didn't, you had him killed and stole
the *Hirondelle* necklace." Merlin fumed, clenching his
fists. "How could you!"

"So how did the necklace end up with Mr. Hawthorne?" Todd asked.

Brandon stepped forward. "I'm the heir of the
Mournays. Felix planned to marry Cynara, thereby
take care of her and Estelle for the rest of their lives.
They would never know about the treasure. He

wanted me dead, however, and the safest place was to have me rot in some prison. He figured he wouldn't be tied in to the theft of the *Hirondelle* necklace. Eventually, I would have been hanged. Lady Fidalia would have sworn that it was her necklace, wouldn't she?"

Felix nodded, his face ghastly pale.

"She needed money to support her heavy gambling, so you gave her funds to assure her help." Brandon crossed his arms over his chest. "However, the *Hirondelle* necklace was one of a kind, designed by Louis XIV's jewelers, so it would be easily recognized by someone familiar with the story behind the necklace." He turned to Estelle. "Mother knew that story, but didn't—until lately—tell us, since she figured we would never see that necklace."

Felix groaned, his head slumping forward.

"A tidy little plan, Mr. Seymour," said Todd, pulling out his handcuffs purposefully. "I believe that no judge will show you any mercy after this. You've planned the death of two people besides executing Jean yourself."

"Three," Merlin said. "He had my driver killed after Father's accident. The driver knew I was nowhere near Father's coach when it crashed over the side of the ravine."

Todd's face was red with anger as he untied Felix and placed the handcuffs around his wrists. "We'll take these two birds back with us to London now." He turned to Muggins. "What did you want out of this?"

Muggins was slumped forward in his chair. "I wanted a new life for myself in America, freedom, riches." He gave Merlin a contemptuous glance, then spat on the floor. "I didn't want to muck out stables for the toffs any longer. Master Felix promised to set me up in style overseas."

Todd nodded, pulling his lips into a grim line. "Lead the way to the dungeons," he said to Bramble as the butler stepped into the room. "Show me the strongest of the cells. These two"—he pushed Felix and Muggins toward the hallway—"shall ponder their sins in darkness while I arrange for their delivery to the capital."

"One more thing," Merlin said. "Who shot you in the copse at Stormywood, Felix?"

Muggins replied in Felix's place. "He wasn't shot! Another groom—the one you fired, Mr. Merlin—was hidden in the woods and shot in the air. After Felix spoke with Squire Henry on his 'deathbed,' he took some drug that would make him seem dead. That's when you saw him, Master Merlin."

"They spent all this time in a cove a mile east of here," Cynara explained. "I was a prisoner there until tonight." She turned to Muggins. "But how did you discover that we'd gone to London with the purpose of rescuing Mr. Hawthorne?"

"I overheard your plans to go to London, and I knew it wasn't a trip of pleasure, so I followed you." Muggins clamped his mouth shut. "I had orders to do away with you along the way. I'm tired of this!" He kicked a chair as the lawmen led him outside.

When the runners and the two villains had left, Cynara threw herself into Merlin's arms. "I'm so glad it's over."

He cradled her close. "It truly will be over once we've given our accounts at the trial. Then we can take up where we left off." He nuzzled her cheek. "We shall stay in bed for a week. The servants will think we're taking a much-needed rest."

They laughed and went to sit by Estelle, who looked dazed. Brandon was holding one of her hands, and Cynara took the other. "Mother, what will you do now?"

Estelle shook her head. *"Mon Dieu,* it's so strange. With the return of the family jewels, I look back and remember my childhood." Her voice quavered. "It's almost as if I can hear Father's booming laughter, and Mother's rapid French. It's all coming back to me." She fingered a lovely strand of pearls. "Mother used to wear this so often. It was her favorite necklace."

"I'm sure they would be delighted to know that the Mournay jewels are back where they belong—around your neck, Estelle," Merlin said. "I'm sad to say that my uncles squandered most of the Mournay gold though."

"There's enough here to bring Bluewater into its former elegance," Brandon said. "But how will you keep up this crumbling heap?" he asked. "I'm sure Felix—who now is the earl again—will be sentenced to death for his crimes. Then you will be the Earl of Raven once more."

Merlin laughed. "A lot of juggling of titles, that's for sure." He took Cynara's hand. "With the help of my lovely wife, I shall bring the estate back to prosperity. In fact, since the revenues are coming mostly from the farmland, I shall put my efforts into rejuvenating the existing farms, and try some newfangled ideas for greater crops. But there's a chance we might find more copper lodes, and I shall look into that." He sighed and gazed deeply into Cynara's eyes. "I feel that with

Cynara at my side I shall not fail. The moment she became my wife, she changed my life for the better. From now on, with the suspicion gone from my name, we shall live happily and fulfill our plans for Black Raven."

Estelle's eyes glittered with tears, and she embraced her daughter and Merlin. "I'm so happy that your marriage turned out to be a blessing," she said, choking. "It's a burden off my shoulders."

"Well, Mother, now you have to find me a bride," Brandon said lightly. "Seems that you're good at one thing—matchmaking."

Estelle slapped Brandon's wrist. "You have yet to grow up, my son. No more gambling, no more late nights, no more—"

"I hear, I hear," echoed Brandon, and he stood. "I also hear that the Duck and Willow serves excellent ale. Do you want to wet your whistle, Merlin?"

"No . . . I have better things to do." He pulled Cynara with him to the door. "Brand, don't flirt with the redheaded barmaid," he threw over his shoulder as he closed the door.

The following night, when all was at peace, and the villains were gone from the castle, Cynara rested in Merlin's arms. They were lying naked in his bed, the carved and canopied bed where dozens of Seymours had been conceived. The aftermath of their lovemaking was a sweet glow, a contentment that tied them together so closely that they could almost anticipate each other's thoughts.

Merlin stroked the silky skin of Cynara's back. "I

take it you will complete the refurbishing of the castle now?"

She nodded. "Yes, room by room. Then I shall open a village school, and my first student will be Bobby."

"A school?" He sounded surprised.

She traced his hard chin as she rested on Merlin's shoulder. "Yes . . . I think that since you're going to improve the lands of Black Raven, I shall improve the minds of the people. Everyone ought to know how to read and write."

Merlin nodded slowly. "I agree, but where will we find the time to have that London Season you missed? We'll be stuck at Black Raven for a long time if we implement these plans."

"I intend to bring out our daughter in style in London! No forced marriage for her, and that's my final word."

"A daughter?" His eyes widened in delight. "Are you pregnant?"

She gave him a seductive smile. "No . . . but I'll soon be once we keep as busy at night as we plan to keep during the day."

He raised himself above her on one elbow. "I intend to hold you to that, my sweet. Starting tonight."

Cynara thought that was an exceedingly good idea, and resolutely pulled his mouth to hers.

Dear Readers:

My next release is a Georgian romp, MIDNIGHT LOVER, November '94, a story very close to my heart. For you who remember Charles, Lord Mortimer, in FOREVER LOVE (1989) this is his story. Did you know he supports his crumbling estate by secretly writing bestselling poetry? I didn't think so, but you'll get a taste of his poetry and his inventive games of seduction as he pursues his long lost love, the mysterious Marguerite Lennox—who has always been his secret inspiration.

Romance and highway robbery are the ingredients of the spin-off, coming in 1995. Charles's best friend, Nicholas Thurston, whose grin will melt your hearts, got more than he bargained for when he robbed a coach and had to take the lovely, but infuriatingly haughty, Miss Serena Hilliard hostage. His patience is sorely tried as he has to wear down her pride, teach her how to cook, coax her to trust him and open up her heart. All this while protecting her from her murderous uncle. A lesser man than Nick would have given up a long time ago . . .

I would like to point out that the title "Lord Merlin Seymour" as written on the back of this book is erroneous. It should have been Merlin Seymour, Lord Raven, or the Earl of Raven.

I wish you all a wonderful summer with lots and lots of good reading. I love to hear from my readers and you may write to me c/o Zebra Books.

Fondly,

Maria Greene

YOU WON'T WANT TO READ
JUST ONE — KATHERINE STONE

ROOMMATES   (3355-9, $4.95)
No one could have prepared Carrie for the monumental
changes she would face when she met her new circle of
friends at Stanford University. Once their lives intertwined
and became woven into the tapestry of the times, they would
never be the same.

TWINS   (3492-X, $4.95)
Brook and Melanie Chandler were so different, it was hard
to believe they were sisters. One was a dark, serious, ambi-
tious New York attorney; the other, a golden, glamourous,
sophisticated supermodel. But they were more than sisters — they were twins and more alike than even they knew
. . .

THE CARLTON CLUB   (3614-0, $4.95)
It was the place to see and be seen, the only place to be. And
for those who frequented the playground of the very rich, it
was a way of life. Mark, Kathleen, Leslie and Janet — they
worked together, played together, and loved together, all behind exclusive gates of the *Carlton Club*.

*Available wherever paperbacks are sold, or order direct from the
Publisher. Send cover price plus 50¢ per copy for mailing and handling to Penguin USA, P.O. Box 999, c/o Dept. 17109, Bergenfield, NJ 07621. Residents of New York and Tennessee must
include sales tax. DO NOT SEND CASH.*

DISCOVER DEANA JAMES!

CAPTIVE ANGEL   (2524, $4.50/$5.50)
Abandoned, penniless, and suddenly responsible for the biggest
tobacco plantation in Colleton County, distraught Caroline Gil-
lard had no time to dissolve into tears. By day the willowy red-
head labored to exhaustion beside her slaves . . . but each night
left her restless with longing for her wayward husband. She'd
make the sea captain regret his betrayal until he begged her to
take him back!

MASQUE OF SAPPHIRE   (2885, $4.50/$5.50)
Judith Talbot-Harrow left England with a heavy heart. She was
going to America to join a father she despised and a sister she
distrusted. She was certainly in no mood to put up with the in-
sulting actions of the arrogant Yankee privateer who boarded her
ship, ransacked her things, then "apologized" with an indecent,
brazen kiss! She vowed that someday he'd pay dearly for the lib-
erties he had taken and the desires he had awakened.

SPEAK ONLY LOVE   (3439, $4.95/$5.95)
Long ago, the shock of her mother's death had robbed Vivian
Marleigh of the power of speech. Now she was being forced to
marry a bitter man with brandy on his breath. But she could not
say what was in her heart. It was up to the viscount to spark the
fires that would melt her icy reserve.

WILD TEXAS HEART   (3205, $4.95/$5.95)
Fan Breckenridge was terrified when the stranger found her near-
naked and shivering beneath the Texas stars. Unable to remember
who she was or what had happened, all she had in the world was
the deed to a patch of land that might yield oil . . . and the fierce
loving of this wildcatter who called himself Irons.

*Available wherever paperbacks are sold, or order direct from the
Publisher. Send cover price plus 50¢ per copy for mailing and
handling to Penguin USA, P.O. Box 999, c/o Dept. 17109,
Bergenfield, NJ 07621. Residents of New York and Tennessee
must include sales tax. DO NOT SEND CASH.*